Milly Johnson was born, raised and still lives in Barnsley, South Yorkshire. A *Sunday Times* bestseller, she is one of the Top 10 Female Fiction authors in the UK, and with millions of copies of her books sold across the world, Milly's star continues to rise.

Milly writes from the heart about what and where she knows and highlights the importance of community spirit. Her books champion women, their strength and resilience, and celebrate love, friendship and the possibility of second chances. She is an exceptional writer who puts her heart and soul into every book she writes and every character she creates.

Milly Johnson

let the *bells* ring out

SIMON &
SCHUSTER

London · New York · Amsterdam/Antwerp · Sydney/Melbourne · Toronto · New Delhi

First published in Great Britain by Simon & Schuster UK Ltd, 2025

1 3 5 7 9 10 8 6 4 2

Simon & Schuster UK Ltd, 1st Floor,
222 Gray's Inn Road, London WC1X 8HB

Simon & Schuster Australia, Sydney
Simon & Schuster India, New Delhi

www.simonandschuster.co.uk
www.simonandschuster.com.au
www.simonandschuster.co.in

The authorised representative in the EEA is Simon & Schuster Netherlands BV, Herculesplein 96, 3584 AA Utrecht, Netherlands. info@simonandschuster.nl

Simon & Schuster strongly believes in freedom of expression and stands against censorship in all its forms. For more information, visit BooksBelong.com.

A CIP catalogue record for this book is available from the British Library

Hardback ISBN: 978-1-3985-4706-3
eBook ISBN: 978-1-3985-4707-0
Audio ISBN: 978-1-3985-4708-7

Typeset in Bembo by M Rules
Printed and Bound in the UK using 100% Renewable Electricity at CPI Group (UK) Ltd

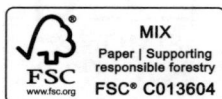

FSC
www.fsc.org

MIX
Paper | Supporting
responsible forestry
FSC® C013604

In memory of a beloved couple: Grace and Bobby Campbell of Irvine, Ayrshire. Grace, Mum's cousin, was gentle but resilient, kind, beautiful and a lady who was passionate about her reading. She said a final goodbye to her beloved Bobby in January this year and then followed him onwards only five weeks later.

Bobby, an HGV lorry driver who stayed at our house so often over many years, brought joy and fun with him whenever he walked through the door. My draught board was always waiting for him, even though his wins were always the result of unashamed cheating.

Travelling up to Glasgow in his wagon with Mum, calling in at truckers' cafés for cheese and onion sandwiches, are among my happiest childhood memories. The best and loveliest of people – of family.

Bobby and 'Bobby's Girl' are now together again for always. It was an honour to know them and to love them. God bless them both.

23 December

*Yesterday is history, tomorrow is
a mystery but today is a gift*

Chapter 1

The snowflakes started to fall on the windscreen as soon as Vincent Diamond – of Diamond Service Taxis – had turned onto the A7501 towards Whitby, as if they had somehow been triggered by his change in direction. Within the minute, he'd had to notch up his wipers from the intermittent setting to the steady swipe to maintain his vision of the road. He couldn't remember there being any warning of this on the weather forecast, which he checked every morning, especially when he had a long journey in the diary. And super especially when he had a long journey to make in the bleak midwinter.

The drop in temperature inside his cab was probably his imagination working overtime in response to the sudden snowfall but he reached over to tweak up the heating all the same.

'You warm enough back there?' he called over his shoulder to his passenger.

'Yes, thank you,' she replied.

Miss Elizabeth Dudley, whom he was chauffeuring from Reading to Durham. Her voice matched the rest of her:

ladylike, cultured, honeyed. She was probably the most beautiful fare he'd had in the back of his cab, and that was saying something as he'd picked up a lot of actresses from theatres in the West End. His eyes flicked up to the rear-view mirror to see her looking out of the window to her side, weighing up this sudden change in weather. Then her mobile phone claimed her attention: no daft ringtone, just a classic *brrr-brrr*.

She pulled it out of her bag, answered it. 'Hi,' she said. Even with just that short word, the recipient of it must have felt she really wanted to speak to them, Vincent mused. He thought she looked like an Elizabeth. His mum had been an Elizabeth, and his gran, and so he was predisposed to the name being synonymous with lovely women.

She leaned forward to ask him: 'Excuse me, how far are we away from Topston?'

'About two hours, with holiday traffic,' Vincent answered. He didn't say, *and the weather,* because he presumed this was just a rogue flurry or the weathermen would have said otherwise. Metcheck had given the forecast as cloudy, rain changing to sleet mid-afternoon, and a constant one centigrade temperature, though on his dashboard it was showing as minus six outside. It wouldn't hold them up, he was sure of it, just a temporary pocket of cold front. He hoped it wouldn't, anyway, for he had to drive back in it as soon as he'd dropped her off on the outskirts of Durham. Topston Manor, one of those piles that made footballers' houses in Alderley Edge look like gate lodges. His old mum, ever the pragmatist, would have looked at the pictures of it and said, 'How much would the window-cleaning bill be for that every month?' God bless her, wherever she was. Looking down at him, no doubt, still worrying about him, still loving him.

'About two hours,' Elizabeth repeated down the phone.

There was a lull while whoever was on the other end of the phone spoke again.

'Well, it is—' Elizabeth attempted to answer but it seems she was interrupted. Another long lull.

'I know you told me to come up before but I couldn't. I had things I needed to do ... I know it's important I ... yes, I understand that ... Gregory, please let me speak, I—'

'Gregory' wasn't letting her get a word in. Vincent gathered he wasn't a happy bunny. He visualised someone that made Darth Vader look like the Dalai Lama.

Vincent's foot pressed gently on the brake. The snowflakes were getting fatter and faster and they'd already started to settle on the road. He turned on the blower because the windscreen was misting up and reducing visibility.

'Gregory, can you just listen to me for a moment, what's the weather like there because here the snow is really bad ... Oh, you don't have any?'

Well, that was good, thought Vincent, eavesdropping. Just a localised storm, in that case. It would make its presence known and then melt quickly away, with any luck.

'Yes, I'm sure we'll be there well before seven ... but I can't help the weather can— Gregory ...? Hello, are you still there?'

Gregory clearly wasn't. Elizabeth rang him back but it went to answerphone and she was forced to leave a message.

'Hi, Gregory, it's me. I'm not sure if we got cut off or you'd finished saying what you had to. I'll keep you posted on where we are. See you soon ... Bye.'

Vincent slowed the car down even further. The wiper blades were operating at full pelt and the snowflakes were as big as pennies. The cars in front of him all had iced roofs now and had it gone suddenly darker or was he getting snow-blind?

'I'm supposed to be at a party at seven,' said Elizabeth, her words riding on a long drawn-out sigh.

Vincent's eyes snatched up the time on the dashboard clock: five to three. 'I'm sure you will be,' he replied. He wondered if at any point in the conversation Shouty Gregory had told her to be careful and get there when she could – and safely.

Chapter 2

Jane Wutheridge was glad she'd had the foresight to wear her old snow boots to travel in, not that there was a hint of snow when she left their Derbyshire house but because they were snug and warm and gripped the ground like a limpet. She still called it *their* house, even though it had been solely hers for just under a year, but it wouldn't be theirs – or rather hers – any longer in less than four weeks, because contracts would soon be exchanged and then completion on the sale of it would follow. They were reliable and safe boots, comfortable, solid as a rock . . . her boots had all the qualities her life was presently lacking.

She hadn't wanted to make this train journey. She wanted Christmas alone, a last one in the rectory before the new owners came in. She was cross she'd been pressured into spending it elsewhere. And the disruption just put the tin hat on things. She wasn't frightened of snow like some old people; she loved it. She and Clifford had taken many winter holidays; in fact, they'd been hundreds of kilometres past the Arctic Circle and then down to Antarctica, where they wanted to go again, but life got in the way of their plans. Or rather death did.

The conductor entered the carriage and stood by the sliding door.

'Can I have everyone's attention, please? Sorry, the tannoy isn't working. We've been informed that we have to divert to Selton. For services west, you need to get off at the next stop, Derringbury, for the connecting train to Eskford. I repeat, we are now no longer calling at Eskford on this train.'

'Chuffing hell,' said the loud man behind Jane, whose voice hadn't dropped below a hundred decibels since he got on. 'One leaf or a snowflake and the trains go to absolute cock in this country.'

The conductor ignored him and announced that they'd be at Derringbury in a few minutes.

Jane reached into her bag for her brown bucket hat. Clifford had bought it for her, one of his last presents. 'I thought it was about time we started buying each other practical things,' he'd said with a twinkle in his eye, though it wasn't as bright a twinkle as the one in the diamond ring he'd tied to the label inside the hat. It was on her finger now. An eternity ring, even though they knew their time was running out – at least here on earth. But Clifford was that rare being, a scientist who believed in an afterlife and he knew they'd share that eternity. The irony was that she, a creative, a romantic, believed that life, consciousness, everything, ended with the last breath.

Jane put on her gloves and made her way to the storage rack for her suitcase, declining the help of the conductor because she wasn't ready to start playing the old-lady card just yet. She'd packed fairly lightly and luckily had sent the presents on ahead. She hadn't gone over the top with them either, this year, because, for as long as she could remember, she'd spent far too much time trying to match the gift to the person only to get the lazy options in return: chocolates with a suspiciously close sell-by date, a market-tat brooch in a cheap box, a manicure set. She'd had at least ten manicure sets in various forms over the years.

Clifford would have said that this interference in plans constituted an adventure. But Clifford wasn't here to share her fears and take the reins; she was all alone and there was no excitement to be had.

Further down the same train, Frank O'Carroll and his wife, Grace, were preparing to disembark. They should have been getting off at Eskford but as it was having to divert, they'd have to get yet another connecting train – their fourth on this journey. He was beginning to think this trip was cursed from the get-go. Firstly he'd buggered up his ankle and couldn't drive – and Grace didn't have the confidence to drive this far – so the only way they could reach their country cottage getaway was by public transport. Plus the place he really wanted had been double-booked and they'd had to take the option of another which wasn't the cosy, olde-worlde with log-fire one he'd put his deposit on. Mistletoe Nook might have sounded idyllic but the photos showed a modern bungalow full of the brown and orange décor that was a signature of the seventies. At this late stage, it was accept that or nothing, so his hands were tied and not even the part-refund made it sweet. His mum always said bad luck came in threes: *more like a hundred and threes*, thought Frank as they headed for the storage bay where their two suitcases were situated. Grace hadn't said a word and by not saying anything, she said everything. Frank could feel annoyance pumping out of her pores like toxic fumes from a faulty air vent. She hadn't even wanted to come away for Christmas, he'd been the one to suggest it, push for it, because he knew if they stayed at home, by the new year one of them would have moved out. A romantic cottage with a log-fire was his last desperate attempt to save their thirty-three-year relationship. The modern substitute cottage wasn't going to have any restorative magic, he just knew it.

The train edged out of the tunnel into a world that seemed much whiter than it had been when they'd entered it. Frank looked through the window at the snow falling hard. The hills in the distance were totally covered and had smudged into the sky.

He turned to Grace.

'It'll be fine, just another blip to test us. We'll be in Eskford in no time and then it's just a short walk to the cottage. I'm not worried. It'll be all the cosier for this messing about.' His smile was bright, covering up the worry he said he didn't have.

Grace didn't look worried at all though, she just looked . . . *resigned* was the best way of putting it. Whether they reached the cottage and it was warm and inviting or they ended up stuck all Christmas in a train station in the middle of nowhere, he believed she'd wear the same expression.

The train slowed and they passed signs announcing the name of Derringbury station. He spotted a waiting room, thank goodness, because he didn't fancy standing on a freezing, uncovered platform until their connection arrived.

'Can you manage?' he asked his wife who was wrestling with her suitcase handle.

'Of course I can,' she answered him, that ever-present snap in her voice. He wasn't even sure she knew it was there, it had just become her default way of talking to him. The

Grace of old would have waved away the booking debacle and be searing his ears with giddy questions: *What do you think is the first thing we should do when we get to the cottage? Shall we go to the local pub for tea? Should we get up early to go to the farm shop and buy too much food?* Little Miss Chatterbox, he used to call her. These days she only seemed to speak when she needed to and though her incessant talk used to drive him bonkers, he missed it. He missed the old Grace; she was like a shell emptied.

It appeared there were just them and another passenger who were alighting: a small, aged lady had just stepped onto the platform and Frank thought she looked as if she'd climbed out of a Miss Marple book with her slight frame, stompy boots, hat and tweed coat.

Frank helped Grace to 'mind the gap' and then he called over to 'Miss Marple', pointing at her suitcase.

'Can I help you with that?'

'Thank you, that's very kind, but it's on wheels and easy to steer.'

He could at least get the door into the waiting room for her. He held it open and she thanked him as she walked through. Grace followed, a heavy dusting of snow on her shoulders and on her long tied-back auburn hair, which melted instantly in the warmth that met them inside.

The first thought that came to Frank was that he'd wandered onto the film set of *Brief Encounter* because, apart from the bulk of a large modern machine for the distribution of hot drinks in the corner, the place couldn't have had a refurb for decades. It smelt fusty, but in a comforting way, like the smell of old books.

There was a long bench opposite a couple of rusty storage heaters mounted on the wall that were pumping out hot air, effectively too considering how ancient they looked. Grace took a seat near one of them, leaving a gap between her and Jane.

'Shocking weather, isn't it?' Frank said to her.

'Awful,' Jane replied. 'At least it's nice and warm in here. Are you changing at Eskford as well?' She really wasn't sure that she'd done the right thing, getting off here in this tiny station. She should have stayed on until the major junction at Selton and decided what to do from there on. Returning home would have been the most sensible option of all, of course.

'No, Eskford is our final destination. We've booked a cottage. For Christmas.' Then Frank looked around and spoke to himself, but aloud. 'There must be some timetable around somewhere.' Did they still have those in stations? It showed how long it was since he'd been in one that he didn't know. Maybe paper ones were a thing of the past and everything was on computers and phone apps now, which was all very well until you had a situation like this. His phone was saying there was no internet, no Wi-Fi available. There was a lot to be said for hard copy data. Nothing for it but to wait then.

Frank stood up and went over to the coffee machine. He couldn't see a coin slot, or prices. He tried his luck, pressed a button that said 'Hot Chocolate' and to his surprise, the machine dropped a cup below and obliged him.

'Blimey. It's not often you get something for nothing these days. Anyone else want one? Hot chocolate, chicken soup, tea, coffee with or without milk?' No fancy lattes or flat whites as an offering. There was a small table adjacent with spoons and sugar sachets and paper serviettes. Jane mouthed a silent no-thank-you. 'Grace?'

'I don't want anything if there's a train due,' she answered.

'Well, maybe if you get a drink that'll hurry the train along. Sod's law and all that,' said Frank with a smile that was wasted because she had turned away from him, her eyes instead roving over the flaking vintage green paint of the walls and the intricate, but heavily chipped, ceiling cornice.

He carried the plastic cup back to his seat. He offered his wife the first sip from it but she shook her head. The old Grace would have tried it and claimed it and he'd have laughed and had to get himself another. She could never resist a hot chocolate. He'd bought her a fancy machine to make them a couple of Christmases ago and it was still in the box. He hadn't encountered the old Grace for years and maybe it was a mistake to think she was still in there somewhere; maybe she had gone forever, leaving only this husk he lived with.

They sat in silence, waiting. Then Grace got up without saying anything and headed towards the door with a toilet sign above it.

'So where are you travelling to?' Frank asked, striking up conversation with Miss Marple. He would later be amused when he found out her name was Jane.

'Lancaster,' she answered him, with an accompanying sigh.

'Lancaster?' Frank puffed out his cheeks. 'How long is that going to take you?' He guessed over three hours from here, without hitches and there was a very big hitch outside in the form of all that snow.

'I don't even want to think about it,' said Jane. She really should have gone on to Selton, she felt it more with every minute that passed. There was a large hotel attached to the station that would surely have a vacancy – even at this time of year; a room reserved for emergencies. That was one advantage of being old; people tended to go the extra mile for pensioners.

'Aren't there any staff here?' asked Frank, with a sudden burst of frustration. 'There should be a stationmaster around. Should we be worried?' He dropped a small laugh, but it was only half a laugh and it wasn't a very convincing one at that.

Chapter 3

'Oh dear, I don't like this at all, Des,' said the woman in the front passenger seat of the car, for the twentieth time at least – a rough estimate, because Ruby 'Roo' Cooper had given up taking a tally after thirteen. Nora and Des Woolley, friends of Roo's neighbour, were travelling north to spend Christmas with her sister Sandra and they'd offered her a lift to Whitby en route. But if Roo had known how much Nora talked, she'd have taken her chances hitching a lift from a dodgy lorry driver with an axe on his dashboard. The woman didn't stop to draw a breath. And it was all nonsense, trivia, word soup, which was a bit unfair on soup. Des was driving and in his own little steering-wheel world, cut off from Nora after forty-plus years of refining the art.

In the last three-quarters of an hour though, Nora's tone had altered from chirpy chirpy cheep cheep cheerful to worry worry weep weep which was even harder on the ears.

The snow looked as if it was falling horizontally, such was the wind-force outside. The snowflakes were like swan's feathers, huge and downy.

'Oh deary, deary me,' said Nora then, throwing in a bit of variation on a theme. 'What do you think, Des?'

For once, she left some space for Des to actually answer the question she'd posed.

'I think we should turn back, that's what I think,' he said after some moments of contemplation, then grumbling under his breath that they'd have been there now if they'd set off this morning as he'd wanted to.

'Sandra's got a twenty-pound turkey in though,' Nora answered with a gasp. 'She's made her own stuffing.'

'We won't be able to eat it if we're dead,' said Des to that, his irritation with his wife clearly evident in his tone. 'I don't even like flipping turkey.'

'Yes, let's make an executive decision and go home.' Nora nodded decisively, then, as if she remembered they had a passenger reliant on their goodwill, she gave a little start. 'Oh, Ruby, where will that leave you?'

Up shit creek without a paddle, Roo didn't say. Another two hours of Nora's incessant babble would do her head in, but that was the least of the reasons why she didn't want to return home with them. Anything but going back. But she couldn't expect them to carry on their journey when it was dangerous. 'Erm . . . well . . .'

Then she saw it through the window – the left-arrow sign with a train graphic on it and 'Derringbury 500 yards' written underneath.

'Des, can you drop me at the train station please? I'll get to Whitby that way.'

'Ooh. Are you sure?' Nora said. 'Train.' She screwed up her face as if the word was rotten-fish-flavoured. She didn't do public transport or mix with the hoi polloi.

'You could come back with us,' Des offered.

It would be the wisest option by far to just go home. She could hole herself up, read books, drink wine, eat crisps and keep the TV switched off so she wasn't bombarded with the sounds of jingle bells, carols, and Paul bloody McCartney singing about him having a wonderful Christmas, nor the sight of celebrities in red fur-trimmed hats making an arse of themselves on game shows for charity. But . . .

She scrabbled in the side of the bag for her coin, gave it a rub, tossed it into the air and slapped it on the back of her hand. *Do I risk the train?* she silently asked the cosmos, before lifting her hand to see the YES facing her. Decided then.

'Thank you, Des, but my friends are expecting me.'

Des insisted on getting her case out of the boot at the station, even though Roo had told him to stay in the warm. He pipped the horn as he drove off, his wheels roaring as they struggled for purchase on the ground. Roo's suitcase wheels had the same problem. She didn't suppose anyone had thought of inventing suitcase wheels designed for British winters. Maybe they had them in Norway though, where snow was a way of life.

She headed across the car park towards the small station and, through the windows of the waiting room, she could see people inside which boded well.

She opened up the door and walked in to find an old lady and what she presumed were a couple – middle-aged, him swiping his finger across the screen of his mobile.

'Excuse me,' Roo began after wiping her mouth clear of snowflakes. 'Do you happen to know when the next train is due and where it's going?'

'That, I'm afraid, is the million-dollar question, love,' the man answered her with something that was – and yet also wasn't quite – a smile.

Chapter 4

Tim Grant loved his Jeep. It had never let him down in the three years he'd owned it, but now he was swearing at it like a trooper. The thing was a bloody tank and it had just had its big all-singing, all-dancing service, but it was coughing its guts up as if it had been a fifty-a-day smoker. The engine cut out for the third time; the strain on the battery was audible when he had to restart it. In short, it wasn't going to make it up to Newcastle and he *needed* to be in Newcastle. He hadn't even a clue where he was because the satnav had decided that if the engine was going on strike, it was going to come out in brotherly support and the screen had died miles ago. He'd come through a village and ended up in the back of beyond with nothing in front of him but snow and a thickening, darkening mist. He didn't fancy the chances of a recovery vehicle finding him when he couldn't even tell them where he was. He made the decision to pull in at the next place which might offer him shelter and work out his plan of action from there. The same thing had happened weatherwise five or six years ago when the country was blanketed in unforecast snow for the whole of the Christmas period. He hoped whatever this was would be more short-lived, but it did pose the question: what Mickey Mouse course did meteorologists go on these days, and which bigger idiot was saying they were qualified at the end of it?

The engine cut out yet again and Tim muttered another choice expletive under his breath as he slipped into neutral and twisted the key in the ignition. It fired, but under obvious protest. He pushed forward and saw something ahead at the side of the road: a sign, growing clearer the closer he got to it. *Hallelujah.* There was a railway station nearby.

Change of plan then, not that he had much choice. He just hoped and prayed the station was one with shelter from these infernal elements.

The giant car rolled down the gentle slope of road by gravity and not by engine power because it popped, stopped and wouldn't be started again, as dead as a dodo. Tim twisted the steering wheel gently to the left, hoping he wouldn't stall on the bend – he didn't – and came to a halt in what he presumed was the station car park. He jerked on the handbrake and watched the snow fill up the windscreen in seconds. He was about to say *This bloody country*, when a rogue thought visited him about a potential life in a much kinder climate at the other side of the world, which was definitely not where his head wanted to go. He gave it a rattle to shoo it away, before getting out to relieve the boot of his two suitcases. Another car was drawing up beside his, albeit one with a working engine. If he'd been as lucky, he'd have ploughed on.

Derringbury. He'd never heard of the place, not that it mattered. There was indeed a waiting room and he could see people inside it which he took as a good sign that there was a train due. He'd get to Newcastle one way if not the other. He didn't like to let anyone down. He'd done enough of that before now to last a whole lifetime.

Chapter 5

Vincent tried not to eavesdrop but it was impossible not to, even given how quietly Elizabeth was speaking into her phone. This was the third call she had taken from her fiancé Gregory in half an hour and he could tell she was fighting exasperation. She'd just apologised to him for sounding terse, even though from what he could hear, it was Mr Fiancé who was the one at fault, cutting off her every sentence.

'I don't think you know how bad it is, Gregory,' she was now saying. 'I've tried to send a photo but it won't let me . . . Sorry, what? I can't hear you, I keep losing . . . Hello, hello . . . Gregory. Are you still there?'

Elizabeth took the phone away from her ear and dropped a heavy sigh.

'Can you tell me where we are again, please? Sorry,' she asked Vincent, the strain evident in her voice.

'According to the satnav, we're about to go onto Spaghetti Junction in Birmingham,' he answered her. 'I have no idea what the satellites have been drinking, but I wish I had some for later.' He caught sight of her in the rear-view mirror and saw her worried expression. 'Apologies, that wasn't helpful. I wish I knew.' He hadn't seen a sign for a few miles now. He hadn't seen anything but snowy fields flanking the road. Surely there must be something due up ahead soon: a pub, a garage, a village.

'I don't think my fiancé quite believes the snow is as bad as it is,' Elizabeth said. 'It's just starting to fall up there.' She sort of hoped that it would fall with the same speed so he'd accept she wasn't exaggerating. *He's stressed about the party*, she told herself. He wanted everything to be right. He was used to things going his way, it was part of his make-up. *You'd have made a rubbish King Canute*, she once joked to him on one of their early dates, and he'd laughed.

Vincent narrowed his eyes to take in what he thought was a shape in the distance, but he could have been hallucinating. Snow blindness, akin to extreme thirst in the desert where people imagined oases of drinking water. No, there was definitely a shape, a big car was up ahead. And then he spotted a sign on a left-facing arrow denoting a train station nearby. He seemed to be gaining distance on the car in front even though he hadn't increased his speed any. The car indicated and that, he thought later, maybe influenced his decision, a primal *safety in numbers* move.

He made a hasty alternative plan: he'd abandon the car, escort Elizabeth by rail to Durham and then figure the rest out from there. He'd lose money on this job because he'd probably have to stay overnight in a hotel but he had nothing or no one to get back for – apart from his cat. She could get into the kitchen via the cat flap and there was always a bowl of kibble on hand to sustain her, though she'd probably go to his neighbour and plead starvation, as she was wont to do.

He told Elizabeth what was now going to happen and she'd merely nodded, accepting he knew best. He hoped he did.

The car in front – a massive Jeep – was rolling slowly down the hill. Vincent parked nearby to it when it stopped and opened his window to call to the large bearded man who got out of it.

'Any idea where we are, mate? My satnav thinks we're on Spaghetti Junction.'

'Somewhere not far from Whitby, that's all I know, sorry,' replied Tim, hefting two cases out of his boot before heading towards the station. He didn't want to be sociable. He just wanted to get to Newcastle.

Not that Vincent took any offence at his curtness. It wasn't the weather for hanging around and chatting and rogue conditions like this had a tendency to shorten tempers, as demonstrated by fiancé Gregory.

He got out of his car, a brand new solid Mercedes estate, and lifted Elizabeth's luggage and his own bag from the boot. He always kept an overnight 'just in case' holdall with a couple of changes of clothes and toiletries in there. Plus a snow shovel, a woollen throw, a foil blanket and a pair of dependable Timberlands because his mum had told him to. She was the most resourceful woman he'd ever met and he recalled from his childhood days that her handbag had everything in it from a screwdriver to a lollipop. Even when she was in her later life, he'd ask her why she felt the need to carry so much around with her and she answered him with a tap on the side of the nose and a 'Just in case'. But her ways had rubbed off on him because he was always prepared for the unexpected *just in case.*

He tapped on the back window and spoke through the glass.

'You stay here in the warm until I've taken these into the station.'

'Absolutely not,' Elizabeth replied, opening the door. 'I'm a passenger, not a princess.'

The irony was that she sounded exactly like a princess though with her cultured voice and all her vowels rounded, unlike his that had been flattened by a steamroller. But she wouldn't take no for an answer, so he was forced to concede, though her cases wouldn't roll through the thick snow so he had to lift and carry them while she followed with his lighter bag and boots. The wind had swelled and they had to push their way through it and the spit of snowflakes. He'd promised to get her to her party, but he was starting to wonder now if he really could.

Chapter 6

The man with the Jeep was already sitting down in the cosy, old-fashioned waiting room when Vincent and Elizabeth walked in. It seemed as if he had picked the seat that was the furthest away from the rest of the people in there, to create distance. There was an elderly lady huddled in tweed, a middle-aged couple and a young woman wearing a fluffy pink teddy-bear coat, an arty white stripe at the front of her dark hair. Jeep man was the only one who didn't look up when they entered.

'Blimey, am I glad this station's got shelter,' said Vincent to everyone. 'Can anyone tell me where we are? My satnav ain't playing ball.'

'Derringbury, which I would estimate is somewhere south-west of Whitby,' replied the elderly lady. 'We're wait-ing for the train to Eskford where allegedly we'll be able to get our connections.' She held up crossed fingers of hope, even if her word 'allegedly' didn't seem to have much of it attached. She still wasn't convinced the conductor on the train had given her the correct advice.

'The coffee machine works and it seems to be giving out

freebies,' said Frank. He thought he recognised the new-comer's accent, a fellow Kent county-man, he'd put money on it. He noticed how he turned to his lady and asked her if she wanted anything. She was very lovely, expensive camel-coloured wool coat, quality from top to toe. Grace had been wearing a coat like that when they went out on their first date. It had been snowing and he didn't think she'd turn up, she'd use the weather as an excuse. He could still recall how his heart seemed to expand in his chest when he spotted her coming from around the corner, blowing into her hands as she walked towards him.

'Cheers,' said Vincent. Elizabeth didn't want anything but he took advantage of the free gift of a white coffee. He took a sip and sat down. Jane was pointing out to Elizabeth where the loos were and Roo followed them both in. She figured if a train was due, she might as well go here. Train loos had a tendency to be a bit grotty, in her experience.

'So where are you headed?' Frank asked Vincent.

'Near Durham. Place called Topston, if you've heard of it.'

Frank shook his head. 'Hotel?'

'House. My fare is going up to her fiancé's family for Christmas.'

'Oh'. Just a small sound, but it was obvious to Vincent that Frank had thought they were a couple. *If only.* Elizabeth Dudley was way out of his league. He'd have had more chance of landing Kate Middleton.

'You?' Vincent threw the question back at him.

'We've got a cottage booked for Christmas near the next station, but I buggered my ankle and can't drive,' replied Frank. 'The whole thing has just been beset with disaster, hasn't it, love?'

He turned for affirmation to his wife, who nodded and

added, 'You could say that.' Her tone said, *And it's all your fault.*

'Got to think positive,' said Vincent with some conviction. 'We'll all be where we are supposed to be in no time,' but he didn't feel that his optimism was shared by anyone else in the room. He gulped greedily at his coffee, which was surprisingly good, and wished the machine distributed biscuits as well because he was bleedin' starving.

Just as the three women came out of the loo, he cocked his ear, sure he could sense a faint rumble in the distance.

'Is that a train?' asked Jane, tilting her head also.

'I think it might be,' said Frank, standing, listening.

'Finally,' said Grace with impatient relief. She grabbed her handbag and extended the handle on her case, ready to drag it outside.

It was definitely a train, the sound getting louder with every passing second. Everyone was shifting, preparing to leave the snug waiting room for the arctic platform. In half an hour, Frank thought, they'd be in Eskford and the people here would already be a fading memory.

Tim put his phone back in his jacket pocket because Derringbury was in a black hole as far as telecommunications was concerned. No telephone service, no internet, no chance to assure the Princess Royal Hotel in Newcastle that their Santa was running late, but he was on his way and wouldn't be letting them down.

Chapter 7

As if the day hadn't been out of the ordinary enough, the train that pulled into the little Derringbury station still managed to top it. A steam locomotive, pulling carriage after carriage past the platform, the top half painted vintage cream and in the centre of the midnight-blue bottom half, in gold lettering, the name *Yorkshire Belle*. Tim counted ten such cars after the engine head, the windows offering tantalising glimpses of opulent interiors: heavy tapestry curtains, wood-panelled walls. When the train finally came to a stop, they all found they were level with the back of the last posh carriage and the front part of the eleventh, which was burgundy, workaday and shabby, bearing the black initials of South Riding Trains. It looked like a poor relation cadging a lift.

When Frank said, 'What the bloody hell . . . Is it royal?' it summed up what was going through Tim's, Roo's and Vincent's heads too. They waited, silent, perplexed as to what was happening. Was this the train they were meant to be getting on? Then the door of the burgundy carriage opened and a man in a smart dark blue uniform hopped out. He looked a bit togged up for a mere guard, they all thought.

'Everyone for Eskford,' he said, waving them on, clearly not wanting anyone to dawdle, but no one wanted to anyway. The wind started biting as soon as they'd left the waiting room.

The interior of this carriage was very different to the ones in front: rows of hard seating, half facing forwards, half the other way. South Riding Trains must be in dire straits if they were still utilising carriages this ancient, thought Vincent.

The guard checked the platform was clear, then blew the whistle that was on a cord around his neck. Then he stepped on, slammed the door shut and dusted the snow off his jacket. It had a YB stitched in gold on one lapel, shiny gold buttons, and two gold stripes running down the outer seam of his trousers. This wasn't a uniform, it was livery.

Jane fumbled in her bag for her ticket so she had it ready to be scanned. Roo pulled a pained expression.

'I haven't got a ticket,' she said. 'I wasn't expect—'

'I wouldn't worry about tickets today,' said the guard. 'We can only take you one stop anyway and besides, I haven't got the equipment to sell you one.'

'What's the train?' asked Vincent, nodding forwards.

'The *Yorkshire Belle*,' replied the guard. 'We're going to Scotland for Christmas, picking up staff at various points along the Lochlann line. We'll drop you at Eskford and at least you'll get your connections from there.' He grabbed hold of the back of a seat for support as the train bucked forwards, as if the driver was a learner, not yet au fait with his gears. He pointed to the stitching on his jacket. 'The *Yorkshire Belle*,' he repeated, surprised that the name met with no reaction. 'You've not heard of it? It's been in all the newspapers. Pullman designed all the carriages. One of the top ten most luxurious trains in the world. You should see it.' He sighed wistfully and gave his head a small shake. 'Millionaires, eh?'

You'd need to be more than a millionaire to afford this setup, thought Frank. He'd be a millionaire if he liquidised all his assets and he couldn't afford to own even one of those posh carriages, never mind ten plus an engine to pull them.

'Maiden trip,' the guard went on. 'We are meeting Mr and Mrs Ingleton and their friends at Glasgow. You'll have heard of Dwight J. Ingleton, of course.'

Their blank faces seemed to further stupefy the guard who tried again to jog their memories. 'American businessman? Very *very* rich businessman at that. Iron and Steel – surely you've read about him?' Still nothing.

'And he's bought himself a train,' said Frank. 'Like you do.' And not a Hornby set either, but a life-size one with Pullman carriages.

'In a nutshell,' said the guard. 'And we're travelling around Scotland until the New Year. I know it's work for us, but there are worse jobs.'

'I hope he's paying you all well,' put in Roo. She'd done steward work and they'd treated her like a slave.

'He's a very generous man,' said the guard with a knowing wink. 'We get our perks. No shortage of people wanting to work for him, even over Christmas.' He smiled fondly then. 'He's taken quite the shine to Yorkshire and his wife's ancestors were from Scotland, hence why they decided to go there to christen the train. Some folks live in another world, it makes the Orient Express look like a cattle truck.'

'I'd love to see it,' Jane said.

'Can't show you, alas,' said the guard, shaking his head. 'No access via this carriage; besides, we can't have people stamping their shoes through it before Mr Ingleton.' He shuddered then as if someone had walked over his grave. 'Sorry about the temperature, there's something wrong with the heating in here, but you'll be off and on your way in about twenty minutes and at least it's warmer in than out.'

Roo would have questioned that. She blew out her cheeks and saw the ghost of her breath appear like ectoplasm.

Frank placed his hand over Grace's and whispered, 'I think he's having a laugh, don't you, love?' Hers didn't move, didn't make an effort to flip and curl her fingers around his; it remained stiff. He kept it there though, because she was cold and he wanted to comfort her, defrost her. If only it were as easy as holding her and transferring some of his heat, but she was frozen beyond her bones, beyond her soul.

'Can I just ask, how big is Eskford station? Are we really likely to get our trains from there?' asked Elizabeth, leaning forward to speak to the guard who had taken the seat in front of her.

'Well, the station itself is about the same size as Derringbury, but just because it's a little station doesn't mean it's not as well-connected as the big ones. More than one line goes through it, hence its full name: Eskford Junction.'

Its full name was music to their ears because it sounded busy and reliable. Hope settled in their hearts and stayed there for ten glorious minutes, then the train juddered and ground to a sudden hard stop, the main lights were extinguished and the emergency lights came on.

Chapter 8

'Is this a joke or a bad dream?' asked Tim to no one in particular, the tone in his voice reflecting his incredulity. One step forward, two steps back, which seemed to be his life pattern at the moment.

The guard walked to the end of the carriage, took from a hook a heavy greatcoat and a hat with ear flaps and put them on.

'I'll find out what's going on. No need for anyone to panic,' he said then, heading out of the door into the dancing snowflakes.

The travellers watched him through the windows, trudging forward to the head of the train.

'I hope it doesn't suddenly set off without him,' said Roo.

'Fat chance,' grumbled Tim.

Only minutes passed but it felt like an age. No one could do anything but wait; it didn't look good.

Tim huffed. 'Should have stayed in the bloody waiting room.'

'Hindsight is a wonderful thing,' Frank almost said, but kept quiet because it wouldn't have helped really.

'He's back,' said Roo, finally seeing movement outside. Sure enough, the guard, accompanied by a second figure, came into view jogging towards their carriage. They boarded, snow heavy on their hats and shoulders and it was indicative of the temperature inside the carriage that it took its time melting from them.

The guard addressed them. 'I'm sorry about this, every-one, but we've encountered a problem.'

'You don't say,' Tim commented, with heavy sarcasm.

'What sort of problem?' asked Vincent.

'It's the braking system and we can't go anywhere with that seized up. It means you'll have to sit tight for a while. Myself and Leonard – the driver here – will have to walk on to the station and get the engineer. Don't worry, it's not far.'

'Eskford?' Frank drew the obvious conclusion.

'No, St Hilda, immediately after Eskford. He's waiting there for us to pick him up. About ten minutes' walk—'

'More like twenty, Albert,' Leonard the driver disputed.

'Aye, maybe that's more like it,' agreed Albert the guard. 'Twenty minutes then, as the crow flies.' He waved his hand in the general direction of St Hilda and looked as if he was shaking hands with an invisible man.

'What – you don't have a way of communicating with the station other than by walking to it?' Jane queried. 'Not even a radio?'

'Well . . . radios and . . . this sort of snow . . .' Albert began an explanation about moisture and signal unreliability but abandoned it. His pained expression did all the answering for him without him needing to go on.

'Technology, eh?' said Frank, once again looking at his phone screen, but no amount of tapping at it was going to magic up some bars of signal.

'Anyone got a network that's operating?' Vincent asked, replicating the same actions on his huge foldable phone.

'Nope,' said Tim, seemingly speaking for everyone.

'It won't take us long, I'm sure. It's a brand new train, you see—'

'It's a more modern system than I'm used to,' butted in Leonard. 'That's why we're carrying a dedicated engineer. Mr Ingleton insisted, in case of . . .'—his voice withered—'emergencies.'

'Except he's not on yet.' Grace found she couldn't stop the snidey comment.

'No,' replied Albert, contritely. 'But please, just stay put and wait. It'll be sorted. It's most likely down to the weather, he'll know what it is as soon as he sees it. He's an expert.' He reached into his deep coat pockets and pulled out a big, leather glove from each side. 'The sooner we get there, the sooner we get back with him.'

He gave them a semblance of a smile, meant to be encouraging as he slipped on those gloves. Leonard the driver switched on the bulky torch he had in his hand and together they got off and started walking across the snow and the train passengers watched them until they disappeared into the wintery darkness, the light of the torch swallowed up by it also.

Inside the carriage no one said anything for a few minutes. Then Tim's voice broke the silence.

'What next, I wonder? Plague of frogs?'

'I dread to think,' said Vincent. It seemed to be growing colder by the second and 'next' was probably them all freezing to death. The chill was finding its way through even the thickest of their coats.

A full half-hour passed very slowly. Then Jane asked anyone who might care to answer,

'Do you think I would be allowed to use the toilet when the train is standing? I'm not sure you're supposed to but I don't fancy going outside.'

She was answered by a chorus of variations of: 'Sod what's allowed' and 'If you need to go, you must.' She stood up and stumbled. Roo got up quickly to aid her, escorting her down to the bottom of the carriage where the loo was. 'I'm sorry, I stupidly didn't eat before I set off.' Clifford would have been furious at her for that. *We don't expect vehicles to run on empty, so why would we expect people to?* Sometimes it was as if he was next to her speaking the words in her ear, but that was because they had spent so much time together over the years and she was still acclimatising to not having him around, looking out for her, so her silly imagination was filling in the gaps.

'This is ridiculous,' said Grace, shaking from cold. 'We'll either freeze or starve to death at this rate.'

Without saying anything, Frank rose from his seat and headed to the back door.

'Where are you going? Not out there, Frank,' his wife said.

'Well . . . I'm going to see if there is any way we can get on the main part of the train.' Never mind rich Americans wanting their toy to be pristine when they got on it at Glasgow, this was a needs-must situation and not only for toilets. Or Mr Dwight J. Ingleton's maiden trip was going to be blighted by a death on his hands.

'I'll come with you,' said Vincent, pulling his woolly hat out of his pocket. His mum had knitted it for him years ago and it was still going strong. Everything she put her hand to was built to last, including her son.

*

The two men braced themselves against the blizzard and wondered if the guard and driver had got to their destination yet because the conditions were treacherous. How could they even see where they were going in this, and torchlight wouldn't have made much – if any – difference. The first door of the *Yorkshire Belle*'s rear carriage was locked, so they pushed on to the next door – also locked. But the door of the next carriage was mercifully unlocked. They stepped inside and entered another world: the floor with its thick custom-patterned carpet, the wood-panelled walls, the gleaming brass door handles, the exquisite cut-glass light fittings; an inimitable smell of newness greeting them. Even this small vestibule was twenty times grander than the carriage they'd come from.

'Wow,' said Vincent.

'Jesus,' Frank echoed the sentiment if not the exact word. How the other half lived indeed. But the opulence took second place to the joyous light and warmth. They opened the door into the main saloon part of the car and gasped like kids as they found themselves in a bar area, with claret and ivory curtains at the windows, co-ordinating upholstered chairs and bench seats, and tables polished to a high shine. In the far corner was the bar itself, crafted from mid-brown wood, with burr walnut inlay. Crystal glasses sparkled on their shelves, bottles stood shoulder to shoulder ready to serve.

Frank looked at Vincent.

'I could do with a drink after today,' he said.

'I think we should get everyone in here and avail ourselves of something from behind that fancy-dancing counter. Purely for medicinal purposes, of course,' said Vincent with a cheeky grin.

'That sounds like a plan,' replied Frank.

Chapter 9

'Right, folks, this is what's happening,' said a snow-encrusted Vincent as soon as he'd got back onto the dark, cold, crummy South Riding Trains car. 'We're all getting onto the front part of the train. It's warm, it's certainly more comfortable than here and seeing as we have no idea how long it's going to be before we set off again, I think Mr Ingleton is just going to have to like it and lump it that he and his friends aren't the first people to check out the amenities.'

'It's not a long walk, though it might feel like it, but every step you take is one nearer to a much more comfortable situation,' Frank added, brushing the snow from his head with his meaty paw. 'Come on, everybody.'

'We can't do that, Frank,' said Grace.

'Yes, we can and we are, love, so up you get. Leave the cases, ladies, we'll come back for those. Just get yourselves out of here and into civilisation before you catch hypothermia.'

When Grace stood, she realised how stiff her limbs were from the cold that had already settled in them. Even if she felt uncomfortable about the decision to trespass onto someone else's property, she'd do as he asked, for the old lady's sake if not hers because she shouldn't have to put up with this.

'Let me help you,' she said to Jane, taking her handbag for her. She and Elizabeth aided Jane down the steps and they all linked arms as they walked towards the unlocked second *Belle* carriage as directed. The wind seemed insistent on blowing them back and, just as Frank said, the journey seemed much longer than it actually was. The relief was sweet when they finally climbed aboard, breathless from the effort of fighting with the elements, their faces smarting from the snow that had stung their skin like small icy insects. Jane flopped down onto a plush wine-coloured couch and then immediately stood up again, looking for a cloth or throw to put underneath her so she didn't dampen the beautiful brocade.

'It'll dry out in no time,' said Elizabeth, 'I wouldn't worry.' She looked around. What a difference between this carriage and the one they had just vacated. Not only in comfort, for it felt as if they had crossed a timeline, been transported back to an art deco world of decades ago.

Vincent hefted two suitcases through the snow, delivered them to the bar and then returned for more. Frank was on his second trip and Tim was doing a check around the unlit end carriage to make sure they had everything.

'I hope we aren't expected to bring it all back in five minutes because I shall flatly refuse,' Tim said.

'I think we all will,' agreed Vincent.

The three men trudged forward with the remainder of the luggage and when Vincent, the last man on, closed the

Belle's train door, the warmth of the carriage felt like an embrace. They stood in the vestibule to shake the snow off their coats before joining the others. The fat upholstered seats in the bar were a million miles kinder on the bottom than the hard ones in the South Riding Trains car.

'Just look at that,' said Jane, marvelling at the weather outside, which seemed to have grown worse in mere minutes. The snowflakes were diving chaotically, being whipped up again by the wind before they had the chance to rest upon the ground.

'Was this even forecast?' asked Grace.

'Rain turning to sleet when I checked,' replied Vincent.

'It's just like what happened a few years ago, isn't it?' said Elizabeth. She remembered it well. At the time, her father had a stomach bug and she'd moved back into the family home from her flat above the company offices to look after him over Christmas. They'd been trapped together and he'd been more bad-tempered and ungrateful than ever before, and it was quite a feat to better his best at being hard to please.

'I suppose we should make some intros, seeing as we are going to be spending a little time with each other,' said Vincent, starting the ball rolling. 'Vincent – or Vince, I answer to either.'

'Ruby,' said the woman in the pink coat with the badger flash in her hair. 'Though I prefer Roo.'

'Frank,' said the strong, square-shouldered man who looked as if he must have done some boxing in his time. 'And this is my wife, Grace.'

The old lady next. 'Jane.'

'Tim,' said the tall man with the surfeit of white hair. He said his name as if he had given part of his soul away at the same time.

And finally, the woman in the camel coat, golden hair pinned in a perfect French plait: 'Elizabeth.'

They all wondered collectively how much time they'd be spending with each other. How often they'd need to use their names.

'I could murder a coffee,' said Grace.

'I think a round of warm drinks would do us all good,' added Roo.

'Or something stronger, perhaps.' Frank tipped his head towards the brass and burr walnut bar in the far corner.

'Absolutely not,' said Grace to that. 'What if the guard comes back? He'll throw us off.'

'I'd like to see him try.' Jane chuckled. 'I'm willing to take my chances.'

'So am I.' Vincent nodded and so did Elizabeth.

'Count me in too.'

Grace threw up her arms in a small surrender; it seemed like she was outvoted.

'Allow me.' Frank stood up and walked over to the bar. He lifted up a flap to get behind it. The newness shouted at him, everything pristine and ready for a very rich family's use. His eyes took in the many bottles on display – there was nothing they didn't have. He opened up various cupboards under the counter which were stocked to capacity.

'Well, what would everyone like? They have your favourite here, Grace: Grand Marnier.'

Grace opened her mouth to say that she wasn't sure but her husband was already pouring it.

'My husband Clifford used to love that,' said Jane, unwrapping the scarf from around her neck. 'He always used to say that it was Christmas in a glass. But as for me, I'd like a brandy, please.'

'Courvoisier? Calvados? Armagnac ...?'

'Ooh, a calvados sounds wonderful,' trilled Jane. 'Apples, one of my five a day.'

Frank picked up the bottle and read the label: *Adrien Camut*. Prestigious at that. His eyebrows rose involuntarily. He knew how much this aged bottle would cost. He should have felt guilty about being the first to break into it, but he really didn't. So many things had gone wrong on this journey, a little respite was needed. And if Ingleton was rich enough to buy a train, a measure from a three – maybe four – hundred pound bottle of apple brandy wouldn't break him. He only hoped Mr Ingleton wasn't some sort of gangster who took violently against anyone christening his virgin train supplies. Too late; his hand twisted – the seal was broken, the damage was done. He lifted one of the crystal brandy balloons from the holders above his head and tilted the bottle over it.

Roo left her seat and approached the counter. 'I'll be your waitress for the day.' She smiled.

'Thank you,' said Frank, slipping easily into his role of bartender. Home from home, of course, but this was a few notches above his little place by the sea.

Roo delivered the weighty crystal glasses to Grace and Jane. Drinks always tasted more delicious in this sort of receptacle, she thought, although her dad would have been equally blissed out by drinking Bacardi from a tea-stained mug.

Jane put her nose inside the balloon and inhaled the fruity, warm aroma. It reminded her of sweet pastries being sold in a sunny Normandy market; her first holiday of many there with her beloved Clifford. She let herself savour the little bubble of happiness the memory brought – the *glimmer* – before she let her lips touch the dark, rich liquid.

Grace coughed as the orange fumes of her Grand Marnier hit the back of her throat. Frank remembered the first time she'd tried it – at his parents' house one Christmas. She'd coughed just like that, and Frank's dad had said, *let me get you something else instead, love,* and went to take it away from her and she'd snatched it out of his reach and said, *don't you dare, Mr O'Carroll.* She'd made him laugh. She made him laugh so much in the years that followed too, until it had all ground to a halt. Until their lives had ground to a halt.

Elizabeth had a Courvoisier, Vincent a Jack Daniels. Then Frank poured an Irish whiskey for Tim, Roo and himself.

There was a shiny silver ice-bucket on the counter, the name of the train etched in fine scroll on the side. Its insulating qualities must have been second to none because it was full to the top with ice and none of it had melted. All in preparation for the rich Mr Ingleton, no doubt, when he boarded and someone poured him a welcoming snifter so he could toast his colossal, expensive, iron toy.

Frank joined the others sitting around one of the wooden tables, inlaid with the same marquetry as that on the walls. Someone had distributed square leather coasters, half off-white, half dark blue with the *Yorkshire Belle* name in gold, just like the outside of the train. Mr Ingleton was a man who liked his merchandise copious and tastefully branded, it seemed.

The carriage seemed extra snug for the crazed weather view from the windows. They could have all been in a snow globe that a giant had just shaken.

'I hope the guard and the driver aren't lying out there somewhere,' said Roo, unfastening her pink furry coat now that she was finally warm enough to do so.

'Me too, but it would be downright stupid to go out there

and try to look for them,' said Grace. 'We just have to hope they knew where they were going and got there safely.'

'Shhh, everyone,' said Jane, holding up her hand. 'I can hear someone.'

They fell silent to listen. There was a man's voice, faint, in the distance. Then a chuckle. Tim got up and walked down the carriage, hunting the source of the sound. It was getting louder, closer. He traced it to the corner. A vintage box radio was sitting on a shelf full of leather-bound books, looking like a tatty interloper. He wasn't one for interior design but maybe this was a feature; something so shabby it became chic.

'It's a radio that's been left on,' said Tim, picking it up, tweaking up the volume.

'Bring it over,' said Frank. 'There might be some travel news.'

Tim set it down in the middle of the table.

'That of course was Nat King Cole. I imagine we are all putting some coal on our fires tonight, aren't we?' said the disembodied voice coming from the radio speaker, with a chuckle at the end for his pun. 'Goodness me, what weather.' A gentle voice, older, someone missing most of – if not all – his teeth.

'You're listening to BBC Radio Brian. The real BBC. That's Brian Bernard Cosgrove, not the British Broadcasting Corporation. Coming to you from the very snowy moors of Yorkshire. I hope you're all safe and sound in your houses. Blimey, it's wild out there, isn't it?'

'BBC Radio Brian,' repeated Tim with a humph. 'I wonder how many listeners he's got.'

'Well, seven at least,' said Jane.

'I think we need one of the main news stations,' said Tim,

twiddling the knob first one way, then the other, but apart from white noise and a very very faint unstable connection to a foreign station, he found nothing. So back to Brian he headed.

'Considering that we seem to be cut off from the rest of mankind, he might be the only way we have of finding out any information. I vote we keep him playing until his battery runs out,' he said.

'They'll have spare batteries somewhere, I expect,' said Roo. When you were rich to train-buying standard, surely you had people who thought of all the details, all the things you would be in danger of running out of.

'Very pretty, isn't it, though? I'm sitting here in my studio and my wife, Mrs BBC – Cath – has just brought me a lovely cup of hot chocolate laced with a little medicinal brandy because it's a bit parky in my attic . . .' Radio Brian continued. All seven of them had roughly the same idea of what Radio Brian must look like sitting in his chilly top-of-the-house enclave, looking out at the snow, sipping from a huge mug. A man much older than his years by the sound of him, imagining himself as the Shipping Forecast providing an essential service to a million listeners.

'The snow is over the whole country now: Galashiels to Godolphin Cross. Apparently it's come from Siberia. They always blame Siberia, don't they? About that broken-down lorry I told you about earlier on the B1234 – that sounds like a made-up road, doesn't it? – anyway, I'm happy to announce that the driver walked to the Dog and Duck where he is going to stay for the night, so he's snug as a bug . . . So to celebrate that, let me play you a little festive-themed tune – "Let it Snow" sung by Vaughn Monroe. Do you know, this song was written on one of the hottest days of the year. Isn't that amusing?'

Jane preferred the Dean Martin version. 'Dino' recorded it on a sweltering August day in 1959. But it was in the winter of that year when she'd first heard it playing on the radio at the exact time when Wilfred Maltravers turned up for the first time at the door with a sack of coal over his shoulder. He was seventeen, from Italian stock so he had thick black hair like Dean Martin and the face of a god and it was love at first sight – at least it was for her. His obvious disdain for the gooey-eyed little soon-to-be-sixteen-year-old girl didn't put her off. But then no one took that much interest in the young Jane and so that was par for the course. Until she met David Carteret the year after, of course, then she didn't know what to do with all the attention. And that was why she fell so quickly, hook, line and sinker. He was a glass of water to a permanently parched throat.

'You must have some good memories attached to this song,' said Frank, watching the smile spread on Jane's face.

Jane clicked back into the present world, embarrassed slightly that her innermost thoughts might have manifested themselves.

'Mixed,' she answered him without elaborating. It was strange how life turned out really. She'd been secretly in love with Wilfred for twelve whole tortured months when she overheard him telling Mrs Blenkinsop from next door that he was going to the Christmas ball in the village hall. She'd begged her best friend, Susan, to go to it with her. But it snowed and Susan fell and hurt her leg and rather than let Jane down, she'd sent her older sister along with her ticket. Blonde, beautiful Kitty, who had more curves than a country road. Was it any wonder that when the cool, iceman coalman Wilfred clocked Kitty, he defrosted on the spot. Jane left them jiving on the dance floor and went outside to cry and there she met David Carteret having a cigarette. She knew him by sight, but he was older – a man, as opposed to a boy, and he really wasn't her type at all, but she was hurt and her feelings were all over the place and they got talking and she said yes when he asked her out to the pictures. *I'll show that Wilfred Maltravers that I'm someone to be desired.* And the rest was history.

'Where were we all supposed to be going then?' asked Frank after taking a sip of his whiskey. My, it was a good one, coating his mouth with an immediate grain hit, though his nose caught a light honey when he lifted the glass. Just what a discerning doctor would have ordered for such a night. He remembered then that Jane said she was going to Lancaster and Vincent was heading to Durham to drop off his passenger. 'Grace and I have a cottage booked near the next station. We were staying there for Christmas and then coming home on the twenty-ninth.'

'Sounds nice,' said Elizabeth. 'I'm going to just outside Durham, to my future in-laws' house. It's my official en-gagement party tonight. Vincent was driving me there.'

Roo had also presumed that Vincent and Elizabeth were a couple: her posh and him a bit of rough with his unruly brown hair, stubble and cheeky face, perfect opposite at-traction. Ridiculously, considering she didn't know them at all, she found herself a little disappointed that they weren't.

'Diamond Service Taxis, that's me,' said Vincent, flut-tering a pair of jazz hands. 'Guaranteed to get you to your destination on time, though I might need to alter that tag line.'

'I don't think anyone would sue you under the Trade Descriptions Act, given the extreme circumstances,' said Jane with a smile. 'I'm supposed to be going to Lancaster, to spend Christmas with my stepson and his wife.'

Elizabeth wasn't the only one who picked up on Jane's tone as she delivered the line, which was akin to saying she was off to the dentist for a root canal procedure.

'And I'm off to an Airbnb in Whitby for Christmas with friends,' said Roo. She turned quickly to her side. 'What about you, Tim?'

'Newcastle. I'm Santa at a corporate party for families.'

That surprised no one, because he looked exactly like a Father Christmas with his big build and thick white hair and beard. Although it had to be said, his manner was more Grinch.

'Do you play Santa a lot?' asked Roo.

'Only at Christmas,' came the clipped reply, as if Roo had asked him the world's most stupid question. It put her off him immediately because there was no need for that smartarse answer. She'd live happily without knowing who made his costume or if he looked naturally like that or had to have his hair bleached, questions she might have asked him in the course of conversation to pass some time. Or if he changed up his miserable face when he was in front of a load of kids.

'I think they'll have cancelled the party if that makes you feel any better,' said Vincent. 'Sounds like the snow's not limited to around here, if the radio man is telling the truth.'

Tim gave a shrug by way of an answer, as if he wasn't committing to believing it or not.

'I suppose your party will have had to be cancelled as well, Elizabeth.' Jane gave her a sorry smile.

'Yes, I expect so.' It was easier to agree than explaining that the Pennington family wouldn't have cancelled the party even if there had been a nuclear war. Elizabeth's name would be mud for not moving heaven and earth to

accommodate their laid-in-cement arrangements, for not
circumventing any possible disturbance to them. Most of
the key people would have arrived that morning because
they would be staying over Christmas: Gregory's aunt and
cousins, plus friends of the family who considered themselves relations. The best man lived in Durham and would
have got there early. Elizabeth's father arrived the previous
night and would be furious that she hadn't accepted the lift
he offered her but instead stayed home to snatch a meet with
an old university friend who was in the area for a few hours
only. The staff doing the catering and serving were a mix of
live-in and locals. The only people really missing were the
non-essentials – and the newly affianced woman, of course.
She looked down at the diamond on her ring; it was huge,
heavy, showy. It kept swinging around and digging into the
next finger. It wasn't the one she'd picked. She didn't know
why he'd even asked what sort of ring she'd like if his plan
was always to override her choice.

'I'm getting a report of a train stuck near Derringbury,'
said Brian.

'That's us. Shh, everyone,' said Grace.

'Let's hope the passengers are listening, shall we,' Radio
Brian went on, '. . . because there will be no rescue tonight.
So the message to them is if you are by some miracle hearing
this, you hunker down and stay as warm and comfortable as
you can. Let's hope there's some provisions on that train for
those folks. Some sandwiches in the dining car, maybe. I'm
always partial to an egg and tomato on a train personally.
And I'm also told there's no electricity in Eskford at the
moment so I hope everyone who lives there has candles in
copious supply . . .'

'Oh great,' said Grace. 'So even if we did get there, we'd

have nothing to see with or cook on. Not that we have any food anyway.'

No point in us taking anything like that, we'll just buy it when we get there, Frank had said. He'd envisaged a trip out to the local farm shop and buying everything they needed there, lovely indulgences to make up for the second-best living arrangements.

He sighed. He didn't think things could have gotten any worse, but his old mum used to say that just when you'd hit rock bottom, someone was sure to come along with a pick so you could keep digging down.

'So the guard and driver must have made it to wherever they were going, then, if the guy on the radio has had a message about us,' said Elizabeth, patting her chest where her heart lay. 'That's something we can stop worrying about, at least.'

'What if we hadn't just heard what we've heard?' said Roo. Her 'what if' nerve was cranked to the max. *What if there had been no way of getting into the front of the train and they'd had to stay in that frozen back carriage? What if they'd felt duty-bound to go looking for the missing guard? What if . . .*

Elizabeth cut off her torturous thoughts. 'Well, we *did* hear, and we have enough to worry about without extra things, so put them out of your mind.'

'Are you all right, Jane?' Grace noticed that Jane looked a little . . . 'wilted' was the word that came to mind.

'I think I might need a biscuit or something,' came the answer.

Roo unzipped her cavernous cloth shoulder bag and hunted around in it, pulling out a mini Mars bar.

'Here you go, I've always got choc stocks in my bag for emergencies.'

Jane's hands were visibly trembling as she reached over for it.

'If you're sure, thank you, dear.'

'Here, let me,' said Roo, opening it for her. 'When I have one of those low blood sugar moments, I'm no use to anyone either.'

'Thank you.'

Frank polished off the last of his glass because that little scene had galvanised him into action. His own stomach had just done quite the grumble.

'If we're in here for the night, then we'd better find out what's what, as Brian says.'

'I'll check out the facilities with you,' said Vincent.

'I'll come along as well.' Tim stood. And Roo immediately thought that he was going primarily because he didn't want to stay with the women. He had a bit of a problem with the fairer sex, did old Santa, she'd bet anything on that.

Chapter 10

The end carriage, the one that was locked when they'd tried to gain access to it from outside, had a polished plaque next to its door: *Maria Gloriosa*. It was a lounge with very light wood on the walls and all the upholstery and carpets were in pale tan. There were shelves dotted around full of old bound books, most with gilt lettering on their spines, probably chosen for their vintage look rather than their readability, Frank surmised, noticing some of the titles: *The New Book of American Politics, The Curious Beetle of Jung, Great Bells of the World*. The windows looked larger in here than the ones in the bar and the back of the carriage was almost entirely glass. That the sofas were mostly positioned facing the windows was a pretty clear indication of the purpose of this room: an observation coach, a quiet coach for reading and contemplation, sitting and just 'being'. What a luxury.

They doubled back, telling the ladies what they'd seen and then headed forward. Vincent noticed that the area in which they'd set up base was called 'Lutine'; there was a brass plate at the side of the door they'd missed when they first walked in. The next carriage, according to the signage, also had a name: 'Old Tom'.

'Bet that's Ingleton's cat,' said Vincent.

The first part of it obviously served as a dining area as there were two central tables, one shorter than the other and spread with a blue cover and place mats with the name of the train printed on them, waiting in readiness for the first diners. They discovered a galley took up the rest of the coach. They entered to find an immaculate working space, ovens, gas hobs, cupboards everywhere crammed with crockery, cutlery, pans and cooking utensils, and though this might have seemed the obvious place to find food, the fridge was empty. Vincent silently hoped that it wasn't all getting picked up with the crew en route or they were going to be surviving on a very potent liquid diet until they were rescued.

'Liberty' was next; another lounge, the décor very dark wood and muted blue and gold upholstery. At the far end was a black iron fireplace with a ridiculously ornate cream surround. Two detailed classical figures were carved into the marble, differing only in their countenances – four of them, for each had two heads facing in opposite directions. In the corner was a Christmas tree, a real one with thick dark-green branches – not yet decorated – its top nudging against a hand-painted ceiling that made the one in the Sistine chapel look like an amateur attempt.

They forged on. At the front ends of each carriage were compact toilet rooms with sinks, but at both ends of the strangely named 'Uglich', there were bigger washrooms with showers. This carriage was comprised of four bedroom cabins. They were all more or less identical, give or take the colour scheme as two were sage with creamy birch wood, two gold with a rich mahogany contrast. There were twin single beds in each, made up ready for weary guests. The bedding was whiter than the snow outside the windows, the pillows fat as clouds. Tim could have just sunk into one of those beds.

The next car, 'Sigismund' only had two rooms, both doors to them locked. Maybe these were the luxury cabins, the suites, Mr Dwight J. Ingleton's hangout and space for himself and his most important guests. 'Mingun' had seven cabins, obviously smaller; maybe rooms for the staff, they had to surmise because these were locked too. Another bathroom introduced the next car with the intriguing name of 'Yongle' which was made up of another two smallish cabins, again locked, and beyond them floor to ceiling cupboards full of linen, towels, toiletries, cleaning equipment, all sorts of odds and sods, sacks and sacks of wooden logs ... and – *bingo* – three enormous fridges packed to the gills with food.

'There is a God,' said Tim on a long outward breath of relief.

'Gentlemen, we are not going to starve,' said Vincent, with equivalent sentiment.

There was a pantry on the other side, the shelves laden with jars and bottles of everything from mustards to jams, honey, spices and seasonings, flour, sugar, bread, eggs ... every grocery component one could think of, and at the bottom a store of all manner of fruits and vegetables.

The penultimate carriage, 'Pummerin', was a bit of a hotchpotch car; it housed two desks, tables and less opulent furnishings leading them to believe this might be the staff mess. They couldn't go on as the door to 'Dhammazedi' was locked, but they could see through the glass that it housed a considerable amount of equipment, possibly the generator that powered everything – and they hoped kept powering it. They'd found what they needed to and walked back to tell the others.

'It's getting worse out there,' said Jane, worry gripping her insides, squeezing them. 'I don't know where it's come from.' She didn't say it for fear of coming across like a doom-monger, but it's what she imagined the end of the world would look like. She was hardier than she appeared, but that didn't mean she wasn't a little frightened by the ferocity of the weather. It wouldn't be easy for her to walk in the footsteps of the guard and the driver if they had to and this amount of snow wasn't going to melt overnight. So it was with some relief that, when the three men returned, they were all smiling.

Vincent clapped his hands and rubbed them together. 'Well, the good news is, ladies . . . we ain't gonna starve.'

'And the bad news?' asked Jane, because his phrasing suggested there might be some.

'The bad news is that we might starve if we're here for longer than a month.' Frank grinned.

Jane felt that worry loosen its hold a tad. Clifford's voice whispered in her ear: *'Don't you start doubting me now. I said I'd always look after you, and I will.'*

If only.

'I am going to rustle us up something to eat. My stomach thinks my throat's been cut,' said Frank.

Elizabeth was not the only one who presumed Frank's wife might have stood up at this point and offered to help him, but she didn't. So she volunteered herself.

'Would you like a hand?'

She noticed Frank steal the briefest glance at Grace before he answered.

'If . . . you . . . feel as if you would like to help me locate a kettle, then yes please.'

'I can do that.' Elizabeth got up.

'Anyone got any food allergies or things they can't eat?' Frank asked.

There were mutterings and shakings of heads by way of answer.

'Good, that makes it easy. Come on then, Elizabeth.'

They made their way to the next carriage.

Elizabeth paused by the brass sign and wondered who 'Old Tom' was. She took in the tables and the plush velvet chairs and thought how wonderful it would be to dine in this coach as it traversed the countryside. She loved trains, though Gregory didn't do public transport if he could help it. He wouldn't go on a plane if it meant he had to turn right.

She gave a small gasp as she walked into the galley. 'My goodness, how pristine. I'd like to bet that no one has so much as chopped an onion in here.' She opened a cupboard and peered inside. Then another.

'The food storage is right at the front of the train. I'll go and bring some things down and put them in the fridge.'

'I'll come with you,' said Elizabeth. 'Four hands will be better than two.'

She followed Frank through the various carriages, marvelling at the sheer opulence, the painted ceilings, the sumptuous soft furnishings, no corners cut, everything top-notch, everything created, fitted and painted by the best craftsmen.

In the pantry Elizabeth found a large basket which she filled with various items to put in the galley fridge. Frank piled foodstuff into a fruit box including a ham, a large pie, cheese, bread and a huge cooked chicken. They took them down to 'Old Tom', almost giddy that a proper meal was soon to be had.

In the galley, while Frank was assembling sandwiches, Elizabeth was pulling plates out of the cupboard; beautiful blue and gold plates with the name of the train in fancy scroll across the middle.

'Damn, I forgot the salt and pepper,' he said. 'I'll go back.'

He made his way through the carriages, and as he entered 'Yongle' it was the oddest thing because he could have sworn he heard a door ahead shut. He called out, 'Hello. Anyone there?' It wasn't a surprise that no one answered, but still, his skull started prickling with a low thrum of unease, and he wasn't a man for such fancies. He didn't linger. He took the large silver salt and pepper pots and a jar of mustard for good measure, and headed back to the galley.

Elizabeth had found a kettle by the time he returned. It was a large-bellied steel one that sat on a stovetop and heralded its boiling with a celebratory whistle. Frank knew that because his mum used to have one just like it when he was growing up, although hers was smaller and bashed and buckled with age and use. She used to tell him that there was an old bird that she'd rescued from the cold and he liked nothing better than to be snug and warm inside the kettle and that was his song of happiness when it boiled. She was full of such stories, every one of which made him smile. Occasionally, as now, something unexpected − like a gift − would drag a memory connected to her out of the store cupboard and he'd smile again. God, he'd been lucky with his parents. He'd been luckier than Grace had with hers who were frozen to the core, not an ounce of fun in them, not a single chuckle.

'Blimey, you don't hang around, do you?' said Frank. Elizabeth not only had the plates ready, but she'd set trays with elegant china cups, saucers and cutlery ready to take through.

'I think hunger is galvanising me,' she replied. 'I haven't eaten at all today. I was supposed to be having a six-course supper tonight and so I kept my stomach empty.'

Frank pulled in air through his lips. 'You should always have breakfast, you know. Most important meal of the day. My breakfasts are the stuff of legend. People might be finding that out in the morning if things stay as they are.' He stole a glance at the window, the snowflakes lashing at the glass as if they wanted immediate entry. He'd like to bet he would be playing breakfast chef come daylight.

He turned on the tap and washed his hands.

'You're a cook? Chef, Frank?'

'Self-taught, but yes,' Frank said. 'I grew up in a pub. Always knew I'd have my own one day and now I have. I like to be hands-on, so you'll find me behind the bar and doing the breakfasts for any guests, not dictating orders to staff. I find it easier to do than delegate.'

'And what's your place called and where is it?'

'You won't have heard of it, little seaside village in Norfolk called Seapoint. Beautiful it is. Inn's called The Salty Cockle.'

Elizabeth chuckled. 'Sounds lovely. Although that's not a Norfolk accent you have.'

'No, I'm a Chatham boy and my wife is a Gillingham girl.' Frank began to carve the ham into thin slices. The knife was a beauty and slipped through the meat like butter.

'That's close to where Vincent is from too,' said Elizabeth.

She'd found out that he was from Kent when they'd been chatting in the car.

'I thought as much. Recognised the Estuary.'

'How come you ended up in Norfolk then?'

A beat – a telling one. 'Oh, we just . . . fancied a change of scenery. A quieter pace of life,' he replied, a perfectly feasible answer but that initial pause made Elizabeth feel there was something more to his story.

'My Grace knows that the kitchen is my territory. That's why she didn't volunteer to help me.' He dropped a small laugh. 'In case you were wondering.'

'Oh, I wasn't at all,' Elizabeth fibbed, thinking that he sounded too keen to answer a question that hadn't been asked.

'I do all the cooking. It helps me get my head straight.'

'I like to walk,' said Elizabeth. 'That does it for me.'

There was something about walking that freed up her brain, but sometimes it asked her too many awkward questions in the attempt to sort her out.

The kettle started to flex its lungs and Frank thought again of the small contented bird preening its feathers and preparing to sing through the spout. Who would have known then when he was a happy little boy, as warm and content as that bird, just how much coldness and unhappiness there was waiting up life's road for him?

Chapter 11

Roo came to help and together the three of them took everything to the dining table. Elizabeth bobbed her head into the bar carriage to tell the others that dinner was served.

'Come on, Jane, get yourself sat down here, love. You've got first pick of the sandwiches. Some stand pie as well there, darlin', if you fancy,' said Frank.

'You're a star,' said Jane, her voice brimming with gratitude. When her eyes came to rest on the tower of sandwiches that Frank had made, she added, 'My goodness, when do the rest of the five thousand arrive?'

Frank pulled the chair out for Jane and then tucked her under the table. Roo poured her a cup of tea and when she lifted it to her lips and sipped she sighed. 'I don't think I've ever tasted better.'

'It's *Yorkshire Belle* blend, according to the tin,' said Elizabeth. 'Can you believe they have their own tea and coffee?'

'Well, you would if you could.' Roo passed the sandwiches to Tim and it really wasn't her imagination that he grunted a thank-you as if torn between being polite and dismissive, manners slightly winning out. She felt her nerve endings bristle as if something primal within her sensed an enemy.

The rapture showed on Frank's face as his teeth bit down into his cheese and pickle. The bread tasted as if it had come out of the oven less than an hour ago.

'I don't usually get this much pleasure from something I've put together myself but on this occasion . . .'

'Absolutely delicious,' said Roo, through a mouthful, then apologised. 'Sorry, I know I shouldn't talk with my gob full but credit where it's due, Frank.'

Frank couldn't help beaming watching everyone tuck in. He enjoyed feeding people. He was one of life's carers and nurturers. It ran in the family, his lot had all been the same.

'There's plenty of food anyway, so at least we are not going to wither away. And let's hope and pray the generator keeps working.'

'There's a fireplace in the lounge, though, and there's a store of logs so we at least have a source of heat if all else fails,' said Vincent. 'And if we have fire, and we have bread we can have toast and warm up our insides as well.' He smiled. Elizabeth tried not to think how nice his smile was. His face defaulted to that smile, she'd noticed.

'Goodness, listen to that,' said Tim, as a flurry of hailstones hit the train windows behind him, sounding as if someone had thrown handfuls of rocks at the glass.

'It makes being inside extra cosy, don't you think?' said Frank. He turned to Grace. 'You all right, love?' He handed her the pot of pickle and she knew that he'd probably searched the stores to find it because she liked it on every sandwich, regardless of what it was. A picture flashed up in her mind of her once peeling back the top slice of bread on an egg mayo sandwich and spooning it on and Frank shaking his head, but smiling. She'd made him smile a lot over the years, but she couldn't remember when the last time was.

'Vincent said there are some bedrooms made up,' said Jane, reaching for another sandwich. Soft buttered bread and salty chicken had restored her.

'Yes, four of the cabins are unlocked and we should seriously think about using them tonight. We can't sleep on sofas with blankets wrapped round us. We might be here for another full day at this rate,' said Frank. 'There's plenty of linen stocks and I'm pretty sure that it won't take Mr Ingleton's staff long to change the beds. Our needs are here and now and I for one am sleeping supine with a pillow at my head tonight.'

'Four rooms and seven of us,' echoed Elizabeth. 'That's Frank and Grace in one . . .'

'I'll fly solo, if no one minds. I snore like a drain,' Tim butted in, which threw the ideal sharing arrangements out immediately.

'I'll share with one of the ladies then,' said Grace.

Tim winced. 'Sorry, I wasn't thinking. I don't mind sharing but they might. It's a bit embarrassing . . .'

'I have no qualms at all in sharing,' Jane said. 'In fact, I'd prefer it. Grace?'

'Yes, of course. I'll come in with you, Jane.'

Elizabeth looked towards Roo who put her thumb up by way of an answer as her mouth was full of ham, bread and mustard. Elizabeth would be a good room-mate, she thought. Nice company. She didn't want to be alone either.

'Looks like you've got the short straw with me, mate.' Frank pointed to Vincent. 'We can talk about Kent and how annoyed we get when people think we're cockneys.'

'Ha, you're on.'

'Oh, the weather outside is indeed frightful,' said Brian's voice from the radio speaker. 'I'm going to be ending this broadcast very soon. I hope Mrs BBC has got the warming pan ready for the sheets . . .'

That caused some titters around the table.

'Warming pan? Even we had electric blankets when I was young and I'm now eighty-one.' Jane reached for a slice of pie. She hadn't enjoyed a meal as much in a long time; simple fare but absolutely delicious. Roo picked up the pot and went around the table filling the tea drinkers' cups up. Grace did the same with the coffee.

'Only joking, of course, although according to the other BBC, the weather update for this region is a little bit grim, I'm afraid. More snow is on the way. I'm shaking my fist in the general direction of Siberia for everyone so you don't have to bother.' Brian chortled. 'I'm having a very warming hash supper tonight. Best beef, our own home-grown potatoes and carrots. Mrs Cosgrove makes the best. And I always ask her to put a few sprouts in it as well . . .'

'That sounds good.' Vincent found himself thinking about coming home from school, pushing open the door to be greeted by the aroma of his mum's best beef hash, served on a massive fried pancake that overlapped the plate. That was his favourite tea of all time.

'I'm presuming he doesn't mean wacky baccy hash,' put in Roo.

'Shh.' Tim directed the sound at Roo alone. She was despising him a little more with every passing minute.

'Hope you're all warm and snug. Here's Winter Wonderland, but don't anyone go out and build a snowman – not in this. So, until tomorrow, everyone. Goodnight and god bless.'

'You have heard of hash before, haven't you, Roo?' Vincent's voice was soft and she knew it was an attempt to counteract Tim's snap. He had no need to though, she wasn't a drip, but she was glad he recognised that the big beardy git was a knob. More Wanker Claus than Santa Claus.

'I'm presuming it's some sort of stew?' Roo answered him.

'It's probably different things depending on where you're from. I'd have said it's somewhere between a fry-up and a stew. I think some of that might be on the menu for tomorrow if the rescue party hasn't been. I spotted some beef in the fridge.' Frank looked at the window he was facing and the chaos of snowflakes being buffeted by the wind. The idea of them being a rescue party's priority in this seemed ludicrous.

'Please put some sprouts in it. I love sprouts.' Roo gave him her most hopeful smile.

'I will. Christmas Eve hash-stew,' said Frank. 'The best of comfort food.'

Christmas Eve, thought Roo. If ever there was a day when she needed some comfort food – tomorrow was it.

Jane stood up to clear the plates until Elizabeth kindly, but firmly, told her to sit back down – she and Grace had this. Vincent and Tim got on with rolling people's luggage down to the cabins. Roo and Elizabeth had cabin one, next door Jane and Grace, then Frank and Vincent and Tim in the fourth.

When Grace went in to get her regular nighttime magnesium tablet from her case her jaw dropped when she saw how gorgeous the bedroom was, with its green and gold blinds and curtains, mirrors polished to a perfect shine, cut-glass lamps and carpet almost thick enough to bounce on. There were storage cupboards everywhere, with inset hinges so they were flush to the walls in order to be invisible, every inch of space either decorative or functional. There were two adjacent single beds in the cabin and a separate dressing area with a sink that sat inside a large wooden cabinet with curved doors and shelves full of stoppered bottles of toiletries that promised the highest quality contents. Adjacent, there was a heated brass towel rail with fluffy snow-white towels draped over them, *Yorkshire Belle* in golden scroll embroidered along the bottom of each.

There was a thick white robe folded into a parcel on each bed, tied with blue and gold ribbon. It wasn't hard to imagine how comfortable and welcoming that bed would be, even without the sort of day they'd had. Nodding off on a sofa wrapped in a blanket versus this bed; there was really no competition between the two options on offer.

Jane came in when Grace was taking the T-shirt she used as a nightie out of her case.

'Oh my goodness,' she exclaimed, looking round. 'How beautiful.'

'Isn't it?'

'I've stayed in some lovely staterooms in hotels and on ships, but this beats them all,' Jane told her. 'There's a shower next door if you didn't know. It's *compact* but there's no slipping of standards.'

'I think I'd very much like a shower before I turn in, it's been such a long day.' Grace yawned then, hit by a wave of tiredness.

'That sounds like a plan, Grace.'

'Plenty of warm towels in that little side room, Jane. I hope you don't mind, I've claimed this bed under the window. I thought the other might be slightly warmer for you. There's no draught, of course, but that one just looks cosier.' Grace leaned over the bed and pulled down the heavy blind, shutting out the expanse of black sky and white snow outside.

'I really don't mind but thank you for the consideration,' Jane replied. She noticed the robe parcel on the bed. 'My, that looks as if it would be a luxurious wear. I'm not sure it would be right to, though.'

'Yes, I agr—'

'Then again, we're using everything else, aren't we?' Jane cut her off. 'And these are "extenuating circumstances" after all.' Her lip kinked at the left side.

Jane pulled the ribbon, killing the bow, and lifted up the robe, shaking out the creases. 'Look at that. I'm really not going to be able to resist putting it on.'

'Well, if you are . . .' Grace undid the ribbon on her robe.

The sound came from far away, low but still enough to cut through the weather and reach Jane. She always did have very acute hearing that hadn't diminished as the years had gone on; if anything, it had sharpened. An audiologist had once told her that she could hear an ant walking in bedsocks across a woollen quilt. Clifford had called it a gift, but there had never been any major advantages to it so she would have disputed that.

'Do you hear that, Grace? A bell, in the distance.' Its tone consistent and rhythmic: ring-ring – pause – ring-ring . . .

Grace strained her ears and moved her head around but she couldn't hear a thing, then a knock at their cabin door broke their concentrations and made them jump.

Jane opened it to find Frank outside.

'Sorry to disturb you, girls, but my toothbrush is in your toiletry bag, Grace.'

Grace unzipped her bag, pulled it out and handed it to him.

'I suppose you'll want the toothpaste as well.'

'No, you keep it. I've found some in the cupboard underneath the sink,' Frank replied. 'Yep, they've even got *Yorkshire Belle* branded tubes of toothpaste. Not that I'm surprised; are you?' He addressed the question to Jane.

'Not one bit, Frank.'

'Is there anything else of yours in my case?' Grace asked him, almost impatiently.

'No, I don't think so, love.'

Jane had already noticed how different his tone towards her was to the tone she used towards him. It was as if he were treading carefully on eggshells, his voice always subdued, reverent, in fear of shattering them.

'Everyone's having a nightcap before we turn in,' said Frank.

'Right,' said Grace.

'That sounds like a good idea,' enthused Jane. 'Though I don't think I'll have any trouble sleeping in this bed.'

'See you down there then.'

'You will indeed,' said Jane.

'Grace, you coming?'

'Yes.' The word flat, emotionless.

Frank pulled the door to. And Jane thought, *there is a marriage in trouble.*

Chapter 12

Roo apologised for saying 'Wow' yet again, but this room really did have the wow factor. It had turned her into a giddy puppy from a bog-roll commercial. She'd only intended to dump her big bag and coat and go back to the bar but the lure of all those cupboards with surprises inside, so many of them, was too much to resist. She looked everywhere and opened everything. It was like the train version of a luxury advent calendar.

'*Yorkshire Belle* toothpaste? Who has their own toothpaste? I bet the royal family doesn't even have that.'

Elizabeth laughed. She'd had the same intention, a quick visit to check out where she was spending the night, but Roo's discoveries were keeping her too entertained, her wows and gasps of delight and 'Will you look at this' exclamations.

'Oh my god, toothbrushes in here. Total cock-up on the ergonomic front – why aren't they with the toothpastes?'

'You should leave them a note. Write one for Mr Ingleton on the *Yorkshire Belle* stationery,' said Elizabeth. Stationery that Roo had discovered in a drawer: pens, ink, envelopes, notepaper and a jotter, all with the train's name in gold lettering somewhere on them. What's more, when she pulled it out fully, a flap magically appeared and it became a writing desk top. Elizabeth thought that Gregory's mother would have deep logo envy. She had the family coat of arms plastered everywhere that would take it, but she didn't have it on her toothpaste. Not yet anyway, but no doubt when Elizabeth told her about it, she'd immediately investigate the costs. Not that they would be preventative, for she had the sort of money to splash around on small, expensive runs of things, especially when she knew it would impress people. The Penningtons were all about that.

'You coming for a swift one before we turn in or do you have other plans?' asked Roo, making Elizabeth smile yet again. She had taken to this young woman from the get-go.

'Well, I did have, but I'll cancel them, Roo. Please lead the way.'

They were the last to arrive in the Lutine carriage. Frank was behind the bar serving up drinks. Someone had turned off the radio; there would be no more news tonight anyway, they figured. Not now Brian 'the real BBC' was tucking into his hash.

'Anyone using their robe?' said Roo. 'Asking for a friend.'

'Well, I most definitely am,' replied Jane, lifting the very generous measure of calvados to her lips. It never failed to bring back the best of recollections.

'It'll probably be too small for me,' said Tim.

'I doubt it, they're massive,' said Roo to that. *Shit.* 'Not that I'm implying in any way you're . . . over . . . sized.' That exchange wouldn't exactly thaw the already frozen relations between them.

'I think we can find a happy medium between being respectful to Mr Ingleton and the need for us to keep warm and comfortable at this time,' said Jane. 'I don't want to forecast anything but I would be very surprised if the owner of this train is going to be having his Christmas dinner on it as planned.'

'You reckon we'll be having ours on it then, Jane?' Vincent posed the question.

'I think it's a distinct possibility.' She cast her eyes over to the window. There were so many snowflakes they almost joined up in a sheet.

'Well, if we do, we won't be having cheese sandwiches, I can promise you that. Not if I can fire up the ovens. I'll check that out tomorrow morning,' said Frank, coming from behind the bar with two glasses of Grand Marnier, one for himself and one for his wife. It was too much to hope that it would rekindle any happy memories for her, as it did for him. Sometimes he thought that all he had to look forward to was remembering the past, how it had been when they were happy; and they had been *really* happy. They used to talk about one day holidaying on one of the great trains: the Trans-Siberian railway, although that plan was up in smoke now with the world being as it was. But there were still a few other trains to go at: the Rocky Mountaineer, the Transcantábrico Gran Lujo, but the Venice-Simplon-Orient-Express had always been their hot favourite.

Frank had told her in no uncertain terms what he'd do to her while the train was rocking and make it rock a lot more and she'd told him to make the booking *NOW.* They didn't have the money back then though, not to do it properly, splashing out on every luxury. They had enough spend now, but they didn't talk about it any more. It all seemed so long ago, even if it wasn't: eight, nine years, but also another lifetime, when they were different people. Or at least when she was different. He hadn't changed, he hadn't lost himself. He had been as bruised and broken as she was but at his core, he was the same man with a great capacity to love, one who wanted to make the world a better place and enjoy this gift of life as fully as he could; and he hoped he always would be that man.

'I'll be making breakfast for everyone in the morning. I think we'll need something warm and substantial inside us for whatever the day brings,' Frank announced.

'We can take turns in catering, mate,' said Vincent.

'No one object, please. It's what I do. It'll keep me busy.'

'I'm not going to object, Frank. Not one bit. I'll be your sous chef if you like,' said Roo. 'I'm crap at cooking but I'm keen.' She made an exaggerated salute.

'Roo, you crack me up, gel,' said Vincent with a chuckle.

'Frank's breakfasts are what pull our customers back time and again,' said Grace then. Frank grinned as if warmed by the compliment. It seemed to Jane that she had surprised him with it, maybe because her praise was a rare occurrence. *Damn you, Clifford Wutheridge,* she then thought silently. Living with him for so many years had given her a compulsion to analyse people. He used to say that she'd overtaken him in those stakes.

'You got a hotel?' Roo directed the question at both Grace and Frank.

'A little inn in Norfolk: The Salty Cockle,' explained Frank. 'We don't do lunches or dinners as such, just occasionally some catering for a special event but there's always a big breakfast for the paying, staying customers.'

'I really like Norfolk,' said Elizabeth. 'I had a friend

Drusilla from uni who came from Wroxham. I used to go and stay with her in the holidays. I loved all the pretty little villages around there, so many of them. I think I've always been a village girl at heart, despite coming from a large town.'

'Which town would that be?' asked Grace, because she couldn't place Elizabeth's accent. It was one of those neutral accents that spoke of money and class.

'Reading. I come from Reading.' Although she had lived her whole life there – apart from the three years at uni – she didn't feel connected to the place. She'd been to boarding school there too, despite the family home being only a few miles away: St Padre Pio's Establishment for Girls. It had been a centre for those who exhibited educational excellence, but also for the daughters of rich people who wanted to buy their way in and bask in the reputation of the school, which is how Elizabeth came to be there. It was no coincidence to her that St Padre Pio advocated suffering to bring him closer to Christ because she'd been thoroughly miserable for most of her time there. And no, it hadn't brought her any closer to Christ; if anything, it had converted her into being a fully-blown agnostic.

She wasn't a natural academic like most of the other pupils and the teachers hadn't been particularly motivating or memorable. But she had studied hard, she'd worked over and above anyone else in her year to keep up and got the grades at A-level to get into one of the more prestigious universities in the country. It was amazing how much a flower can grow when watered with encouragement. Her tutors there were rousing, inspirational and she discovered a true love for the English she was reading at St Edythe College, which extended to far more than just an intellectual interest. In the second year she and three other girls stayed in a cottage in a nearby village and it was her first taste of living in a small, intimate community. She had grown particularly close to Drusilla from Wroxham.

Elizabeth felt real happiness for the first time in that period of her life, when she had fun and experienced friendship from people who really seemed to value her company. But it was always expected of her to return to Reading after she had graduated and join the family firm – R. W. Dudley and Sons Exports, which was even more dull than it sounded. Her father didn't have any sons, just her, but he'd thought adding it to the company name gave him more credibility than 'daughter' would have done. She sometimes thought that he considered Gregory the son he'd never had: Gregory Murdoc Pennington, nine years her senior, who had been lured in to serve by an enormous salary. No one had been more delighted than Roderick Dudley to see a romantic spark develop between his new whizz-man MD and his heir. And when the engagement was announced, it was almost as if Gregory had proposed marriage to him rather than his daughter.

'If you like little villages, you'd love where I live,' said Vincent, pulling Elizabeth away from her thoughts. 'Cary's Pond, it's 'bout thirty miles away from Reading. I was a bit like you, country boy at heart, always hankering after a cottage with roses round the door sort o' thing. Then about eighteen months ago I had a fare and by chance my driver was off sick so I did it myself: St Pancras to Cary's Pond, city gent visiting his old mum. You'll think I'm nuts if I tell you that as soon as I landed in the place, I thought I'd come home. Village green with ducks, couple of pubs, row of shops, little school, park, houses that looked as if they'd been made out of gingerbread. Six months later, I'd bought an old farmhouse that came up for sale there and we moved in and that's where my office is now. Never been happier.'

Elizabeth noticed he said, 'we'.

'It enhances your life no end when you're happy in your castle,' said Frank.

'How come you two ended up in Norfolk then?' asked Vincent.

That beat, that pause again, before Frank answered.

'I . . . was looking for a pub to buy and that one just came up. We didn't know anyone there at first, but you soon get to know people when you sell beer. We just fancied a change of scenery, didn't we, love?' Frank turned to his wife for confirmation. She gave a tight little nod by way of response.

'What about you, Tim? What line of work are you in?' asked Elizabeth.

'I was a director in a Japanese firm. A jet-setting, hand-shaking, clean-shaven, schmoozing seller of world-leading technological equipment,' he answered, which came as quite the surprise to them all. Roo especially. She could see Tim in a fur-trimmed red ensemble swearing at reindeer, but oiling and greasing around other execs in sharp suits, eating canapes and 'talking turkey' – nope.

'I loved it,' Tim went on, 'travelling business class all over the world, getting off on making multi-million-pound deals.'

His words were at odds with his tone, Roo thought though. The bloke was an enigma. He was probably making it all up to impress them.

'I took early retirement two years ago. It was my fifty-eighth birthday present to myself.' Then he addressed what he knew must have been running through their minds. 'Yes, I know I look older. I'll drop ten years at least when I shave all this off at the end of the season.' He flicked at his splendid beard. 'I started going white-haired when I was in my twenties.'

'Same here with this bit,' said Roo, pointing at the thick white flash running from her left temple and sitting stark against her dark, dark brown hair. 'It's not fake. I think my mum read too many Catherine Cookson books when she was pregnant and turned into one of them Mallens.'

'I loved those books,' said Jane. 'It was very wrong to fall in love with Thomas Mallen, but I confess I did.' She'd had a few book boyfriends; her unrequited passions had needed somewhere to go back then, before Clifford.

Elizabeth shuddered at the name, remembering the teacher Miss Mallen at her school: a dried-up stick of a woman who looked exactly like a mummy she'd once seen in a museum. She'd called Elizabeth a 'talentless, stupid, privileged brat' when she found out she'd got into the university of her choice. Later Elizabeth found out Miss Mallen hadn't reached the grades to get in there herself. She taught pupils she was insanely jealous of, resented, despised and the resulting poison she produced leaked out of her every pore. Coming from a moneyed background warped how some people interacted with you. She found it so at work, as the 'nepo baby'; some refused to see past it and give her credit for what she could do. They didn't want to see her for who she really was.

'And what do you do with your time now you're retired?' Vincent asked Tim.

'Not a lot.' Tim's tone indicated he was done with answering questions, though Roo would have liked to know why, if he'd loved it so much, he'd stopped doing it. But she couldn't be arsed asking the old goat, even if sixty wasn't old these days.

'I think I'm going to turn in,' said Jane, finishing the last of her drink. 'I want to have a wash and put on that lovely robe.'

'Well, there are plenty of bathrooms. The first shower is just next to your cabin, Jane, and there's a few more going forward. You go and fill your boots. Leave your glass, love, I'll swill it out with the rest when we've done.'

Jane stood. 'Thank you, Frank. I shall bid you all good-night,' she said.

Her leaving acted like a cue for the rest of them. It had been a long day – the longest any of them could remember for some time.

Chapter 13

Grace collected the rest of the glasses with Frank and they went behind the bar to wash them up in the sink there.

'You going to be all right sharing with a stranger?' Frank asked her.

'I'll be fine,' she said.

'Still, it would have been nice for you and me to be together. I mean, here we are on *this train* and when are we ever going to get the chance again to be on something like it?'

'Well, we can hardly ask everyone to swap around now, can we?'

'Maybe we could book a trip on a train in the summer. Across the Alps or some'ing. Like we said we would, when we had the money.'

'Frank, I've already had enough of trains to last me a lifetime, thank you.' Grace huffed as she plunged another glass into the soapy water. 'I certainly don't want to think about paying to holiday on one.'

You mean you don't want to think about holidaying with me, he didn't say, because she would just fly off, accuse him of reading meaning into her words that wasn't there – except it was.

'I said we should have stayed at home,' she muttered then, putting the crystal brandy balloon down on the draining mat too hard and knowing she had been lucky not to break it, this constant mood of hers bleeding out in rough gestures, barks, noises of frustration.

'Yes, well, we're all a lot wiser in retrospect,' replied Frank to that, a rare impatient tone creeping into his voice. His reserves of endurance had worn out long ago and he was now running on a ghost-like residue of them. 'I didn't know there would be all this snow, *you* didn't know there would be all this snow. The experts didn't know. No one knew there would be all this snow, Grace.'

'The moment they told you they'd made a mistake with the booking, you should have insisted on getting your money back, like I told you. Mistletoe Nook – ha. Looks like my granny's house in the nineteen seventies.'

'I wanted us to have a nice break, Grace. A change of scene.'

She turned fully to face him.

'Talking of "change of scene", is that really why we moved to Seapoint?'

'What do you mean?'

'I've thought about this quite a lot recently, how you pushed to buy that pub more than any of the others you'd looked at.'

'We chose it together,' Frank said, hoping she hadn't seen him swallow, hoping she hadn't seen his Adam's apple rise and fall like the weight on a fairground high striker machine.

'You pushed it hard on me. More than the rest. I felt obliged to choose it.'

'Because I thought you'd be happiest there,' said Frank.

'How can I be happy anywhere with—'

She cut off the word, but he could work out what it was: *you.* He'd given this years to burn out, for her to start recalibrating, healing, and they were no further on from day one. The chasm between them was never going to be bridged by a cosy Christmas in a cottage with smoked salmon and champagne in the fridge. It certainly wasn't going to be bridged by a Christmas spent in the middle of god-knows-where with a bunch of strangers in a stranded glorified link of metal boxes, however luxurious. Something in the quiet creaked and it felt as if the sound came from deep within him, like something about to break, to give way under too much strain.

Grace pulled the plug out of the sink.

'Whatever you thought I was going to say, I wasn't,' she said quietly, meekly, as if found out and trying to plaster up the damage.

'I'm going to check around and make sure everything's all right,' Frank said, flatly, as if he didn't believe her and needed distance between them. 'Goodnight, Grace.'

He was close enough to place his lips against her cheek. He always gave her a kiss goodnight, but tonight he didn't and she minded more than she thought she would about that.

In his cabin, Tim undid his suitcase and pulled out his toiletry bag. He shouldn't have said he'd have a cabin to himself. He was sick of being alone and yet he shunned company when it sought him out. He felt as if he had built a wall around himself with no exit. He was a mess. A mess of his own making and unless he found Doctor Who's TARDIS in his Christmas stocking to take him back in time, there wasn't a damned thing he could do to change it.

The shower was warm and more powerful than Jane imagined it would be. She didn't linger too long in consideration for her fellow passengers, in case there was only a limited amount of hot water, but she allowed herself an extra fifteen seconds, breathing in the beautiful scent of the milky shower lotion that was there available for use. She'd been unashamedly liberal with it. Another marvellous *glimmer.* And another with the softness of the white towel she used to pat herself dry. And another smoothing on the silky 'Après' lotion in the glass bottle at the side of the sink, it felt like double cream against her skin and smelt of apricots and spices. And yet another delicious moment after she'd slipped into her nightie: pulling the robe over her shoulders which was every bit as plush as she'd hoped it would be. She wondered if Mr Dwight J. Ingleton would have savoured that first shower aboard his new toy with as much joy as she just had. He couldn't have savoured it more.

The *present* really was so well named, the gift of the here and now, all anyone was really sure of. And Jane's here and now was infinitely more preferable to what she knew she had to come in the near future.

Frank walked to the end of the train, more to burn off some negative energy than to 'check that all was well', as he'd intimated to his wife. If he'd been at home, he'd have lifted some heavy weights or taken himself off for a jog around the block, whatever the time of day or night, but he couldn't exactly venture out in this and he did need to calm his irritated nerves. 'Liberty', 'Uglich', past the locked cabins of 'Sigismund' and 'Mingun'. Then it was around here that he felt it again, a change in atmosphere that made his skull tingle as if it had been doused in icy water.

'Anyone there?' he called ahead of him, as he opened the door to 'Yongle', stole past the locked cabins and into the space where the fridges and the linen stores were. Nothing replied to him, but he'd gone far enough and didn't want to venture on into 'Pummerin'. There was no need. There was obviously no one in there, how could there be? The Abominable Snowman himself couldn't have crossed the snow to get to them.

Maybe a night away from his wife would be a blessing in disguise, thought Frank, as he made his way down the train. At least it would save him from the sight of her back as she turned from him in bed, as purposefully as she once used to turn towards him.

Chapter 14

Grace was reading in bed when Jane entered the cabin.

'Well, I can highly recommend the shower,' said Jane. 'And the toiletries – like liquid silk.' She blew a chef's kiss into the air.

'I'll take one in the morning instead,' said Grace. 'If I have one now, it'll wake me up.'

Jane took off her robe and laid it at the bottom of the bed.

'Don't you go anywhere, I'll be needing you tomorrow,' she addressed it with a small chuckle before folding the quilt back and climbing in. The mattress was the perfect mix of firmness and giving, the duvet had just the right amount of comforting weight to it when she pulled it up around her.

'Oh my, someone took their time to research the best bedding available to modern man, didn't they?' she said, snuggling down. Good bedding was something Clifford had always insisted they buy, whatever the cost, but this was leagues in front of what they had. For a moment she imagined him lying where Grace was, giggling like a child, horizontal dancing like Michael Flatley on amphetamine between the smooth sheet and the duvet. They should have had more time to do what they had planned. So many things on their wishlist.

'Did you say you were going to family for Christmas, Jane?'

Jane nodded. 'My stepson and his wife. They're the only family I have left now.'

'I hope you can get a message to them soon. They must be worried sick about you.'

Jane didn't reply what was on the tip of her tongue: that they were probably rubbing their hands with glee at the possibility that she might have perished in a snowstorm.

She said instead, 'I'm sure they're anxious for news of me,' an answer which covered all bases.

'Do you mind if I read for a while or will the light annoy you?' asked Grace.

'It won't annoy me one bit,' said Jane. 'I'd be asleep in no time even if the room were floodlit.'

'Huh. You're lucky. I've forgotten what it's like to be able to drop off so easily.'

'Menopause?' Jane inquired. She aged Grace around early fifties.

'No, not that.' Grace didn't elaborate and Jane didn't push, though she was intrigued. She lay with her head against the fat, downy pillow having a conversation in her head with her late husband, the like of which they'd had so often when he was alive because they talked a lot: they were friends as well as husband and wife, as well as lovers to the end.

'*So what do you think the dynamic is between Grace and Frank then, Jane?*'

'*I think she can't forgive him for something, Cliffy.*'

'*Affair?*'

'*No, I don't think that's it. Something he couldn't help, and that's why he can't find the way to atone, because no apology would fill the hole that's between them, though it won't stop him trying.'*

What could it be? It was none of her business, of course, but she was very in tune with her senses. She had liked Frank from the off, he was a rough diamond type, but kindness exuded from him like benign radiation, whereas his wife was coming across as colder than the climate outside the train.

'What are you reading?' Jane asked.

'Something I can't get into.' Grace shut the book and put it on the shelf at the side of her bed. 'It's a murder mystery. I don't like any of the characters. I'm finding more sympathy with whoever did it than the woman it was done to. But I'll have to finish it.'

'Why's that?'

'Sorry?'

'Well, why would you force yourself to finish a book you aren't enjoying?'

'Because . . .' Grace's voice trailed off. It was a reasonable question to which she had absolutely no answer other than the one she gave: '. . . because I always finish books.'

'And how will you feel at the end of it then?' Jane realised she might be sounding a little invasive and so apologised for it. 'Forgive me for asking, I'm just interested. You don't need to answer.'

But Grace did answer, although she had to search inside herself for her reasoning.

'I suppose it's a sense of commitment. Or a hope that it'll improve.'

'Do you feel as if you don't want the book to win? Is that it?' asked Jane, getting it.

Grace thought about that. 'Yes, maybe . . .'

'As if by abandoning it you feel you'll have wasted time. So you waste more time to justify the time you've spent on it.'

'I . . .'

Jane shook her head at herself. 'I'm sorry for interrogating you, it's a terrible habit I've picked up over the years. My husband was a psychologist. Over the years his burrowing into heads rubbed off onto me. *People are puzzles and they can always be solved*, he used to say. Ignore me, Grace, please. Goodnight.'

'Goodnight, Jane.'

Jane had already solved this puzzle anyway. Grace needed to control, even something as trivial as reading her book. And that, whispered Clifford into her head, was probably because there was something very big in her life that she couldn't control and she was clawing for the ability to do so everywhere else that she could. Not having control panicked her, made her feel that if she didn't hold herself in tight, that she'd burst her banks like a dynamited dam. That was why she carried on reading a book that was infinitely more interesting when it was still growing in a forest somewhere, and the result at finally finishing it was a lost leader, a Pyrrhic victory.

Jane closed her eyes and heard Grace drop a sigh as she reached over for the book she wasn't enjoying to carry on reading it.

Next door, Elizabeth pulled the quilt up to her chin and made a noise of bliss. Even her future mother-in-law didn't have bedding like this and she bought hers from the same place that supplied the Savoy.

What would they all be doing now in Topston? How

much would she have been ripped apart in her absence? Vincent would get some of the blame, of course, for his guarantee that he would get her there, even though he couldn't have managed that if he'd been driving a snow plough. They probably wouldn't even pay him. She'd make sure, if that were the case, that she would pay him herself.

As if her thoughts of him had traversed the dark, Roo said, 'I assumed you and Vincent were a couple at first.'

'Did you?'

'He's lovely, isn't he? How old is he, do you reckon? Mid-thirties, I'd say.'

'I don't know. I only met him for the first time today.'

'You looked good together when I saw you in the waiting room at the station . . . just saying. I'd have matched you up.'

Elizabeth shook her head, but she was smiling.

'Oh Roo, stop. You've only known him – and me – for hours. He might be a serial killer.'

Roo would like to bet he wasn't. And though Vincent was a bit ragged around the edges, like a friendly scrapyard dog, and Elizabeth was like a pedigree Persian cat, she could easily see them as a couple. He and Frank were the sort of men who looked after their ladies, she could tell. Old-school gents. The type that opened doors for women and carried their shopping and stood up for them on buses.

'What's your fiancé like?'

He likes people not to interrupt his best-made plans, Elizabeth answered in her head. She was glad that the phone had no reception because she would be saved from his diatribes. She'd listened to the couple of voicemails he'd left when he obviously couldn't connect to her in person, but in neither had he said: 'Are you all right, Elizabeth? You must take care and get to me when and only when it is safe to do so.'

'He's tall, dark and very handsome,' she said instead. *'You're going to have great-looking kids,'* her PA had said to her in the office. Kids that she just knew she'd have a battle to keep with her when they reached the age to go to boarding school. Gregory, like Elizabeth's father, had had an infinitely more successful experience at such an institution than she had and she knew she'd be up against both of them when the time came for enrolment.

Power was very sexy, of course, and Gregory was very powerful. Oh, she knew how women envied her having landed the big important fish, Gregory Pennington. People all his life had spoiled him and stroked him and never said no to him and had sculpted him into a Roman emperor. He savoured his potency, his ability to make grown men feel as if they'd been blessed to gain his approval or to have them quiver in their boots when they'd met his censure. Elizabeth had been totally seduced by his confidence, the force of his personality, because he was impenetrable to everyone except her, because he was different with her and that made her feel beyond special, valued. At least, she'd wanted to believe it was *her* – Elizabeth, the woman, rather than Elizabeth, the heir to the mega-successful R. W. Dudley and Sons export firm. They'd be a power couple, her beauty, breeding and fortune lumped together with his money and intelligence and looks and ambitions because he was gearing up for a leap into the political arena. He was everything the behemoth MP John F. Mayhew should have been a few years ago had he not fallen prey to his own weaknesses and believed his own infallibility. Sex was so often the weak screw in the armour of powerful men, a flaw that wouldn't affect Gregory, despite the fact he might have been a lot of women's (and men's) carnal fantasy. His accomplished flirting certainly led one to believe he would be hot, insatiable even, between the sheets.

'What does he do, for a job?' asked Roo.

'He's the MD of my family's firm. We deal in exports.'

'Exports of what?'

'Anything anyone needs to export. They are very good at ... circumventing costs and duties and taxes. In short, they're expensive to use, but they'll still save companies a fortune. And yes, it's the right side of legal. I wouldn't work for them if they weren't.'

'So are you having a big, fat wedding then?'

'I expect so,' said Elizabeth. 'We were going to formalise plans after the big, fat engagement party up in Durham.'

'That where he comes from?'

'Yes, that's right.'

'I love that accent.'

'He doesn't have one, I'm sorry to disappoint you.'

'Ah, I bet he's got one of those really posh, neutral accents hasn't he?' Roo drew the conclusion.

'Yes, he has.' Gregory actually had the accent of someone with a mouth full of hard plums. No flat vowels would be allowed to pass his lips. He made Jacob Rees-Mogg sound like a barrow boy.

'Mind you, so have you. But your voice is really lovely.' It was too, thought Roo, she wasn't giving false praise. 'If I could scoop it up and put it in a jar, it would look like best honey.'

Elizabeth laughed at that.

'Old money? Or nouveau riche?'

Elizabeth had never been asked as many questions about Gregory and the wider circle of the whole Pennington clan.

'Well, his father came from the impoverished branch of

the family but in his thirties he inherited the estate – and fortune – from a childless relative.'

And apparently overnight he slipped into the role as if 'to the manor born'. But without the class of old money, and all the pretensions of the worst of the nouveau riche.

Roo whistled. 'Lucky bugger. I thought that only happened in films. And one day will it all be yours then when you get spliced?'

'Yes, one day.' And it looked as if that would be sooner rather than later too because Gregory's mother was 'delicate' and his father was a frail wisp of a man now, albeit one with a waspish tongue. In all the time she'd known him Elizabeth had never heard him say a kind word. He had too much in common with her own father which was probably why they got on so well. Elizabeth just hoped that Gaylord Pennington wasn't a future version of Gregory. She'd do everything in her power to prevent that. It shouldn't follow that children became their parents; she most certainly hadn't.

'Wowee.'

'To be honest, Roo, I can't think of anything worse,' said Elizabeth. That had slipped out; Roo was too easy to talk to, or maybe she was just too ready to talk.

'Really? Why? I'd kill to own a mansion.'

'Trust me, it's not what it's cracked up to be. Every time they have all the windows cleaned, you can wave goodbye to over two thousand pounds.'

'Gulp.'

'The rooms are enormous to heat, so they don't. It's freezing.' Although Gregory's mother, Elspeth-Ann, would have made sure they were heated for the engagement party so no guest would be talking behind their backs. She'd had the decorators in too to spruce up the reception rooms. A lick of fresh paint over the flaky old.

'Bit stingy are they, his mum and dad?' Roo levered herself up to listen to more. This was a glimpse into an alien world and she was rapt.

Elizabeth opened up her mouth to say no, of course not. She shouldn't be indiscreet, disloyal to her future family, especially not to someone she'd met only hours ago, but she was hardly giving away any of the unsavoury family secrets they'd managed to keep hidden, such as Gaylord getting the housekeeper's granddaughter pregnant when he was seventy and she nineteen. And them holding a celebratory soirée when they found out she had a 'blighted ovum' pregnancy.

'It's odd, Roo, because they blow money like it's going out of fashion on some things and yet on others they skimp to a ridiculous degree. Top-of-the-range cars: Gaylord's got four Ferraris and he shouldn't be allowed to drive any of them. Extravagant curtains and linen, but the cheapest of furniture from antique auctions; wildly expensive jewellery, wardrobes full of high-end clothes that they've bought but never worn, horrendous wigs . . .'

Oops, that also slipped out. Roo obviously loved that detail though.

'What? Wigs!'

'They both have hair, they haven't lost it or anything. But they just . . . for some reason, favour . . . wearing . . . awful, cheap wigs.'

They had a whole section of their respective dressing rooms reserved for the display of them. Gaylord's favourite was block-brown and completely at odds with his natural fair colouring. It was parted in the middle and he wore it so low it went into battle with his shaggy grey eyebrows.

Elspeth-Ann favoured a variety of midnight-black coif-
feured towers that made her look like the illegitimate child
of Joan Collins's character in Dynasty and a busted sofa.

Picturing it, Roo burst into laughter in the dark, apologising at the same time, which set Elizabeth off giggling.

'I've offered to take them somewhere decent and be
fitted for proper ones, but they just won't.' Elizabeth's voice
dissolved and she thought of the last time she had laughed
talking to someone like this and it had been her uni friend
Drusilla, ten years ago when she'd been nineteen and they'd
been in a tent at Creamfields, off their faces on the home-
fermented parsnip wine they'd brought with them, bought
at the farm up the road from their student house.

'Do your mum and dad like Gregory?' asked Roo when
their laughter eventually subsided, though it took a while.

'My mother hasn't met him. She lives in Madeira with
her new husband. She's not really interested in my life. My
father adores him. More than me, I think.'

Roo wondered if Elizabeth meant that her father loved
Gregory more than she did, or that her father loved Gregory
more than he loved her. If she'd asked, Elizabeth might have
answered that both were true.

'Sweep you off your feet, did he? Am I asking too many
questions? Tell me to shut up, I won't mind. My life is so
boring and yours is so interesting, I'm just fascinated.'

Elizabeth smiled again, but had the light been on, Roo
would have seen it was a sad sort of smile. She wasn't tired
and it was nice to talk. She hadn't got any close friends these
days that she could natter away to, not with any honesty,
not without feeling that they might store anything that was
off-piste as future gossip currency. If only Roo knew how
boring her life really was, how grey and dull and unfulfilling.

'I was very attracted to him from the off. He oozed style and confidence and he seemed to be very taken with me when we met.' Sometimes, when thoughts tormented her, she pulled their first meeting out of the store cupboard in her head. He couldn't have faked his reaction when he first saw her, a look of instant intoxication. She had wondered about it since, when she was in a contemplative self-doubting zone, but didn't want to believe it. It was two years ago and her mother had just announced she'd married her long-term lover, the man she'd left them for ten years previously. *'I didn't ask you to the wedding, darling, because it was just a small affair and I thought it might put you in a spot with* him.' *Him* was Roderick Walter Dudley, her ex-husband and father of her only child, but she never referred to him by name after abandoning them, without any warning, for the Portuguese owner of the tennis club she attended. Elizabeth had never visited their house in the Madeiran hills nor met Luis Lemos, because she had never been invited. *'It would make it awkward for everyone, darling.'* Penelope Dudley (Lemos now) flung the word 'darling' around so liberally that it had long since lost its value. But then Elizabeth saw photos of the wedding, which looked a hell of a lot bigger than her mother had said, complete with smiling bridesmaids: Luis's three daughters. Elizabeth had been beyond hurt, her heart had been punctured actually to the point where she didn't think it could get any more battered. Enter stage left, a dashing knight, proficient in the courtly code, primed to flatter, someone whose attentions were salve for her wounds. Oh, he wined and dined her, he bought her jewellery, he introduced her around as his *lady*. He met every need she didn't know she had. She had never been quite able to work out when the change occurred, when his patience with her began to wane, when her 'little endearing odd ways' became her 'infuriating annoying ways', when she felt the blow of a cold wind in their relationship. But they were creatures trapped in the same aspic and it was beneficial for everyone they made a success of it.

'But does he make you laugh, Elizabeth?'

Roo had no idea of the impact such a question could have on her temporary room-mate.

Silence. She couldn't lie and say he did. He'd never made her laugh, not really laugh until her sides ached and she could barely breathe. He wasn't the sort. But did people in her position really still laugh like that anyway? The questioning was making her think too much and she aimed for deflection.

'Never mind about me,' said Elizabeth. 'What about you? What do you do?'

'Not much,' said Roo. 'I'm just wading through life trying to find a coat that fits. I work in an office at the moment, sorting post, making tea. Doing a job at twenty-four that I probably should have done at sixteen. Told you I was boring.'

'Silly. Anyone special in your life?'

'Absolutely no one.' Roo yawned. 'Blimey, all this chit-chatting has knackered me out, I might have to shut my eyes in a minute. Incidentally, what's Santa's problem with women?'

'Pardon?'

'Tim. Haven't you noticed how he talks to women differently to men?'

Elizabeth hadn't. He'd been fine with her. He was the least talkative out of all of them, admittedly, but she hadn't picked up on what Roo had.

'I can't say I have, to be honest.'

'Well, it's probably just me he has a problem with. Sorry, I'm talking too much and keeping you awake. Goodnight. See you in the morning.'

Thinking about it, he hadn't used that clipped tone when he'd spoken to Elizabeth, maybe because she was beautiful, with her long golden hair and perfect face. Some people put a lot of stock on looks. He wouldn't have been rude to Jane because she was old, or Grace because she was with Frank and he might have lamped him. Just her then, thought Roo in the dark. But Santa always had been a tosser, she'd had no need to try and get on his right side like the lied-to kids who one day grew up to find out all their efforts to be good for him had been nothing but a total waste of time.

Chapter 15

'You're doing a lot of sighing,' said Jane with some amusement, turning over to face Grace.

'Was I? I'm so sorry.' Grace closed the book, calling it a night. She'd tried to read the same page five times now and on each occasion her mind had wandered off.

'Everything all right?'

'Yes, fine,' Grace answered, none too convincingly. 'Well . . . I had a slight row with Frank and I feel a bit bad about it.' He had never not ended their day with a kiss or a kind loving word. Even during the thick of everything when she'd spat at him like a cobra, he had held her and told her he was there for her and he'd get her through.

Jane didn't say anything. Clifford had once told her that saying nothing was the best way to eke out all the information one needed from another. There was something about silence that people found so uncomfortable they felt obliged to fill it.

'I'm aware that I'm . . . blaming him for this . . . debacle.' Said aloud, Grace realised this admission sounded ludicrous and petty. 'He wanted to make this Christmas nice, special and it's been ruined. He hurt his leg and couldn't drive us and then the cottage firm told us they'd double-booked and offered us an alternative that didn't look a fraction as nice and I should have insisted that we didn't go because look at us now.'

'On one of the world's most luxurious trains free of charge, yes, I see your point,' said Jane with a trill of laughter. Then, 'Forgive me for being facetious.'

Yes, she was indeed being 'facetious', thought Grace with a nip of annoyance. There was nothing 'glass-half-full' about the situation they were in. The silly old lady had no idea of what she'd been through and why she might not want to count her blessings. She felt that ever-present spitting cobra open one eye, as if priming to uncoil inside her again.

'I lost my son five years ago, my only child,' Grace blurted out. 'It feels sometimes as if the whole universe is constantly against me, doing everything it can to wreck any chance I have at ever being happy again, so I'm not being rude, Jane, but maybe that will explain why I don't share your optimism. Unless you've lost a child you can't imagine the storm in my head, it's worse than what's out there and unlike what's out there it won't abate, it just keeps on without any chance of respite.' Grace flicked the reading light off above her head.

A few moments passed before Jane said, 'I'm sorry to hear that,' the buoyancy in her tone much reduced.

Grace was cross at herself now, bringing Jane down. And she was cross at Jane for driving her to give part of herself away to shut her up. 'Forgive me. I shouldn't have said ... Look ... It's been a very long day. I hope tomorrow brings some good news and ... better weather. We can but hope. At least, like you say, we're in comfort and safe from the elements. Goodnight, Jane.'

'Goodnight, Grace.'

Jane lay in the dark processing their conversation, processing Grace. Processing all those 'my's' and not 'our's'. She knew exactly what Clifford would have said to them, how he would have raised his steel eyebrows. How she missed him. How she wished he *was* in the ether somewhere and not just residing in her head as a figment of her imagination.

Vincent walked into the cabin shower-fresh, flip-flopping in his white train slippers that he'd found in one of the dressing-room cupboards. There were four pairs and one of them just happened to be his size. 'I think I'm enjoying this a bit more than I should be.' He sat down on the bed as if he were Goldilocks discovering the baby bear's perfect bunk.

'What would you have been doing if you weren't here then, Vince?' Frank figured Vincent wouldn't have been doing that much if being marooned in the middle of nowhere with a group of people he didn't know was such a delight.

'Well, I should have been having a couple of days off, catching up with paperwork and counting my profits.' Vincent grinned. 'Busy time for taxis, Christmas. Not that I do much of the actual driving myself these days. But one of my lads . . . his kid is poorly so that's why, last minute, I ended up with Elizabeth's job.'

'So how does it work then, running a taxi firm if you live in the back of beyond?'

'Well, I eventually learned the art of delegation, as my ex-missus nagged me about. I put a manager in my place in the city office, good girl she is, young, keen, loyal. She deals with all the black cabs. See, I buy 'em and rent 'em out. I co-ordinate my little fleet of prestige taxi vehicles from the countryside HQ, namely Chuckle Farm, Little Lane, Cary's Pond. Very macho. I keep thinking I should change the name, man it up a bit. McClaren Farm, Lambo Manor. What do you think?'

'You're talking to a bloke who lives in Salty Mussel cottage, son. I don't think I'm the right person to ask.'

Vincent hooted.

'You don't live in your Salty Cockle pub then?'

'It's an annex, with its own front door, so it's joined on but separate if you know what I mean, so we can shut off from work occasionally. It's important you do that sometimes. I've learned that over the years.'

'You been in the pub trade all your life then?'

'Naw. My dad was a landlord and so I spent my formative years in a pub but I was a boxer when I was younger. And no, you wouldn't have heard of me. I was what they call a journeyman: reliable but not outstanding, though I had my moments. I was never good enough to be one of the big names and that was fine, because I earned more money being the fill-in, putting on the show. And, when my day was done, I went into the pub game and bought a gym to train young boxers up. Johnny Kendall's one of my lads. And Paul Khan, he's just signed up with Frank Warren.' He grinned proudly.

'I have heard of them. I follow the boxing. Heavyweight, Khan, inne? Kendall – cruiser?'

'Yeah, that's right. I miss it. I miss working with young people. I miss ... making a difference. I've got some ideas for the pub floating around that I'd like to do. Some of the kids who used to come in through my doors didn't know what discipline was, couldn't follow a rule if it was tied to their fronts. But somehow, by putting a pair of gloves on and discovering a craft and getting hit in the face, they learn how to respect others – and themselves, how to focus. They learn perseverance and self-control, and find a purpose. Kendall was in with a gang and he'd be in prison for sure by now. And once you're in there, the system swallows you up.'

'You give your gym up, Frank?'

'Yeah. Life got too busy, you know how it is.' He didn't elaborate.

Vincent nodded. 'The girl who's my manager, the young one, she was an ex-prisoner. Made some stupid mistakes as a teenager. I took a punt on her when they asked me if I'd be willing to employ her to make the tea and sort out emails. Best investment I ever made – in that person. She's a blinder. If I ever sell up, her job security will be part of the buying package. Got to take a chance on people sometimes. I have in the past and it's not paid off but when it does . . . it means the world, making a difference like you say.'

Frank nodded. It was nice to meet someone with the same mindset. It made him think that the ideas he had he shouldn't shelve, as Grace had wanted him to.

'How many cabs you got then?'

'Ten,' said Vincent.

'Ten!' Frank whistled. 'That's some serious coin.' He wouldn't have put Vincent at more than mid-thirties. And he knew how much *one* of those cabs cost.

'I passed the knowledge just before my twentieth birthday. My mum, my dad and my nan all helped me buy my own cab. And I saved and I grafted and I borrowed a bit and bought another and rented it out. Then another. Nan left me some money and I ploughed it into my business and just kept building.'

'They still around, your family?'

'Naw,' said Vincent. 'Dad went not long after my nan, lost my mum six years ago and my missus left me four months after. I find that keeping busy stops me being lonely.'

Frank didn't say that he kept busy for the same reason, but it hadn't stopped it for him.

'We weren't right for each other really, more friends than anything else and we'd met and split up all in the space of two years. We didn't take anything from each other, just walked away nice and amicable. But, she did give me that invaluable piece of advice about learning to delegate and she was right because I was running myself into the ground.' Vincent smiled. 'She didn't want kids when she was with me. It was one of the many things that weren't right. But she's got three now. I'd have loved to have kids.'

'You've still got loads of time, Vince. What are you — thirty-five?'

'Thirty-six in Feb. Getting old, Frankie boy. The tadpoles are starting to thin out.'

'Give over. Look at all them ancient rock stars still giving it large.'

He'd have a child again tomorrow if Grace had been able, despite what they'd been through. Yes, the joy their boy had brought them had been worth it. He knew though that Grace didn't think the same.

'Life, eh?' Vincent huffed. 'We lose people but the world keeps turning and we have to keep on keeping on however much we try and resist it.'

Frank nodded but he wasn't quite sure that was entirely true. His wife's world had stopped turning five years ago and for all his efforts to get it shifting again, the brake remained stubbornly on.

*

Grace was long asleep but Jane was uncharacteristically still awake, thinking about too much. It was just when she found herself edging into the hinterland of sleep that she heard it again, in the distance and it jolted her back to full consciousness, that ring-ring, pause, ring-ring. A deep, serious knell: a signal. A distress call from someone stuck in the snow, perchance? *Who just happens to be carrying a huge bell?* Clifford's gentle ribbing in her head.

She closed her eyes and attempted to slip out of this world and into one of her imagination, her usual method of finding sleep when it evaded her. One of the trips she and Clifford had planned to make but didn't get round to, so she took them both there in her head. Tonight they were queueing up behind fellow passengers to disembark their cruise ship in Casablanca. The heat of the sun hit them like a wall of fire when they walked out onto the gangway.

The rattle of the bouncy metal in her mind disguised the sound of the soft footsteps moving cautiously outside the train cabin, pausing at the door, before moving on.

Christmas Eve

*Christmas Eve, the night when a magic
wand is waved over the world in the
hope we will feel the cheer, the peace and
goodwill, the joy within our hearts*

Chapter 16

Roo was up first, dressed and stole out of the cabin with her notebook and pen so as not to wake Elizabeth. She couldn't believe she'd slept as soundly as she had given all that was going on in her brain.

Christmas Eve. It wasn't how she expected it to start and she wasn't sure if that was a blessing or a curse. At least she was living with people and not in her own head, which wasn't a good place to be at the moment.

She headed into 'Liberty', the lounge with the fancy fireplace, and sat on one of the sofas, pulling cushions around her because it was cool in there this morning. There wasn't much of a view through the windows, in fact there wasn't *any* view because the vista had been swallowed whole by a white haze of freezing fog. More snow was falling. Had it even stopped and given itself a break from yesterday? she wondered.

It was eerily quiet, more silent than silent but just after she clicked on her biro to write something, in the distance she could have sworn she heard the faintest of ringing sounds – rhythmic, ring-ring and then a pause before ring-ringing again. She tilted her head all ways to see if it disappeared, but it was still there. At what age did tinnitus start? Could be that. Everything else in her life was tits up; her brain fooling her into hearing things that weren't there would be a cherry on her cake of shit.

It was a little too chilly to work, she decided. She needed proper warmth — inside and out. She dumped her writing pad on a chair, left the comfort of the sofa and bent to the fireplace. There was a pile of old newspapers, kindling and matches as well as a stack of logs and she'd been adept at making fires since she'd been a kid. The first place she'd lived in with central heating had been three years ago when she'd rented her bedsit. Once experienced, she had no idea how she'd ever coped without it.

She made some tight twists out of the newspaper, piled the kindling and a couple of the smaller logs on top and set it aflame. She waited until she saw the wood burning steadily before heading down through the dining car to the galley in 'Old Tom'. There, she put the kettle on the stove to boil some water. She really needed something much stronger than coffee to get through today but she wouldn't go down that road. She'd seen the damage done when turning to substances to numb the mind. She also knew it was human nature to hurt oneself when the legitimate target was unavailable.

She heard a door shut along the passage. Someone else was up and probably heading this way for a coffee too. She only hoped it wasn't Tim. She didn't want to see his miserable face first this morning. She called 'Hello' but no one materialised. And when she left the galley to go back to the lounge, she was met with only that still superlative silence.

Santa Claus
Wanker Claus
Jolly old St Prickerlas

It was quite satisfying how many names Santa had that could be distorted. It wasn't her finest work, admittedly, but it did give her a giggle as she was writing it and that was a Christmas miracle in itself, thought Roo. Then in he walked himself: Tim, Tim, the Brother Grim. Roo opened her mouth to say 'Morning' but, on seeing it was just her in the lounge, he carried on through, passing her before she could even form the word in her mouth.

'Sweet baby Jesus,' said Roo to herself. And not in any meaning associated with the nativity. The distant ringing bells might have been in her imagination, but him being a total rude misogynistic tosser was as real as could be.

In the galley, Tim found the still-warm kettle on the stove. A voice in his head said, *'It wouldn't have killed you to say good morning.'* What was the matter with him? Well, he knew that. The closer it got to Christmas, the more he'd have to activate his 'ho-ho-ho' muscle for the benefit of others while inside he would retreat further and further into the dark cave of himself. At least now, not having to perform for a massive group of people and excited kids, he could allow his inner Krampus to ooze out of him unhindered. But it should only be poisoning himself, no one else was deserving of that.

He'd just lit the gas under the kettle when a chirpy 'Morning' from behind cut off his thoughts. A word brimming with all the cheer that daren't visit him for fear of being told to eff off.

'Oh, good morning, Frank.'

'You beat me to it. I thought I'd be first up.'

'And young Roo has beat us both. I've just spotted her in the lounge. She's got a fire going.'

Frank rubbed his hands together as a shiver claimed his shoulders. 'I know, I saw. Have you seen it outside – proper pea-souper?'

'Yep. I didn't know if it was fog at first or if we'd been buried alive in the snow.'

Frank opened the fridge for the milk and his eyebrows rose. 'Aye aye, I think someone's had a midnight feast.' The rest of the chicken he'd brought from the storage fridge in 'Yongle' had been obliterated, clean bones left on the plate and what remained of the big ham had been ripped into by hungry fingernails by the looks of it. And the same person/creature had bitten straight into the remaining pork pie. That wasn't on, though he couldn't think which of the train people was likely to have acted like this. Roo? *Naw.* Tim might have been his first choice if someone had held a gun to his head; only because he could have sneaked out of his cabin unseen, unlike the others, but he looked as shocked as Frank when he saw the carnage.

'Bloody hell, is there a wolf loose?'

'Who'd do this?' said Frank.

'My money's on Jane,' said Tim. He didn't intend to crack a funny, it surprised him as much as it amused Frank, who chuckled.

'It can't be any of us, Frank. But who else?'

'Weird.' Frank shook his head in confusion. He tipped the savaged food into the bin though. He didn't want to eat anything that someone else's gnashers had been all over.

'Tell you what else is weird, Tim, but a couple of times going up to the front of the train, I've felt . . . as if I wasn't alone. Now I don't believe in all that supernatural bollocks but ... something made the hairs on the back of my neck stand up.'

'I don't think ghosts are partial to pork pies,' said Tim.

Someone was, however, and Frank didn't want to be wasting any more food, so he'd find out who the culprit was and warn them off. If that had happened in his kitchen in the Salty Cockle, he'd have had their hands in the bacon slicer.

Grace feigned sleep until Jane had left the cabin because she felt a bit awkward after their exchange last night and didn't really know what to say to smooth things over. She'd snapped at Frank when he suggested that maybe it was time she had some therapy. She'd snapped at him more than she had at her sister-in-law when she'd said the same. She'd turned Frank into her whipping boy and she hated herself for it. She hated herself more than she hated him, than she hated the world. And she hated God most of all and that's why he was punishing her probably. She was hate person-ified, everything else had been boiled and burned away except that emotion. She had no love, no joy, no cheer left and no way of generating more. She ate and breathed only to feel pain and anger and she was tired of it, so very tired.

She washed and dressed and then, hearing voices in the next carriage, walked into the lounge to find most of the train people sitting around the fireplace drawing warmth from blazing logs and mugs of tea and coffee in their hands. Frank wasn't there though and neither was Tim.

'You all look like a Christmas card,' she said, trying to say something nice and positive. Especially in front of Jane. Jane smiled at her though; she hadn't quite written her off as a horrible person then, the way she had written herself off.

'Your old man's in the kitchen,' said Vincent. 'We all offered to help, but ...'

'Oh, I know,' replied Grace. 'He can't share his kingdom.'

'We're all discussing who the phantom midnight scoffer is,' said Jane. 'Apparently someone had a bit of a meat feast during the night. I can vouch for you, Grace, because if you'd stirred, I'd have heard.'

'Hit the fridge like a famished fox apparently,' added Roo with relish.

'Really?' Grace didn't know these people but she wouldn't have had any of them down for that sort of behaviour, especially as Frank had put together quite the supper for them all.

'Where's Poirot when you need him?' Elizabeth stood up. 'Can I get you a coffee, Grace?'

'No, you're fine. I'll go and see Frank. He won't want me hanging around him if he's in chef-mode so I'll probably be straight back. He says I can't boil water without burning it.'

Jane watched her leave; she could tell from her gait she was carrying weight on her shoulders as well as in her heart. She'd thought a lot about what Grace had said to her the previous night. Maybe she could help her. Even if it did mean she'd have to make herself bleed to do so.

Grace could hear Frank singing as soon as she entered the coach named 'Old Tom': 'I Wish it Could be Christmas Every Day ...' He had a voice like a foghorn. Billy had inherited his father's tone-deafness and it had been Frank who went into school to have a quiet word with the music teacher and tell her that their son might not be able to hold a note with a pitchfork, but ridiculing him about it, making him feel bad about what he couldn't do when she could have been praising him for what he could do – i.e. knock the spots off anyone playing the guitar – was not good teaching. Frank never shouted. His quiet, gentle, husky tone got where shouting never could and he'd still managed to eviscerate that teacher more than any raging parent had before. Grace had never heard him raise his voice in all the years they'd been together, even when she'd been screaming like a harpy at him, blaming him.

'Morning, love,' he said on seeing her framed in the doorway. She thought he might have given her the kiss he hadn't given her last night, but he didn't. He just carried on beating up eggs.

'The others said something about someone having a midnight feast – that right?'

'Yeah, get this. Some scruffy bleeder attacked the food in the fridge. Every one of them with a poker face though. I can't work it out. Something funny's going on in this train.'

'Well, it wasn't me.'

'Love, I know even if you were starving, you wouldn't sink your choppers into a pork pie. I had your back.'

'Thank you.'

He was a good man, he'd always have her back and he loved her, Grace knew that. They'd been so happy but she knew that they never would be again. She was going through the motions of her marriage, waiting for him to tell her it was over because she wasn't brave enough to do it herself.

'Sleep well?'

'Yes, the beds were lovely, weren't they?'

'We should sell up the inn and buy our own train, Gracie. What do you think?'

She humphed. 'Another wild idea of yours?' God, she

really couldn't stop herself. The needle always poised, waiting for a passing balloon.

'I was ... only joking, you know. As if we could buy a
train.'

'Yes, sorry, I know you were.'

She'd wiped the smile off his face though. He carried on
beating, but no longer singing.

'I'll go and lay the table,' she said, opening the drawer,
taking out the cutlery.

Hiding underneath a midnight-blue cover in the top corner
of the dining area, Elizabeth had discovered a large shiny
brass bell on a stand. To summon diners, she guessed. She
wasn't sure Tim would hear it as he'd wandered off to check
out the books in the end carriage, 'Maria Gloriosa', but
still she pulled the chain and rang it anyway and shouted
'Breakfast is served' like the ancient butler who was part
of the Topston staff. He was way past the age of retirement
but soldiered on and would most likely drop on the job.
Her in-laws would probably have him stuffed like they had
all the animals they'd hunted and killed and then mounted
on the walls. When she became mistress of the manor,
Elizabeth would tear them down and give them a decent
burial. Country life to her meant judging jam competitions
and making sure people who lived in the estate cottages
were fine. She would draw the line at slaughtering innocent
creatures and Gregory wouldn't convince her otherwise.
She remembered having the conversation with him when
they had first started courting and he'd told her that any
wife of his would have to immerse herself in all the family
traditions whenever they were at Topston. 'Silly, kind girl,'
he'd called her then when she'd told him why she wouldn't

and smiled as he'd touched her nose. Fast forward to a recent conversation when he said, *There are two types of people in the world, Elizabeth, those who hunt and oversentimental idiots.*

'Roo, can you give Tim a shout, please?' asked Frank. 'He won't have heard the bell down in "Maria Gloriosa".' He deliberately infused the coach name with his thickest Estuary accent for comic effect.

'No problem,' she said, wondering if Tim would thank her for summoning him. She'd risk her non-existent life savings on the answer to that one.

She found him reading in the quiet of the carriage. A big heavy tome that nevertheless looked small in his giant hands.

'Breakfast is served,' she said when he looked up.

He didn't say anything by way of response as he stood. She'd had enough of his twattiness now. Especially because she was the only one to whom he seemed to direct it.

'Thank you, don't mention it,' she snapped loudly.

'Pardon?' *The cheek of him to look affronted.*

'I said, thank you, don't mention it.' She threw up her hands. 'Do you have a problem with me, Tim? Have I done something to offend you? Only it seems as if you have a decent word for everyone but me and I'm pretty sure I ha-ven't been in the slightest bit rude to you to warrant you being a—' She didn't say the word, but it was quite obvious if it wasn't 'dick' it was akin to it.

It annoyed her even more that he had the nerve to stand there with his features arranged in a smacked arse formation. And today really wasn't the day for him to be pushing any of her buttons.

'Yes, you,' she said, as he then had the cheek to turn slightly as if she might be addressing someone behind him instead.

'I really hope that the kids you were going to entertain today would have got to see you less . . . wankery . . .' *Oops, bit far,* said a voice inside her but she told it to shut up because all bets were presently off. 'It's bad enough me being here without having to wonder what I've done to piss off Father sodding Christmas. I mean, he was never a pal of mine in the first place. When I was a kid, I was always on his bloody naughty list without him giving me a single clue what I'd done to end up on it, so I'd really like to be spared the head fuck of all that palaver again now I'm an adult.' She stopped, took a deep breath and recalibrated.

'Anyway, *Tim*'—she said the name as if it sat on her tongue like a handful of salt—'your breakfast is ready. You're welcome.'

She spun a perfect one hundred and eighty degrees and grabbed the door handle, but Tim's boom of a voice arrested her.

'I'm sorry, it's just . . . you remind me of someone.'

She looked back at him, bit off the temptation to say something sarcastic.

'My daughter,' Tim went on. 'You remind me of my daughter.'

'Hate her, do you?' Roo opened the door, moved through it.

'You couldn't be more wrong,' said Tim to her wake.

'Well, isn't this lovely?' said Elizabeth, taking some toast and butter from the plates of breakfast feast Frank had prepared. 'I mean, give or take the acropolis happening outside.'

'Acropolis?' questioned Roo. 'Have we ended up in Greece?'

Elizabeth laughed, and her laugh was like a bell, a

tinkly, shiny bell full of joy and the sound of it penetrated Vincent's chest like an arrow. That's all it took, he would remember later. That laugh after getting the word wrong for everything inside him to shift, change, open.

'Oh goodness, what do I mean?' Elizabeth said, appealing to everyone around her. 'Help.'

'Akrapovič,' suggested Frank, his grin lop-sided.

'Nooo. Oh my lord, what *is* the word? Acrop . . . no, that's what I've just said.'

'Abramovich?' Vincent nudged her shoulder with his own.

'Stop it, Vincent.'

His name in her mouth. Why did it taste like a sweet?

'Ibrahimović?'

'Oh Jane, I expected you to be on my side.' Elizabeth wagged her finger at the old lady. *Elizabeth's laughter,* thought Jane. Another glimmer, such a beautiful pure sound.

'Djokovic,' said Tim, joining in as he took the only un-occupied seat, opposite Roo who blanked him.

'Stop it, you rotten lot.' Elizabeth tapped her head, hoping to dislodge the word from a shelf in it. 'Ac . . . Ap . . . Apo . . .'

'Apoplexy?' Frank chuckled.

'Apocalyse.' Elizabeth beamed triumphantly. She tried not to spoil the moment by imagining Gregory across the table rolling his eyes at her. She blinked the vision away.

'I've forgotten now why I even said what I did.'

'You were talking about what was happening outside,' Jane reminded her. 'Intimating that maybe it's the end of the world.'

'Oh lord, I hope not,' said Frank. 'I've got a delivery of

beer coming in a few days. I'm supposed to be trialling an open mike night for New Year.' Another of his schemes, 'a wild idea' as Grace put it. He was going to do it anyway despite her misgivings, providing they got out of here alive, of course. There was nothing like it in the area and he wanted to pull in some young people to bring some cheer and life to the place. Grace didn't want him to set up another gym, teaching people to fight, but he didn't think she'd object to him wanting to make them laugh. He'd been hurt then that she'd derided his brainchild. But this time, she wouldn't stop him.

'That sounds fun,' said Roo.

'I thought so.' He didn't look across at Grace, he didn't want to register any scorn in her expression. 'The world needs more laughter. I would like to be instrumental in bringing a bit more to our little corner of Norfolk.'

'I always wanted to be a stand-up comedian,' said Roo. 'My careers teacher said that was the funniest thing she'd ever heard. And not in a good way.'

Frank tutted. 'Teachers can do a lot of damage to a kid.'

'And they can do a lot of healing too,' said Tim. 'My daughter's a teacher. One of the good ones. She cares about them.'

Roo piled some scrambled eggs onto her toast while thinking, *Was this the daughter she reminded Tim of then*? Didn't sound like it really. He'd have been nice to her if that was the case; he must have another whom he couldn't stand the sight of.

'I had to have a word with a teacher at school for showing up my little boy, having a pop at his singing. He wasn't exactly Aled Jones, shall we say, but I gave her a taste of her own medicine. Kids . . . when they get damaged little, they can't process it and it might cause them all sorts of bigger problems when they get older,' Frank told them.

Yeah, that's why I can't stand Santa effing Claus and his Christmas extravaganza, thought Roo.

'That was very catty of your careers teacher, Roo, to try and stifle your ambitions. I hope she didn't succeed in doing that.' Jane went back in for another forkful of grilled tomato. She couldn't remember the last time she'd tasted one so flavoursome – another glimmer.

'Well, I'm a glorified office junior in a plastic injection-moulding factory that makes poop scoops and litter trays, so what do you think?'

'Doesn't matter what job you do, so long as you're happy doing it, gel.'

'I'm not though, Vincent, I hate it. I still want to be performing on a stage.' Roo smiled, albeit a watered-down version of a smile. 'Not jokes though, I sort of evolved into stand-up comedy poetry.'

'I love poetry,' said Jane. 'Clifford and I used to go and see John Cooper Clarke whenever he was performing. They knew each other quite well when Clifford was a professor at Manchester University.'

Roo's jaw fell open, impressed. 'Oh wow, Jane, JCC is my inspiration, my *god*.'

'"Chickentown".' Jane had a twinkle in her eye. 'Clifford could recite it backwards. The extra-sweary version.'

The thought of an elderly academic reciting all those profanities amused Roo no end.

'This is a quality breakfast, Frank.' Vincent raised his cup of tea in a toast to the chef.

'I was thinking it might serve as fortification for our

rescue,' replied Frank, 'but looking at all that outside, I'm not convinced the situation has got any more hopeful.'

'And inside, we have a ghost that's scoffing our grub,' said Vincent.

Frank smiled, but he was bothered by it. And he would get to the bottom of it one way or another, even if he had to stand guard in the galley all night.

'No such thing as ghosts. Maybe we have a sleepwalker among us,' said Jane, sweeping her eyes across her fellow guests and concluding that none of them seemed the type to tear into a chicken like a starved animal.

'You don't believe in ghosts, Jane?' This from Roo, who was surprised by her statement.

'No, I don't, Roo. I think once we are out of this world . . .' She pulled her words up short before she could impose her beliefs on others, but she'd said enough to make her reasoning clear. 'I'm a humanist, that is to say I concentrate on making the best of my time on earth.'

'Is that because you were married to a scientist, Jane?' Grace asked.

'Ironically, no. I was brought up a heaven-and-angels, god-fearing Christian but my beliefs whittled away over the years. My husband Clifford was a scientist who did believe in an afterlife. He didn't used to, but then he had a . . . an experience.'

She had the interest of everyone at the table but she didn't go on until prompted by Frank.

'You can't leave it there, love. You're going to have to fill us in.'

Jane's hand stalled while putting marmalade on her toast. She shouldn't have opened herself up for interrogation, this subject for debate.

'He had a near death incident. He actually "died" on an operating table during a heart procedure. A rather typical story of heading towards a bright light, of being met by a loved one who told him to turn back. His mother, with his childhood dog'— *Jane needs you, go home, Cliffy. It's not your time*— 'Of course most of it could be explained quite simply, the things he heard . . .'

'They say the hearing is the last sense to go, don't they?' Elizabeth said.

Jane swallowed, wondered if she should go on, decided she should.

'It wasn't so much what he heard . . . as what he purported to see when he . . . felt his spirit leave his body and look down at himself, at the mad activity happening from doctors intent on not giving up. Things the surgeon confirmed, details, conclusions that couldn't have been reached just from joining the dots between the available information. That's what gave his account a credibility no one could dispute.'

Jane flapped her hand to indicate she thought she was going on too much and needed to wind it down. 'In short, he was absolutely convinced after that there was something beyond life and no one could sway him otherwise.' *Faith transcends all evidence,* he told her. *I was there, Jane. It was no dream.* He connected with other eminent scientists afterwards who had experienced similar; those who believed nothing truly disappears from the universe and consciousness extends far beyond physical reality. *My darling Jane, I wish I could gift you what I saw,* he'd said, because he knew the pain that still ached below her scars. But she couldn't make herself believe, even with his unswaying testimony, and she had undergone nothing herself that had ever altered her conviction that all anyone truly had was the here and now. Even though she often felt Clifford with her, she knew it was only something deep in her psyche trying to bring her comfort, doing its desperate best to keep him near and in time it would fade.

'What sort of scientist was he, Jane?' Roo asked.

'A psychologist, with a list of qualifications after his name which was longer than his name itself: Clifford Terence Bartholomew Horace Wutheridge.' Jane smiled proudly. 'Mind you, he was the first generation in his family to break ranks and not follow a legal career, so he had something to prove – and boy, did he. My Clifford was a very clever man. And one able to inspire students and make science digestible for people like me who had a much more dominant right side of the brain. He was very loved. And when he retired – finally – he found a new unexpected career on the TV. I was quite wary for him about it because I thought they wanted to wheel him out as a dusty old fart but he was quite the hit.'

Roo made a small gasp. 'You don't mean ... Dr – Professor – Cliff . . . Rutheridge, do you? The fella who was one of the experts on *Love in the Sun*?'

Grace snorted at the suggestion. 'I wouldn't have thought—' But she was as surprised as the rest of them when Jane nodded, pleasure showing in her expression that her husband had been recognised.

'You watched him then, Roo?'

'Oh my god, I never missed it. The aftershow was better than the main programme. He was brilliant and spot-on every time. I remember when he said that Baz didn't really like Kelsey and listed about a million indicators and everyone thought he was bats because it was *obvious*'—she wiggled a pair of quotation marks in the air with her fingers—'he was bonkers about her. Twenty-four hours, he'd dumped her like a hot turd for Shaunelle.' Roo gasped again in sheer awe. 'And that was your fella? He was ace.' Her smile closed down. 'I was so sorry when he . . . There was a programme of all his best bits.'

Jane beamed. 'Thank you for that, Roo. That's so kind of you to say. Now you must tell us about you wanting to be an entertainer. Maybe you could help pass the time and perform some of your poetry for us,' Jane went on. Roo looked horrified.

'I couldn't.'

'Then how will you get on a stage and perform in front of hundreds, Roo?' This from Elizabeth.

'I won't,' she replied. 'I might still want it but it ain't going to happen. Not now.'

Jane shook her head. 'Because of that awful careers person? I wonder how many other people's dreams she ruined. You should do everything in your power to prove her wrong – convert her criticism into a fuel that will launch you like a rocket at the stars.'

'Too late now.'

'Because you're so ancient?' said Vincent. 'What are you? Twenty-two?'

'Flatterer. Twenty-four. Just.'

Vince mused. 'Yeah, heading up to that quarter-century, I see your point. Bit past it.' Then he winked and smiled at her and Roo thought what a great smile he had. She'd only known him less than a day and yet it felt like much longer. He was lovely, a proper catch. He wasn't Harry Styles sort of handsome, his hair was a bit all over the place and his nose was too crooked for that sort of flawlessness, but it couldn't have been more perfect for his face. His eyes were twinkly though, kind and hazel and full of fun. Aaron's nose was straight and perfect, and his eyes were . . . She cut that thought off right away and turned her attention back to her eggs.

Grace laid her cutlery down on her plate. 'Well, that was lovely, thank you,' she said to her husband, with the polite formality of a stranger and Jane thought, *She's out of sync with him and can't find her way back.*

'I'll second that,' added Tim. He stood. 'My turn to wash up, I think.'

Roo handed her plate to him and made a point of saying a pronounced thank-you when he took it from her.

'I might go and find some decorations,' she said. 'I im- agine that the staff will have enough to do with the beds and things when they get on so I can save them a job while passing a bit of time. And if by any chance we're stuck here all Christmas, then it'll be nice for us.'

She said it but really she didn't believe they'd be here that long. When the fog cleared, they'd see green fields out there by later this afternoon. Fog meant the temperature was rising, she was sure she remembered that from school. Then again, the geography teachers were as uninspiring and useless as the careers advisor woman so maybe not.

Chapter 17

It was through pure mischief that Roo did a U-turn on the way to the stores in 'Yongle' because she decided, on a whim, to help Tim with the clearing-up first. She'd force him to engage. That could be her distraction for today, because sure as hell she needed one. As she passed it, the beautiful wooden clock on the wall in the lounge started revving up to announce the hour. A door opened underneath the face and a lady sashayed out holding a bell, then a man met her from the other side with a hammer in his hand to strike it – ten times. *Two hours to go.*

Roo had learned from someone once that sometimes the most effective way to really piss off an enemy was to be nice to them; they couldn't handle it. Even when you were itching to leap on them with your nails curled into tiger claws, you should rise above your instincts because then you robbed them of claiming any moral high ground. It had been a lesson learned too late, though, with Aaron. She was lucky he hadn't had her arrested for assault, but in mitigation she hadn't realised her aim with a football trophy would be quite so accurate. He ended up with a very impressive black eye – a 'poor me' Insta pic saw him looking like half a panda, but the trophy survived. AARON EWERIN, TOP SCORER OF THE YEAR, the engraving had said. They weren't wrong there.

'Here I am to help you, Tim,' Roo burst into the galley and announced her arrival in a manner so bright and breezy she made Anne of Green Gables sound like Wednesday Addams. He didn't respond. *Knob.*

She picked up a tea towel from a stack in a drawer, all of them special *Yorkshire Belle* issue. The name was plastered everywhere from the carpets to the ceilings; she was only surprised it wasn't printed on the loo rolls. Jane came through carrying some cups and Tim, voice as soft as the tissue of those luxury loo rolls, asked her to just put them down on the work surface and he'd sort them, so Roo knew he hadn't gone temporarily mute.

He rubbed the first plate over with the cloth and put it on the draining board, not even attempting to make conversation with her though. It was going to be a long five minutes, Roo concluded.

Elizabeth went forward into the 'Liberty' carriage, to stoke up the lovely fire Roo had built. It was still going but a touch hungry.

'Here, let me,' said Vincent, who had followed her there on his way to fill up the log basket from the stores at the front. 'Don't want you burning yourself.' Then he hesitated. 'Not that I think you aren't capable of doing . . . I don't want to insinuate that . . . Oh hell, these days, you're scared to have manners in case you insult . . . I . . .'

He was getting himself in a knot and she rescued him, smiling inwardly.

'I'm very happy to be in the company of a gentleman, always, Vincent. If you had a seat on a bus and stood up to allow me to sit down, I'd thank you and take it.'

The thought of Elizabeth on a public bus tickled him. His parents had always raised him to be a gentleman and it threw him when women passengers more or less slapped his hand away when he lifted up their suitcase to load into the boot, snapping, 'I can manage.' More often than not then, as he was standing back and watching their bodies buckle with the strain, they'd drop it, relent and say grudgingly, 'I suppose you should do it.' What a palaver.

Vincent put the log on the fire with the tongs.

'Yeah, I guess you could have done that without killing yourself.'

Elizabeth laughed. 'You did it better than I could have though. A very masculine technique.'

'Flatterer.'

His grin was lopsided, she noticed. She could easily imagine him as a small boy with a smiley, cheeky face on his school photos, his light-brown hair thick and defying his mum's attempts at taming it with her brush. Girls at her school weren't allowed to smile on the annual photos and, coupled with the frilly collared blouses that were standard uniform, the result was they ended up looking like dead people on Victorian post-mortem photos. They were stuck in a drawer somewhere in the family home, still in their envelopes. They'd never been out on display once. Had she been her mother's horse though, she'd have been in a silver frame.

'Not got any better out there,' said Vince, standing by the window, straining his eyes to see anything beyond the fog other than more snowflakes falling. They were fine ones first thing that morning, now they were fat again. 'I think I might be in trouble with your fiancé for not delivering you to Durham.'

He made her sound like a parcel, a commodity. Maybe that's because she was.

'I really shouldn't worry, Vincent. You can't be expected to work miracles. It's not your fault I'm not there.'

It was all *her* fault though, that's what they'd be saying, the whole of the Pennington family. She could have travelled with her father had she not been so pigheaded and now look at the debacle she'd caused. She wished she had a magic mirror, like Beauty, to see what was going on up there. Her ears felt as if they were burning as much as the logs in the grate.

'Looks like you might have to spend Christmas with a group of strangers and not with your loved ones,' said Vincent, sighing on her behalf.

Loved ones. If, by some miracle, she did get there for Christmas dinner, she'd be in the company of an old curmudgeon who was pleased by nothing, his intolerable snob of a wife who would no doubt be wearing a wig that would dwarf a King's Guard's bearskin and be caustic as lye with her. Elspeth-Ann's sister would be there too: 'Namedrops' as Elizabeth had nicknamed her, for her constant namedropping. *As I said to Lady Collingwood, we can't come to you in Cannes this year as we've been invited to Monaco with Prince Albert and I really must catch up with William Gates . . . we never call him Bill.*

The future best man would be present too, someone Elizabeth just didn't feel comfortable around. She suspected he was jealous of her relationship with Gregory; it would certainly explain his cattiness, though it didn't explain his overfamiliarity if they were ever alone – and she made sure she avoided ever being alone with him. There were the schmoozing 'minor royals' as she thought of them: the extended family who were always invited, who sucked up to the principals for glory by association. And then there was her father who would be in his element, greasing, net-working, circulating among everyone except his own flesh and blood who was in his blind spot. But he would give a rousing speech at some point to a captive audience about how thrilled he was that his beloved daughter had found her match. There would be copious amounts of champagne and caviar on blinis, birds stuffed into other birds and roasted together, golden candlesticks on the tables, more festive flowers than Elton John could have thought decent.

And there would be Gregory, who she knew would be in a foul mood because, no matter what the extenuating circumstances were, the stress she had caused them for fucking everything up would be grounds for sending her to Coventry on a business-class ticket. Of course he would be charm personified with everyone but her and she would have to withstand feeling his ire discharging from him like radiation from a leaky nuclear power plant. Getting there at this stage in the proceedings would afford her no brownie points; no one would be pleased to see her, the damage was done because of her selfishness in insisting she put a friend she hadn't seen for years above them. Maybe they had a point. It would be a contest to see if they could beat her up more than she could herself. *Loved ones.* Vincent had no idea. But she nodded and said, 'Yes, I just might have to.' She sat down on one of the sofas, nudging aside the notebook that was there. 'What about you? Where were you spending Christmas before all this happened?'

'By myself this year,' he replied. 'Not that I haven't had my fair share of invitations, but ... naw.' Last year he'd gone to a friend's house. He'd had a wonderful dinner with them, a jolly time playing charades and party games, the beer, wine and spirits had flowed but it had just been too much being part of the happy family scene, watching their gorgeous kids open their presents, feeling the love bounce between them, feeling on the outside edge. Feeling alone in the midst of them, like the maypole around which all the players danced.

'Oh.' Elizabeth hadn't been expecting that. He'd definitely said '*we moved in*' when he was talking about his farmhouse. She couldn't really probe further though for it might sound too flirty asking if he had a partner. She didn't want him to think she was enquiring out of intimate interest.

As if he had heard her internal machinations, he said, 'Just me and the cat: Snowball, appropriately enough. Luckily, she goes round to the old lady nearby if I'm ever away on a job and she gets spoiled rotten on salmon. I mean, who always keeps salmon in the fridge in case the neighbour's cat fancies it? I'm thinking about moving in there myself.'

Ahhh ... a cat – hence the 'we'. Well, that was rather sad that someone as nice as Vincent Diamond had no one to spend the holiday with. Her imagination threw up a picture of what a Christmas with Vincent might be like in his country farmhouse. She bet he'd have a real tree and loads of lovely things in to eat. There would be a fire much bigger than this one and *Home Alone* on a massive TV and he'd be the type who'd want to snuggle up on a squashy sofa ... *Stop that, Elizabeth.*

She picked up the notebook at her side to distract her wayward thoughts and opened it. It was half-full of scribblings, crossings out, notes in margins, couplets. She guessed it belonged to Roo.

> Santa Claus
> Wanker Claus
> Jolly old St Prickerlas
> Foreskinterklaas
> Piss Kringle
> Welcome as a pus-filled pimple
> Mr Jingle bell-end
> Father Shitmas
> Don't kid yourself, you're not my friend
> Please stick your presents up your ass

Hardly a typical Christmas verse, thought Elizabeth, her eyebrows raised at the vitriol.

'What's that?' asked Vincent.

'Roo's poetry, by the look of it,' she replied, turning the page, reading to herself.

> Lovely Lizzy with the long, golden hair
> Are you aware . . .
> You have sad grey eyes
> Wearing the ring of your not-really prince
> If it came to a vote, who'd be your dreamboat
> I think we'd all quote, 'Dump him and pick Vince'
> He's caring, protects
> It's not that complex — try him for size
> Don't marry a man who puts clouds in your eyes
> I bet you'd have great sex
> Before it's too late, Lizzy, pack your suitcases
> Your kids would be gorgeous — but with smiley faces

'Let's have a look then.' Vince held out his hand. Elizabeth shut the book quickly.

'We shouldn't really pry,' she said. 'I'll take it down to the cabin for her.'

'Who do you think the phantom pie-scoffer is then, Tim?'

In the galley, Roo tried yet again to engage him in conversation but Tim was resolutely sticking to monosyllabic answers.

'No idea.'

Ooh, a two-syllable word there, she thought to herself. He was defrosting.

'You must feel a bit better that there is nothing you can possibly do about missing your Santa gig?'

'Yes.'

Tim opened one of the cupboards above his head to put the last mug away.

'I get it, you don't like to let kids down on one of the most important days of their year. Their parents are just going to have to do a bit of work instead, aren't they? Let's face it, some of them just can't be arsed so it won't kill them to push themselves for once.'

Roo saw Tim freeze in the action of closing the cupboard door, then he shut it with undue force and strode out of the galley, leaving Roo wondering what inference he had taken from her words that she hadn't put in them.

Chapter 18

Everyone but Tim was in the lounge in the 'Liberty' car when Roo went back through. They had kept the fire fed with logs and someone had fetched the radio which was perched on a small occasional table. Vincent had been up to the stores on the hunt for batteries and found some so there was no chance of 'the real BBC' Brian running out of voice, which was good because he was presently their only bridge with the outside world. Roo arrived just in time to hear the last few bars of 'Blue Christmas', but not the Elvis version that she recognised. It was certainly a blue Christmas for her all right – so blue it was almost black.

'Well, that was Doye O'Dell singing "Blue Christmas",' Brian commented when the song was finished. 'He's a particular favourite of my wife, Cath. Though what she'd do with him if he landed in her Christmas stocking, I just don't know.'

'I bet he could hazard a guess if he put his mind to it,' Frank said.

'I feel a bit sorry for all the kiddies expecting to go to church today for their Christingle services because it's not going to happen for them, is it? They're going to miss out on their oranges and sweets, aren't they, thanks to this weather? And there's no let up, is there? Not yet anyway. In fact, the *meaty-logical* office is telling us to be prepared for even more. I don't think we will get to Midnight Mass tonight either, sadly. We live very close to the church but I don't think the vicar is going to open up just for us two.'

Roo's sharp intake of breath resulted in a gurgling noise in her throat which she coughed away.

'Do you think all the churches will be shut today?' she asked to no one in particular.

'If the rest of the UK is like this, I can't see many being open, Roo,' Frank answered her.

'It must be awful for those who had a funeral or christening planned. What would they do?' said Jane.

'Or their wedding,' added Grace.

'Must be really awful for them, what a shame,' Roo commented, though it had to be said, without much conviction. Then she clapped her hands as if she meant business. 'Right now, I really am going to try and find some decorations to tart up the lounge,' she said, her tone artificially bright.

Down in 'Maria Gloriosa', Tim was ensconced in a large armchair that seemed to have been made for his substantial frame, reading a book he had chosen for its relevant title: *Great Bells of the World*. The owner really was running with a theme on his toy. It was a grand tome with yellowing pages and a comforting old book smell. There were accompanying black and white photos and drawn illustrations and though he'd expected to flick through it with cursory interest, he'd quickly become engrossed. Tim liked to read. He'd been brought up in a house where there were always books around because his mum was an avid reader and encouraged him to find pleasure in books. He had so many memories of her reading to him at bedtime, special times between a parent and a child, and yet not enough memories of him reading to Fleur.

He cut off thoughts of his daughter abruptly and carried on with the chapter that had most caught his eye: 'The Bell that was Executed'.

Roo found some trimmings in the store cupboard next to where the linen was kept in 'Yongle'. There were bags of garlands and ornament clusters, enough to decorate the whole train twice over by the look of it. It wasn't as light in this carriage, or as warm, and had an oddly different feel to the rest of the train, but then up at this end the luxurious gave way to the practical, the functional. She loaded two hessian sacks full; she'd have to come back later for the big box of tree decorations.

There were luckily plenty of lamps and hooks and racks and rails to wrap the leafy, glittery garlands round in the 'Liberty' carriage, although she had to enlist the help of Vincent because she was too short to reach them, but he was more than willing to be Roo's servant. At over six foot, Vincent was tall enough to do the job. Tim would have been taller still but he was AWOL (good) and she wouldn't ask him anything ever again.

Jane watched Vincent being micro-directed by Roo and smiled fondly. They reminded her of herself and Clifford fancying-up the rectory together. The ceilings were high there and he'd been up and down stepladders, obeying her every command. He wouldn't have thanked her for cautioning him to be careful at his age and he'd been fit as a flea until the first day of February. He'd left her quickly, too quickly, no chance to prepare, no warning. It was the smallest of blessings because he would have made a terrible patient; he wasn't built for infirmity. The heart op he'd had years before, and his temporarily 'crossing over' had given him a new lease of life, mentally as well as physically; in fact, he'd become titanium.

Last January in the sales she had replaced lots of their older, tattier things with new shiny ones for this Christmas, but she'd donated them to charity, their packaging unopened. She hadn't the heart to put them up, not without him there. When he'd gone, the rectory felt cavernous, even though it had been the perfect size for them both. She didn't want to live in it without him, it had been the right thing to sell it. But still, the prospect of moving into a 'granny flat' wasn't thrilling her one bit.

'That was the Mormon Tabernacle Choir singing "Joy to the World",' said toothless Brian from the radio. 'I've always thought what a funny word Tabernacle is. Tabernacle apparently means a place of worship, for those of you who didn't know, and also a very large box for putting the communion artefacts in.'

'He's very educational, isn't he, old Brian?' said Frank. 'I reckon we could learn a lot listening to him.'

'I shall miss the Christingle service though today, myself and Mrs Cosgrove do love that at our local church. It won't be the same not bringing home our orange with the candle in the top. It's not just the kiddies who'll be disappointed.'

'What actually *is* Christingle?' asked Roo, attaching a garland to the mantelpiece of the fireplace. 'I've heard the name but I don't know anything about it.'

Brian's next words seemed to answer her question, as if he'd been listening in.

'It's our favourite of the Christmas services. The kiddies love making the Christingles, although I suspect that's more to do with the sweeties and I'd like to bet they eat more than they put onto the little sticks. For those of you not familiar with Christingle, the orange represents the world. The red ribbon around the middle is the blood of our Christ, the four skewers are the four corners of the world – or the four seasons, or maybe both. The sweeties and the raisins on them are all the food God provides and what do you think the candle in the top means?'

'I'm guessing light, Brian,' said Roo.

'That's right, the light of the world, our Lord Jesus saviour.'

'He can definitely hear us,' Vince nodded pointedly towards the radio.

'It's the tradition in our church that we light the candles in the dark and sing "Away in a Manger". It gets me every time.'

Away in a manger. Billy dressed as a shepherd with a chequered tea towel on his head secured with parcel string, holding his Christingle to present to the old Tiny Tears doll in the makeshift manger. His face split into a grin as he spotted his mum in church and she'd smiled and cried at the same time. The image was too much; Grace got up, strode down the carriage, muttering something about going to the bathroom, but Frank's eyes followed her, guessing where her thoughts were as Bing Crosby started to sing the carol. It got him every time he heard it too, but he was better at covering it up.

The clock on the wall began to whirr and Roo looked at its face to see both hands together at the top. The lady appeared with her bell, the man with his hammer to announce the mid-day. Would the marriage of Aaron Andrew

Arsehole Ewerin and Amber Hope Bitch Booth be cancelled or would it somehow have gone ahead? Amber wanted to be married before the baby was showing too much; Aaron had filled her in on that choice detail. And Roo had asked if that was because she wanted to appear respectable, because if so it was a bit late for that with her shagging her best mate's fiancé. Would snowflakes fall like nature's confetti on them as they emerged from the church as husband and wife? She imagined them laughing about it, figuring it would make a story to tell their grandchildren one day.

'It looks very festive in here now, thanks to you, Roo,' said Jane, diverting Roo's thoughts from the allotted hour. 'And Vincent, of course.'

The last chime of the twelve sounded.

'I'm going to fetch the box of tree decorations,' said Roo, hurrying out of the carriage before her face gave way to the turmoil going on behind it. She had never been one for public emotional displays: she'd learned over the years to shove her feelings behind a façade, out of public view – give or take chucking that trophy at Cockface. There were only disadvantages to exposing your underbelly.

'Hark! Hark, the angels sing. Today the Christ is born . . .' trilled Roo as she strutted down the coaches, dragging her thoughts away from where they wanted to take her. It was just as well there was no internet coverage because she knew she wouldn't have been able to resist dipping onto Insta to torture herself. She could just about hold it together when there were people around, forcing her to keep her upper lip stiff, but up here in this part of the train she was completely alone and her hurt tore its way out. Tears started spurting out of her eyes as if there was an industrial pump behind them.

'Let the bells ring out on this first Christmas Day . . .' she made herself carry on, her voice jelly-wobbly, in the hope that singing words – even these wrong ones – would drive away the image of the man she adored, who told her – totally out of the blue – that he didn't want to marry her any more. Not only that but that he was going to marry someone else – and quickly. She thought he was joking, because he was a convincing winder-upper. *'We didn't plan it, it just happened.'* Then he told her who the other person in that 'we' bracket was. *'We didn't mean to do it.'*

'Yeah, I get it, I'm always just opening my legs when I don't mean to,' she'd replied. And she couldn't even talk it over with her best mate, because Amber Booth, the woman Aaron had impregnated, had been that best mate.

Roo pushed open the door to 'Yongle' and crossed over to the cupboard where she'd seen the tree decorations earlier.

'Hark! Hark, let wise men come, the star will light their way or maybe not, maybe it just can't be bothered because Christmas is a total pile of shit' – her brain was gone now. This was her favourite carol, all folky and rustic, and she couldn't even remember the next line but she needed to sing because while her mouth was moving, it helped to stop the reel of perfect pictures in her head of the love of her life in a slick suit slipping a wedding band on the finger of the glowing pregnant bride dressed in virginal (ha!) white. She dashed the tears away from her eyes, told herself to get a grip and picked up the box of baubles. It was as she was about to head back that her attention was grabbed by a movement in the corner of the car. She saw a boot and not only that, a boot attached to a foot, attached to a leg and whoever the whole assembly belonged to was hiding behind the tall towel cabinet, because she saw that leg retract slowly to join the rest of its body.

Roo went as cold as if someone had just tipped a bucket of icy water down the back of her neck.

Don't panic and keep singing, said a voice within.

'Hark! Hark,' she hung onto the tune, 'all hail to God on high.' She turned, trying to look as unbothered as someone going through customs with absolutely nothing to declare, but her feet were getting faster and faster towards the door and as soon as she was through it, she dumped the box and ran.

Chapter 19

Tim was just heading to his cabin when the far door into the 'Uglich' car was thrown open forcefully and he saw Roo bombing down the corridor. She didn't stop when she got to him either, but careened into him with such force that, slight as she was compared with his bulk, she knocked him into the window.

'Tim,' she said his name in a whispered fluster. 'I think there's someone hiding in the carriage with the larder. I *know* there is. I've just seen his leg. I'm not imagining it, it moved. A big boot ... it ... I saw ... he's behind the cupboard.'

She was visibly shaking as she was rambling. Holding her by the tops of the arms, he could feel the vibrations coursing through her. His initial response was to go and check out her suspicions, but they were quickly overridden by a more guarded one. If there was someone else on this train, as Roo insisted, then there had to be a reason why they hadn't shown themselves. Maybe a little caution was needed and there was a lot to be said for safety in numbers.

'Let's go back into the lounge and tell the others what you've seen,' he said, pushing her gently towards 'Liberty'.

'I know what I saw, and it was a boot and it was attached to a leg that was very slowly trying to tuck itself out of sight behind the cupboard with all the towels in it,' said Roo. She was scrunched up defensively in between Elizabeth and Grace.

'Well, that explains a couple of things,' said Frank, having listened to her: one, the unmistakable feeling that he wasn't alone when he was at that end of the train, and two, the carnivorous 'ghost'.

He picked up the poker from the companion set at the side of the fireplace. Vincent looked around for a suitable tool and decided the hefty metal salt grinder would deliver a suitable clubbing. He handed its brother – the pepper mill – to Tim.

'Ladies, you stay here,' said Frank. The ladies didn't argue.

The three men walked down the carriages: 'Uglich', 'Sigismund', 'Mingun' and then halted in the vestibule before 'Yongle'. They checked with each other that they were ready. There was no point in pussyfooting around, the plan of action was to storm in as if they meant business.

Vincent opened the door and charged, followed by the others.

'Okay, we know you're in here, so out you come,' boomed Tim, in the moment more Satan than Santa. He marched over to the towel cupboard but if there had been anyone behind it, they were gone now. Vincent and Frank both searched around but there was no other presence. Then they all heard the sound from 'Pummerin', like furniture being shifted.

They moved forward, weapons at the ready, in preparation for confronting who had been living among them unseen. The blinds had all been pulled down in here since they'd last visited this carriage – and not by any of them.

Frank's turn to bellow now, although he was never any good at volume.

'Come out and show yourself. We aren't leaving until you do.'

Nothing. Then a slight shuffling. Then a pair of hands appeared from under a table, held up in surrender.

'I'm here,' said a voice, male, weary. A figure rose, dressed in a long, dark cape coat with brass buttons. A large scar covered the whole left side of his face.

Vincent released a couple of the blinds which sprang up noisily and gave them some more light. Now they could all clearly see the man who was standing in front of them and looking far thinner than the bulk of his coat might suggest; it was sizes too big for him. It wasn't a scar either on his face but dirt or dried blood. His sandy hair was matted with similar above his left eye which prompted Frank then to ask, 'You all right, mate?'

'Am I okay to sit?' asked the man, as if the effort of standing had been too much. 'I'm . . .' He touched his head as if that might explain his situation.

The men lowered their weapons. This injured interloper was no threat, that was pretty clear.

'How long you been on the train? Where did you come from?' asked Vincent.

'I . . . I don't know . . . Last night, I think. The train was standing here. I was in pursuit . . .'

As they came closer still, they could see that the coat was a uniform with a number stitched above the top right pocket.

Vincent noticed a cap on the floor where the man had been sitting, a peaked cap. Army, was he? Police? All winter edition garb from the look of it, heavy-duty and woollen.

'My name is John Brown. I'm a prison officer.' He had a north-east accent, they noticed: not as strong as full-on Geordie but heading up there.

'We had a break-out. I think I must have fell when I was running and banged my head. I was trying to get back . . . I must have gone miles out me way because there's no train tracks anywhere near us.'

'You were lucky,' said Frank. 'You could have died lying out there. Is there anyone else with you?'

'No. I went on ahead. There was just one who got away but they must have caught him, he wouldn't have got far in this weather.'

'Well, you did,' countered Tim.

'I'm dressed for it though, he wasn't.'

'I hope they caught him, for his sake,' said Vincent. He shivered then because this car was cooler than the rest. God knows how cold it must be outside – John Brown was indeed lucky.

'I think we'd better get you down to the warmth and sort out your head,' Frank told him. That cut looked in dire need of cleaning up. He hoped it was just a flesh wound because there wasn't a cat in hell's chance of them getting some medical attention out here, other than what they could provide between them. Even if there was a way to contact the air ambulance brigade, they couldn't fly to them in the snow soup out there.

The shock registered hard on the faces of the women on seeing four men enter the car, when only three had left it. John was leaning heavily on Frank who was the best to support him, being roughly the same height, and also the strongest of them. If you were ploughing a field and missing an ox, Frank would have made a good substitute. He deposited the newcomer down on the couch nearest the fire and he slumped against the cushions as if his spine were made of rubber.

'Ladies, this is John ... John Brown. He's an officer at a local prison. Apparently someone broke out. John was following them, fell, bumped his head, got totally disorientated and somehow ended up with us. He's lucky, don't you think?'

Jane thought of those far-off bells she'd heard and wondered if that was a signal from the prison. The sound travelled well if it was, but maybe there was little around to get in its way.

'There must be a first-aid kit around somewhere. They've thought of everything else,' said Roo.

'There's one in Maria G, mounted on the wall,' said Tim. 'I'll get it.'

'No need, I've got one in my suitcase,' said Jane. 'If you've had the sort of life I've had, you don't travel without a portable hospital.' Jane stood. 'I think some warm water is warranted.'

'I'll get that then,' said Tim. 'There's a bucket in the galley and some cloths in a drawer.' He went one way, Jane the other.

'How long have you been on the train, John?' Elizabeth asked.

'I'm not sure. It was dark. I remember trying a few doors before I found one that I could open. I must have just ... collapsed when I got in. I don't know what I did then. I think I ate something ...'

No one said anything to that, but they all knew they'd found the phantom pie-scoffer. At least there was no ghost to freak them out.

Jane soon arrived back with a zip-up square case and a towel. She foraged inside and took out what she needed, then wriggled her hands into some thin latex gloves and inspected John's wound.

'Well, the good news is that it's a superficial cut and it appears to have partly sealed itself up. The trouble is there's so many blood vessels in this area that I imagine there was quite the blood flow. Did you lose consciousness, John?' she asked him.

'No, I don't think so. I went dizzy, I felt a bit sick. If I did pass out, it wasn't for very long.'

'If it had been for very long, you wouldn't be walking around, you'd be buried out there. There's grit or something in the wound, not sure how you've managed to find something to hit your head on not covered in a foot of snow.'

'I can't remember.'

Tim walked in with a tin bucket full of tepid water which he set on the carpet at Jane's side.

'Are you a nurse?' John asked Jane, as she began gently dabbing at his head with some swabs.

'No, but I've done a fair bit of nursing in my time,' she answered him. 'I'm actually an artist. Well, I was.'

'Were you, Jane?' Roo gave a little gasp. 'Although I don't know why I sound surprised, because I'm not at all. I thought you looked like a bit of a creative.'

That amused Jane and she took it as a compliment.

'Did you sell . . . exhibit . . . your paintings . . . sculptures?' asked Elizabeth.

'Paintings. Yes, years ago. I don't think Van Gogh was

looking over his shoulder at the competition, but I was able to supplement my income as a secretary and then when I met Clifford, I found that being his secretary became more important than flogging my wares and that allowed me to paint for fun rather than food. Painting was a small passion of mine rather than a grand passion. Clifford was that to me.' She smiled and Elizabeth suddenly felt in danger of filling up at the loveliness of the sentiment.

'That's got me in the sweet spot,' said Roo, echoing her thoughts.

'Ouch.'

'Sorry, John. You had a stone stuck in your head. We don't want that there.' Jane took tweezers from her kit and teased out some debris which she laid on a tissue on the table.

'Can I get John something to eat or drink?' Frank asked Jane for permission.

'I don't see why not,' said Jane, adding a little cheekily, 'It's not affected him so far. Would you like a little brandy, John?' She asked it as if an affirmative answer was a foregone conclusion.

'Thank you, I would.'

Vincent volunteered. 'I'll go.'

'I think maybe I should rustle up something for lunch,' said Frank. 'Are we all ready for a bit of nosebag?'

'I could force something down. Want a hand?' asked Tim.

'No, you're good, mate. I'm going to prepare that Christmas Eve hash for later and as for now, how does soup sound to everyone? Soup and cheese toasted sandwiches? I found a great big tin of tomato soup in the pantry.'

'That sounds divine,' replied Jane.

'I'll help you,' said Elizabeth, raising a warning finger at Frank. 'I'm not taking no for an answer.'

'No, I will.' Grace left her seat. 'I know you don't like me in the kitchen with you but maybe in these circumstances . . .'

'I won't turn you down . . . in these circumstances.'

Though Frank had never said that he didn't want Grace in his kitchen, that was a 'Mandela effect' conclusion she'd drawn for herself. A convenient misapprehension she chose to believe.

'You've got too much hair, John. I'm not shaving it to put a plaster on so let's keep our eyes on it but I think it'll be fine. I've cleaned and sterilised it as best I can and it's already started to knit so you're obviously a good healer, but don't be tempted to scratch it as the chances are it might itch as your nerves wake up.'

Jane had done all she could. She zipped up her first-aid case and wrapped all the wipes, cotton wool and bits of grit together to put in the bin.

'Thank you,' John said. 'You'd have made a good medic, I think.'

'I was always very thorough when I needed to put my nurse's hat on, I'll give myself that.' She smiled at him.

'Who did you nurse?'

'My sons,' Jane said. 'When they were children.'

'I remember my mum staying up all night and putting cold cloths on my head when I was poorly once,' John recalled. 'I must have only been little but I remember it, clear as day.'

Elizabeth tried to imagine her own mother doing similar and failed. Penelope Dudley couldn't bear to put herself out for anyone else, not even her own daughter. She'd had a nanny when she was younger although Elizabeth had no fond memories of her, like so many people had of theirs. She was called Olwen Uzzle and had long hairs growing out of her nose. She was snappy and impatient and smelt of yeast and cheap soap and slapped Elizabeth's hands and legs for the slightest misdemeanour, with the full permission of her parents who were of the 'spare the rod and spoil the child' mentality. That was the only saving grace of having to go to boarding school, because the services of stinky Olwen (as Elizabeth referred to her in her diary) were finally dispensed with.

Roo started to ask, 'How many son—' but was interrupted by Vincent walking in with a nip of brandy.

'Here you go, John. Purely medicinal.'

Both of John's hands came out to take it and Jane registered the look on his face: *Rapture.*

'Oh my, that smells good,' said John, breathing in the bouquet before he placed his lips to the glass and sipped as reverently as if it were communion wine.

'You look as if you've not had one of those in a while, John,' said Jane.

He let the brandy sit in his mouth before swallowing, before answering her.

'There's none of this in jail.' He took too large a mouthful then, coughed and laughed at himself. 'That's strong stuff that. Smooth though.'

'Ten-year-old cognac according to the bottle,' agreed Vincent. He doubted Mr Ingleton had anything on his shelves that was akin to some of the paint-strippers he'd had on nights out.

'Do you stay in the jail yourself then? As staff?' This from Tim.

'Well, it's a bit out of the way so yes ... we're holed up there for weeks at a time.'

'And you got the short straw working over Christmas?' asked Jane.

'Aye.' Shifting the glass between his hands, John slipped one arm out of his coat sleeve, then the other. 'That's better. I've warmed up now.'

He had on a blue-grey shirt and black trousers that were a much better fit than the newly divested coat.

Tim lifted it from the sofa. 'I'll hang this up; it's still damp. It looks too big for me, never mind you.'

'It's not mine. I just grabbed the nearest one when the alert went off.' John Brown took another gulp from his glass. 'This a royal train, is it?'

'No, it's called the *Yorkshire Belle*. It's going to Scotland for Christmas. Well, at least it should have been. Do you want to dry your boots as well? Take 'em off and put 'em by the fire. I can go and find you some slippers,' said Vincent.

'I will in a bit,' said John. He closed his eyes. 'I'm rather tired.'

'Why don't we leave you for a while to have a rest?' said Jane. 'We'll give you a call when lunch is on the table.'

'Aye, that'd be grand. Just five minutes.' He already looked half-asleep, though the brandy glass was locked between his two hands.

They moved down to 'Old Tom', except for Vincent who went to find a spare pair of the complimentary slippers. Looking at the size of the boots John had been wearing, he was going to have to source a pair big enough to fit Coco the clown.

In the galley, Grace was gently warming a huge pan of soup while Frank was dicing the onions and chopping up carrots for that evening's supper. The beef in the fridge was far too

good a quality for a hash but as there was no chuck steak
to be had, they'd have to suffer yet more superiority. He'd
cook it low and slow with some gravy he'd made from the
powder he'd scooped from a labelled tin and later add the
veg and the potatoes that were presently parboiling. He'd
throw in the sprouts for Roo at the last minute or they'd
end up like his old mum's used to. She'd put them on to boil
for the Christmas dinner in late September. He couldn't do
with a mushy sprout.

'Well, this is nice, innit?' he said. 'I might let you help
me in the pub now we've proved we can share a kitchen.'

'I'd rather clean,' replied Grace. He didn't comment but
she knew how he'd have taken that. She might as well have
said that she didn't want to breathe the same air as him.

Frank put the cheese sandwiches Grace had made into
the hot oven.

'I wonder how everyone's getting on back home. I mean,
if the weather's like this there, I don't expect them to keep
it open.'

He'd left the pub in the capable hands of two of the bar
staff who had worked in the pub for years before they'd
taken it over. They knew the place inside out and were as
reliable as the country's meteorologists weren't.

'I'm not even thinking about it,' said Grace. 'What would
be the point when there's nothing we can do?'

He wondered what she *was* thinking about though. He
had no idea what was in her head these days. Once upon a
time they were on such a wavelength, they'd finish off each
other's sentences.

'What do you make of this new guy then? The pie
scoffer?'

'I think he's a very fortunate man,' said Grace, nudging

down the heat under the soup. Then she stuck a spoon into it and tasted it. 'You might need some more Worcester sauce in this, you can't taste what you've put in.'

'Hark at you, Nig-*ella*.' He hadn't meant to put the emphasis on the latter part of the name, but he had. *Of all the chefs to pluck out of the air . . . Of all the ways to say it.*

He tried to gloss over it, smother it with other words, actions. He lifted up the bottle of sauce, screwed off the lid.

'Everyone says Worcester but it's Worcestershire. Gobful, though. No wonder people—'

'Has she been in touch?' Grace asked, tight-lipped.

Frank shook some more of the bottle into the soup. This was a conversation he didn't want to have, not now, not here. He had planned to build up to it with small, tentative but sure steps, but with one stupid slip of the tongue he'd just ruined all that.

Since he didn't answer immediately, because he was thinking what was best to say, he effectively answered her.

'She has, then,' Grace said. 'I knew it.'

'Let's not do this now, Grace.'

'*Now?*' she said, honing in on the word. 'So when were you going to inform me what's been going on behind my back? When you'd got me trapped alone in a cottage with no means of escape so I'd have to listen to you?'

He sighed. 'I haven't heard—'

'You're a liar.' Grace's lips contracted over her teeth. She was in fight mode. Again.

'I—'

They were interrupted by Vincent and Tim appearing in the doorway.

'There must be something we can do. That smells bloody gorgeous,' said the former.

'Yep, we are just about ready to serve up,' said Frank, switching on his public persona. 'Grace, if you'd start to ladle the soup in the dishes, Vincent and Tim, our waiters *du jour*, will take them through.'

Grace did as he requested, her face stone. Frank flipped the sandwiches in the oven, the hand gripping the spatula shaking with the effort of holding himself together. God, what a mess. And less than ten minutes ago he'd thought there was a glimmer of light on the horizon, but it was just the shimmering mirage of an oasis in the desert, conjured up by stupid hope and desperation.

Chapter 20

The fog was clearing outside, not that it increased any visibility because the snow saw to that. The wind was beginning to get up again too, even if they couldn't feel it in their cosy, extravagant surroundings. Radio Brian was playing his gentle Christmas tunes of yesteryear and in between he was gabbling on about the full English breakfast he and Mrs Cosgrove had enjoyed that morning, and his baubles, some of which, apparently, he'd had since he was a boy.

'There's plenty more where this came from if anyone wants it,' said Frank, which was just as well as John was already on his second toastie before anyone had eaten their first. His spoon was dipping in and out of his soup so fast it was almost a blur.

'Do you eat the same food as the prisoners, John?' asked Elizabeth.

'Mostly,' he replied, pausing his spoon for a moment to answer. 'There's never any flavour in the soup, it's nothing like this. You can't tell a fish broth from a beef.'

'Do they get their five a day?' asked Roo.

'Five what?'

'Fruit and veg.'

John shrugged. 'I dunno. I've never counted.'

Grace coughed because a bit of toast went down the wrong way and Vincent noticed that no one had put any drink provisions out.

'I'll get some water,' he said, giving Grace a tap on her back as he passed her.

'I think we should have wine,' said Roo. 'Have you seen the amount of bottles in the bar and the pantry? They won't miss ten.' She grinned.

'Ten?' Frank chuckled. He wiped his mouth on his serviette. 'But you do have a point, it's Christmas Eve. I think we can do better than water. I'll go and grab a couple.'

'I'll get the glasses,' said Roo. She left the table and opened a nearby oak cabinet that had a lamp standing on it with a beautiful bell-shaped stained-glass shade. She'd discovered a store of them in there when she'd been poking around looking for things; glasses, more tablemats and serviettes on the left side, games on the right. 'Oh, if anyone is interested, there's a chessboard in here. And draughts, cards, ludo, backgammon, paints, brushes, and a Monopoly board,' she was reminded to tell everyone.

Vincent cleared his mouth of toastie and then said, 'Brian was talking about Monopoly earlier on. He and Mrs Cosgrove were going to play it sometime today.'

'Who's Brian?' asked John.

Tim waved his spoon over at the radio.

'The real BBC. He's our only connection with the rest of the universe. Brian Bernard Cosgrove.'

John Brown's brow creased and his lips moved over the name. He stroked the right of his forehead as if it would help bring down the thought in there that wouldn't be reached.

Elizabeth sought to aid him. 'Maybe you listen to him in your office at work?' she suggested.

'Although he's more likely to be on in the background rather than you listening properly to him,' said Vincent, not unkindly, because he was very grateful for Brian's comforting, if quirky, delivery and his perfect pick of tunes.

'I'm getting very fond of Brian,' said Roo, depositing a glass down in front of everyone. 'He's like one of those uncles who doesn't do much but it's always nice when you see them.' Or so she imagined, as she didn't have any uncles herself.

Frank returned with the bottles of wine and began to pour. Rather conveniently, there were four of them for red and four for white.

'You're spoiling us, Frank. And this soup has a proper tang to it. It's absolutely delicious,' said Jane, who couldn't quite believe she'd eaten so much of it, especially after the breakfast she'd had.

'I agree,' added John.

'Worcestershire sauce,' replied Frank, 'elevates any ordinary dish. I put a splash of it on the cheese toasties as well. The taste just about comes through without overpowering everything else.'

Although he doubted that John's mouth had had time to register any flavours, for the toasties – and he was now on his third – couldn't have touched the sides.

'I'm off for my lunch now, but I'll be back in an hour and I'm going to do a first on air: I'll be making a Christingle seeing as we can't get to church today,' said Brian. 'Why don't you grab an orange and a couple of cocktail sticks, some red ribbon, a candle, small squares of tin foil and some sweets and join me? I bet we've all got plenty of sweeties around at this time of year. Ours are in the Christmas cupboard which I'm sure Mrs Cosgrove won't mind me accessing for entertainment purposes today. Shall we all convene at three?'

'I think that's a great idea and I will join you, Brian,' Roo said to the radio. Anything to keep busy, anything to drive her thoughts away from today. She addressed the table. 'We could have a craft class.'

'I'm going to read,' said Tim, dismissively, as if her suggestion was absurd.

Roo thought that he might have warmed a little towards her given she'd sought out his help when she'd seen John Brown's moving boot, but it turned out that was just a temporary *entente*, then. The devil nudged her shoulder. She wanted to find out about this daughter she reminded him of so much.

'You got kids, Tim?' she asked brightly, knowing full well he had at least one.

'A daughter,' he replied flatly, without looking up.

'And were you going to be spending Christmas with her?'

'No.'

Frank, Jane and Vincent all raised their heads at his gruff tone and Roo was secretly glad that they'd borne witness to his rudeness. And Tim, to Roo's glee, must have been suitably shamed by that because he immediately apologised.

'I'm sorry for snapping, it's a sore subject.'

'S'fine,' replied Roo, enjoying being smugly magnanimous. But then she chucked in her advantage by asking, 'Why though? Have you fallen out?'

Vincent leaned in and whispered, 'Roo . . .' giving her a warning shake of his head.

'It's all right, I'll answer her,' said Tim. 'She lives in New

Zealand. She met a man over there and she married him. She's having her first baby in the new year.'

'How lovely, Tim.' Jane smiled. 'Have you been over to see her?'

'No, I haven't.'

'Scared of flying?' Roo was aware she was pushing it.

'No, I'm not scared of the flying.'

'Why then?'

'Roo, maybe Tim doesn't want to talk about it,' said Frank now, jumping in to gently admonish her.

'Tim brought it up,' said Roo.

'Because I'm a shit father, that's why, Roo,' Tim flung at her from across the table. 'And I don't deserve to see her. That answer the question?' He picked up his spoon again.

'Not really,' said Roo, aware now that she'd totally tipped the scales against herself, but she was unable to leave well alone, even if she could see Jane, at Tim's side, sending her a 'shh' message by lifting her finger and tapping it against her lips.

'Okay then, I'll tell you. I worked too much when my Fleur was little. I wanted her to have the best of everything: bedroom, puppy, kitten, riding lessons, nice school, clothes ... so her mum did all the caring stuff and I did the easy thing and stuck my hand in my pocket. I didn't read stories to her because I was never there at bedtime, I was schmoozing at conferences with strangers and zipping around the world enjoying the hospitality. I didn't take her to the park or to parties or to the cinema. I missed her school plays and her sports days and seeing her getting the prizes she won for coming top of her class. And then when she'd grown up, my wife left me because she said the holidays and the presents and the big house and the money in the bank had never been enough. She said I wasn't there for them, that I'd got it all wrong. And when I was ready to make it up to my girl, spend time with her, she . . . decides to go travelling and met *him* and moved *there*. I missed my chance to be a good dad and I can't get my time back and I'm ashamed of myself and can't do a thing about it.'

He locked eyes with Roo and she saw the gleam of water in his, the threatening glisten of it before he blinked it away. She'd pushed him too hard and now it was her turn to feel sorry.

Tim looked down, feeling the hand on top of his own, warm and kind. Jane's.

'Tim, as parents we do our best. We inevitably get some of it wrong. But when what we do is done with love, we must not beat ourselves up so much. I bet your daughter appreciates what you did for her more than you know.'

'She wants me to go and stay. She wants me to be there when the baby arrives,' said Tim. 'It's me that's being a stubborn old git. My anger at myself is coming out as anger at her.'

'Then you should swallow that anger and go, because we always think we have more time than we have.'

'I've told her that I'm not going, Jane. I said things I shouldn't have. I had no right to tell her that she shouldn't live her life and be where she wants to be. I'm jealous, that's what it is. I should know better. And now I've gone and spoilt everything.'

'I'm sure you haven't, Tim,' said Elizabeth. 'Daughters are very forgiving.'

More than fathers, she wanted to say. She loved hers even though he hadn't really done that much to earn her love, other than perform some nepotism in giving her a top job in his company. She was all too aware that so long as she behaved and conformed, she'd stay in favour and she didn't want to lose him from her life; he was her only family really, because her mother cared less about her than he did. She'd tried to broach the subject with him weeks ago that she wasn't sure she was ready for the engagement and he'd shut her down, more angrily than she'd been prepared for. *Was she mad? Did she realise the advantages for her of marrying Gregory Pennington?* He hadn't asked her if she loved him. She wasn't sure what she'd have said if he had. She'd loved the attentive, gentlemanly Gregory he'd been at the beginning. But, she'd begun to think recently, what if that face of Gregory was a veneer to lure her in? What if his charm was like the fresh, cheap paint they'd sploshed all over the ceilings in Topston Manor that kept flaking off, revealing the mould and rottenness underneath? What did true love even feel like? And why, if this was love, did it not make her smile more? Why did she have those clouds in her eyes, as Roo had seen?

Chapter 21

After lunch, Roo went on a hunt, to gather up the components for her Christingle craft session. She'd managed to find a reel of red ribbon in the stock cupboard where all the decorations had been kept. There were plenty of clementines in the pantry and some long tapered candles that she snapped into smaller pieces; there were cocktail sticks in the bar and a jar of maraschino cherries. She had the sudden urge to open it, stick her finger in and hook one out. She burst it between her teeth and a shot of sticky, rich liquid hit her tastebuds. They reminded her of Christmases past and one of her dad's barmaid girlfriends, who'd sneak her a slug from her bottle of snowball when they were in the pub, top it up with lemonade and then drop a cherry in it for her.

Vincent had found some slippers for John, but they were sizes too big. Alas John's feet were about half the size of his boots. All the prison-issue footwear was on the large side, he'd explained, they just had to wear extra socks to pad them out. John's thin, worn socks, however, wouldn't have helped him fill those big boots. Vincent gave him a pair of his own thick woolly ones to tide him over. The socks John took off were fit only for the bin. One more wash and they'd have disintegrated. Mind you, his feet looked as if they would as well. Those boots must have rubbed him raw. John stuffed them hurriedly into the fresh new socks but Vince had spotted they were a mess.

'What was that song you were singing when you walked into the carriage where I was holed up?' John asked Roo when they were both sitting around the fire drawing warmth from it.

'"Hark! Hark", that one?' she replied. 'It's my favourite carol.'

'You've got a lovely voice. I haven't heard that one before.'

'It's an old folk song. Carols once were meant to be sung in pubs and houses, you know, not churches. Not quite sure I sang it properly though, I was a bit thrown by your leg moving.'

'Ah yes, my leg,' said John, flexing it. 'I was trying to keep still and not alert you but my knee hurts. Old age.'

'You don't look that old, John. I mean, you'll probably look younger when you've had a wash.'

That made John hoot.

'I feel a bit grubby. I could do with a bath. Is there one on here?'

'Not that we've found, but there are great showers.'

Roo didn't want to say that he could indeed do with one. His clothes were whiffy and half his hair was matted. He'd looked much bigger when she first set eyes on him with that heavy coat and boots and she suspected he was much younger than the forty-something she'd guess he was. He was just a little shorter than Frank, five nine, maybe, but string-lean. Jane could have probably overpowered him if he'd lied to them about being a prison guard and was actually a psycho. He wasn't though, she could tell. He had nice eyes, kind, friendly, even if the rest of him looked a bit 'weathered'.

'I expect you'll be bunking up with Tim now. He's already warned everyone he snores, so good luck there.'

'We'll see, Roo,' replied John. 'He might not want to share with a stranger.'

'We're all strangers. We only met yesterday. The train broke down taking us to Eskford and the driver and guard got off to fetch an engineer and haven't been back. If that hadn't happened, we would have all gone on our merry way and not given each other a second thought.'

'Ah, interesting. I presumed you were a party travelling somewhere together for Christmas.'

It was amazing how quickly you did get to know people though, when thrown together, thought Roo then, seeing them all through John's eyes. Maybe he presumed as much because of her goading of Tim, something you might not do unless you knew someone a little better than one did.

She'd felt bad about Tim since, annoyed with herself for pushing him to reveal far more of himself than he probably wanted to. She looked at the clock on the wall and saw she had fifteen minutes before Brian came back on the radio to make his Christingle.

'If you'll excuse me, John, I'll be back.'

Just outside the car, Roo took her coin out of her pocket, closed her eyes and asked the question.

'Should I do this?' She tossed it up, slammed it on the back of her hand to find the YES facing upwards. She was glad about that because she felt it was the right thing.

Roo made her way down the carriages looking for Tim. She popped her head in the galley, but there was only Frank in there, mixing something in a bowl and singing – if you could call it that – 'Jingle Bells'. She reminded him about the sprouts in the hash, but he said he hadn't forgotten. She had an idea Tim would be in 'Maria Gloriosa' reading again and he was. Alone – good. She walked in, he looked up, gave her a slight nod of acknowledgement and returned to his book, presuming probably that she wasn't in there for him. She surprised him though by sitting down near him on the sofa.

'Can I have a word?' she said.

'If you must.'

He laid the book down at the side of him; it was a large one with yellowing pages and a brown cover, a gilt outline of a bell on the front. Then he waited to see what word she wanted with him.

'What you were saying ... earlier ... about your daughter ...'

He shuffled uneasily. 'I don't really want to discuss—'

She spoke over him.

'I'm not asking you to, I would like you to listen to me. To my story. Please.'

'All right.'

'You'll have to bear with me, I'm not very good at précising things,' she began.

'Okay.' His face said he hadn't a clue what she was going to come out with. Roo smiled and began.

'My mum left us when I was really young. So my dad was lumbered with me. We didn't have a lot of money, Dad didn't have a job. He said it was because of his back, but there wasn't much wrong with it when he was doing a bit of work on the side, not that he did much. Occasionally he'd have a girlfriend, dunno how; most of them were quite nice, rough but kind, not that they lasted long. One of them taught me how to use our old twin tub so I took over the washing duties because Dad used to just dip stuff in the sink and it was never properly clean and I'd get made fun of at school: Ruby Pooper, they'd call me, or Poopy Cooper. But I found out early that making people laugh, poking fun at myself a lot, got them off my back. A defence mechanism. That's why I thought I'd quite like to make people laugh and get paid for it, when I grew up.

'I had free school dinners which didn't help the name calling, and there was never anything in the cupboards which is probably why I'm the height I am and why my body doesn't store fat, because it doesn't know what to do with it. Alien substance.' She gave a small laugh, one devoid of any real humour.

'He loved me . . . I think, in his own way, and I loved him. I was pretty upset when he died, because he was my dad.'

She could have told him so much more, and she would if she needed to, but these bare bones would probably suffice.

'I'm aware that this might sound as if I'm talking about Dickensian London and not sixteen years ago in South Yorkshire, but some kids still live like this today, survive under the radar.'

She took a deep breath before continuing. It never got any less raw remembering how it was.

'On the run-up to Christmas, Dad would find a bit of work so he had some money in his pocket. Not for presents, for boozing. I remember racing downstairs to see if Santa had been and finding some of my old toys wrapped up, and a scruffy old book that some kids had already scribbled on, a KitKat. I remember feeling absolutely heartbroken. Of course then I didn't know it was my dad's attempt at presents, I thought it was Santa and he hated me. And then going back to school and everyone talking about what they'd had. I was on tenterhooks for a whole year, hoping Santa would make up for it the next Christmas, but he didn't. There was nothing. Not a thing under the tree. My dad had got wrecked and couldn't remember where he'd put stuff. He gave me a tenner and told me that Santa had sent it for me so I could get myself what I wanted.'

She coughed. She could still recall how devastated she'd been, she could still tune in to the hurt of *knowing* she'd pissed Santa off somehow and hadn't a clue how to put it right.

'Mad, I know, but even when I found out there was no Santa, I carried on hating him as if he was real, I still had all those feelings. Maybe because I didn't want to hate my dad, so I transferred them. My dad, who was always around, I saw him every day. Every. Single. Day.'

Tim shifted, obviously uncomfortable. This was not what he wanted to hear.

'Yep, he was always around, Tim. Well, nearly, because he was in the pub a fair bit. But if he wasn't there, he'd be watching the telly or pissed asleep on the sofa and I'd throw a blanket over him before I went to bed. He didn't have money for presents, for healthy food, but he always had money for beer, cigs, spliffs, betting, his mobile phone and we had a massive telly. Huge thing.

'And though he was never rotten to me, never hit me or anything, he wasn't that great to me either because there was only ever one person on his planet, unless you count the barmaids and the bookies. My point being, that I would have killed for a dad who wanted to provide his best for me, who sacrificed his time with me for the greater good, who put me first, who worked so I'd be comfortable and warm and filled my belly with nice food. That's real love, that is. Don't think that your girl can't see that, whatever your ex-missus said. So if she wants you to go over and be with her for the birth of her baby, that's telling you she loves you right back, Tim.'

Tim wasn't looking at her any more, he had dropped his head but she could see his eyes blinking, processing the words she had fed into his brain.

Roo stood up, ready to leave.

'We're making Christingles with Radio Brian in five minutes on the table in 'Old Tom'. Plenty of oranges to go round.'

She'd said all she needed to and she hoped it might help, because she bet that Tim had never thought of it all from the other side. Her miserable younger life had come in handy twice, then: for today, as well as for developing her comedy muscle. If only she had the guts to flex it.

Chapter 22

Everyone, apart from Tim and Frank, was already sitting at the table in 'Old Tom' when Roo arrived there. Frank was preparing the veg for tomorrow and he didn't want any help, he'd told those who offered. In truth, he just wanted to be by himself. Being in the kitchen helped him think, helped him sort out his head the way dog walks or ironing or lying in the bath did for other people. And he had a lot to think about.

'Baby, it's Cold Outside' was playing from the radio that someone had set up at the head of the table.

'They've ruined this song for me, saying it's about coercive control,' said Grace. 'I always liked it before.'

'Is it really?' Roo raised her perfect brace of eyebrows.

'Well, they can read anything into everything these days, can't they? They'll be giving trigger warnings for Rudolf the Red-Nosed Reindeer next because of the bullying,' said Vince, tutting.

'Thinking about it, I suppose if you were of a mind to, you could actually interpret the words as being a little . . . insistent,' said Jane, tilting her head in cogitation. 'But then again, I remember Clifford winning me round when I said I wouldn't go out with him when he first asked, not taking no for an answer and so I eventually gave in and it was the best decision I ever made.' Jane didn't add that she knew the difference between a man who had his limits on how far to push and one who didn't.

'Where did he take you, Jane?' asked Elizabeth.

'A little Greek restaurant just outside Manchester. It wasn't anything impressive décor-wise, but my – the food. We had a meze, the food kept coming out and coming out as if the chef was under the sorcerer's apprentice spell. Clifford said it had been his plan to seduce me afterwards but neither of us could move.'

She laughed at the memory. 'I was fifty years old at the time. I thought my days of being seduced were well and truly over and it was quite a lovely surprise to find out they were just beginning.'

'Jane, you mucky pup,' Roo exclaimed, while thinking that was lovely, even if she didn't want to think too much about people generations above having sex.

Elizabeth had never liked the song anyway and she hadn't needed to be convinced that the male in it wanted his own way and be damned, especially as she was in the sort of relationship where her opinion was of little value and so there wasn't much point in her giving it. But she had to accept that Gregory was a strong personality, someone who wanted to be the driver on the control bus, that's why he was so successful. Like with the engagement ring situation, for instance. It was even more annoying to wear since she had lost some weight and it needed resizing. She made an executive decision; she pulled it off and stuck it in her jeans front pocket. She felt the relief instantly.

'I've got the Monopoly board all set up for later,' Brian said as the tune ended. 'I always end up having to pay Mrs Cosgrove a lot of rent for her hotels. She's missed her calling, I think, she would have suited being a business typhoon so much more than she would a cleaner at the school in St Hilda.'

Jane's ears pricked up. 'St Hilda? Isn't that where they were picking the engineer up from?'

'Did he just say "typhoon"?' asked Vincent.

'An interesting fact you may not know about Monopoly. It was invented at the beginning of this century by a lady and originally called The Landlord's Game. Elizabeth somebody or other.'

Vincent gave Elizabeth a pointed look across the table.

'Not guilty,' she said. 'And I think Brian's got his centuries a bit mixed up there.'

'I do it all the time,' put in Jane.

'Shh, you lot,' said Roo with playful disapproval. 'This is interesting.'

'Anyway, it was originally half-game, half-educational tool and much copied with people doing their own versions of it, even though Elizabeth had a patent on it. Now skip forward about twenty-five years and along comes someone calls Charles Darrow who ended up playing this Landlord's Game at a friend's house when he and his wife had dinner with them. Anyway, what does the crafty little beggar go and do? He pinches the idea and makes his own version, calling it . . .' Brian left a gap for people to fill in the missing word which they did.

'Monopoly,' came a chorus of voices.

'And the game people, Parker brothers, buy it from him.'

'Little beggar indeed,' Jane tutted.

'That's not the "b" word I would have used,' said Roo.

'Now, Parker finds out that Elizabeth has patented the game so they fob her off by buying the rights for five hundred dollars, only that. And she was never given the credit for inventing it. And Mr Darrow became the first millionaire games inventor in history. And they say crime doesn't pay. Poor Elizabeth. Excuse me.' There followed the sound of a nose being blown. 'I always get quite emotional when I tell that story. I'm just going to have a moment before we make our Christingles so I hope you've got everything ready. I think a little bit of "Adeste Fideles" by Ol' Blue Eyes himself, Frank Sinatra, will sort me out.'

'Blimey, I never knew that,' said Vincent, turning to John. 'Obviously crime does pay, doesn't it? Although not so sure it must feel like that if you get caught. Is it a cushy number in prison, John? Mind you, if you've got blokes trying to escape in this sort of weather, maybe not.'

'Who was it that ran off?' asked Jane. 'A lifer, presumably?'

'No, he'd done eight but he had a few years to serve still,' replied John. 'He wasn't one of the ones they watched, never caused any trouble. He was part of a gang of seven up in Middlesbrough who were accused of robbing a train in which a guard was clobbered and sustained significant injuries. The police knew who'd done it, someone blabbed, and three were arrested, four got clean away.

'Smith, the lad who broke out last night, was only small-time and . . . he realised he was in over his head with that lot and legged it before they'd even stopped the train. And yet, months later, when the guard had recovered, he picked him out in a line-up as being the one who injured him. One hundred per cent, no doubt in his head.'

'Why would he lie?' asked Vincent.

John shrugged. 'Someone got to him, that's why. I guess he was given a ... sweetener for his troubles to mete out the punishment to Smith for running off. Not a very wise thing for Smith to do, especially not with the sort of people he got himself involved with. The idea being they'd force the rap on him and the others would get lesser sentences: robbery but no violence. Except it didn't work out like that because the judge was determined to make the three of them pay equally for the full seven. One of them, Tommy Andrews, couldn't take it, he was just a bairn, and after five years ...' John left a suitable gap for them to fill in. 'The third member, a fella called Jimmy Grimes, got poorly, no chance of a recovery, and he coughed up a confession in September. Didn't want to go to his grave carrying the burden that it was him who hit the fella. I think he felt bad about young Andrews as well. Sang like a canary, backed up everything Smith had said, including about him not even being there. But the government decided to do nothing with this new info. Henry Smith would serve his full time and not a day less. So, I suppose it just got to him, being in prison for something he hadn't done when now he could finally prove that. But nobody was listening.'

'Well, if he is innocent, I hope he got away and contacts the newspapers,' said Elizabeth. 'He should make as much noise as possible so that someone at least investigates. He needs a good legal bod.'

'And what would he pay them with?'

'There are many legals out there who would take on such a case, *pro bono*. For all sorts of reasons: for the PR, the expo-sure but also for sheer altruism,' Jane answered him. 'My late father-in-law for instance. He was wealthy enough to work for the mere thrill of fighting for the underdog sometimes.'

She smiled at the dusty memory of August Wutheridge QC, his stout Charles Laughtonesque figure and his voice that had the ability to extract the truth from a witness by stroking or scaring it out of them.

'The more people who hear about it, the more chance he's got of getting help. There are good people in the world as well as knobheads,' Roo added, although her world was more densely populated by the latter, including the mack daddy of all knobheads, Aaron Ewerin.

'That was the smooth tones of Mr S,' said Brian, after the closing bars of the song. 'Are we all ready to make Christingles?'

The door to the coach opened and in walked the large frame of Tim.

'Room for one more?' he asked.

In the galley Frank had stuffed the turkey with the sausage meat he'd found in the pantry – good quality stuff it was too, rich with the aroma of fresh sage and garlic. He had cut the carrots into batons, peeled the potatoes, some ready for mashing, some for roasting. The parsnips were small, young and didn't need the core taking out, which was lucky because it wasn't his favourite job.

He'd trimmed the bottoms of the sprouts and not wasted his time putting crosses there like his mum always did. Then again, she wasn't the best cook, but like his dad said one day when they were battling through her attempt at a Keith Floyd fish curry, she needed to have a couple of faults or she'd be an angel and be whipped up to heaven away from them. She was a world expert on Yorkshire puddings, though and, because they were in the county, it would be unforgivable not to have them tomorrow, so he'd made a bowl of batter and put it in the fridge. And he'd just finished preparing a dish of cauliflower cheese with sprinkled chopped onions on top, because he knew that it was something his wife particularly liked. Yep, he was aware he was still seeking her approval, still hoping to find that one something that would break the spell cast on her and bring his Grace back to him, but he was losing faith and he knew the point was nearing where he had a decision to make: stay with Grace or continue to see Ella. But Grace had given up on her marriage, and he couldn't save them alone.

He pulled his cotton hankie out of his pocket and wiped his eyes, but it wasn't the onions that were making them water.

Chapter 23

'Here you go, Tim, there's all your gubbins.' Roo set the components of the Christingle down in front of him, once he had taken a seat.

'Thank you, Roo,' he said, his tone much softened, and she knew he wasn't just saying thank you for an orange and some cocktail sticks.

'So firstly, wrap your red ribbon around the middle of the fruit, securing it with glue or pin or even a knot,' instructed Brian. 'I've done a little preparatory work already and skewered my Dolly Mixtures with the cocktail sticks . . .'

Hark! Hark, the angels sing. Today the Christ is born . . .

'That's your carol playing in the background, isn't it, Roo?' said John, sticking cherries and chopped-up dates onto his cocktail sticks.

It was indeed, a folk group singing acapella, four harmonising voices.

Let the bells ring out 'cross every land, all hail this blessed morn.

'I love folk music,' said Elizabeth. She'd once bought two tickets for a Steeleye Span concert for herself and Gregory and he'd sat through it as if he was enduring a long boring court case. She'd thought at the time that had they gone a few months earlier, he would have made a convincing effort to have enjoyed it. Now she knew that a few months later and he wouldn't have gone at all. He didn't listen to music, he listened to pompous literary fiction, dry military history and politics audiobooks. The things they didn't have in common far outnumbered the things they did and having even this short time away from him was like drifting up into space and seeing their world as it was: full of dried-up seas and arid brown where there should have been rich, green foliage.

'Let heaven and earth rejoice and sing, welcome, welcome, little king,' Roo trilled, prompting Jane to tell her – just as John had done earlier – that she had a lovely voice.

'Give over, Jane.'

'You should take the compliment and not bat it back,' Jane admonished her, though she knew that most women didn't know what to do with a compliment. Accepting them was uncomfortable, a contradiction to an entrenched negative self-perception. It had taken Clifford quite a few years to succeed in having her value herself, as he valued her.

Frank walked in. He needed company, his thoughts were racing around in his head like motorcyclists on a wall of death. He forced out his best smile.

'Don't let me interrupt, I'm here in an observational capacity.'

'There's a spare orange if you want one. We can help you catch up,' said Roo.

'Oh, go on then, if I must.'

Roo quickly tied on a section of ribbon and rolled it across the table. 'Cocktail sticks and cherries at your side there.'

Frank looked to his right for direction from Jane.

'Are we ready for sticking our four corners of the world into the orange?' asked Brian. 'I mostly use sweets I don't like so I'm not tempted to eat them. Mind you, there aren't really any sweets I don't like.' He chortled. 'Though I confess I am not that fond of the raspberry in a Fry's Five Centres bar. I always have to give that to Cath.'

'What's that?' said Roo, through a mouthful of maraschino cherries and their juice.

'History, that's what that is,' said Frank. When they were first courting, he used to buy Grace a Fry's Five Centres bar when they went to the pictures. If he'd looked to his side, he would have seen Grace steal a glance at him, remembering the same. He'd refuse her offer to share it, so she had to pretend she was full when she gave him the last section.

'I do think old Brian may be living somewhat in the past, though who can blame him,' said Jane with a wistful sigh. She had a picture in her head of him in his attic, talking into his microphone, not getting out enough to realise the world was moving at a ridiculous pace. She wished it would stand still more sometimes. 'Maybe Brian is in a delightful bubble of memorabilia, a world where Quality Street came in proper tins with shiny wrappers. It was like opening a box of jewels once upon a time.'

'And the smell of Christmas used to rush out at you when you took the lid off,' said Frank with a nostalgic sigh. There was a tin of those for him under the Christmas tree every year, along with a pair of slippers and a *Beano* annual. His mum was still buying him his 'holy trinity', even after he was married.

'Progress, eh?' said Vincent, wondering how he had managed to cock up sticking four sticks into a bleedin' satsuma.

He'd made it look like a wheel that had lost half its spokes. He would never have got a job on *Blue Peter*. He held it up to look at it from all angles.

'What the hell is that?' said Tim. 'You a flat-earther, Vince?' And he guffawed and Roo thought that the Tim who had walked in after their talk seemed lighter, jollier. She'd done that and she allowed herself a moment of smugness for it.

'What's "a flat-earther"? asked John.

'People who believe the earth is flat and not round,' replied Vincent, 'but we all know for sure that's bollocks because the people who went up to the moon saw it was round and took pictures.'

'Allegedly.' Roo held up a finger to stop that theory in its tracks.

John chuckled and shook his head. 'They want to get their trains to run properly in all weathers before they even start thinking about putting men on the moon.'

'Absolutely,' Roo said to that, recognising a fellow cynic in John.

Vincent looked over at Tim's impeccable effort.

'I've got serious Christingle envy, Tim,' he said. Even his red ribbon line was like a perfect equator.

'Why an orange, I wonder, and not an apple or a pomegranate?' Grace said, checking all her sticks were equidistant.

'Juice,' answered Roo.

'Eh?' Vincent pulled a 'you're bonkers' face.

'I think it's because it's full of juice.'

The look on Vincent's face said that he wasn't convinced so Roo explained further.

'Because it's like God's given it to us so we can squeeze

as much sweetness as we need out of it. You can't squeeze an apple, can you – or a pomegranate. The seeds would fly all over the place.'

'Right,' said Vincent, with a conceding tilt of his head. 'That might make sense if I force it to.'

Roo knew he was teasing her and so she told him to shut up.

'Now for the exciting part,' said Brian. 'I always put a little bit of tin foil around the bottom of my candle before I stick it in. I'm not sure if I remembered to tell you to get that, but, if not, I'm sure you've got some in for tomorrow's roast.'

'Yes, don't worry, Bri, you did say,' Roo replied to him. They all proceeded to wrap the bottom of the candle stubs before sticking them in the top of the clementines. Frank had just about caught up, with the help of Jane and her best cherry-spearing skills.

'So now, we light the candles and praise baby Jesus, the light of the world, bringing hope to those in darkness.'

'Hallelujah, brother,' said Vincent, making them all laugh by raising his hands in the air as if he were at a big religious convention in a field.

They lit their candles from a match and Tim turned the main light off. And from the radio came the soft rolling harp notes of 'Balulalow'. Jane knew the song, knew what the Scots lyrics were about: a homage to the Virgin Mary singing her lullaby to her baby as she rocked him in her arms, and in the flickering candlelit dark the piercing voice of the soprano found a place in Jane's heart that had hitherto escaped being broken and broke it. She remembered holding her first son, unable to stop marvelling at his perfect face as he slept, his tiny fingernails, his thick brown lashes. She didn't think that any baby who came next could stir such emotion in her, but it did twice more – each time that won- derment, that riptide of emotion that carried her willingly away. *Never mair from thee depart.* If she had been debating whether it was the right thing to do to talk to Grace when the opportunity presented itself, then she had just found her answer.

Benjamin Britten's ethereal harmony, the pin-sharp voice of the soprano, the soft dark of the train carriage and the eight of them together with their candles lit, caught in a strange crystallising moment; they all felt it, as if they were held in time, in the cup of its hands, fleeting, uniting, pure but none of them said it for fear of appearing daft.

Vincent looked across the table at Elizabeth: she appeared even more beautiful by candlelight; her eyes were shining as if they were made of diamonds. *That Gregory is a lucky fucker*, he thought. He hoped the man realised that. A pic- ture rose in his head of he and Elizabeth close on his big sofa at home in front of the TV, watching an old festive film, his favourite one about the angel who comes down to earth in the form of Cary Grant and falls in love with the bishop's wife, coffee table in front of them with two big glasses of mulled wine on it scenting the air, Snowball snoring contentedly in between them. Pipe dream, of course. Elizabeth Dudley was the caviar-on-blinis type, not Doritos dipped in a sour cream dip. And if anyone rubbed all the rough edges off him, there would be nothing left but a pile of sawdust.

The last bars of 'Balulalow', the final cadence that left its enchantment in the air. Elizabeth lifted up her eyes to find Vincent's, his gaze intense and sparkly as if there was laugh- ter captured in the irises. She smiled, a little embarrassed.

And Roo, seeing that moment of connection, slapped her hands together and said, 'Well, I was going to tart up the tree now because it needs doing before tomorrow, but I might go for a lie down instead. Any volunteers – Elizabeth? Vincent?'

Jane followed Tim and John who were heading off to the cabins in the 'Uglich' carriage.

'Honestly, I don't mind sharing,' Tim was saying. 'I might snore, I'll warn you.'

She listened, dawdling by her door. She heard John reply, 'Bloody hell, it's lovely in here, isn't it?'

'There's a robe and towels, toothpaste, soap, everything . . .'

'Aye, I might have a proper wash now. But I think I'll just kip down on a sofa in that end bit. I'm not a good sleeper either and it'd be nice to have a bit of space and silence around me for once.'

'Up to you, John. Feel free to use here as a base and if you change your mind, well, the bed's not going anywhere.'

'Thank you, Tim. I'll take the quilt with us and the pillow, but I'll be all right.'

'I've got a spare shirt and pants but they might drown you.'

'Don't you worry. Frank and Vincent have given me a couple of their things.'

'Take the robe and the towels if you're going for a shower.'

'Aye, I will. Thanks very much, Tim.'

Jane slipped into her room. She heard John padding past singing the 'Hark! Hark' carol, or at least as much of it as he could remember, filling in the rest of it with la-di-das. He sounded content, but then she supposed he would be, seeing as fate had delivered him to the train rather than leave him out there in the snowy wilderness. The happiest of chance, or something else? And though she didn't believe in that 'something else', she knew that even the greatest of intellectual minds had argued over its existence.

'I could cut you down a twenty-foot Douglas fir, drag it back to your house and set it in a pot,' said Frank, 'but ask me to decorate it, and I'm scuppered.'

'So that's a no, you aren't helping us do the tree.' Elizabeth grinned dipping into the box and pulling out a beautiful little drummer boy, coincidentally the title of the tune that was now drifting out of the radio.

'I'll fill up the log pile, that can be my contribution to the afternoon's duties.'

Elizabeth loved his voice, it was like gravel wrapped in silk. And his down-to-earth Kent accent. Vincent's too; honest and unaffected, *what you see is what you get*.

'I'll help you do up the tree,' said Grace. Her accent was still present but less pronounced. Some people's were more easily ironed out over time, she knew. And some increased in pomposity. Elspeth-Ann's sister, for instance. She had become a caricature of her former self with her ridiculous word distortions.

Vincent carefully draped the tinsel round the branches. Despite living alone, he always went a bit mad on decorating his house at Christmas, a vestige from his childhood, he reckoned. His parents always made it lovely; he and his mum would sit at the dining table and lick and stick paper chains and he went with his dad to pick up the tree and they always bought one that was way too big and stuck three foot out of the boot on the careful drive home. He'd felt the loss of them at this time of year more than at any other and dressing the tree dipped him in a warm pool of memories.

If he could have crossed the membrane that separated this world from the next, he'd have leapt there, even for just long enough to give them both a hug and a kiss.

Vincent, the only one tall enough to reach, was put in charge of placing the baubles on the higher branches, while Elizabeth took the right side, Grace the left.

Elizabeth picked another ornament from the box. Every one was wrapped in tissue to protect them. Some were made of glass, some carved from wood and hand-painted. She marvelled at the glittery snowflake in her hand that would hang on the tree from a fine, golden ribbon.

'They're beautiful, aren't they?'

She wanted to find a house that had a ceiling open to the upper floor so she could have the most enormous Christmas tree in the hallway. She'd get one with a root ball so she could plant it in the garden afterwards and over the years a small forest of them would build up. And when they had a Christmas party everyone would have to bring a bauble, rather than a bottle, to make a memory. She and Gregory had been to view a few houses and couldn't agree because she wanted an old place with beams in the suburbs and he wanted a penthouse in the city. She was sticking her heels in but no doubt he'd get his way in the end though, because he seldom didn't.

Grace reached into the box and unpeeled the tissue to find a wooden Santa carved in a saluting pose. What were the chances? she thought, casting it a look that told the taunting universe exactly what she thought of it, then she hung it at the back of the tree, out of sight.

'After this I'll help you in the kitchen,' said Vincent to Frank.

'Everything's done, mate. But tomorrow will be a different story, it'll be all hands on deck.'

'Yes, we'll have to get organised and allot duties,' Elizabeth added, unable to keep the thrill out of her voice. It would be fun,' everyone pitching in, having Christmas dinner on board this lovely train. She felt she knew and liked these people more than those she had planned to spend the day with.

'Lovely in here, isn't it?' said Vincent, looking around but talking as much about the feeling of the place as the décor. It made him think that when he got home he'd give his sitting room that overdue lick of paint. Maybe he'd use the same colours, so they'd remind him of this unexpected Christmas in years to come. Maybe even steal a couple of other design ideas. He wasn't so sure about the marble fireplace though, he preferred his large inglenook, but it was a stunning piece nevertheless.

'Some craftsmanship gone into that, isn't there?' he said, indicating the carving. 'Two heads are better than one, eh?' And Vincent laughed at his own joke.

'I reckon that's Janus,' said Elizabeth.

'Hugh Janus?'

'Vincent, behave,' Elizabeth tutted at him with an accompanying smile. 'Roman god of gates and doorways.'

'I know. We learnt about him in school,' said Vincent. It was a long time ago but good teachers had a way of making you remember things. 'One head facing towards the old year, one towards the new one. That's why he's associated with portals, because it's all about transition, time, saying goodbye to the old year and hello to the next one.'

'New beginnings, he was all about the new beginnings was old Janus ...' said Frank. His voice trailed off because he could feel Grace's eyes on him and he knew that she was reading meaning into his words that he hadn't put there.

The look on her face told him he was right. Without pre-
amble, she turned from them and strode towards the door,
smashing the jolly air in the room by doing so, and Frank's
eyelids dropped as if they wanted to shut out the world.

Chapter 24

Jane was just emerging from her cabin when John came back down the corridor, still singing his cobbled together version of, 'Hark! Hark.' The timing wasn't a coincidence.

'Just the person,' she said and he smiled at her. 'How was the shower?'

'It was fantastic,' John replied, towelling his head. 'That tiny bathroom is grander than any other room I've ever been in in my whole life. I feel like a new man.'

'Then would you like to join me in the bar for a little post-wash brandy?'

John appeared puzzled. 'Is that a thing?' he asked, as if it really could be a custom in the world of the intelligentsia brigade.

'I think in the situation in which we all find ourselves, we are entitled to believe it is indeed *a thing*,' Jane answered him with a trill of laughter.

'I'd rather have a whisky if I had a choice.'

'Of course you have a choice. Everyone else is busy and I don't like drinking alone.' She put on her best manipulative sad face.

'I'll keep you company then.'

'No need to change yourself, just come as you are in your robe, Mr Smith,' said Jane, leading the way to Lutine.

Vincent was looking at Elizabeth and vice versa as if they were telepathically trying to work out what had just happened.

'I'm sorry,' said Frank, resignedly. 'It was nothing you said.' It wasn't the first time Grace had taken a perfectly innocent comment to be a bullet with her name on it. He didn't 'owe' them an explanation but he gave it to them anyway, because it was frothing inside him and he needed to let it out.

'Five years ago our son died. Grace has never gotten over it.'

Vincent searched inside him for some suitable words but were there any?

'I'm not telling you that to make you feel uncomfortable at our expense, but just to give you a bit of context,' Frank continued. 'He was a soldier. She was terrified he'd be killed in action one day; I think she was waiting for it to happen from the moment he joined up.'

'I'm sorry for your loss, Frank,' said Elizabeth. 'I'm not sure how you'd truly get over that.'

'Well, you don't. You learn to live with it because you have to,' said Frank.

'I'm sorry as well, Frank.' Vincent didn't even want to think about getting your head around that. He remembered his mum saying to him when she was at the end, *It's how it should be, Vinny, because I couldn't have lived if you'd gone first.*

'She's become a different woman. If you knew the Grace before you wouldn't recognise her today. She was always laughing, fun to be with, like a ray of sunshine. I feel like I don't know her any more.' His voice wobbled and brought him up sharp. He sounded like a man on the edge.

'Oh, Frank, how very sad for you both,' Elizabeth said, for the want of saying something, even though she knew that anything would sound lame, trite, inadequate.

'I better go and find her,' said Frank, getting up quickly, aware he was giving too much of himself away. He would do again what he had so many times before, knowing it would change nothing because his wife had built prison walls around herself and she wouldn't let him in. And also she refused to come out.

'That's quite a measure, John,' said Jane, lifting her eyebrows in surprise at the tumbler he had just brought over to her. 'I'll be on my back if I drink all this.'

He had poured himself the equivalent measure in whisky as for her calvados and had no such qualms. He sat next to her on the sofa and looked out of the window. The snow had stopped, the fog had cleared a little but any visibility had been swallowed up by the early winter dark now. And right on cue she heard it again, cutting through the distance, that bell ring-ringing, in the distance.

John pressed his back into the sofa and closed his eyes.

'It's like heaven, this,' he said after savouring it for a few long moments.

'Do you believe in heaven?' Jane asked him.

His eyes jerked open and he turned to her.

'Don't you?'

'No, I'm afraid I don't. I think this is all we have and so we should make the very best of it.' Jane took a sip of the calvados. It was as if she could taste her memories.

'You believe in God then, Jane?'

Her turn to throw the question back at him. 'Do you?'

'Yes.' There was not an iota of doubt in his voice. 'You know when I was a boy you just say it, don't you, *I believe in God* without thinking about it. You go to Sunday school and learn all about the Bible. And then you grow up, and you start to think, "If there's a god, how come he let this bad thing happen?" And somehow, along the way, you stop saying that you believe in God. But if you're lucky, you meet someone who tells you that the bad stuff isn't God's fault, he gave us a world to make the best of and the worst of . . . and we have. We can't blame him for it all when things go wrong. But I like to thank him when they go right.'

He took a long sip at his whisky, pulled his thick robe tighter around himself and made a sound of real contentment.

'Who was it who enlightened you?'

'A priest in the prison. We've had a couple of them over the years, but this one . . . there was something special about him, Father Joseph, a goodness that came out of him. He didn't try and ram religion down anyone's throats, didn't breathe fire and damnation, but he could hold you in the palm of his hand just with his presence. He is the man I want to be.'

'A priest?' Her tone said she didn't believe him.

'You see a lot of life in prison, Jane. You see how the smallest of actions can change people for the better and the worse. Father Joseph was like a balm on everyone when he was there, and he was only there for a couple of months, but his legacy was long-lasting. He made a real difference.'

Jane wet her lips in preparation.

'I called you Mr Smith earlier on and you never noticed.'

John jerked a little. 'Did you? No, I didn't.'

'It was just a name plucked from the air, wasn't it? John Brown, easy enough to remember. May I call you Henry now so we can be done with the pretence?'

Frank presumed Grace had gone to her cabin but when he knocked on it, there was no answer and so he opened it but she wasn't there, ignoring him, which would have been entirely plausible. He pushed on, through 'Sigismund' and 'Mingun' where the cabins were all locked so she could only be in 'Yongle', and she was. Standing in the far corner, facing it, like a child who had been admonished by a teacher.

'Grace,' he said softly, going through the too-familiar motions of trying to soothe her, even though he knew he wouldn't manage it. His hand came out to her and when it made contact she sprang away as if his touch revolted her.

'Don't.'

He didn't know what to say because everything had been said and nothing had made a difference. Nearly everything, because he had always dressed up the truth in warm clothing and the only thing left was to strip it back, expose it even though he knew what the consequences could be.

'Billy—' He got only as far as the name before she rounded on him.

'Don't say his name.'

'He was my son too. *Billy O'Carroll* and no one is to blame for what happened to *our* son.'

Grace stabbed her finger at him, her face a mask of fury.

'You and your cowboys and soldier games, shooting at each other, making him guns out of wood. YOU feeding him all that macho crap . . .'

It was an old argument and his answer to it had always

been the same: that the childhood games they had played which had brought them so much pleasure, dressing up as sheriffs and outlaws and soldiers had nothing to do with their twenty-five-year-old son dying.

'He drove himself, Grace, he wanted to be the top. Whatever he did, he would have pushed himself to the limit, beat his own bests, made—'

'He wanted you to be proud of him, that's why he pushed himself beyond what his body was capable of,' she spat.

'I was already proud of him and he knew I was, he had nothing to prove to me.' Frank's voice rose beyond what it had ever done when talking to his wife. 'It was no one's fault, Grace. Not the army's, not mine, not yours, not—'

She laughed, a hard, brittle sound. 'Why would you even say it wasn't my fault? I never wanted him to go into the army, I begged him not to. YOU encouraged him.'

Frank's voice was at its highest pitch. 'Because that's what he wanted to do. He'd never wanted to do anything else in his life but join up. Do you think I didn't want him to be safe? Do you think I didn't worry?'

'Not as much as you should have done.'

'HE WAS MY SON.'

'HE WAS *MY* SON MORE THAN HE WAS EVER YOURS. I carried him'—Grace's hands folded over her stomach—'in *here*.'

Frank thumped at his heart with his fist.

'And I carried him in here and I always will. My boy, my little boy, and I feel his loss every single day. My heart keeps breaking and trying to mend but you don't see that because I hide it, I'm trying to be strong for both of us and I'm tired of it, Grace; I'm tired of this same scene between us. We brought him up to live his dreams – *his* – not yours, not mine and he did that. Don't you think I would have been happier if he'd been sitting at a desk? But we gave him a life to do with as he wanted and he did and he was happy.'

Grace's face contorted. 'How can he be happy being *dead*?'

'He lived, he loved, he had a beautiful woman, a beautiful child on the way—'

'Don't you dare mention *them* to me, I don't want—'

But Frank did, because it was time.

'She's gorgeous, Grace. Ella wants you to see her. Billie May O'Carroll. Our son's little girl. Our granddaughter.'

Grace slapped her hands over her ears. 'No no no NO.'

'She is his, she is ours. Come with me next time.'

Next time.

The words stood out in the air as if someone had drawn a highlighter pen over them. And Grace jumped straight on it.

'Next time? What do you mean next time?' She knew, of course; there was no misinterpreting them. 'You've *seen* her? In person?'

How could he deny it now? He didn't want to carry the burden of secrecy any more.

'Yes, I've seen her and I will carry on seeing her.'

Grace visibly gasped. Something drifted across the front of her mind.

'Where is she?'

The moment he had dreaded. 'Cromer. She's in Cromer.'

The penny dropped. A huge, lead-weighted penny.

Grace's voice now, the volume ripped away but no less rabid for it.

'That's why you wanted the pub as much as you did. Because it's about five fucking miles away from them.'

'Yes,' said Frank. There, it was out.

Grace's eyes widened as thoughts zapped around her head, fizzing and sparking fire like live wires. 'You manipulative bastard,' the insult cold and quiet.

It was half the truth but not the whole of it. He hadn't liked the other pubs they'd been to see, but as soon as he had walked into the Salty Cockle, with the cute-as-buttons Salty Mussel cottage at the side of it, he knew it was the right place, he felt it. And it was, not the least because the locals had accepted them, and they were a bunch of insular funny buggers but they had totally folded the O'Carrolls into their community. And living there, he could easily sneak away and see Ella, the woman his son loved, and her child – Billy's child. And it had been like having a version of him back because his son had made her and would always be part of her and Frank would not give them up. He didn't want to hide that he was seeing them any more; he didn't want to *sneak* off to visit as if they were a dirty secret – it was too big, too important, too precious a relationship.

'She has his blue eyes, Grace.'

'That makes it worse, don't you understand? I don't want to see them in her, I want to see them in *HIM*.'

'He's gone, love.'

'Don't you think I fucking know that?'

The look on Grace's face was one he hadn't seen before and he thought he had seen every combination her features were capable of creating. She was like a wild, wounded creature, stripped of her skin, unable to breathe without pain.

'Please. See her.'

'No, I won't ... It would ... kill me to be reminded of what I had lost, seeing him in her face, but it not being him and he is all I want to see. Don't you get that?'

'I thought it would too but it didn't, it was the opposi—'

'No no NO.' She sliced her hands, cut off his words, took a breath. 'You should respect my feelings.'

Frank took a breath. 'And you should respect mine. I'm not stopping seeing them, Grace.'

'Then you have a choice to make, Frank. Them or me.'

And he answered grimly, his anger on a rein but it was straining more than it ever had before with her. 'Don't make me choose, Grace,' the inference clear. Then he turned and walked away from her.

Chapter 25

John froze for a long moment. Then he opened his mouth to speak then shut it and sighed before it opened again, full of different words from those he had been about to say.

'How did you know?'

Jane gave a small laugh.

'I don't think I needed to have been my husband's best pupil to work it out. I didn't buy the large coat and big boots story for a minute, not to mention the state of your socks and feet. Then there's the attack on the food in our stores. And you hiding yourself away – would a prison officer really have anything to fear from us? No idea how you got that injury to your head, but it certainly wasn't from a fall in the snow. And the surprising detail in your story about Henry Smith, it's almost as if you knew him intimately.' She raised her eyebrows at him. 'Plus you wouldn't share a room with Tim, perhaps because the first chance you get to spend a night of true freedom, you don't want to be cooped up in a small cabin with another *cell-mate*. And I keep hearing a bell, I presume it's from the prison which would lead me to believe the absconder is still out there. Shall I go on?'

Maybe some of her deductions were weaker than others, conjectures, but together they made a pretty strong argument.

John – Henry – didn't deny it. He fell silent for a long half-minute, lots of thoughts climbing over each other in his head. Eventually, with a croak in his voice, he asked:

'Will you tell the others?'

'I think I should. When there is the possible threat to their lives.'

He moved his head from side to side, with slow deliberation.

'Jane, there is absolutely no threat to you and your friends from me. Everything I told you about Henry Smith is true. I was a bit of a crook, but poverty can make you like that. And I mean proper poverty. When my da' upped and left, we had nothing. Petty thieving to put stuff on the table for me mam was the only reason I did any of it. The train . . . it was the first time I'd been involved in a big job and even with the promise of what I could have brought home, I had a bad feeling about it. I was at war with myself, and when push came to shove I . . . I couldn't go through with it, even knowing I'd be in for some trouble for letting people down that you really shouldn't let down.

'But, and this is going to sound really strange, I know . . . what I've come to realise over the years is that everything that happened to me, happened for a reason. I don't know what that reason is yet, but I'm *sure* I am being guided. I thought Father Joseph would laugh me out of town when I told him that, but he never. He said if I felt it that strong, I was probably right. Then Jimmy Grimes confessed and proved me innocent and I could taste my freedom, except they buried the truth. I *had* to clear my name now I could, it was important for me, and for me mam. And I knew then that the only way was to get out and shout. But it was a massive risk because if I did get out, there were no guarantees anyone would listen to me and chances were I'd end up far worse off than I was before. If they just caught me and threw me back, I'd lose all my privileges I'd built up over many years. And they'd add time on for me running off.

'But then the snow happened, from nowhere. The prison officer count was down with illness as well, so they locked everyone up, apart from a couple of us trusties, cooking and cleaning. And I find a door left open and ... that never happens. And there's a coat hanging up, boots there as if they're waiting for me. And I knew what I had to do, I had to take me chance. All that lot happening together couldn't have been coincidence.'

Coincidence. Jane could almost hear Clifford musing on the word at the side of her.

'I have to keep pinching myself that I made it here because it feels a bit like a dream, although this whisky certainly tastes very real, I have to say. I must have given me head a proper clunk because I still feel dizzy if I move it too much.'

'How did you bump it?' Jane asked him.

'I once, must have been two years ago, went down the cellar with a guard, can't even remember why, but what I never forgot is that there were rocks piled up against an old sluice gate. I knew it was a weak spot. I knew that if I could somehow get to scrambling up 'em and dislodging the grid, I'd be on the outside. I checked after and saw that the perimeter wall's at its lowest point there. Couldn't have been more perfect. I kept my weight down and my fitness up.

'Of all the doors that could have been left open, it was the one that allowed me access down there. But also, I could have gone *up* from there, hidden myself in the maze of passages in the roof which I imagine is what they thought I'd do and probably bought me some time. It couldn't have gone smoother: up the rocks, kicked out the grid, over the wall, as if it was meant to be. Apart from the fact it was more of a drop on the other side than I anticipated and I fell hard, scraped all my head on the way down. I think adrenaline must have fuelled me until I found the train because as soon as I was on it, I dropped as if I'd died.'

Jane believed him. She'd felt he was lying when he had been; she didn't feel that now.

'If this is true, then there are people out there who can help you.'

'Do you think the others'll throw us out there when you tell them?' There was a note of genuine worry in John/Henry's voice.

'I doubt it very much. I shall stand in your corner,' Jane replied.

'Thank you, Jane. No better to have behind me.'

Then they relaxed further back into the sofa and drank in companionable silence.

'I did wonder what was going on with Grace and that answers it,' said Vincent. 'She didn't look a very happy woman from the off.' He didn't say it, but he'd thought that Grace's face was never going to be troubled by laughter lines.

'Frank's lovely.' Then Elizabeth realised what she might be intimating by that. 'Not that I'm saying Grace isn't, but Frank is a little easier to get to know.'

'He's a geezer, inne?'

Elizabeth nodded, not quite sure what he meant but knowing it was a compliment.

'Pass me another snake, will you please?'

This riddle she could work out. She lifted up some tinsel. It was – unsurprisingly – exquisite quality, like everything on this train.

'I'm really sorry you missed your party, Elizabeth.'

'It would have been very dangerous to continue driving.'

'I'll get you there though, better late than never.'

'Look at this sugar-plum fairy, isn't it beautiful?' Elizabeth changed the subject as she lifted the decoration up for him to see. She didn't want to think about Topston. Gregory's annoyance with her would be gaining hourly interest, and her father would be fuelling the fire. No one was on her side, that was the problem. She dreaded the 'welcoming' committee when she did finally get to them. She knew their priority would be to vent their frustration at her, rather than throwing their arms around her with relief that she was safe.

'You okay?' Vincent asked, seeing her expression, wondering what was causing her brow to scrunch and that thoughtful look in her soft grey eyes.

'I was just thinking about having to leave here and go back to normal life.'

'Me too.'

Elizabeth made a silent wish that the snow wouldn't thaw overnight. It was quite lovely not being able to do anything about the situation they were in. It felt so Christmassy in their little bubble and it was as much to do with Radio Brian, the log-fire, the gentle camaraderie and Roo's artistry with the decorations as it was with the expanse of snow outside.

From the radio Bing was singing that he would be home for Christmas.

'I won't, though. I'll be listening to you, Brian,' said Vincent. He had the sudden urge to take Elizabeth's hand and twirl her around the room. His mum had taught him to dance when he was a boy. 'It'll come in handy one day, you mark my words,' she'd said, overriding his sulky reluctance. He couldn't, of course, it would have been an imposition, but there was that kind of feeling around that they were in an old Hollywood film where people burst into song and dance as part of their normal routine. There was a sparkle in the air, as if someone had swirled it with mince-pie-scented glitter.

'Brian sounds as if he really enjoys what he does, doesn't he?'

'Gotta be happy in your job though, it's important.'

'Are you, Vincent?'

'Yeah, I love it. I love my people, got a good crew. What about you? What do you actually do, Elizabeth?'

'I work for my father, he owns an export company. We export anything anywhere and I'm the pen-pushing director of admin.' She did her best to inject some enthusiasm into her words but failed, and from what Vincent said next, it was quite obvious that her effort hadn't landed.

'That sounds . . . er . . . interesting.'

It made her laugh. 'Vincent, it couldn't be less interesting.'

'Doesn't float your boats, I'm guessing.'

'My boats are well and truly welded to the mud.'

'So why are you there then? What would you do instead, if you had the choice to do any job in the world?'

Why am I there then? It would sound pathetic to say that it was expected of her to be there. That she'd be the world's biggest ingrate if she hadn't taken the position and been appreciative of it. Vincent hadn't had her life, hadn't been brought up and conditioned to only gain approval for doing what she was supposed to, but to say as much would have made her sound like the gutless jelly she was and she didn't want him to think that of her.

She was uninspired, unchallenged. Any effort she made to change things was thwarted and she could have made improvements because she had a good eye for business. She couldn't make her mark there, she just had to toe the line and leave the decisions and the deal-breaking to the men. Her father was still living in a bygone age. If she hadn't been his daughter, she'd have probably been making everyone tea and plating up biscuits. She was a director in name only and felt the coldness behind her back, the resentment of her being the 'nepo baby' who had a not-too-demanding job but was paid a lot more than those who did more work. *Golden handcuffs.*

'Duty, family loyalty, I suppose, Vincent. As for what I'd like to do . . . I want my own venture, something to sink my teeth into. I want to open a second-hand bookshop. But not just any old shop, a reading centre which would bring people in to learn, to talk, a little café in the corner, a breakfast club for children, a real community support project. I have ideas that would make it profitable enough to sustain itself with staff, but it would be about so much more than the cold, hard cash. And if it works, and I'm sure it would, then I'd roll them out to other areas that needed them.' Elizabeth's voice was full of rising passion. 'Stories, books are so valuable, the ability to read has a real knock-on effect on society, on industry, on health, on the whole of . . .'

She trailed off, because she didn't want him thinking

she was a 'goody two-shoes'. She'd hoped to get Gregory onside to back some local charities. She had managed it too, because it was good PR, big business looking after the little guys, except he'd selected corporate-friendly little guys and not the most needy. He picked glam causes, run by schmoozing chief execs who held glitzy events and spent too much of any monies raised on their swanky office furniture and first-class transport.

'You should do it, Elizabeth.' Vincent could see Elizabeth reigning in a book-filled kingdom.

'One day,' she replied, doubting that day would ever come. She was trapped in her obligations, as much as Grace was evidently trapped in her grief.

Chapter 26

The Christmas Eve hash was going down a treat.

'Perfect sprouts, Frank,' Roo threw across the table.

'I've had worse compliments.' Frank winked at her and made her laugh.

'What you been doing while we was busy decorating the tree?' Vincent asked her. 'Did you have a lie down like you said?'

'No. I was writing some poetry,' said Roo. *And crying*, she didn't add. The poem was as raw and exposed as the Santa one she'd started, although she'd scrapped that one now that she and Tim were on a cordial footing.

> *Once you were my Christmas parcel*
> *Now you're just my Christmas arsehole*
> *And despite the knobhead words I've spoken*
> *I miss you, A, my heart is broken*

It hadn't been cathartic attempting to put her feelings down on paper, it just brought it all back, highlighted how much she hurt, how lonely she felt and she'd stopped writing and wept hard into her pillow instead. Then she'd washed her face and put some make-up on because she didn't want to have swollen eyes and have everyone ask her what was up. She'd gone to the lounge for some company but there was no one in there except the radio playing a quirky song called 'All I Want For Christmas Is My Two Front Teeth' and it had both cheered her up and given her an idea.

'Are you going to give us a burst?' asked Frank.

'Well ... maybe. Actually, I've been thinking. What about tomorrow ... we have a talent competition,' said Roo.

The idea was met with less reaction than she hoped for.

'There's a problem there, gel, I ain't got any talents,' Vincent replied.

'Yes, you have,' Roo insisted. 'Everyone has. It's not an audition for BGT, it would just be us passing a bit of time. It'll be fun, even if you're crap. As I'm sure you will be.'

'Just for that, I'm going to show you.' Vincent wagged his finger at her and matched her grin.

She had a surprise ally in Tim, who backed her up.

'I can contribute.' He was going to tell them all what he'd been reading about but it would make a novelty act. Especially if he dressed up as Santa for the occasion as well. Shame to waste his costume.

'Grace can fold towels into the shape of any animal you can think of,' said Frank. He hadn't spoken to his wife since earlier, but for appearances' sake, he would keep up the façade of them being a couple, even if he wasn't sure if they would be by the time they disembarked.

'That's a bit of an exaggeration. I can do a swan and—'

'Don't tell us,' said Roo, shushing her. 'Save it for tomorrow.'

'I suppose I could tell some jokes,' Vincent thought aloud. 'But don't be expecting to laugh.'

'I wasn't,' replied Roo cheekily, then she turned to her side. 'Elizabeth?'

'I have a party piece.' *Dare I though?* she thought to herself, feeling a quiver of excitement in her stomach.

'Well, I have something I can share with you all as my act. It might change your life,' said Jane, smiling enigmatically, which raised a chorus of *Ooohs*.

'I'll do a bit of magic,' said Frank. 'If I can remember. Might have to brush up before tomorrow.'

He'd learned the tricks his dad used to do on him and in turn he'd fascinated Billy and his friends. And then he'd taught Billy so that one day he could do them for his kids, but he'd died before his daughter had drawn her first breath. So he would be the one to show them to his granddaughter. If he had a choice to make, he'd made it that afternoon.

'That leaves you then, John,' said Vincent, clearing his mouth of a gravy-soaked piece of potato. 'You going to give us a talk about some of the prisoners you have to deal with inside?'

From the side, their newest addition felt Jane's eyes on him.

'Well . . .' he began, then swallowed. 'There's something I have to tell you about that.'

'. . . and that's the truth and the whole truth.'

Henry Smith looked up to find every eye in the room fixed upon him. There was a wake of silence after his last word until Tim broke it by saying, 'I did suspect something was amiss if I'm honest. The boots, the coat. I mean, I know the country's fuc— . . . in a bad way, but I didn't think things were quite so bad that prison officers had to walk around in boots five sizes too big.'

He also didn't say that for a man at only thirty, Henry Smith looked at least ten years older. He had the face of someone who had lived a much harder life than a prison guard.

'I'm sorry I didn't tell you the truth before,' said Henry, as they had to think of him now. 'I'm not a good liar, I was surprised I got away with it for as long as I did. I didn't want to scare anyone. I mean — escaped convict ... that's not threatening at all, is it? And I can't prove any of what I'm telling you but I am a Christian and I'll swear on the Bible if you want me to. But I would say that, wouldn't I?'

Henry's brow creased. He really wasn't doing a great job of convincing them.

'I won't mind if you all lock your cabins tonight.'

'Blimey,' said Vincent eventually. 'I didn't twig. I must be thick.'

'Or trusting,' said Elizabeth. 'There are worse qualities to have than seeing the best in people.'

'I can understand why you didn't want to share a cabin now,' said Tim. 'I'm guessing you would feel like you were sharing a cell, albeit a rather grand one.'

'Aye, that's it, Tim. Trust me, it wasn't the prospect of your snoring and I did hear it the first night when I was looking around. My cell-mate would put you to shame in that respect so I've learned to switch off. But I realise I'm telling you quite the tale and if you want to keep me shut in one of the end rooms away from you all, I won't feel offended.'

Frank prided himself on being a good judge of character. He wasn't taken in much, he'd been around too many years, seen it all and more. And he didn't write people off for their past mistakes. He'd witnessed what changes the power of kindness was capable of.

'You jokin'? Locking you up with the food?' he exclaimed. 'You'd do it all in one night. You went through the fridge like a herd of bleedin' locusts. I think the safest place for you is in the middle of us, son.'

Henry smiled and dropped his head, suddenly upset, humbled by their benevolence. He was wearing a shirt of Frank's and a pair of Vincent's underpants and tracksuit bottoms, plus his socks and Roo had given him a pair of hers as well as a spare. When Jane had first challenged him, having worked out his identity, she had been ready to tell the others who he was. But the more they sat and conversed, the more she thought it would be better coming from him; it was his truth to share, after all.

'You have no idea how much relief I feel for you knowing.' Henry pressed his chest as if to indicate the lightness there, a burden removed.

'I suggest you enjoy this time while you have it,' Tim said. 'We will fortify you with good food and company and anything we can help you with for what lies ahead.'

'Thank you,' said Henry, drowning the rise of his emotion with a large gulp of red wine. It couldn't have tasted better if Jesus himself had turned it from water.

Every plate was cleared, which Frank took as a great compliment. Even Grace's – and hash wasn't her favourite and he found himself trying to read some meaning into that. Once upon a time his wife's feelings sat on her sleeves, but they had been driven deep underground this past five years. He had to work out what was going on in her head through a series of cryptic clues and he was exhausted by it, at the end of it all now. For the first time he let in the thought that he would have to consider the logistics of them splitting up. But when they sold the pub, he knew he would be staying in Norfolk near to his granddaughter.

As the others gathered up the plates and brought them through to the galley, Frank arranged a box full of mince pies onto a plate and stirred some brandy into a jug of cream. They were fresh, from a farm shop according to the label, so they needed eating sooner rather than later to taste at their best.

'Ooh, Frank, mince pies.' Roo drooled.

'You might be disappointed, love, there's no sprouts in them.'

'You bake them yourself, Frank, in between peeling all the spuds?' asked Vincent, grinning.

'Yep,' Frank joked. 'I tell you, kneading that pastry doesn't half get all the dirt out from underneath your fingernails.'

Roo pulled a face. 'Gross, Frank. I'm only having three now after you've told me that.'

She admonished herself for trying too hard. She was forcing herself to be jolly while in the background her thoughts were running on one track and one track only and she was fighting them from taking over her head.

They'll be husband and wife by now, drinking a glass of champagne, toasting their first day as a married couple, Mr and Mrs Aaron Ewerin.

They'd have done it somehow. The church was within a walkable distance, the vicar lived next door to it. They'd have scraped two witnesses together from somewhere. *Amber wants to be married before the baby's showing too much.* And what Amber wanted, Amber fucking got.

Roo reached for a mince pie and then a glug of wine

and dried to drown the visions of her one-time best mate and her soft swelling bump, Aaron's hand lovingly laid on it. She knew it wouldn't work though because she'd drunk harder and longer than this over the past weeks only to find those masochistic head pictures had a habit of floating like a polystyrene Michael Phelps.

'So how many of you will have breakfast tomorrow then? Or will you save your appetite for the big meal?' Brian's voice came out of the radio while they were all quiet and eating the very buttery mince pies. 'How many of you are having turkey tomorrow? I must confess that I find it a bit dry and so we're having a joint of beef from our local butcher. I highly recommend Hollybury Farm produce if you're ever in the area. I think I enjoy the cold-cut sandwiches the next day even better than the big meal, but please don't tell Mrs Cosgrove that because she'd have my guts for garters.'

'Well, if we are still here tomorrow, we'll be having turkey, Brian, and I rather think we will be,' Frank answered him, wiping pastry crumbs from his mouth. 'I must remember to set my alarm so I can get up and put the oven on.'

'Frank, one of us will take on that duty, you've done more than your fair share,' said Jane.

'Jane, never interfere with a chef and his plans.' Frank shook the remainder of his mince pie at her and Jane held her hands up in surrender.

'I think we'll slow things right down now, from The Toomey Sisters. But did you know, they aren't sisters at all, unlike the Beverley sisters, two of whom were twins. Anyway, this is "Alone For Christmas".'

A string introduction ensued and then a mellow voice.

'Last year you and I were together
Making plans for the rest of our life

This year you're not here and I'm crying
And someone else is your wife . . .'

The room seemed to recede for Roo; Frank and Vincent sank into the distance as they were laughing about something, along with Jane chatting to Grace as they took a second mince pie from the plate, Tim, Elizabeth and Henry far away, deep in conversation. The radio swelled into the foreground, sucking all the air out of it.

'I'm lonely, so lonely this Christmas . . .'

Aaron and Amber, their champagne flutes chinking together.

'I don't know where my love's going to go . . .'

'What do you think Roo's doing now, Aaron darling?'

'It will wait in my heart for you always . . .'

'Roo who?' Ha ha haaaa.

The song cut off to be replaced by Brian's voice.

'I've just had an urgent message from my wife saying that I have not to play this song, it's way too miserable . . .'

But the damage had been done. Roo's banks burst; she dropped her head onto her arms on the table and she sobbed.

'Darling, what's the matter?' said Elizabeth turning to her, putting her arm around her.

Roo was mortified. As soon as she'd given way to her emotions, she bucked against them. She looked up to find all eyes were on her. No wonder, as she'd just made a total fanny of herself.

'I'm so sorry,' she said, trying to recover, even though her tear ducts were clearly rebelling against her efforts. Whoever was working them had clearly been promised double Christmas rates. As fast as she was wiping her tears away, they were replaced by more. She couldn't stand the intensity of being such a centre of attention, not in this way anyway. If she were on a stage performing then it would be different, but now she felt raw and stripped bare. She attempted to stand. 'I'll get out of your way,' she said.

'You absolutely will not,' said Elizabeth, pushing her back down.

Jane passed a tissue down the table and Roo blew her nose on it before she drowned them all in snot. God, she must look a total sight. She couldn't look at them. What must they be thinking?

'Dear me, I hope I haven't moved anyone to tears with that song. I didn't realise it was so dour until Mrs Cosgrove pointed it out,' Brian was now saying, full of contrition. 'I don't think we'll be playing that one again any time soon. Let's go for Rudolf and his red nose, that always cheers me up and I hope it cheers you up too.'

That didn't help because Roo knew when she cried her face went red, especially her conk. Brian really did know how to wound.

'What was he playing that he had to apologise for it so profusely?' asked Jane, who hadn't really been listening, but whatever it was had had a brutal effect on young Roo.

'Something about being lonely at Christmas,' Henry said. 'Sounded a bit of a dirge.'

'I'll go and make some coffees or something,' said Roo.

'No, you'll sit there,' Elizabeth insisted.

'You ain't going anywhere,' Vince echoed the sentiment if not the same words. 'Start talking, gel.'

Oh, what the hell. If she could have pulled out her coin and asked it if she should tell them what was up, she knew it would come up YES.

She sniffed before beginning. 'My fiancé got married today to my best mate. Or at least if they didn't, they were supposed to, but she's the type that everything goes right for so they would have. I didn't know anything about it until a few weeks ago. They wanted to act quickly because she fell pregnant.'

A few small sounds of sympathy rippled around the table, then Tim said, 'Well, they sound a pair of shits.'

And Roo laughed, even though she didn't think she had a laugh in her.

'I can understand why you were going away with friends for Christmas now,' Grace said and Roo pulled a wincey face.

'I lied. I would have been by myself. My pals are all busy, there's just me on the scrapheap.'

'Surely they would set another place at the table for you,' said Vincent.

'Well, it's a bit awkward really. They're friends with all three of us. They didn't want to take sides.'

Look, it's a mess, but Amber and Aaron are our friends as well as you and . . . they've asked us to be the witnesses. That from her second-best friend who, it seems, knew all about it but it 'wasn't her place to say'. *Not fun being trapped in the middle,* she'd snapped and Roo had snapped back harder, *It's not exactly a barrel of laughs being where I am either.*

'Sounds like you need a whole new bunch of mates,' said Tim. 'If I were your dad I'd have gone round and thumped the little twat.'

'I'd have come and held your coat,' added Vincent.

'Well, Roo, you are not going to be lonely this Christmas, because you are with us here on this wonderful train.' Jane smiled at her.

'With your own personal chef,' said Frank, dropping a reverential bow.

'And you didn't have a clue?' This from Grace.

'Nope. When he was fessing up, we had to break off the conversation because the delivery of boxes had just arrived for me to pack my stuff up so I could move into his house. Neither of them dared tell me so they just didn't bother . . . until they had to. I had a wedding dress fitting booked. Amber was going with me.'

'Dear god,' said Tim. 'What a pair of spineless . . .'—he hunted around for a fresh expletive—'arseholes.'

'Where's the respect?' Frank threw his hands up in the air. 'If you fall out of love with someone, you can't do anything about that, but you can act like a gentleman about it. And this . . . what's his name?'

'Aaron.'

'Never liked that name,' said Frank to that, which may or may not have been true.

'Aaron Ewerin.'

'And this Aaron—' Frank's brain caught up. '*Urine*?' He wrinkled up his face in disbelief.

'It's spelt E-w-e-r-i-n,' replied Roo.

'Still pronounced the same way though, innit?' said Frank. 'You'd have been Ruby Ewerin? Sounds like a complaint you'd go to the doctor with. Blimey, you had a lucky escape there, gel.'

Vincent snorted and apologised, which made him snigger more and he set off the rest of the table.

'Amber Ewerin sounds a little bit healthier,' said Frank. 'Although the doctor would probably tell you that you weren't drinking enough water.'

Even Grace was infected with the comedy banter and was smiling.

'Cuts down the names they can call the kids. I mean, you wouldn't want a Misty Ewerin, would ya?' Frank went on.

'Or a Max. What about Cat?' Vincent added.

'Yuri. Lulu.'

'Stop it, you two,' said Roo, wiping her eyes again, this time from mirth.

'You're better off without the lot of them,' said Tim, thinking that if anyone had hurt his daughter in such a way he really wouldn't have been able to keep his nose out of it. His son-in-law Eugene was a good man, decent, principled and a provider. He'd be around for his wife and his baby, unlike Tim had been. He'd get the balance right.

'How long were you together, Roo?' asked Jane.

'Three years. I got with him on the rebound. My first boyfriend was a right wanker. I didn't think anyone could be worse than him.'

Jane nodded sagely. 'Rebound relationships, they have a lot to answer for.'

'I'm staying single from now on.'

'Roo, you're a lovely girl and someone someday will come along who deserves you and you don't settle for anything less than the top prize.' Frank wagged his finger at her. 'If he's a proper man, am I right, gentlemen?'—Frank's eyes flitted from Tim to Vincent to Henry for confirmation—'he will treat you like a queen, with respect. He won't go knobbing your mates or lying to you. He'll want to look after you and hold your heart in careful hands.' Frank cupped his hands as he spoke and his eyes drew towards Grace and locked with hers. And in that moment Grace felt his love punch through the barriers she had erected around herself. Frank, who had never cheated on her, never treated her less than respectfully, never given her cause to doubt him.

'I'd ask you out myself if you didn't have such funny hair,' said Vincent, making her hoot.

'Here, have the last mince pie, they've got medicinal properties.' Tim pushed the plate over to her.

'Don't you cry over a man, Miss Roo. Someone you love shouldn't make you shed a single tear,' said Frank, who had himself cried too many times over the person he loved.

Chapter 27

They went to the bar after all the plates were washed up. Roo volunteered to be on drinks duty. She mixed an excellent pink gin and tonic for Elizabeth and a snowball for Jane and then she mixed one for herself because she knew its sweet frothiness would hit the spot. Frank must have kept the ice bucket topped up, she decided, because it was full to the brim. She reckoned his pub, The Salty Cockle, would be a great place to visit. She'd always found the sea very healing, which is why she'd thought Whitby might be a good idea. Then again, she wasn't entirely sure she'd been going there to heal.

Outside, the snow was falling but in tiny feather flakes. Inside, they were all sitting in companionable silence in the same places they were in when they first sat down on the train, breathless, cold and covered in snow. Was that really only yesterday?

Roo had lit their Christingles which would burn out soon enough, but there was something about candles and their light that brought much more comfort and warmth than the capacity of their small flames would suggest.

'Well, I am now leaving you for the evening,' said Brian.

'Mrs Cosgrove has prepared all the vegetables for tomorrow. I'm very partial to a parsnip, I have to say, and we only ever have them at Christmas funnily enough. Why is that? We are going to relax with our game of Monopoly and no doubt I will be bankrupt in an hour. Let's hope I can get out of jail when I need to.'

Heads swivelled to Henry who was oblivious to what Brian was saying because he was too busy savouring the malt whisky in his crystal tumbler as if it were nectar delivered from the gods.

'So until tomorrow, the exciting big day. I'm going to leave you in the capable hands of the Andrews Sisters, who also were sisters like the Beverley Sisters but not like the Toomey Sisters. I'm sorry again for that song I played earlier and if you are lonely this Christmas, remember that there are worse things. Better to be alone than with the wrong person. Alone and lonely can be two very different animals. Goodnight, everyone.'

'You listening, Roo?' asked Jane.

Elizabeth was listening too. Being alone wasn't something she would be worried about; in fact she quite liked the stress-free periods with her own company. She often looked on Rightmove, fantasising about moving out of the cold, clinical flat above the offices and into a crumbly little cottage somewhere out in the sticks. It wasn't lost on her that she fantasised more about this than moving in with Gregory and she fought against analysing it too hard because it could be very telling of the state of their relationship.

'That's more like it, Brian,' said Grace as the Andrews Sisters started to sing about Christmas candles and their light being reminiscent of the light of the star that led the kings and shepherds to the stable.

'Do you think it happened?' Elizabeth asked. 'Jesus and the stable and Mary? I hope it did.'

'There was a historian called Flavius Josephus who was born only a couple of years after Jesus was said to have been crucified, and he knew people who had seen and heard him, and recorded it. He describes a man who did amazing deeds and was condemned to death by Pontius Pilate, and I believe Tacitus also was convinced of his existence.' Jane then explained her knowledge. 'My late husband took a great interest in the history after his . . . *experience.*'

'But you remain unconvinced?' asked Henry. He knew about Clifford's changed beliefs, as Jane had told him when they were here earlier, enjoying each other's company after his big reveal. They'd covered quite a lot of ground.

'I remain . . . intrigued,' she answered him. 'I believe there are germs of truth in old myths, but as to how big those germs are . . .' She shrugged, expressing her uncertainty.

'Faith transcends all evidence,' said Henry and Jane's head snapped round to him, because he sounded exactly like Clifford in that moment, even down to the exact words he had used to her.

Roo licked her lips. She'd made a good job of her snowball. She didn't want to finish it but she'd put five cherries in the bottom of it as a consolation prize for when she did.

'You looked right at home behind that bar, Roo.' Frank stuck up his thumb at her.

'I think I'd enjoy being a barmaid more than I enjoy being a skivvy,' she said, wrinkling up her nose. 'Maybe I need to change my life up in the new year. I don't want to live there and bump into Mr and Mrs "Urine", and I don't want my so-called friends avoiding me because they're frightened to pick sides . . .'

'Sounds like they've already picked, Roo.' Tim put his big meaty paw over hers. 'You deserve better, love.'

'You absolutely do.' Frank clapped his hands together as if he meant business. 'So . . . tomorrow then. I thought about two o'clock for lunch, that work with everyone? I can fit in with your plans if you were thinking about visiting relatives in the morning.'

He'd said it to be humorous and then realised that also could be open to misinterpretation by Grace. He didn't even glance at her to see if such a thought was registered in her expression.

Jane yawned and set off a chain reaction.

'Goodness, it's hard work doing nothing, isn't it?'

The song on the radio ended and cut to silence. Brian would be playing Monopoly now with his Cath. Roo thought he sounded like the sort of bloke who wouldn't buy the hotels because he'd feel guilty about charging her the rent. Cath, however, would have no such qualms.

Roo couldn't really imagine growing old with Aaron and him getting out a Monopoly board. He liked games, but computer ones, he was obsessed by futuristic shooting games and killing zombies. How often had she moaned to Amber about the time he spent loading up his virtual guns? And Amber had said it was pathetic, but Amber must have been banging him at the same time. She shook her head, hoping to dislodge thoughts of him, although she did allow herself to imagine him leaving the marital bed to sneak in a crafty game of *Hitman*, as he did with her sometimes. She'd really thought that the only rivals she'd ever have to worry about were animated ones. Pathetic indeed. She *was* better off without him, without them both, she knew this. It was just that her heart needed to catch up with the knowledge that her brain was way ahead of.

They talked a little while they were finishing off their nightcaps, nothing deep, nothing serious, flotsam and jetsam words. They were all weary, as if their stresses and strains had caught up with them and were forcing them to power down. Frank was last to say his goodnights. Grace didn't linger behind to claim her kiss, or even a word, but went to the cabin when Jane did. He was oddly okay about that because today had been the start of the end of them, he'd felt it, and no doubt it would hit him like a ton of bricks soon enough, but for now he was conveniently numb.

He bent to pick up a coin on the carpet outside the bathroom in 'Sigismund'. Weird thing, with YES on one side and NO on the other. He'd ask around tomorrow to see who it belonged to but he could do with a magic version of that coin to tell him what to do. 'Should I end my marriage?' he asked it in his head and flipped it in the air, caught it on the back of his hand and slapped the other hand quickly over it. He couldn't bear to see the answer, so he pushed it in his pocket for the morning.

He made his way to the head of the train to check everything was okay, just making sure things were secure and as they should be. The odd feeling of being watched had disappeared, he realised, as he entered 'Yongle'. But then it would have, now that Henry Smith was part of them and no longer a hidden presence in the shadows. Luck really had been on his side, getting him to the train. Frank hoped it continued to stay with him for all he had to face with the authorities.

He filled a hessian sack full of logs for the fire while he was there; it seemed daft to waste the trip. He caught sight of his reflection in a window as he was returning and he reminded himself of Santa with the haul over his shoulder.

Grace had made him a Santa suit years ago and he used to dress in it, sneak into their son's bedroom on Christmas Eve. He'd never done it quietly because he secretly wanted Billy to wake up and see him, but his boy never had. He wondered if it was still there in the loft, though Grace wouldn't have thrown it away, he knew that, because she'd kept his childhood in boxes: his school reports, his drawings and paintings, every card he'd sent her – every card Frank had sent her for that matter too. She'd always clung on to the past as if one day scientists might discover such things were a ticket to travel backwards in time. Twenty years ago tonight was the last time he'd worn that suit. And though Grace had accused him many times of moving on where she couldn't, she didn't see that given the chance to go back to that night, he'd pay the price to do so – whatever the cost.

Chapter 28

'Are you and Frank all right?' asked Jane. Her light was off but Grace's was on because she was reading, although Jane hadn't seen her turn a page yet.

'As right as we ever are these days,' replied Grace, her eyes still on the words of her book. Then she let loose a long, long breath. 'I think that we are probably at the end of the road of our marriage, Jane. I think we have been there for quite some time, if I'm honest. This trip we took was a . . . an attempt to turn things back but it's been a disaster.'

'Frank seems like a lovely man.'

Jane might as well have thrown a match onto a three-foot-high pile of dried straw.

'Because he laughs and jokes and smiles.' Grace's face contorted as she spoke. 'We should have been on the same page where my son was concerned and we weren't and look at the result.'

'How did he die, your son?' The question pulled no punches but Jane asked it all the same.

'He joined the army. We couldn't stop him and believe me, I tried,' Grace began.

*

'Do you mind me asking about your son, Frank?' said Vincent, after he had finished brushing his teeth.

'I don't mind at all. He was a lovely boy,' Frank said, his face breaking into a smile. 'Grace had such a rough time being pregnant and then giving birth, it buggered her up, she couldn't have any more so he was extra precious. And I know that mothers and sons are supposed to be the thing, but Billy was a real little daddy's boy. Followed me everywhere, always wanting to do what I did. He had a tool kit like mine and a toy lawn mower, baby boxing gloves so I could take him on the pads. I bought him a little army uniform one Christmas and if he wasn't in his school uniform, he was in that – for about a year.' He smiled anew at the memory. He couldn't remember how many times Grace had to mend it, from all Billy's 'manoeuvres' in the garden, climbing over logs and grass to shoot the enemy with the wooden rifle Frank had made him.

'He'd always had an addictive personality, they'd probably stick a label on him these days, but whatever that kid did, he threw himself into it. And from the moment his brain clicked into the army, it never left it. He was a junior soldier at sixteen and set. Grace was terrified, of course. I was torn because I wanted him to be safe, but we give our kids lives to lead and we can guide but we shouldn't dictate. My dad told me that. He used to worry himself stupid when I climbed in a boxing ring, but he never let me know until after I hung me gloves up.'

'My eldest boy always wanted to go in the army too,' said Jane.

'I couldn't bring myself to encourage my child to be willing to die for his country.'

'I wouldn't have stood in my son's way if that had been his decision,' Jane said, her voice soft, telling her own truth without wanting to sound judgemental. 'I gave him his life and with that the freedom to make his own choices. What happened to Billy, Grace?'

'He had a heart attack on exercise. He'd completed a marathon carrying a thirty-kilogram weighted backpack and he kept on running and he collapsed and there was nothing anyone could do, though they tried to bring him back. For a long time.'

It was not what Jane had expected to hear. She had presumed he had been killed in action, which would have been a death more brutal – because some deaths were easier to accept.

'He was a proper soldier and he'd have made a damned fine officer,' said Frank. 'He wouldn't have told anyone to do what he couldn't do standing on his head. He pushed himself, for himself. He wanted to be better than the best and he was. But his heart let him down. He had a weakness in it no one could have known about. A time bomb, they told us after. It could have gone off when he was sitting adding sums up in an office. If he'd put his dreams on hold to please his mother, and she really put some pressure on him not to do what he knew he was born for, he'd have still probably died young, but unfulfilled, living half a life. In a mad way, that made me feel better, if anything could: that he stuck to his guns.'

'Frank can't possibly feel the same as I do. He might be able to move on but I can't. I don't even want to try.'

'He was Frank's son too, Grace,' said Jane, gently.

'With respect, Jane,' Grace replied, her politeness vying with her anger, 'as I said, unless you have lost a child, you *cannot* know what a mother who has carried that baby can feel. You think you can imagine it, and it will be a very pale imitation of reality, trust me.'

The time had come.

'Grace, I have carried three sons and I have raised three sons. And I have lost them all,' said Jane.

Chapter 29

'Roo, are you okay now?' asked Elizabeth in the dark, hearing Roo sniff.

'I'm fine,' replied Roo, guessing why she had asked. 'I'm just sniffing, not crying, honestly. Today helped. I think if I ever meet the real BBC, I might buy him a pint for playing that bloody awful song.'

'He burst a spot that badly needed bursting, I think. But you'll still hurt. It was very cruel what they both did to you. Gutless. You need more of a man than that.' *How easy it is to give advice, so much easier than taking it,* said a voice in Elizabeth's head.

'The thing is that I know if he came back crawling, I couldn't forgive him. I just couldn't ever trust him again.'

Elizabeth nodded, she couldn't forgive someone being unfaithful to her either. Gregory wasn't that type. She didn't think he liked sex that much for it to be a driving force. She felt it was more obligation than pleasure for him, something he was expected to do for himself as proof of his virility and to 'perform' for his partner. One day, the act would be a means to procreation and she would find her fulfilment in their child.

In the industry he was known as a *machine:* hard, unfeelingly efficient, duty before emotion, business before passion. In bed, he was exactly the same. She had squared it with herself though. Better to have someone like that than the standard big wheel who couldn't keep it in his trousers, the mould so many of them had been cast into because power and sex seemed to go hand in hand. Was it necessary for him to desire her in a primal way? Was it important that he didn't 'hold her heart in careful hands' as Frank put it, when everything else lined up?

'You deserve better, as Tim said, Roo. No one should be treated like that. Especially not by someone who once purported to love them.'

'Tonight is the first night where I have felt just a little bit better, thanks to everyone here.'

'Good.'

'Can I tell you a secret, Elizabeth? I didn't know what I was going to do in Whitby. I was that low, I . . . I was having trouble seeing a way out.'

Elizabeth sat up quickly. 'You're not saying what I think you're saying, are you, Roo?'

'I went to the docs and they gave me some anti-depressants but they take six weeks to kick in and I thought, *what's the point of me even being here*? I didn't want to exist any more.'

'Roo, stop.' Elizabeth was horrified. She might have been more horrified if she'd known that it had crossed Roo's mind at one point to flip her YES/NO coin to decide her fate. At least, in that distilled moment, realising she had gotten so low to have even contemplated that option hoicked her rudely back from the brink, from the dark web of her mind.

'Please tell me that you don't feel like that now.'

'I don't.' The whole train debacle had probably saved her. Spending Christmas alone where she'd live in her head and torture herself wasn't the best idea, so thank goodness now she'd never know how that would have played out. She still wasn't exactly dancing on cloud nine but she could see some sunshine on her horizon in the shape of plans, change, hope. When she went home, she would upend this non-life she was presently living. There was nothing to keep her in South Yorkshire where she was bored and lonely. She'd find somewhere else to go where she'd probably be as bored and lonely to begin with but at least she wouldn't be in danger of bumping into *them* or see any of the rubbish friends scurrying around corners to avoid her because they'd thrown in their lot with the other side.

'I'm okay, honestly. Anyway, I'm fed up of talking about it, so tell me, what will your married name be, Elizabeth?'

'Pennington.'

'That's nice and classy.'

In the early days she used to practise writing 'Elizabeth Pennington' but she didn't any more.

'Elizabeth Diamond sounds better.'

'Roo, stop that. You're very naughty.'

'He likes you. Trust me, I'm very good at working people out, give or take the knobs who were under my nose. I've built all my comedy routines on observational humour.'

'I like him too. As a good person,' replied Elizabeth, attempting to disarm Roo from thinking on those lines. There was no point in evaluating Vincent in any other way than a ship that she was presently in the process of passing in the night. No point in giving her head the permission to go there.

Roo chuckled. 'Were you listening when he and Frank

were talking about how a gent should treat a lady. Wasn't it lovely? Grace is a lucky woman, although someone should tell her face that.'

'Their only son died five years ago,' Elizabeth told her. 'Frank told us earlier that she can't get over it.'

'Oh god, I feel awful now,' said Roo, propping herself up on her elbow. 'I thought she was just a misery guts.'

'I think maybe she's allowed herself to be consumed by despair, by grief. I get the feeling that . . . that they're almost broken as a couple.'

'It's a lot easier splitting up from someone when you don't have a house and a business,' Roo said eventually. 'Luckily, all we had were things at each other's places, clothes, toiletries, stuff. I didn't bother asking for mine and I put his in a skip down the road.'

'Good for you.'

'I've only got a cheapo bedsit. I was looking forward to moving into his nice semi until we found somewhere that we could buy together, somewhere that was "ours". You live with Gregory?'

'Not yet. We can't agree on what we want, but if we split it would be every bit as complicated.'

'Because you work together, you mean?' asked Roo.

'Not just that,' said Elizabeth. 'If we were to break up, I'd be throwing my life as I know it away. I'd lose my job; my father wouldn't lose Gregory from the business so I'd be the one to go and he'd engineer it so I did. And I'd lose my father because he wouldn't be able to bear the embarrassment' – *or the disobedience.* 'Everyone wants it to happen. On paper we are absolutely perfect, you see.'

Compliant Elizabeth, broodmare in the making, who would look good on his future-politician's arm. Heir to the massively successful company he would eventually own via their union. Every box ticked. For him.

Roo's turn to sound worried now. 'Elizabeth, it looks to me like you've thought about ending it with him. Aren't you happy?'

Elizabeth knew she shouldn't have said anything that invited questions. She was terrified of opening up because she wasn't sure if she started talking she would be able to stop. She forced out a trill of laughter.

'Of course I am. I was speaking hypothetically. I didn't mean to imply that we're only perfect on paper. I was just saying what would happen if we did split. It would be rather awful, but luckily we have no intentions of breaking up. Anyway, goodnight, sleep tight. I imagine you will be glad to see the back of this day.'

'Yes, I will. Night night,' said Roo, wondering if Elizabeth had just pulled up a drawbridge there before what was behind it escaped.

Tim lay in the dark thinking about his daughter, his lovely Fleur and the sight of her in his head brought a sharp pain with it. *There's no fool like an old fool*, even if he wasn't old – but he was acting old, like a stubborn old man, like his dad and that would be his worst nightmare, to turn into him. He'd been as cold and distant as his mum was warm and loving. Tim didn't ever want to be the sort of parent who couldn't show his love for his child, who didn't make them feel treasured. He didn't want to damage his daughter, as he had been damaged by his father's *froideur*. He couldn't help but suspect, though, he'd inherited some of his inability to process his emotions – it would explain why he was acting like such an immature prat that even his own brain was telling him off for it.

As young Roo had said though, would Fleur be making the effort if she didn't care? She was trying to wear him down with persistence. Hadn't she already said to him that she understood why he was hurt at her living at the other end of the planet but she wanted him to come over whenever he wanted to? She said she loved him, that she understood why he'd had to work so much and give them a comfortable life, all the luxuries he'd never had as a boy and he was being silly beating himself up. But she was a lovely kid, and she would say all that, wouldn't she?

At least there was an advantage in her not ringing him at Christmas, at least she wouldn't be hurt again that he wasn't picking up the phone when she rang.

She wrote real letters to him every month, because she thought he might just read those. Calls, he could ignore, emails could be consigned to junk or he could miss them – but he wouldn't miss a letter landing on his doormat. One had arrived on the morning the day he left for Newcastle . . . yesterday – lord, was it only yesterday? He'd dipped in, his eyes had scooped up only a few words: *Dear Daddy . . . I won't ring at Christmas . . .*

He'd torn it into pieces, opened the door of the log burner and watched the flames eat it. He'd pushed her to it and it had happened: she'd finally given up on him, and who could blame her.

Chapter 30

Jane heard Grace's sharp intake of breath scrape against the inside of her throat, but that was the only sound she made and Jane was glad she'd shocked her into silence. She sat up in bed then and flicked on the reading light. Grace's expression was one of someone who had just been slapped and hadn't a clue what to do about it.

'Allow me to start from the beginning,' said Jane. 'You might think I'm going round the houses, but it's necessary. Is that all right?'

Grace nodded, slowly.

'In 1959, I was fifteen and in love with Wilfred Maltravers who delivered coal and who was two years older. I wasn't even a blip on his radar, not that that was anything new because no one noticed me, teachers, parents, boys . . . I was used to it. The year after, there was a dance and I found out he would be there, so I had a plan of action to snare him. But instead he fell in love on the spot with my friend's sister, Kitty. I went outside to cry. And there, sitting on a wall, was David Carteret, thirty-one, cocky, smoking.'

Jane took a sip from the glass of water she'd put at her side.

She was going to need her own throat to hold up for this story. She wouldn't even have gone into this much detail in one sitting with Clifford.

'He was friendly, good-looking and knew it, and he wanted to know why I had a big wet beetroot crying face. He offered me a cigarette and I pretended I could smoke and made a fool of myself coughing and he laughed. He paid me some attention and that's very intoxicating, especially when my heart and my ego were in bits and looking for something to heal them. And when he asked if he could take me to the pictures, I said yes. Not because I fancied him but because I needed to feel . . . wanted. I didn't tell my parents because they wouldn't have let me go with an older man, one twice my age. So, we met in secret.'

It was right that Kitty and Wilfred got together. Everyone thought she was just a glamour puss but in fact she was a hell of a woman. Years later, when Wilfred had a bad accident at work, she fought tooth and nail for compensation for him, way before the blame-game culture – and she got it and she nursed him and looked after him and they loved each other for their rest of their lives.

'Eight months after the dance, Kitty and Wilfred were married and I was one of her bridesmaids. And I got horribly drunk on fizzy wine and I let David Carteret finally do to me what he'd been trying to do since our third date. "You can't get pregnant on your first time," he said.'

She looked at Grace to see if she had guessed what was coming.

'It hurt, my, it hurt. I'd never been told what sex was like. Was that what all the fuss was about? I thought. I certainly couldn't talk to my mother about it and I had no sisters and all my close friends were virgins. My parents were furious and I had to get married. I didn't want to, I was terrified but I felt I had no choice. My parents would have thrown me out on the streets if I had brought shame on them. David wanted children very much; he was older, time was ticking . . . so I was rushed down the aisle and seven months later my baby was born. The official line was that he was a honeymoon baby that had arrived early. Russell. He was the most beautiful thing I'd ever seen, he was perfect. The love . . . it just engulfed me like a tidal wave. I know you know what that's like, Grace. I didn't think I could ever feel anything as powerful again but ten months later, Duncan arrived and twelve and a half months after that there was Alan and each time the love was no less. Those boys were my reason for breathing. David wasn't bad to me, but he wasn't particularly good either. There was no pleasure in sex because he wasn't interested in giving me any. I never felt cared for or valued other than as someone who made the meals, looked after the children, cleaned the house . . . served his needs.

'He had a good job, he provided. He wouldn't allow me to work, but I painted – not that he would have seen that as a job; a little hobby maybe in between dusting and cooking. I had always wanted to go to art college, but I'd scuppered that for myself by opening my legs, as my mother said. What a disappointment I was to her. But David loved the children, adored them and I would never have split up the family, however miserable I was, because I had the boys to think about. I couldn't anyway; where would I have gone? What would I have lived on?

'Russell was four when I noticed that things weren't right. My mother said he was clumsy, but it was more than that, I felt it. And I felt it in Duncan as well, something . . .

not as it should be; he was very crabby and unhappy. We went to hospitals and Russell was diagnosed with muscular dystrophy. We were told he would probably die before his eighteenth birthday. And we were also told that his condition was my fault because there was a correct suspicion it was passed on from the mother. We were devastated. I hoped and prayed that Duncan hadn't got it, but he had. I thought Alan had to be all right, not all three of my boys, please God. Every time Alan fell over, my heart leapt, but he seemed okay, it was a fall, just a fall. And then when he was five, he started to cry from pain in his legs and I *knew* . . .'

Grace's hand pressed against her heart.

'So yes, when I said that if my son wanted to go in the army I would have gladly let him . . . I would have waved him off because he would be living and doing what he wanted because he could. Russell died when he fifteen. Duncan just made it to seventeen. Alan died on his eighteenth birthday. They're all buried in the same grave. David held up for the funerals and then he just . . . let go, he was in such desperate pain. I understood, they were every bit his boys as well as mine; just because I gave birth to them didn't mean they were any less his. He gave them all the love he had to give.'

She left a gap for Grace to absorb this before continuing.

'After Alan died, all David's hatred for me poured out as if it had been stockpiled for years. He blamed me, of course, for everything because people need a tangible target, something to project all their anger onto and he didn't think I deserved to grieve for what I'd caused. They were a terrible two years. David drank to blot everything out. I couldn't stop him, I couldn't save him either but I did try. I took his blows, Grace, mental, verbal, physical, because

I blamed myself too. The last time he put me in hospital I knew that if I stayed, he would kill me and I thought he just might have a chance to rally if I wasn't around constantly reminding him of the damage my faulty genes had inflicted upon his life. So I left him. I went to my parents for help, my Christian parents who told me all of it was God's punishment on me, the wayward daughter. I never saw them again after that. I stuck a pin in a map and moved where it landed: Manchester. I had a small bag with me and enough money to get a room and start again. I'd been there only weeks when David died, fell over a banister, drunk. I'd like to think it was instant, that he didn't feel it; it was only a matter of time before it would happen. I buried him with his boys, with *our* boys.'

Jane blew out her breath to steady herself. She was back there in those dreadfully sad days. She knew her words would be swirling around in Grace's brain. She hadn't intended to outdo her in the grief stakes, but she did want her to believe there was hope after losing someone.

'I met Clifford ten years later. I was working as a secretary at the university and I was drafted to him, the newly appointed Head of Psychology. Our connection was instant, a magnificent force. What a wonderful human being he was, a man who respected me, treasured me, loved me, a partner in every sense of the word. Such a difference from my first marriage. There was true equality in our relationship but also fun, romance, passion. I found real happiness with him. It made me wonder how many women are in relationships where they don't have it, where they think all that is just an idealistic myth and have no idea what could be, as I once thought. Your Frank reminds me of Clifford; there is a reverence, a respect in the way he talks to you. I notice these things.'

She let that sink in too.

'But how ... how did you move forward, Jane?' There was a note of desperation in Grace's voice, as though the answer would be a holy grail.

Jane took another sip from her glass. Even the tap water on board tasted of superior quality: purer, somehow.

'When you are told your child has a life-limiting condition, you can either drive yourself mad by imagining all sorts of scenarios that the future will bring, so many variations of horror, or you can live in the present and enjoy it, treasure each day for the gift it is, and that's what I learned to do. My survival mechanism.' She yawned then because she was tired. She had talked a lot today and it had been wonderful because she could go days now at home without talking to anyone. She and Clifford had chattered away like a pair of lovebirds and she missed their conversations so much – on everything from ancient Rome to *Celebrity Big Brother.*

'I'll tell you more tomorrow, it's late now. I will say that I have treasured memories, Grace, but the present is my focus, where it should be. Don't let the past steal it from you. Sleep tight. It's too easy to do that in these beds, isn't it?'

Grace lay in the dark, her brain racing, sparking. She thought of David blaming Jane, wanting to wound her for something out of her control because howling at the moon wasn't enough and being so consumed by his own pain he couldn't – wouldn't – recognise hers.

'She blames me,' said Frank. 'And for a time, she'd convinced me that I should blame myself too, for not standing in his way. Then I thought about how happy he was – and he really was. And how miserable he'd have been if he'd done something else, "to be safe". But he wouldn't have been really, because if he'd sold cars or pushed a pen, he'd have bust his guts in the evening running, climbing, lifting weights, because that's who he was. She won't listen though. For five years I've jumped through every hoop to try and heal her. She wanted me to give up the boxing gyms – I did. She wanted to move away because there were too many memories, buy a different pub – I did. But there was one thing I couldn't give up.' Frank suddenly realised how long he'd been talking. 'I'm sorry, Vincent, I'm laying all this on you.'

'Honestly, mate, go on, I'm listening. What is it you can't give up?' He hadn't a clue what Frank could mean. It couldn't be a mistress, he didn't seem the type.

'Billy had been seeing this girl in the army. We'd never met her. He just told us about her. He was smitten. He'd had a few girlfriends and as soon as we'd seen them, the next minute they were gone. But this one – Ella – there was something different about how he was with her. We both said, "I bet this is the one" and I think she probably would have been. We met her for the first time at the funeral, she was in bits, though so were we, it was all a bit of a blur. Then, seven months later we got a letter to say that she'd had a baby – Billy's baby. She hadn't wanted to tell us before in case something went wrong, didn't want to give us any more heartache. She'd had a little girl and she'd called her Billie May – Billie, after her dad – and she wanted us to meet her.'

'Ah, that's lovely,' said Vincent. 'Surely that helped?'

Frank shook his head slowly from side to side.

'Grace went ballistic. No, she didn't want to meet her granddaughter at all. She thought Ella was lying, then she thought Ella was after money, then it was that Ella was trying to manipulate us but it was none of that really, she just didn't want to see the baby and be reminded of her loss, of the boy who was gone. I told Ella to give us a bit of time, but I so wanted to see the little girl.'

'And did you, Frank? Did you go?'

'I couldn't get her out of my head. So yeah, I did. I didn't tell Grace though. Ella'd left the army and gone back to her parents' house in Norfolk. Lovely people. She didn't want anything from us, except to be in Billie's life because we're her family. Vince, that little girl . . . it was like having a precious part of my son back. She was the spit of him when he was a baby, the way she pulled some faces, it was like it was him, but not him if you know what I mean; her own person, but she was made from him. She's beautiful. I thought Grace would come round, but she didn't. If anything she dug her heels in more, didn't want to hear a single word about them. So I never told her I went to visit. Ella wrote letters to Grace pleading with her to meet up but she wouldn't even open them.

'Then a pub came up for sale. In Norfolk, near to where Ella lived. We'd been to see a few and they were all right. But this place was by the sea, in a cracking little village and as soon as I walked in, I knew I wanted it. It felt like home. Grace didn't have a clue where Ella lived, she didn't join the dots. I manipulated it, I admit that, but I've never felt that it wasn't the right thing to do, the right place for us to be.'

'Did she . . . ever find out you'd been to see them?' asked Vincent.

'Yeah, earlier on today. And now she wants me to choose between her and my granddaughter.'

'Fucking 'ell,' said Vincent, after rolling that around in his head. 'What you gonna do?'

'I don't feel I've got a wife any more to choose, Vincent.'

Christmas Day

*Being snowed in at Christmas can make
you believe that time has stood still*

Chapter 31

Ironically, it was the silence that woke Henry, his brain telling him that something was awry because he couldn't hear shouts, echoes, clangs and bangs; there was nothing but stillness. He switched into gear a second after sitting bolt upright, swaddled in the feather quilt. He couldn't remember having a sleep of such fine quality for many years. He'd been dead to the world, no dreams – and he normally had a lot of dreams.

He folded up his bedding and dressed quickly. He presumed he must be the first one up because he couldn't hear any stirrings, which was good, because he had work to do and wanted it to be a surprise.

But, as he found, someone had beaten him to it because the bar had already been decorated with clusters of pine cones, berries, bells, and sprigs, headed with red bows tied to the top middle of the curtain rails and garlands hung over the doors at either end. In the dining carriage, 'Old Tom', it was the same story. It looked better than he could have managed, definitely a female touch. His money was on young Roo, who he knew had titivated the lounge so beautifully.

He'd checked out where things were stored the previous day so he could put his hands straight on them, determined to contribute. In the dining room, he set the table for eight: new white tablecloth, dark-blue satin runner placed down the middle of the shorter table. He laid out cutlery and glasses and stuck candles in three candelabras, placing them equidistant on the runner. He rolled red damask serviettes and pushed them through the gold napkin rings, positioned them to the left of the forks and put a cracker from a box he'd found above the dessert spoons. They were huge things, stiff and weighty. The price had been written on the box and he'd marvelled at how some people had money to throw away like that. Finally he put the charger plates in each setting. He didn't think he had much of an artistic leaning, but he hadn't done bad, if he said so himself when he stood back to admire his handiwork. Yep, that would be a lovely sight for his fellow train people to walk in to.

Frank noticed the table set and all the decorations up at the windows in 'Old Tom' when he went to put the oven on. Someone was an early bird then. *Ah, mystery solved.* Heading up to the fridge in 'Yongle', he bumped into Roo coming the other way. She was carrying a sack while walking slowly and looking around on the carpet.

'Well, Merry Christmas to you, Roo,' said Frank, unsure whether or not to accompany his words with a kiss on the cheek, but she took the dilemma away from him by opening her arms and enclosing him in a hug.

'Merry Christmas, Frank.' She let him go. 'I'm looking for a coin with yes and no on it, you haven't seen it, have you?' He saw her brow was creased with worry.

'Ah, it belongs to you, does it?'

He slid his hand in his pocket and pulled it out. 'This the one? I found it last night.'

The beam on her face was almost radioactive.

'Yes, it is.'

'What's it for then?'

He'd think she was a crank if she told him it was her life guide.

'Just sentimental value. It was my dad's,' she lied. She'd found it somewhere so long ago she couldn't even remember where. Had it been her dad's, it wouldn't have been much use as a steer because he made just about every wrong decision in life there was to make.

'Does it work?'

'Well, because of it I'm on here, instead of in a shit Airbnb in Whitby or back home drowning my sorrows, so I'd consider that a win.'

Frank chuckled. 'I think I should get myself one of those. What's in the sack? You look like a burglar.'

'Some more decorations. I've just been to get them from the storeroom.'

'You set the table as well?'

Roo shook her head. 'Nope, that wasn't me.'

'Ah okay, well, I'd better let you get on with it then,' he said. 'I think I can safely say that we will get to the end of the turkey at least, before any rescue party comes.'

They both turned their heads towards the windows. There had been no thaw, the snow was still inches deep on the branches of a nearby tree, but there were no clouds threatening more. The skies were clear and ice-blue, fading to polar white at the horizon. Frank took a step forward.

'Hang on, what's that over there?'

Roo narrowed her eyes to see what Frank was looking at. 'Is it a church?'

'Definitely some sort of building. Blimey, there's us thinking we're in the middle of nowhere and there's probably a city half a mile away.'

He was jesting, all he could see was what appeared to be the top of a tall square tower. An isolated folly maybe, because he couldn't see anything else. It couldn't be the station where the guard and driver had ventured off to because it lay in the opposite direction. Weirdly, he found the idea of being so near civilisation not as welcome as it should have been.

'Well, the turkey is in anyway and—'

He cut off his sentence as Henry appeared at the end of the carriage and walked towards them, smiling.

'Good morning, Henry,' said Frank. 'And a merry Christmas to you.'

'A very merry Christmas to you too, Frank, Roo.'

Frank shook his hand and he seemed rather taken aback when Roo embraced him, an unexpected but welcome gesture. Frank wondered when he'd last felt the sweetness of a kiss.

'That your swag bag, Roo?' said Henry, aware of a blushing heat on his cheeks.

'Ha.' Roo grinned. 'More decorations, actually.'

'Good luck finding some room for them.' Henry winked at her. He was right then, it was her who'd put them up.

'Sleep well?' Frank asked him.

'Slept like a dead man,' came the reply. 'I hoped I'd be first up as I wanted to . . . do a bit of trimming and titivating. I'm just going to the top of the train to get some ingredients. I thought I'd make eggnog for us all to start off the morning, if I can remember me mam's recipe.'

'That sounds lovely and festive,' said Roo. 'Right, I've got stuff to do. See you both later.'

'I'll walk up to the stores with you, you can tell me how you make eggnog because I've never attempted it,' said Frank to Henry and off they went.

Roo started when she entered the dining room. She noticed the table so beautifully laid out and all the decorations hanging up. Blimey, Henry had been busy. Ah well, she decided, she'd better find somewhere to put this lot she'd brought with her, rather than lug them back. There couldn't be too much sparkle this Christmas as far as she was concerned now.

Tim awoke hearing voices outside his cabin. People were up, it was Christmas morning. Maybe it was the sight of his Santa suit hanging up ready for later that contributed to the feeling he used to get when Fleur was little, the fizz that was generated by the prospect of her excitement. He'd always dressed up on Christmas Eve to steal into her bedroom and put a couple of presents in a pillowcase at the foot of her bed. The rest would be waiting for her under the tree downstairs. She'd woken up once and he'd wanted to chuckle at the gasp she'd made, before she must have realised she had to stay very quiet or Santa would disappear. He'd so wanted to have a conversation with her in the dark but he couldn't risk her realising he was her dad and ruining the magic; kids were way too clever. He gave himself a solitary brownie point for always being there for the Christmas holidays. He used to fool himself that that made him a good father.

He got out of bed and released the blind onto a snowy world but one, at least, with pale blue clear skies and a watery sun. He pulled out a clean jumper from his suitcase and with it a pastel pink envelope that fell on the floor.

'What the hell . . . ?'

No, that couldn't be. It was a letter, his address in Fleur's handwriting, a Christmas stamp in the corner. It was a letter he knew he had destroyed. His hands came to his waist as he stood and looked at it lying on the carpet as if expecting it to disappear for the illusion it was. He retraced his thoughts; he had definitely ripped it up, then he had put a match to it in his log burner. So how come it was there now at his feet? Was he going bonkers?

He reached down, picked it up, slit it open with his finger, slid the pink fold of paper from it.

Dear Daddy,

Just a short letter to wish you a very Merry Christmas. Eugene and I have decided to take a little break in a cabin by the beach. Not too far away from civilisation just in case the baby does make a very early appearance, but not sure what the phone coverage will be like. So . . . I won't ring at Christmas, but as soon as we are back, I'll phone you . . .

. . . Do you remember the Christmas when I woke up to find Santa in my room delivering presents? I can still recall that excitement even now . . .

. . . Love you, Dad. Come and see us — it's great here. And Eugene is dying to meet you. And I want my baby to know you from the moment he (or she) lands.

Fleur xx

Tim slumped to the bed and his heart felt as if it had been flooded with warmth. She hadn't given up on him after all. The reason she wasn't ringing him at Christmas was because she was going away on a break.

When he got home he would sit by that phone and wait for it to ring and then he would answer it and speak to his girl and tell her that he was coming over to see her the first chance he got.

Chapter 32

'Merry Christmas, everybody,' said Brian from his radio. 'News from the Cosgrove household is that once again Cath wiped the floor with me at Monopoly. I was bankrupt after an hour. She very kindly allowed me to have a banker's loan to tide me over, but there is absolutely no getting away from the fact that I was not put on this earth to be a property mongrel.'

Vincent's head twisted to the radio. 'Mongrel, Brian?'

'I think he means mogul,' said Jane, with a titter. 'God bless him.'

Elizabeth, on a search for everyone, walked into the bar just as Bing started to sing 'Deck the Halls'. She had just been marvelling at how beautiful the dining car looked with the table all Christmas-ready and the decorations at the windows, and here were more.

'Oh my,' she exclaimed, looking around.

'All down to Henry and Roo,' said Frank.

Roo was about to give Henry the credit for the bulk of the tarting up, but her voice was drowned out by him bursting through the door carrying a stock pot with a ladle stuck in it.

'I've managed to recreate the famous Clodagh O'Brien Smith's eggnog,' he announced, pleased as punch. Somehow he'd remembered how she did it, though the quantities were a little experimental. He'd beaten egg yolks and sugar, then set them aside while he ever so slowly heated up cream, milk, nutmeg, cinnamon, a pinch of salt, brandy plus the scraped seeds from a vanilla pod until the mix hit the first stage of simmering then he whipped it off the heat. He recalled how long it used to take her to temper the eggs by adding the warm cream mix to them spoonful by spoonful, then whisking so they didn't scramble. But my, it was worth the labour. The smell drifted up from the pot and brought so many memories flooding back as sweet as the day they were made. It was as if someone had taken the essence of Christmas and served it up as liquid, silky gold.

Just as Frank was giving Elizabeth a kiss in greeting, Grace arrived. She looked tired, thought Frank. He wasn't to know how long she had stayed awake last night with things rolling in her mind.

'Merry Christmas, Grace,' said Frank and she thought, *He's used my name, instead of "love".* He gave her a kiss and she noted it was the same sort of kiss he'd just given Elizabeth.

Vincent was the last to greet Elizabeth. There was a stupid awkwardness there they both tried to ignore. *He smells lovely,* she thought. *Like a pine forest.*

She smells lovely, like a flower garden, he thought, placing his lips to her soft cheek.

Jane tasted the eggnog and it took her back to a December she and Clifford had spent in Austria, drinking *eierpunsch* in a market. They'd planned to revisit it, but they ran out of time.

'I'm going to help my Cath construct the trifle now,' said

Brian, 'but I'll leave you in the capable hands of a gentleman
you'll all know very well. I always play one of his specials
at this time of year and I think it goes down well. No one's
asked me to stop putting it on anyway. Ho ho . . .'

'Oh, bless him,' said Roo. 'I hope he doesn't realise that
probably hardly anyone listens to him. I would love him to
believe he has an audience of millions.'

'It's a couple of years old, but it's my particular favourite of all the *Sir Colin of Castle Street*s and of course I'll be
back later with you all. Ooh, I meant to tell you that Santa
brought me a lovely woolly hat and scarf set. Very dapper.
And a tin of my favourite peppermint patties. What did
Santa bring you?'

'Sod all, Brian,' Vincent answered. 'Alas, I'm not sure our
train showed up on Santa's radar.' Though Tim was wondering, if Santa didn't bring him that letter, who the hell did?

There was nothing else to do but listen to the radio together
and drink eggnog. Roo dropped a couple of cherries in hers.
Frank was only shocked she hadn't put a sprout in it.

'*This episode of* Sir Colin of Castle Street *was first recorded
in front of a live studio audience on Christmas Day 1948,*' said
a plummy male old-BBC announcer voice. Then a tinkly
tune revved up and that live studio audience were prompted
into claps and cheers.

'What's this about then?' asked Elizabeth. 'Anyone know?'

'Sir Colin is a geriatric who believes his grandmother had
an affair with the king and he acts more royal than royal,'
said Jane, with a fond smile. 'He's also very stingy and he gets
his words all mixed up, so plenty of comedy material there.
I used to listen to this on Sundays with my mum and dad.'

It was the only time she really felt that they were a family unit, sitting by the radio every week, and she had savoured it. Her dad didn't laugh much ordinarily, but Sir Colin tickled his funny bone and Jane would wish this jovial father lasted beyond the programme, but he didn't. All she got was that emotional oasis once a week.

Roo was prepared not to be in the slightest bit amused. But maybe it was the jolly ambience, the camaraderie, the heavy slug of brandy in her drink, or maybe it was just because funny humour existed in the 1940s too that she found herself chuckling along with everyone else. Henry had a very infectious laugh when it ramped up. It was nice, they all thought, to hear it from him.

At the end of the half hour, they all started clapping along with the studio audience, their cheeks aching from the workout.

'What the hell have I just listened to?' said Roo, wiping her eyes.

'Joy,' said Frank, glad that it had visited him and reminded him it was still to be had.

A little later, in the galley, Frank was checking on the turkey when Grace walked in.

'Do you need a hand?' she asked him.

'No, I'm okay,' he replied, pushing out a smile that didn't sit comfortably on his lips, as if it didn't want to be there. He could have done with a little help but not from Grace. He just didn't want to be Fred Astaire-ing round those eggshells, not today. He wanted a break from it.

She nodded, stepped out and then, seconds afterwards, put her head back around the door.

'Do you think I could see a photo? If you have one. Not now, later,' she said.

There was no misinterpreting what she meant by that. He tried not to let the fact he was stunned show.

'Erm ... yeah, I'll get it for you.'

'Thank you.'

And with that she was gone and he stood stock still in shock, wondering if that had really just happened.

Chapter 33

After she'd finished her eggnog, Roo went back to the cabin to polish up her poetry for the talent competition. Tim went to the galley to insist on helping. Jane, after two eggnogs, drifted off into a nap. Henry regarded her fondly.

'What a lovely old lady,' he said quietly to Grace.

'Yes, she's quite a girl,' Grace replied. Jane's gentle fragility belied a strength she could only guess at to have survived all she had.

'She reminds me very much of my dear old mam. Compassion of Ruth, wisdom of Solomon personified.'

'Do you have children, Henry?'

'Don't think so,' he replied with a crooked grin. 'If I ever get out I'd like to settle and have bairns. I never thought about the future when I was young.'

'You're only young now.'

'I won't be when I get out, Grace. If my plan doesn't work I'll be facing a lot more years and they'll be extra hard to serve.'

'If it helps, I'll pray for you,' said Grace. She still prayed, every night, not that *he* answered her. She wasn't even sure she believed in God any more. She hadn't analysed it, she just habitually kept on praying and kept on being disappointed.

'Thank you, I'll take your prayers. I had an interesting discussion with Jane about faith yesterday. She believes in different things to me and yet strangely we are very similar. In a way her belief seems stronger than any religion. To be grateful for every moment given to us. To be kind because you can be, without any notion that it somehow puts you in the Lord's good books for what comes after, is holier than holy. Kindness is a much-underrated quality.'

'I don't suppose you get a lot of kindness in . . . where you are,' said Grace.

'Would you be surprised if I said we do, in the form of empathy, respect, listening, goodwill, sharing what we have, especially as we have very little. For many it can be a lot to take in, that loss of liberty, however culpable you are. I think I've seen every walk of life in prison over the years, from doctors to beggars, from those who had all the advantages of life to those who were doomed before they even came out of their mothers' wombs. Prison is a great leveller and every small kindness shines like a diamond in a mine. I say "small"; I found out *very* early in my sentence that there is no such thing as a small kindness. Each one has a tremendous weight.' Henry smiled. 'Your husband is a very kind man, Grace. It emanates from him like a light.'

Another one telling her how Frank appeared to them. It was revealing to see him as others saw him.

'I'm rarely wrong in my judgements. I think I have a gift for seeing people as they are, however convincing their fa-cades may be. For instance, I would say that Frank is a good man, he radiates strength. Tim, also – but someone who sees his faults before his virtues. Roo, a young lady who has no idea of her capabilities and when her bud finally starts to bloom, she will be magnificent. In Vincent I see a man who wants very much to love and in Elizabeth, a woman who wants very much to *be* loved.'

'And me? What do you see with me?' asked Grace, wanting to know, but afraid of the answer too, because Henry, she suspected, wouldn't be someone to sugar-coat it.

'I think you are lost in your own life, Grace. I would also say you are ignoring the guide rope that is in reach of your hand.'

'My son died, Henry. I don't think I can ever get over it.'

Grace swallowed down the huge lump of sadness that rose in her throat.

'I don't think you can ever get over something so traumatic. But you can learn to live with it; then in time it will lose its jagged edges and become like a pearl in an oyster. All that love you had for your son is tearing around inside you with nowhere to go. You must find a place for it, Grace. You must give it a home.'

'Would you have been alone today, Tim, if you hadn't been trapped on a train with us lot?' asked Frank as he lifted the turkey out of the oven, which seemed to sizzle and hiss in protest at the move. He switched the heat up by degrees and put in the Yorkshire pudding tins with the fat in the bottom. They reminded him of Sunday lunches at home when he was a boy, such happy memories attached and he wondered, in time, what sort of memories would be evoked by this Christmas dinner. Mixed, he imagined.

'Yep. I'd have driven home early this morning after the event. Good job I always overpack, isn't it? Vestigial habit from my days on the road, having a spare of this and that just in case. And I had a ready meal in the freezer for today. I'm not that bothered about Christmas any more because . . . well, I think I told you.'

'Have you thought any more about what you're going to do?' Frank shut the oven door and straightened up.

'I'm going over to see her.'

'I'm glad, Tim. What changed your mind?'

Tim opened his mouth to tell Frank about the letter that should be ashes in his grate but had somehow turned up in his suitcase, but he would have thought he was gaga.

'I've had time to think,' he replied instead. 'I don't want to regret anything else. So, however much the ticket costs, as soon as I get home – if I ever do – then I'm packing a case and booking a single ticket to Tauranga.'

'Bloody hell, Tim,' said Frank. 'I've been to Tauranga. Grace's sister lived near there. We went out a few years ago to see her when Billy joined the army; I thought it would cheer her up and stop her worrying. It's beautiful, mate. It's like paradise. You'll love it. Go be with your girl, Tim. I don't want to be a scaremonger, but you never know what's around the corner and I'm grateful that in the last conversation I ever had with my son I told him I loved him and I was proud of him.'

He'd wondered since if he'd had some sort of premonition that made him say it when his boy had rung up and told him he was going on a field exercise, so wouldn't be in touch for three weeks. It had brought him the smallest comfort to recall that their last words to each other had been significant. Billy had laughed and said, 'Yeah, and I love you too, you soft old git.'

Tim nodded rather than speaking because he couldn't. Two days ago, he had been annoyed that the snow had robbed him of a night in a swanky hotel, and a five-hundred quid wage, plus petrol, because he doubted he'd get paid. But what had happened to him instead was priceless.

'Are you prepared for the after-dinner talent show?' asked Elizabeth, as Vincent set up the fire in the lounge for later. All someone would need to do was put a match to it and – job done.

'As I can be,' he replied, his attention distracted by one of the old newspapers he'd just ripped and twisted into screws. 'I hope these weren't part of the décor and we've destroyed them. I mean, look at the headlines: *Timothy Evans hanged. British troops land in Korea. Literary giant George Orwell dies. King postpones trip due to ill-health.* And I mean George the Sixth, not Charles. I'm sort of worried now.'

'I'm sure it will be fine. If they were valuable, they wouldn't be kept here as obvious fire-starters. They'd be in a magazine rack for reading.'

'You don't sound very convincing, Elizabeth.'

'I'm sort of worried too.' Then she burst into laughter, that lovely bell-like sound, bells on a one-horse open sleigh.

'Oh, bloody 'ell.'

'It'll be fine, I'm sure.' She sounded a little more convincing now.

Vincent got up from his knees and moved over to one of the armchairs. 'Lovely, this room, isn't it?'

'Yes, it's beautiful.' Elizabeth's eyes roamed around it yet again, taking in the inlaid walls, the shiny jacquard cushions in varying shades of blue, the heavy brocade curtains, soft velvet sofas and chairs, Roo's expert decorations, including two large nutcracker soldiers at either side of the door into 'Old Tom'. She really had gone to town for them.

'I think they might have to drag me off this train when we finally get going and land at Eskford. Then, depending on what the roads are like, we either train it north or double-back to the car and I drive,' said Vincent, though he didn't really want to think about it. Not yet, anyway.

'You really don't have to come with me if I have to catch the train.'

Vincent gave her his best disapproving look. 'I think we've had this conversation before. Either way, when you get to Topston Manor, I will be carrying your suitcases.' He doffed a pretend cap: 'M'lady', and she didn't like that he'd done that, for a reason she couldn't quite figure out.

'Your fiancé will be glad to see you, I bet; to know that you're safe. He must be going a bit potty.'

'Yes,' she said, with a sigh she wasn't even aware of making. Vincent noticed and it told him too much.

'So when's the big day then?'

'We . . . haven't decided that yet. There are a lot of things to consider, people to consult and a suitable date to be found for all,' replied Elizabeth, in a tone that she realised sounded more as if she were talking about orchestrating a funeral rather than a wedding. Then again, the more she was away from her father, her workplace, her fiancé, the more her vision was clearing, the more it did start to feel like a funeral rather than a wedding. A funeral of her remaining freedom.

'Suitable date for *all*?' Vincent probed.

She didn't even want to say it, the things they'd have to work around: the various shooting seasons, for instance, printed in indelible ink in the Pennington diary. They'd be having their Boxing Day shoot on the estate tomorrow if the weather was clement enough. If it had to be postponed, that would be considered worse than the cancellation of the engagement party. Then, starting on the 'glorious twelfth' it would be the poor grouses' turn. Every June and July were out because Elspeth-Ann and Gaylord went to Valencia to stay with her sister who had married a *conde*. They'd have to avoid the busiest export windows too, the networky-trade gatherings. She'd suggested the following year, but Gregory said there was little point in waiting, so May was a probability. There would be a small private wedding and then a large garden party in the late summer.

May was too close.

'What on earth is the matter with you?' Gregory said on at least two occasions when she had woken up gasping for breath because she was being suffocated in her dreams. It would have taken Freud about three seconds to come to his conclusion about what was going on there.

'I've got a big inglenook, ' Vincent announced. There was a moment of silence and then they both broke into laughter.

'Sorry, that wasn't a euphemism,' he said. 'Fireplace, I mean. I have a big inglenook *fireplace*. Nothing nicer on a winter's evening than to get it blazing and sit in front of it.'

'That's my idea of heaven.' Elizabeth smiled wistfully. 'Thick walls, a creaky staircase, a lovely roaring fire.'

'Cheese toasties for supper. A good box set,' Vince added.

'A shared bottle of Pinotage, a huge tub of popcorn.'

'Salty or sweet?'

'Cinema sweet.' There was no thinking about that for Elizabeth.

'I love the cinema, me. Especially the posh ones with the reclining seats. Lots of space for my long legs to stretch out. Although I need nachos and cheesy sauce *and* salsa.'

'That sounds great. I went to a party once when I was

young. A cinema party, it was fantastic. We all had hot dogs and ice-creams.'

'My kids will have them sort of parties. Loads of little noisy buggers getting excited, making memories.'

'I'd love that.'

'You having kids one day, Elizabeth?'

'I hope so, yes. What about you?'

'I'd love 'em. I'd like to be the sort of dad mine was, you know – hands on, building a tree house with them, taking them to football and being the embarrassing dad on the sidelines.'

Elizabeth couldn't picture him being any other sort of dad. She was smiling at the thought of that future Vincent, then that smile closed up as she thought of what would lie in store for her. She'd be there at every sports day and award ceremony but she'd most likely be alone. Something else would take precedence for Gregory: meetings, business, politics . . .

'Your dad sounds a good sort.'

'Well, he's not with us any more, sadly,' said Vincent. 'They didn't have me until they were knocking on. Mum was in her mid-forties, Dad was well over fifty. They didn't think it would ever happen. I kept 'em young, though.' He grinned. 'Dad used to run up and down at the side of the pitch telling the ref he'd got it all wrong and he was like a spider monkey up and down that bleedin' tree in the garden building my den. When I had to sell their house, I wish I could have taken it with me. And you could hear my dad laughing from a mile away. I could always tell when he was in the audience at a school play. Mum copped for taking me to rugby on Sunday mornings if Dad was on call, and more often than not he'd be sorting someone's plumbing emergency. She used to be freezing, she was only a tiny little woman – like Roo, no meat on her bones to insulate her. Never moaned once about it though. Your mum and dad go to all your things?'

The thought of Roderick Dudley cheering her on at the side of a hockey pitch was ludicrous.

'They were very busy people,' she said, diplomatically. Her mother had promised she'd be there when she was presented with her exams certificate, but in the end it had clashed with a tennis tournament, or so she said. She had a lot of tournaments in those days. As Elizabeth was to find later, her mother was just very busy with Luis Lemos.

'I see,' Vincent said. It was becoming ever clearer why an air of sadness lingered around Elizabeth like an aura.

'Your children will be very lucky,' said Elizabeth.

'So will yours,' said Vincent.

Their eyes locked; something passed between them, intense and warm. Too warm. Elizabeth broke contact first.

'I think I'll go and see if Frank needs any help. I'm sure he must.'

She needed to go before Vincent saw the blush bloom on her cheeks and heard her heart boom because it felt loud enough for the train engineer in St Hilda to have heard it.

Chapter 34

'Ah, just in time, Elizabeth. Yes, I do need your assistance, please ring the bell and summon everyone to the table,' said Frank, dropping the hot Yorkshire puddings onto each plate. He had asbestos hands after years in the job. The chef that worked in his dad's pub once told him that he'd need to have those to be a proper pro in a kitchen.

Elizabeth rang the bell and everyone gravitated to the table: Roo from her cabin, Vincent from the lounge, Grace and a newly awoken Jane from the bar. Henry was already in 'Old Tom', pouring out champagne.

Roo had put three of the Christingles with replaced candles between the candelabras and lit them all with some matches.

'Does it matter where we sit?' she asked when she'd finished.

'Just park your arse on the nearest chair and get this down your neck before it gets cold,' said Frank with mock impatience.

'I don't need telling twice. I'm starving,' she said, sitting down quickly on the end opposite Henry. She inhaled the dinner in front of her and purred aloud. She also noted the enormous amount of sprouts that Frank had piled next to her slices of turkey.

'I wouldn't want to be spending the night in your cabin,' said Vincent, leaning forward to talk to her from the other end of the table.

'That's lucky. You've got about as much chance of that as me headlining in Las Vegas,' she threw back.

Vincent pinched his nose. 'Elizabeth, you have my sympathies.'

Elizabeth smiled at him, bashfully though, just a flick of eye contact. He knew she'd felt it too, that moment back there in the lounge. If she hadn't moved away when she did, he couldn't tell what might have happened. He wished she hadn't and it *had* happened.

'Frank, you sit here opposite Grace,' Tim said, moving to the end of the table opposite to Vincent. Henry tucked Jane under the table next to him.

'Would you permit me to say grace?' Henry asked.

'Yes, I think we should,' said Jane, despite her beliefs.

Everyone bowed their heads.

'Dear Lord, we thank you for this feast you have provided for us and for the people you have brought together around this table. We pray that our eyes be open to the ways in which you are there in our lives so we may see your presence. Be our strength when we are wanting, fill our hearts with love and laughter. Help those among us who need to find peace and forgiveness. And keep our hopes burning. Be there to guide us and remind us what is truly important. Bless us all. Amen.'

He crossed himself and sat to a chorus of 'Amens'.

'That was lovely, Henry, thank you,' said Roo.

'High praise from me too – the heathen,' added Jane with a wry smile.

'It was very heartfelt. You'd make a good vicar,' added Grace.

'. . . When your name is cleared by the king.' Roo raised her glass. 'A toast to the king, let's hope he does right by Henry.'

Everyone raised their glass.

'The king.'

'I like the king, he's a gentle man, isn't he? He sometimes looks tired though, I wish he'd take a rest,' said Roo.

'He hasn't been well in the last year or so, has he?' said Grace.

'Mind you, I'm not surprised having a brother like that,' said Henry. 'The strain he's put him under and the trouble he's caused.'

Elizabeth gave her head a disapproving shake. 'He's done a lot of damage to the institution and set it back years.'

'Plus he's put the king in an intolerable situation with his questionable choice of friends,' Henry added to that.

'He was Prince Charming once upon a time though. How the mighty fall,' added Vincent.

'The king's lovely. I prefer him any day of the week to his flashy brother.'

'Me too, Roo. He's a good, solid, honest king who cares about his people and is committed to his faith,' Henry agreed with her. 'And, when the time comes, his heir will be a great monarch too.'

'I hope that's not for a while though,' said Elizabeth, not wanting to think ahead to such a thing. That was probably the only unifying factor between herself, her father and her in-laws, they were all passionate royalists. But that could have been because the honours system would be obliterated if there were a republic.

'Can we do anything to help you, Henry?' asked Vincent. 'Write to someone for you?'

Henry smiled. 'Thank you, but I have all the support I need.' He pointed above. 'In him I trust.'

'You might need some secular help too, though, as a back-up,' suggested Jane, spearing a roast potato. The crunch was very satisfying.

'You're right, of course. I have a practical plan as well.'

'I'm relieved to hear it.' And Jane sounded *very* relieved about that.

'My sceptical friend.' Henry chuckled. 'Science and God sit together in a glass like oil and water. Science, according to Schrödinger, is an entertaining and useful tool to help us understand our world, but it does not – and never will – have all the answers. That's why I intend to enlist the help of both oil and water: my faith and the pragmatic.'

'Touché.' Jane raised her glass to him and Henry raised his and they chinked. Jane missed the intellectual arguments Clifford and his friends used to have over the dinner table about such things. In the days when there was healthy debate, something the present world should re-embrace, she thought.

'This is a top drop of splosh.' Vincent went in for another drink from his glass.

'Don't get hammered, you've got to perform later,' Roo warned him.

'Don't worry, Miss Roo, I haven't forgotten.'

'There's a lot of champagne in the stores. I didn't think Mr Ingleton would mind if we relieved him of a couple. I wasn't cheeky; I didn't raid his Dom Perignon or his Pol Roger,' said Frank.

He had every intention of leaving Mr Ingleton a note with his contact details on it. If the bloke wanted some recompense, he'd sort it.

As if Frank's thoughts had drifted out into the open, Tim said, 'We should swap contact details in case Mr Ingleton wants to get in touch with us.' His meaning was clear.

Henry blew out his cheeks because he understood why Mr Ingleton might want to do that. 'Not sure I'm going to be able to help you if he does.'

'Don't worry, Henry, we'll cover yours if it comes to that. And Roo's,' said Grace.

Jane saw her smile across the table and experienced another one of her glimmer moments. Things might not have been thawing much outside the window but maybe they were a little in Grace's heart.

Roo hadn't twigged what they were talking about. She was too busy loading her fork with sprouts and turkey.

Vincent picked up his cracker and brandished it at Grace. 'Come on, Gracie, let's kick it off.'

The cracker was so stiff they had to tussle but eventually it cracked and a folded hat, a motto and a present fell out on Vincent's side – much to his delight.

'The red fish,' he exclaimed, ripping into the small package. He placed it on his flat palm and waited. It didn't take long for it to react to the moisture on his hand.

'That's not a fish, it's Olga Korbut.' Frank hooted, watching it curl up on itself.

Vincent picked up the accompanying paper insert with the explanatory key written on it.

'Apparently that means I'm passionate.'

'Ooh, there's going to be some lucky girl one day,' said Roo, giving Elizabeth a cheeky glance.

'Here's the joke,' Vincent read. '*Arthur, spell weather, said the teacher. W-E-I-A-T-H-A-R, replied young Arthur. You may sit down, said the teacher. I have to say, Arthur, that's the worst spell of weather since last Christmas.*'

Groans ensued.

'If you think that's bad, just wait until the talent contest later,' said Vincent.

'Come on, Frank,' said Tim, holding his cracker up to him. Tim won the tug of war: a small metal plane landed on the table.

'You'll be on one of those soon,' said Roo.

'I will.' Tim put it in his pocket so he wouldn't lose it.

Roo's contained a painted metal lion, complete with full, dark mane.

'*What do lions sing at Christmas? Jungle bells.* That's the worst joke on the planet.'

'Trust me, it really isn't,' said Vincent. 'That lion is straight out of the *Wizard of Oz* and it's a sign you need courage, even though you're full of it already.'

Roo was touched by that. 'Aw, thank you, Vincent.'

'I tell you what else you're full of.'

'Vincent.' Jane wagged an admonishing finger at him, but her eyes were twinkling.

'You all right, gel?' Frank called across to Roo and winked.

'I am.' Roo nodded, and she was too. She was warm in the lap of luxury, surrounded by wonderful company with a fantastic sprout-heavy dinner in front of her. She was drinking best champagne with cherries sat in the bottom of her glass and a very beautiful Narnia-like view framed in the windows. She could be a lot worse off. And next time she wouldn't fall in love with someone with a surname that was incompatible with Ruby.

Elizabeth's cracker contained the ancient and rubbish joke about the difference between a snowman and a snow-woman. 'SNOWBALLS,' everyone shouted; and a cute silver whistle that worked, because she tried it.

Then Vincent said, sounding very serious and in a strange accent, 'You don't have to act with me. You don't have to say anything and you don't have to do anything. Not a thing. Oh, maybe just whistle. You know how to whistle, don't you, Steve?'

'Steve who?' asked Roo, totally confused.

But Elizabeth got it.

'Roo, it's one of the most famous scenes from a film ever,' explained Vincent. 'I used to watch the old films with my mum and dad. I picked up all the quotes. Lauren Bacall and Humphrey Bogart.'

'Which one was that supposed to be then? Don't think Rory Bremner has much to worry about.'

'Somebody down that end give her a slap for me. I don't want to soil my hands,' said Vince, making Roo laugh.

Frank had a small silver steam-train engine in his cracker. He'd keep that, as a souvenir, but would he remember this Christmas with tears or smiles, he wondered. Jane, remark-ably, got a beautiful enamel orange with a loop at the top for a chain; it reminded her of the Christingle. Henry got a four-leaf shamrock encased in a glass oval. For luck. It made him smile because he had Irish blood running through his veins – and they were a very superstitious lot. Grace was last to pull. Her novelty was a miniature nutcracker soldier with a moveable jaw. In his red jacket, tall black hat and boots he looked very much like the two very large ones that stood sentry by the doors in the lounge.

Frank watched her studying it in the palm of her hand.

It was more nutcracker than soldier but he wondered if she would think it was another instance of the fates torment- ing her, or if she'd remember instead 'Sergeant Nutty', the wooden Christmas hearth decoration they'd had when Billy was small and he'd laughed until he couldn't get his breath at the 'Nutty and Mummy' show. All Frank's memories of his son were happy ones; Grace's, however, circled the moment of his death on a continuous loop.

Vincent got up from the table to turn on the radio.

'He'll be having his dinner, Vince, leave him be,' Roo called down.

'Yeah, but he'll have left his gentle sounds of yesteryear playing for his loyal listeners, won't he, so shut up, you, and eat your sprouts.'

Sure enough, Brian had made sure his loyal listeners would be suitably entertained in his absence. Judy Garland was singing 'Have Yourself a Merry Little Christmas'.

'I've always loved the words to this song,' Jane mused. 'Especially about being together through the years, if the fates allow. I must confess I was dreading this Christmas.'

'The first one without Clifford,' Grace said it for her.

A beat before she answered. 'Yes.' As if she had considered saying something else instead.

'It's just a shame that you won't be with your stepson and you've got us instead,' said Tim.

'Trust me, I would much rather be here.' Those two brandy eggnogs and champagne bubbles had gone straight to her tongue.

'Oh blimey, Jane. He must be bad if that's the case,' said Vincent, with a cheeky chortle.

'Is he, Jane?' asked Roo, when Jane didn't counter him.

'Michael isn't anything like his father, I'm afraid. His

mother ruined him, used him as a weapon when the marriage ended. Clifford didn't see him for many years, not for the want of trying. He had to wait until the boy was an adult and by then the damage was done. Clifford was denied being a positive influence on him. They did build bridges, but . . . I never quite trusted him. There was always something wily and manipulative about him. He was very good at wrapping his father around his finger, playing the guilt card about him not being around to wheedle "overdue compensation" out of him . . .' Then Jane realised what she was saying and apologised. Someone must have slipped some WD40 in her eggnog as well as the cognac.

'Forgive me, I'm ruining lunch.'

Henry pressed on her shoulder, a gesture of comfort.

'If anyone has any better stories, let's hear them now.'

'Nope, I'm already invested, Jane, I want to hear more about Michael the arsehole,' said Roo through a mouthful of stuffing. She was beyond intrigued. She'd had the son down as a junior Clifford, someone caring, who had stepped up to the plate to look after his stepmother in her twilight years, so Jane's revelations were unexpected.

'I wouldn't know where to start. In my defence, I was grieving . . . at a very low ebb when I agreed to . . . Oh lord, what have I done?' Jane's cutlery clattered to her plate and her hands came up to her head. She looked so genuinely distressed that everyone stopped eating.

'Now, come on, love, you're among friends here,' said Frank. 'What have you done? Then we can help sort it out for you.' His tone was so warm and kind which was, as Grace knew, his default.

They weren't going to turn off the spotlight so Jane started to talk, though cursing herself for her wayward mouth.

'The Rectory, where we lived, was always going to be too large for me by myself. I was expected to sell it, buy something small and give Michael his share of the proceeds. One day he will have it anyway, he has always made sure I know that the money I have is because of his father ...'

'Whoa ... back that truck up,' said Vincent. 'Surely you were a partnership?'

'Well, yes, that's ... right ... I know this, but he had considerably more money than I when we got together. In saying that, Michael's had quite a lot from us. We lent him the deposit for his house and we didn't get it back, but in the end Clifford said he could keep it rather than it cause any upset. Then his business went under and we helped with the debts ... he would have lost his home otherwise. It's far too big for him and his wife really ...'

Frank raised his eyebrows. 'Sounds like he's had quite a bunce already.'

'Yes, he has. We never argued, Clifford and I, but we came close over Michael and his ... ventures. His father propped them up, every time with hope in his heart that they wouldn't fail, but they always did. He has about as much acumen for business as I have for industrial welding.'

Henry gave her a gentle nudge. 'I could actually see you as a welder, Jane. I reckon there's not much you couldn't do if you put your mind to it.'

'Well, thank you, Henry, but even I have my limitations,' said Jane, smiling, grateful that they were being kind to her.

'So, if he's such an entitled knob, how come you were spending Christmas with him? I mean, he's not even blood, is he really?' asked Roo.

'Because I haven't been thinking straight, Roo,' Jane

replied. 'I've felt old and vulnerable without Clifford. And a little frightened. Michael's been making me think too much about the future, about what I have to come . . .'

'Sounds to me like he's been working on you,' said Tim. He was already building up a picture of this Michael and he wasn't liking what he was hearing.

'He suggested he turn the spare rooms he has into a flat and persuaded me that I should move in there with them. So I'll be paying for it to be renovated with some of the monies from the house sale. Like he said, I don't really have many friends left in that area. Some have moved in with their children, some have . . . gone and so when Michael said that I'd be safe living in the house with them because old people living alone are sitting targets for burglars and . . . worse, it seemed like a sensible option. I'd have my own independence. I'm to rent the flat from—'

Elizabeth bounced in now.

'Hang on. So you're going to pay for the renovations and then he's going to charge you rent, have I got that right?'

'Yes, Elizabeth.'

'Have you settled on a figure?'

'Well, not yet . . . he's been rather . . . evasive about it.'

'I'll bet,' humphed Roo. 'He's put the fear of god into you about getting murdered if you don't go and live with him. He's going to suck a load of dosh out of you and then slap you with a massive rent and you're going to be trapped with them, aren't you, because you'll not have enough left to buy a place if you did change your mind. If you ask me, he's only invited you over for Christmas to make sure he can terrify you a bit more so you stump up. The snakey cock.'

'Don't hold back, Roo, say what you think,' said Tim

with some amusement. She really was like his Fleur, no-nonsense, open-hearted, principled. Although Fleur was somewhat lighter on the expletives.

'As he says, though, it's going to be his money one day anyway. And how long have I got left? At least I'd be supervised. I—' Jane growled at herself. 'I should never have drunk all those bloody eggs.'

'Well, I'm glad you did,' said Henry. 'My dear Jane, I've known some crooks in my time but I think your stepson ranks quite highly among the worst of them. That money was left to you by your darling Clifford and therefore is yours to do with as *you* like.'

'I can't do what I'd like to do with it though. It's too late.'

'Which is what?' asked Elizabeth, pretty sure that this Michael had attended the same school of coercive control as others she could mention.

'You'll think I'm a silly old woman.'

'We'll think you're a silly old woman if you go and live with someone who's waiting impatiently for you to kick the bucket,' said Tim, pretty sure he was speaking for them all.

'Clifford and I always wanted to do more travelling when he finally downed tools, but he was a victim of his own success and I didn't mind, he loved his second-wind career. But originally, we were going to sell the Rectory, get on a ship and go around the world and then get on another, or a plane or a . . . a train – ha.'

'What's stopping you doing that by yourself?' asked Roo.

Jane dry-chuckled at the thought. 'I'm not brave enough.'

'You, after all you've survived?' said Grace.

'I always wanted to see the Taj Mahal but I won't go now, of course. It's a monument to eternal love and I don't want to be there without him. I'd end up looking rather sad like Princess Diana did, all alone.'

'Cruising is a nice safe way to travel.'

'I'm eighty-one,' said Jane.

'So your travel insurance will be a bit hefty but sounds like you can afford it,' Frank put in.

Roo, on an impulse, picked up the Christingle in front of her, blew out the candle and proceeded to squash it in her hand. The skin burst and the juice shot out onto her sprouts and down her arm.

'This is your life, Jane, and you need to squeeze all the juice out of it that you can and keep squeezing because you haven't exhausted your supply yet. You are way too young for a rocking chair and a crochet hook.'

She sounded wise beyond her years. Jane's eyes framed the orange in Roo's hand. *Was she right?* Then, feeling the intense heat from all this attention, she clicked out of the moment, picked up her cutlery.

'Please, everyone, eat,' she said. 'It's all too wonderful to go cold.'

They obeyed her but didn't stop talking.

'So, in an ideal world, where would you fancy going to most?' Grace asked Jane.

'I'd like to go back to Antarctica, that was a big one on our list because it was breathtaking. But I'm also very fond of Europe. I think I know Venice more than many of the locals and it's a place that is impossible to tire of. There's a world cruise starting in February, leaving from Southampton docks. A hundred wonderful days. They still have available cabins, I tortured myself and looked. I sometimes imagine that I'm about to do what we planned: sell up and be free.' She sighed. 'I've more or less emptied the Rectory now.

Apart from essentials and Clifford's books; those will be the hardest of all to let go of and I'm not quite ready for it yet.'

'You want to give those to Elizabeth,' said Vincent, through a mouthful of parsnip. 'She wants to set up a second-hand bookshop.'

'Oh, Vincent, it won't happ—'

Jane cut off her protest. 'What a lovely idea, Elizabeth. You must tell me more about that before we get off the train.'

'So, here's the big question, Jane,' began Frank, 'do you really want to go to Lancaster when we start moving? Pretend you're in court, I want to hear yes or no only.'

Jane took a breath, then answered. 'No.'

'Would you like to get on that ship in February?'

'I can't—'

'Yes or no.' Frank was firm.

'Yes.'

'If you didn't go to Lancaster, would you have somewhere else to stay when your house sale finally goes through?'

'I . . . No.'

'Well, I've got an inn and if you want to stay with us until the ship leaves, you are very welcome, Jane. You can get one of them cruise buses to take you to Southampton. I know for a fact they leave from Norwich.'

'We won't ask you to renovate it before you move in either,' said Grace, smiling at her and then glancing at Frank. He saw a flash of the old Grace there, the one with mischief in her eyes – he hadn't seen her for a long time.

'I don't know what to say,' said Jane, absolutely floored by their show of generosity.

'Well, you think about it,' said Frank. 'But if you don't say yes, you're in big trouble.'

Jane burst into a flurry of tears, a short shower of them then recovered just as fast. 'I feel as if a great huge boulder has moved from here.' She pressed her stomach.

'Happy Christmas, Jane,' said Frank, holding up his glass. 'And *bon voyage* when it comes.'

Chapter 35

'Hello, everyone,' said Brian from the radio, just as the blue brandy flames had died on the most enormous Christmas pudding. In the absence of a microwave, Frank had had to steam it for hours. It was the most beautiful pudding he'd ever seen, half-moon slices of oranges, and almonds and bright red cherries on the top bathing in a rich glaze.

'. . . I just thought I'd bob on to see how you're all doing.'

'We're all fine, Brian. And we hope you're having a lovely Christmas,' said Roo, raising her twice-refilled glass to him.

'I've got my new socks on and my new slippers and to-night I'm going to be wearing my new pyjamas. Cath will be wearing her new dressing gown so we are going to look a right pair of bobby dazzlers.'

'Oh, bless him.' Elizabeth smiled at the radio. 'What a sweetheart.'

'We're all snug and are going to watch *A Christmas Carol*. I see that *Cinderella* is on the TV on Boxing Day and I wish it were today. I enjoy Scrooge, but I do like a love story and I'm proud to say that.'

'Good on you, Brian,' said Elizabeth, also slightly squiffy now.

'Anyway, the reason I've come upstairs is to tell you that the temperature is going to rise considerably over the next twenty-four hours. You'll have no doubt seen the start of the thaw this afternoon, but for anyone who is away from home because of the weather, well, you're going to be reunited with your loved ones very shortly. I wanted to bring you the good news. Now I'm off to have a mince pie so I'll see you all tomorrow. I'll leave you with some more wonderful tunes of yesteryear. This one is dedicated to my Cath and it's called "I've Got My Love to Keep Me Warm".'

There should have been a whoop of joy that the thaw was finally happening, though the snow was still thick on the branches of that nearby tree, but strangely, there wasn't.

After the pudding there was cheese. No one had much room for it but, by the magic of Christmas, they found some for the excellent fresh selection that a cheese-loving chef had collated for the Ingleton party. Cheeses with names like no other: Old Cardinal, Auchenshuggle Blue, Shepherd's Warning, Christmas Truffle, Old Pennine, Ten Bells. And it was obligatory to have a little of the train owner's exceptional aged port to wash it down. Though, just a little one because, as Roo reminded them, there was the talent contest to get through.

'Any more alcohol and I'll be telling you all my PINs and passwords,' said Jane, going in for another cheeky sip. Mr Ingleton's food and drinks people really knew their onions.

'I am more stuffed than I have ever been in my whole life,' said Roo, before apologising for the burp that escaped.

'I can't move,' said Vincent, with the smile of a man in a

state of bliss. 'But I'm going to have to.' He forced himself to his feet. 'This lot won't shift itself.' He held up a flat palm at Frank. 'Don't you dare, you've done more than your fair share and you ain't lifting another finger for the foreseeable.'

'Well, I'll go and sort out the fire,' said Frank. 'Grace, would you come with me?'

While everyone else cleared the table, Frank walked off with Grace. She knew he didn't need any help with the fire so she wondered what he might want her for.

'Sit down, please,' he said, when they were in the lounge. He felt more nervous than when he'd brought a ring box out of his pocket to ask her how she'd feel about being Mrs O'Carroll. He'd only got as far as the 'Mrs' when she dived on him, knocked the ring out of his hand and their big moment was spent hunting around in the shallows of a river for it.

'That was nice what you said to Jane, about her staying with us, Frank.'

Nice maybe, but he hadn't thought it through, though; he'd realised that as soon as the invitation left his mouth. Speaking for them as a couple when he wasn't sure how much longer that would be the case.

Frank wrinkled up his nose, cringing. 'I should have run it past you first.'

'I absolutely don't mind. It was the right thing to say. Kind.'

He hadn't brought her here to talk about Jane though.

'I bought you something for Christmas,' he said.

'I thought we weren't . . .' she said. 'You insisted.'

He waved that away. 'It's just a little thing.'

He'd told her they weren't doing presents because he felt, over the past couple of years, she'd just bought him

anything for Christmases, birthdays, for the sake of something to wrap up. It was another nail in the coffin of their
marriage when he'd said it to her this year, to spare her the
obligation.

She sat on the sofa when he handed over the small square
box. She cracked it open to reveal a gold locket with her
initial scrolled on the front. It was beautiful and it wasn't
'just a little thing'.

She lifted it out.

'Open it,' he urged her.

She used her fingernail on the clasp and when she saw
what was inside, her breath caught in her throat. On the
right was a familiar photo of Billy, her baby, his blonde hair
lit by sunshine. On the left, Billy again, his face scrunched
up in laughter, his eyes bright and shiny. It confused her.

'Where did you get this picture of him? I haven't seen this
before.' She tapped it gently.

'It's not him, Grace. It's his daughter.' He coughed away
the dryness in his throat. 'You wanted to see a photograph,
well . . .'

He wasn't going to give it to her but after what she said
earlier, he put it in his pocket to keep there or offer up if the
moment presented itself.

He saw Grace's eyes travel from one side to the other.

'They're so alike.'

'Yes, they are.'

'She's beautiful.'

'She's gorgeous,' he said, gently.

Grace closed the locket and replaced it in its box. He half-
expected her to hand it back.

'Thank you. I'll put it in my room. I'm sorry I didn't get
you anything, Frank.'

'It's all right.'

She stood up. A flicker of a smile twitched her lips, then she walked away from him in the direction of her cabin.

Chapter 36

'Where the hell is Tim?' said Roo with not a little impatience. They were all gathered in the lounge, ready for the talent competition. Tim had told them he wouldn't be long and he'd been ages.

Vincent was just about to go and hunt him down when they heard the crash of a door as if an elephant was barging through the train.

'I think he's on his way,' said Elizabeth, cupping her hand around her ear.

'HO HO HO.'

Tim burst into the carriage in full Santa regalia, carrying a black sack over his shoulder. He looked enormous, taller, wider as if he had swelled into his costume, which was perfect, from the big stompy fur-trimmed boots to the heavy black belt with the polished brass buckle, to the tip-tilted hat with the pom-pom.

'My goodness, Tim, you really are him.' Jane's jaw dropped. She'd taken the children to see a lovely Santa once in a nearby mansion with flush-red cheeks and a thick white beard that he'd encouraged the boys to pull. He bellowed with laughter at their surprised faces when they did and found it attached. But Tim made even him pale into insignificance. He looked more real than the real deal.

'Right, Santa, park your red bum please and we will begin,' said Roo, stealing another look at him. The sight, or even the mention, of Santa usually stirred all sorts of sad things up inside her but here, now, he was part of the bonkers context, an integral part of their group, and she smiled at him. It must have been lovely for Fleur to have such a daddy. You didn't have to see someone every day for them to know they loved you. She hoped she'd got that across to him.

Roo clicked into duty mode, consulted the pad in her hand with her notes on it and opened her arms wide to signify the show was about to start.

'I bid you welcome to the *Yorkshire Belle* grand talent show.' Everyone clapped. 'I have a carefully chosen running order. So first, I think we should kick off with a bang. Ladies and gentlemen, I give you Santa Tim.'

Another round of applause. Tim got to his feet and reached in his black sack, pulling out his own notepad.

'I'm glad you put me first, Roo, because not only would I like to set a most excellent standard but also I'll round things off at the end if no one minds with another slot because, you see, I have so many talents I didn't know which one to pick. Anyway, moving swiftly on . . .'

He took a pair of half-moon gold spectacles from his pocket and popped them on before opening his book.

'A History of Bells by Tim Grant. I found a very fascinating book in the library on board and I thought I'd share what I learned, starting with the fact that all the carriages on this train are named after bells. So from the back of the train:

Maria Gloriosa, cast in 1497, is considered the most beautiful bell in Europe. A huge bell it is too, standing two metres tall. Or, to put it in perspective, the height of four Roos.'

'Oh, very funny, Santa,' said Roo, though she liked this playful jolly Tim and she was rather proud she'd helped to winkle him out of his unhappy shell.

'Then we come to the Lutine bell which hangs in an insurance institution in London as a symbol of their honourable business practices.'

'Insurance and honourable in the same sentence?' Frank bellowed but he was rightly shushed by the others.

'"Old Tom" is not named after Mr Ingleton's cat as some thought,' Tim continued. 'It was the forerunner to Big Ben in Westminster. And I'm sure we've all heard of the Liberty Bell, which is the symbol of American independence. It was made by a British firm, shipped over but it cracked when it was first rung.'

'Like Vince then, he's a cracked bell.' Roo grinned and Vincent narrowed his eyes at her.

'I'll come back to "Uglich", because I want to leave on a high,' said Tim then, slightly worried his bell info wasn't as fascinating to the others as he'd found it to be. He'd edited his speech down substantially, too, as the stories behind the bells were so interesting, if somewhat heavy on detail. '"Sigismund". Named after the king of Poland, and at thirteen tonnes needs twelve bell-ringers to swing it. Or two Franks.'

Frank crunched up his arms to show off his biceps.

'The Mingun bell, at ninety tonnes, was once the biggest bell in the world. And it doesn't have a clapper but is struck. And you'll find it in what used to be Burma. The Yongle bell is now in a bell museum in Beijing but it was cast in the Ming dynasty and named after the emperor Yongle, the ruler who built the Forbidden City.'

'Yongle is right up there with Ewerin as a name,' said Vincent to Roo. 'Ruby Yongle also sounds like something you'd go to the docs with.'

'I hate to tell you all that the name is correctly pronounced *Yong-luh*. It doesn't rhyme with dongle,' said Jane with a chortle.

'Bugger, that's knackered my joke then. Anyway, carry on, Tim.'

'Pummerin is in Vienna. The great Dhammazedi was believed to be the biggest bell ever cast, weighing as heavy as twenty-five double decker buses. It was stolen to melt down and make cannons, put on a raft across a Burmese river ... and I bet you can't guess what happened next.'

Tim waited, Vincent delivered. 'They dropped a clanger?'

'Oh, very good, Vince.' Frank gave him a round of applause for that.

'I want to hear about "Uglich",' said Grace.

Tim grinned. He wanted to tell them about it, though they'd think he'd been at the cooking sherry.

'Let me take you all back to sixteenth-century Russia. Ivan the Terrible dies, leaving behind two sons, neither of which are suitable to rule in Daddy's footsteps. One liked praying and the other was only three. So Ivan was forced to appoint a man called Boris Godunov as regent to the older son and the baby and his mother were exiled to ... Uglich. When the boy was eight, he was found dead with his throat slit. Was there skullduggery afoot?' Tim was relishing telling this; he'd been excited about this part of his speech, knowing it would wake them all up if he'd sent them into a coma. 'The boy's supporters rallied and summoned an uprising by ringing ... the great bell of Uglich. Godunov squashed it but he was furious ... at the bell.

'Now, bells, in the Russian Orthodox faith, were believed to have souls. And since only the living can have souls, a bell was considered human. They thought of them as prominent members of society. They gave them human names. So Godunov decided to punish the bell for having the nerve to call rebels to arms. He had it dragged into the city square where a blacksmith ripped out its tongue – by which I mean the clapper. He had the ears cut off – the part on the top where the bell was hung from – and then he had it flogged.' He added with relish: 'To death.'

'No way,' said Vincent.

'Yes way. Then he exiled it to Siberia. All the rioters who hadn't been executed had to carry it there, fourteen hundred miles – it took them a year. Three hundred years later the bell was pardoned and it was brought home, where you'll find it today.'

Jane turned to Henry. 'If even bells can be pardoned, then that must bring you hope.'

'Why are trains sometimes called 'belle' then, like this one, Tim?' asked Grace. '*Northern Belle*, *Brighton Belle*, *Bournemouth Belle*. I mean, I know it's spelt differently, but is there a connection?'

'Because it comes from the notion they are beautiful, classy. But the word serves a double purpose because we associate the sound of bells with trains, different spelling of course but same pronunciation. The old steam locomotives relied heavily on bells as signals. Part of their code system, if you like. Trains and bells, a beautiful partnership. And that concludes my lecture.' And he bowed and they gave him a hearty clap.

'Tim, that was brilliant,' said Roo, taking his place in front to do her compere bit. 'You've set the bar high, but I'm sure our next contestant will limbo under it very well to a great depth. Everyone – I give you ... Vincent.'

Vincent stood up with a piece of paper shivering in his hand, telling of his nerves.

'Right, be kind,' he said, 'I love a good joke me and so I thought that I would treat you to some jokes what I've made up. So ... Christmas jokes, by Vincent Diamond. Feel free to chuck tomatoes if you so wish but preferably ones that come attached to the top of a pizza.' He read out the first one.

'What do you call five snowwomen who form a pop group?'

He looked up to see if anyone could guess. No one could.

'The Ice Girls.'

He was rewarded with laughing groans.

'What happened to Santa when he was naughty at school? He got candy-caned.'

More groans.

'I started off with my best ones,' Vincent said, mock-affronted.

He certainly did that. But he made everyone chuckle and he went back to his seat with applause that was every bit as warm as the response to Tim's act.

'Thank you, Vincent,' said Roo, taking her place in front of them all at the end. 'Now it's my turn. I thought I'd give you all an example of my poetical leanings and you can judge for yourself if I should be on a stage. So, I have written about what a pensioner might want for Christmas. Jane, please do not hate me.' She cleared her throat and began.

'The things I want for Christmas
Have changed with every year
I used to want some jewellery
Posh shoes, designer gear

But as I've aged the things I wanted most
I don't no more
I'm not interested in Jimmy Choos
Chanel, La Croix, Dior

All I want for Christmas is my two front teeth
Once that would have made me content
Now I need a full set of the bleeders
With extra Fixodent

Santa, take my crows' feet
Whip away my wrinkles please
Let me wake up with a navel
That isn't level with my knees

Can you take some of this cellulite
And turn it back to muscle
Can you make my joints go fluid
So I glide like Darcey Bussell

Can you plump my cheeks again
So they aren't flat and flaccid
Can you sort out my digestion
Stop me burping up that acid

Can you rip away my muffin top
And make my boobs all perky

And tighten up this flappy neck
Stop me looking like a turkey

Can I have a bowel movement
That comes straight out the gate
One of those that feels
As if I've halved my body weight

So Santa, if you're listening
I hope we are agreed
My list for you is crystal clear
These are the things I need

I'll leave you out some proper grub
As wage for you conforming
The best on Marks and Spencer's shelves
. . . But here's my solemn warning

If you bring me cheapo chocolates
Or a bottle of mulled wine
A mug, a throw, a calendar
Or owt that smells of pine

Bubble bath or hand cream
A jam and spoon gift set
Bedsocks or a photo frame
Or something flannelette

Or a rough and scratchy scarf
In all colours of the spectrum
I'll chase you up that chimney
And I'll stick them up your rectum . . .

'. . . I thank you.'

Jane led the applause. She was wiping the tears from her eyes as she did so.

'Bravo, Roo, that was wonderful. How insightful you are. I must have a copy of that.'

'You absolutely should be on a stage, love,' said Vincent. Roo waited for a jokey piece of sarcasm to follow but there was none. Roo beamed at the response she'd received. They all seemed to genuinely enjoy it and Jane definitely wasn't faking those tears of mirth.

'Next up we have our wonderful chef, Frank,' she said.

Frank got to his feet. It was a long time since he'd done this and he tried not to let when that was bleed into his mind.

'Welcome to the magical world of El Franko,' he said, and took from his pocket a packet of cards he'd borrowed from the on-board games cupboard in 'Old Tom'. He shuffled them and asked Jane to pick a card and show it to everyone but him, then he put it back in the deck, averting his eyes. He shuffled them again and picked out a card, announcing that was hers. It wasn't, and she felt a tad awkward saying so. He looked confused, put his hand in his pocket to pull out a hankie with which he proceeded to wipe his brow but a card fell out of it. Jane's card. None of them had a clue how he'd done it and there were impressed gasps aplenty. Then he displayed his empty hand and waved it past Elizabeth's ear and seemingly produced a coin from it.

Grace remembered Frank pulling coins from Billy's ear, his squeals of delight mainly because he ended up with them all and thought they were in limitless supply. When the ice-cream van came, Frank would say that if Billy had a coin in his ear, he could use it to buy a cornet – and there always was one. There was a lot of laughter in their little family of three. She'd grown up in a joyless household and was determined that it would be different for any child of hers. Billy had the best childhood, he was happy and loved and treasured. Father and son were joined at the hip when he was little; Frank was never too busy to read him a story or play games with him or do the 'which cup is the ball under?' trick that he was performing now, and thrilling them all with his sleight of hand. He was the same Frank now that he had been back then, though his sadness showed in the lines on his face and the volume of his smile never quite hit the levels it once did.

Jane was up next and worried that her contribution might be pale compared to the rest.

'Many years ago I realised that most of my life seemed to be regretting the past and worrying about the future and I was ripe for discovering a coping mechanism to deal with those anxieties. And so I forced myself to attune to the present, relish the here and the now as it happens and I find it has helped me so much in life. Especially when I encountered heightened moments which I used to liken to *bubbles* because that's what they felt like to me, little bubbles popping and releasing a fleeting hit of intense joy. Then I read about someone relating the same thing and calling them 'glimmers', which is a perfect word for them. Don't miss them, they're special. Remember yesterday when we were all sitting around the table with our Christingles, did you feel that flash of connectedness, that sublime *synergy*, because I did?'

Jane noticed the reaction to that in the faces of her audience and she knew they had too.

'Or that "mmm" moment when we walked onto this part

of the train out of the snow and sat in the bar? Or when we first put on the white robes and felt the material snuggled against our skin. I savour these bubbles, these glimmers. The more open you become to them visiting you, the more of them you will experience. A mere microsecond of bliss, and yet, once acknowledged, their effect upon you will last much longer. They are reminders that whatever we are going through in life, there is always light to be found. I promise you, they will change your mindset so when one shows up, allow yourself to respond to it, let it ground you, calm you, hold you in the wonder of it .' Her eyes swept over the seven people in front of her, lingering a moment longer on Grace. 'I stand here before you as someone who is testament to their healing power.' Jane smiled. 'You can thank me later.'

Their applause was rapturous because Jane had been fascinating and they all felt as if they had taken on board something extraordinary. If they could have seen into each other's heads, they would have discovered they were all thinking of such a moment they would consider a glimmer. Frank found one almost immediately when Grace stood up to take her turn – and he saw she was wearing her locket.

He had thought he knew what her act would be because she had brought a towel into the lounge with her. She was very accomplished at folding them into different shapes to put on the guest beds in the inn. But she left it on the arm of her chair, said 'Excuse me', dashed off and then came back with one of the two large nutcracker soldiers that stood at either side of the bottom door.

Grace dragged a chair over and sat on it, with the soldier standing at her knee.

'Sorry about that, I changed my mind at the last minute,' she said. 'I'd like you all to meet Sergeant Nutty.'

And Frank felt a glimmer that was the size of a weather balloon pop inside him.

She'd remembered a lot of that old routine, even after all those years. It was no surprise, given how many times she'd done it because Billy wanted the dear familiarity, dissolving early into giggles, anticipating her lines to come. Grace made Sergeant Nutty 'talk', working his jaw with the lever at the back. She was still good at doing the alphabet without hardly moving her mouth and deflecting attention when she had to tackle the difficult 'b's and 'p's.

Someone's squeal of laughter – she couldn't work out whose but most likely Roo's – reminded Grace of Billy's in those early Christmases. He was so young, so very young, wrapped in the protection of her wings, she always thought she could protect him, would give her life for him if she had to. It was as she carried the soldier back to his post that she realised she'd blamed Frank for something that was her fault all along. It was because of Sergeant Nutty that Billy started playing soldiers, wanting to dress up in a uniform. She'd been the one who planted the seed in him, not Frank.

Chapter 37

Elizabeth was next up to the pretend stage.

'This is a song that I last performed ten years ago in a student bar. It's a folk song,' she said with a nervous smile. She'd written the words down on some paper from memory but she doubted she'd need them.

Whatever everyone was expecting it wasn't what followed. Far from being a lilting ditty about milkmaids, ploughmen or sailors coming home, it was a cheeky little number called 'The Bantam Cock'. Two worlds colliding: the bawdy and the genteel with terrific effect. A bantam cock brought in to service a farmer's hens goes on a sexual rampage, 'tupping' everything from the fantail pigeons to the lily-white columbines, a budgie and a visiting migrant swan. Then it dropped dead. Except, when the farmer came to bury it, the bantam opened up his eye and whispered that it was waiting for the circling vultures to come down so he could have a go at them as well.

Elizabeth was delighted to have brought them such jollity. It was so wonderful to let out her corsets because she had never expected to perform it again. She felt truly happy in that moment, lapping up the laughter, and she knew she was in receipt of one of Jane's glimmers, especially on seeing Vincent grinning and clapping the loudest of all.

'Well, Elizabeth,' said Roo with heavy admiration. 'I think I speak for everyone when I say, that was bloody marvellous.'

Elizabeth was beaming as she took her seat again and tried not to think that the bantam cock would stay locked inside her for ever now. The elder Penningtons didn't do anything after dinner except drink brandy, puff on cigars (both sexes) and chew on people's characters. Gaylord had once almost spontaneously combusted when Elizabeth had suggested a game of charades. He'd looked at her as if she were a smell drifting upwards from the sole of his Dunhill velvet loafer.

Henry's act needed some audience participation. He asked them all to forgive him for a performance that would not live up to the others he had seen but he was wrong. Everyone had to sing 'Jingle Bells' while he played the two spoons he pulled out of his back pocket. He was so good they sang it twice to allow him to repeat it and he finished on a wild flourish. It was a skill he had acquired in the prison kitchens, he enlightened them. If they'd had more time, he could have taught them to pick a lock or whittle wood or distil alcohol from sugar, bread, potatoes and rotten fruit.

'And now, before the conclusion of this afternoon's entertainment, I think Tim wanted to round things off with something else, is that right?' Roo said to him.

Tim bounced up from the sofa with a deep, Brian Blessed style 'Ho ho ho, that's right, little girl.' He planted himself on the porter's chair near the corner, legs akimbo and said, 'I want everyone to come up here and sit on my knee and tell me what you want most for Christmas. You don't have to say it aloud if you don't want to, but by the magic of Santa, I'll do all I can to make your best wish come true. Now young man ...' He beckoned over to Vincent, who played the game by going over to Tim and perching on his knee.

'Let me guess ... is it a book?'

'No, Santa. I'm going to say it in my head.'

Vincent closed his eyes and wished. '*Find me a nice woman to love, Santa.*' Then he opened them again. 'You get that, Santa?'

'Loud and clear, little boy, and if I can get that blue bicycle down the chimney, you'll find it under your tree. Neeext.'

'Me!' said Roo, who was a considerably lesser weight. Tim could hardly feel her.

'*I would like to find a place where I belong,*' she said inwardly.

'*I'd like my wife to come home to me,*' Frank said to himself, squeezing his eyes shut as if that would help his cause.

'*I'd like to hold my son, just one more time would do, even if it's in a dream,*' was Grace's silent request.

'*I'd like to find the sort of belief that Clifford had,*' thought Jane. Once formed, it was unbreakable and she envied that he *knew* without any doubt that something existed beyond the secular realm, despite him being the most pragmatic, rational man she could ever hope to meet.

Elizabeth sat on Santa's knee and thought that she'd reached the age of twenty-nine without ever doing that before. Did that mean she had all those years of wishes saved up in readiness? If so, she spent them all in one fell swoop.

'*I'd like to find the courage to do what I must to be happy.*' Even said only in her head, she couldn't quite cite the specifics, but if it involved upending her life, she was going to need the help of a supernatural entity such as Santa Claus.

Only Henry spoke his bid aloud. 'I'd like the life God has decided I deserve,' he said, ridiculously perched on the big man's knee. 'What about you, Tim? What would you grant yourself?'

'Me?' he replied. 'I'd like to hug my daughter as soon as I possibly can.'

'Then you have to do exactly that, Santa,' said Frank. 'And now I think we all deserve a mulled wine, if you'll excuse me. I've got it all set up ready to warm in the galley. Roo, I ain't putting any sprouts in yours, before you ask.'

'Aw, can I have some cherries instead then, please?'

'I can manage that.'

'Henry, your spoon thing was actually brilliant,' said Roo. 'I'd like you to teach me how to do that. I might include it in my act.'

'I will, if you teach me the words to that Hark! Hark song,' he responded.

'Course. The interesting thing about that old carol is that it's one of those songs that you can do CPR to, so yes, we'll cross-pollinate, because it's something worth knowing,' said Roo.

'What's that?' Henry asked, confused as to what she meant.

'CPR?' Roo pushed her hands up and down. 'Cardiac something resuscitation, I think it stands for. Vincent, lend me your body for a moment. Lie down on the sofa.'

Vincent puffed out his cheeks. 'Now there's an offer you don't get every day.'

'Shut up, Vincent,' said Roo and demonstrated lightly on his chest what she meant while singing the carol. 'You can do it with "Last Christmas" as well but I don't like that one. "Hark! Hark" is joyful and that's fitting, isn't it, seeing as it would be a source of joy bringing someone back from the dead. Even you, Vincent.'

'You don't half crack me up, Roo,' said her patient.

'The tune's simple, Henry, I'll write down the words for you. Then you can have some nice memories attached to it whenever you sing it in future. Hopefully with your mum next Christmas, drinking her eggnog in front of the fire.'

'Thank you, Roo,' said Henry. 'And I'll give you a spoon lesson in return.'

Vincent, his services dispensed with, got up from his supine position. 'Hey, Roo, I thought of someone else you aren't allowed to marry: anyone with the surname Barber.'

'Shut up, Vincent,' she said again, smiling.

Frank had just reached the galley when he heard his name being called and turned to see Grace striding after him. She'd been holding it in since she'd finished her routine with Sergeant Nutty but couldn't any more. When she reached him, he saw the tears falling down her face.

'It was me, wasn't it? I put the idea in his head,' she said.

Frank hadn't a clue what she was talking about.

'What do you mean, love?'

'Way before you made him those cowboy guns, before you bought him that army uniform, I did that thing with the nutcracker soldier. I started him thinking about soldiers and the army and—'

She couldn't continue, she just folded into her heartbreak. Frank put his arms around her, pulled her into his barrel of a chest.

'Oh, Gracie, it wasn't anyone's fault. It wasn't yours and it wasn't mine. It wasn't Sergeant Nutty and it wasn't us being sheriff and outlaw. It wasn't his army uniform or his walkie-talkies. People find what they need and Billy needed what he found. His passion had no limits but his body did, that's what let him down, not us. Not you, not me.'

He held her, his poor tortured wife and wished he could take her pain away and carry it himself to save her the burden of it because it had crushed her. He loved her so much and if this Christmas Day had taught him anything, it was that he wasn't at the end of his fight to get her back. To get *them* back as they once were.

Chapter 38

'I meant what I said, Jane, about coming to stay with us,' said Frank as he brought her and Elizabeth a mulled wine. The two ladies had moved into the bar as the lounge was too warm and they were both wilting, though the others had stayed, like the hothouse flowers they were.

'I know you did, thank you,' she replied. 'I promise I will think it over.'

'What's left for you to do in the house before it's sold?' asked Elizabeth, when Frank had gone back to the galley.

'Hardly anything. My local community have been wonderful, helping me pack up everything. What I was going to take to Michael's will now go to the charity shop. There are Clifford's books, of course. I shall rent a small storage unit because there are some things I do want to keep: photos, his papers, a writing desk he bought me, in case I ever do settle down again. I've sold all the big pieces of furniture; the new owners have bought quite a lot of it because it was chosen for the house but almost looks as if the Rectory was built around it. It wouldn't have fitted in the new flat in Lancaster which is poky . . . or bijou as Michael and Alison describe it.'

'What's your daughter-in-law like?'

'Like Michael – oily, disingenuous. They're very well suited.' She made yet another small growl of annoyance at herself. 'I can't believe I was suckered into agreeing to such a . . . a stupid move. Whatever possessed me?'

'As you say, you were at a low ebb and ripe for being manipulated,' said Elizabeth to that. 'Don't be too hard on yourself. Some people are just too good at coercion.'

Elizabeth knew that situation only too well, being in a place and wondering how you got there, and however desperate you were to get out of what felt like a 'trap', in the end it was easier and less painful to stay in it. So much easier to encourage someone else to break free than do it oneself. She envied Jane her courage.

'You're right. Michael is very good at manipulation. My husband was a savvy and emotionally intelligent man, but his son was his Achilles heel. It always sat heavy in Clifford's heart that he hadn't had the chance to influence him for the better when he was young and forming, but he was of his flesh and Clifford loved him unconditionally. I *knew* what Michael was like, I should have been prepared for his game plan, and yet I still managed to let myself be railroaded.'

'Some people can just sense vulnerability, Jane, and they home in on it with primal intuition. Have you handed him any money for the flat refurb yet?'

'No, not so far. But he keeps pressing because he says he's already paid some of the workmen. They were very expensive, apparently. I've asked to look over the bills but he just laughs and says, "Don't you trust me?" He said that his father made him swear to look after me if anything should happen to him, though I'm not sure how true that is. I've no doubt they'd have made sure I was fed and watered adequately, like a Wagyu beef cow. Or at least a much lower grade version, they wouldn't want me out-living them.' She dropped a little mirthless laugh.

'Yes, and they'll milk you of money until they get their hands on the motherlode.'

Jane pulled a sad face. 'I confess after Clifford died, I really didn't want to last much longer, so did it matter who got our money? But finding my glimmers along the path of my grief began to lift me: in the kindness of strangers who helped me box up the house, sitting in my garden in the midsummer listening to the birdsong, watching the swans who choose our riverbank to nest in, the moonflowers that finally decided to grow after years of me trying to cultivate them.' She gave her lip a chew. 'Michael and Alison will be furious when I tell them I'm not going to live there.'

'But what can they do about it?'

Jane thought about that for a moment before answering. 'Nothing, I suppose, except make a lot of noise. Michael doesn't like things not going his way. But ... I haven't actually written my new will yet so he would be very foolish to murder me, wouldn't he?' There was a twinkle in her eye as she said it. 'Thanks to the fortifying powers of such an excellent Christmas dinner, I have formulated a little plan that involves some manipulation of my own.' Then she took a sip from her mulled wine and shuddered with delight.

'Another glimmer, Jane?'

'More of an explosion. Now, Elizabeth, please tell me about this bookshop.'

Elizabeth shook her head disapprovingly and huffed.

'Vincent shouldn't have said anything. It's just an idea I

had about opening up a bookshop that's run to sell but also to give some support to people who need it in the community. I'll never open it, of course.'

'Why not?'

'Because I'd want to do it as a full-time project and I have a job. Even if I do hate it.'

'Then leave and do what you want to. As someone who spent a lot of years on the wrong track, let me tell you life is infinitely sweeter when you switch to the right one.'

'It's complicated, Jane.' She didn't want to load onto the old lady's shoulders what a tangled mess she was in, a fly wrapped up in a web. She couldn't pick and choose which elements of her life to keep and which to reject. It was all or nothing, in or out.

Jane tilted her head at her drinking companion. For just the briefest of moments she saw her younger self sitting in front of her in Elizabeth's form. She recognised her: lonely, unfulfilled, starved of kindness.

'The older you get the more you realise that we are our own saboteurs, creating obstacles in our way, and why? Because we are too afraid of the spectre of change.'

Elizabeth wondered if Jane could see into her head. Her next words intimated that she could.

'Know your worth, don't let anyone feed you crumbs when you deserve cake. And don't settle for a life without love, Elizabeth. You might think you can, but you shouldn't.' Jane leaned forward, tapped her on her knee and held her eyes with her own honey-brown ones which were bird-bright and full of wisdom.

'Now, I want to invest in your bookshop.'

Elizabeth smiled. 'Jane, that is sweet of you, but you can't possibly say you'll invest in the pipe dream of someone you

only met a couple of days ago. I might be such an ace ma-
nipulator that I cast your stepson in the shade.'

Jane laughed at that. She knew people and she would
have bet her considerable savings on that not being the case.

'I don't want my husband nor myself to have worked so
hard for all those years just to see our savings squandered
on Michael's idiotic schemes. He's too idle to make any of
them a success.'

*There she is, the Jane I know. Where have you been hiding, old
girl?* She heard Clifford in her head. And she could see him
in her mind's eye, an amused and approving smile pulling
at one corner of his lip.

'I absolutely refuse to waste another penny,' she went on.
'He's had his fair share and what is left, I want to be used
for something worthwhile. I didn't know what to do with
it until this afternoon, but I do now.'

'*You* are worthwhile, Jane,' said Elizabeth, reaching for
Jane's hand and giving it a soft, warm squeeze. 'Blow all that
money on yourself.'

'Oh, don't you worry, I won't be forgetting myself in the
equation. There's plenty to go round,' said Jane. A mutiny
was rising within her. It would be mad, wild to change her
course so dramatically. But also jolly exciting. *An adventure,*
as Clifford would have said. And no, it wasn't the alcohol
that had possessed her, but something much more potent
and life-affirming. She actually felt as sober as a judge, more
clear-thinking than she had been since last February.

'I'm going to write that will as soon as I get home. And
then I'm going to book a very long holiday. Now, tell me
about your business plan, Elizabeth. I want all the details.'

So Elizabeth did.

*

'You are very funny, Roo,' said Grace, meeting her outside the loo as Grace was coming out of it and Roo was about to go in. 'I loved your poem.'

'Aw, thank you,' said Roo, genuinely touched because she didn't think that Grace seemed like the sort of person who would have said so if she didn't mean it. 'I really enjoyed performing it. It's made me feel that maybe I ... I should go back to the drawing board. I wouldn't like to get old and have all these dreams still inside me, untried.'

Her words rang a loud bell inside Grace. And she found herself nodding.

'Of course, I might crash and burn.' Roo winced.

'Or you might fly,' said Grace.

Roo smiled. A little encouragement went a long way with her. She hadn't had much of it in her life.

'I don't want to settle for second-best. I feel as if I'm just looking at what I want through a window at the moment, wishing it were mine. I'm just existing at present and that's no good, is it?'

Is that what Billy would have thought if he'd done what I wanted him to do? Grace asked herself, though she knew the answer. He'd needed to live his life for him, not for her. And it was right that he had. He'd once told her he was in the place he should be, doing what he was born to do and she hadn't wanted to hear it. At his funeral, his commanding officer had said that Corporal Billy O'Carroll was a soldier deeper than his bones and she'd been too angry to be proud. But would she have really wanted him to live a little life like Roo was presently doing – unhappy, unfulfilled? Why was it that this flash conversation with someone she barely knew could make her see what she never had before?

'You absolutely must, Roo,' said Grace. And she surprised them both by hugging the young woman. It was the hug of approval she never delivered to her boy.

Chapter 39

Elizabeth made everyone a hot chocolate before bed and they assembled in the Lutine bar to drink it. She'd found an ornate tin with French writing on it – *Le Joli Marron Chocolat* – in the pantry when she'd been looking for Horlicks or something suitable for a night drink. In the galley she mixed the powder with milk, a hearty splash of cream and warmed it gently. It filled the whole carriage with the most beautiful nutty aroma. Vincent nearly asked her to marry him on the spot when he tasted it but he stopped himself. He could have joked like that easily with Roo, but there would have been a completely different undertone with Elizabeth.

'Tomorrow, we are going to breakfast like kings on the leftovers, because if you have never had a Boxing Day mash-up, you haven't lived,' Frank announced.

'That sounds intriguing,' Elizabeth said, not quite sure how that would taste.

'Trust me, Elizabeth, it is the *best*.' Vincent made an 'okay' sign with his fingers circled. His dad always made the Boxing Day breakfast, throwing all the remains of the

Christmas dinner into a big pan with butter then flattening it into a giant patty which he'd serve by the slice. Funny but he remembered enjoying that more than the Christmas dinner itself.

'Hello, everyone,' Brian's voice interrupted the music playing on the radio. 'Are you all having a lovely Chis . . . Christmas evening?'

'Wahay, Brian's blotto.' Tim laughed.

'I don't know whether to be happy or sad about the big thaw, do you? It's going so fast now, isn't it, as fast as it came down. I think I've even spotted some grass and it's weird, isn't it, it's like an assault on the eye, that green . . . it seems so bright.'

It was dark outside the train but there was definitely no thaw going on out there. Their benchmark guide was those inches of snow settled on the tree branch and they hadn't budged. They'd presumed Brian lived fairly nearby, but maybe not in that case.

'I just bobbed on, like the red red robin, to say that I'll see you all tomorrow, when normal service will be presumed . . . assumed . . . I mean resumed. Sorry, I've had too much port with my Wensleydale. What a wonderful cheese. If that cheese were a human being it would be the king, wouldn't it? I love the king. God bless the king.'

'God bless the king.' Everyone raised their cups to him.

Then there was a female voice in the background hard-whispering.

'Brian, you're drunk. Come downstairs.'

'All right, all right, Mrs Cosgrove. Listeners, I will leave you in the faithful hands of my gentle sounds of yesteryear. God bless you all and I'll see you tomorrow.'

'*Hark! Hark . . .*'

Roo's favourite carol started up and she began to sing it along with Henry, who was word perfect now. She'd written the lyrics down for him but it was as if he'd always known them.

'Remember, Henry,' said Vincent, doing some CPR on an invisible patient sprawled across his legs.

Henry smiled and mirrored the action.

'I think I'm going to have to turn in soon,' said Tim, still in his Santa costume. He looked colossal in it, much bigger than Tim in his normal clothes. 'Can I just say, I've had the best day with you all. I really didn't expect things to turn out like this when my engine died and I had to roll the car into Derringbury station.'

'Yes, me too,' said Jane. 'I'd like to thank you for listening to me earlier. I probably wouldn't have said anything had it not been for that eggnog.' She had a lot to thank Mr Ingleton's eggs for, plus Henry's ability to turn them into a truth drug.

'Well, I think we are all glad you did,' said Elizabeth, pleased she had been part of a gang that, hopefully, had saved Jane from a fate worse than death.

She'd had a wonderful conversation with Jane over those mulled wines, and she'd found herself joyously infected with the old lady's zest and energy. Jane had told her how much she had survived in her life, and the many knocks and dents she'd endured seemed to have forged her into steel. She hadn't arrived ready-made like that from her mother's womb. And though Elizabeth hadn't traded with stories of her own life, it was as if Jane knew when she told her that however much she might think she could settle for a life without love, she shouldn't.

Jane turned to address the couple at her side. 'Frank,

Grace, I would like to take you up on that offer, please. But I will pay my way.'

Frank said, 'Well, I'm delighted and we'll fight about that when you come to us.'

'It won't be for very long. By the time the contracts are exchanged, there will only be about three or four weeks before the cruise sets off. If I can manage to get on it, of course.'

'If it's meant to be, it's meant to be. And if you don't get on that one, you can get on another.'

'Yes.' Jane smiled. She had few doubts she would get on the ship, she *felt* that she would, which was an odd way of operating for one so grounded and not given to the airy-fairy. She was beginning to wonder if it was more than coincidence that all of them had ended up here together.

Coincidence. One of those subjects that always landed in the middle of a group of scientists, gathered at a dinner party, like a Barnes Wallis bomb.

'*Coincidences bow to the law of statistics, but people are desperate to interpret them in a way that fills them with meaning.*'

'*I have to disagree with you there, my friend. Everything is connected by invisible threads. You are familiar with the story of Jung and the golden scarab beetle?*'

'*Yes, of course I am, Clifford, but—*'

'*A "coincidence" that defies any notion of chance occurrence?*'

'*My dear Wutheridge, coincidences are inevitable when the common laws of chance are at play. As humans, we are inclined to seek patterns and in coincidence we find them. We focus on the connections, ignore the evidence that doesn't fit. Random luck and our compulsion to filter, that is all there is to your "phenomenon".*'

'*In 1898, a novella was written about an unsinkable ocean liner crossing the Atlantic on an April night where it hit an iceberg and sank. The name of this ship: the* Titan, *and it carried an insuffi-cient number of lifeboats to serve its crew and passengers resulting in a catastrophic loss of life. Fourteen years later, April 1912, a ship called the* Titanic . . . *you know the rest. Coincidence? I think not.'*

Both sides of the argument as strong, as fascinating, the most incisive minds of men in conflict with one another. 'Coincidence is God's way of remaining anonymous', Einstein said. Freud disregarded such nonsense: *everything could be explained* was his mantra; whereas Jung believed coincidences were a manifestation of a deeper order in the universe. Certainly, after Clifford's 'experience' he was more inclined to believe in the magic of them. *'Accept the mystery, Jane,'* he'd say. *'I am a happier man for doing so.'*

Was he right? Could it be they were all brought here for a reason? Was Grace meant to hear her story to help her heal? Would Tim have defrosted without them? Was she meant to overdo the booze and tell them all about being railroaded into living in a place she didn't want to go, and be saved? Did Roo understand the impact that squashing that orange and squeezing out the juice had upon her? Was it chance she'd won an orange pendant in the cracker to reinforce that scene, if she should ever begin to doubt herself? She couldn't speak for the others, but she knew that getting on the train to Eskford had changed her life. No, more than that, it had given her back a precious future she thought had been buried in the grave with Clifford.

'You'll have to write a poem about us all, Roo,' Jane said.

'Oh, don't you worry, I will.'

'I quite like the idea of being in a poem,' said Vincent. 'Make sure you put down how 'andsome I am.'

'Vincent, I write the truth in my poetry.'

Vincent grinned.

'You written one about Mr Urine?' he asked her.

'I've written about five hundred. None of which would be fit for reciting in respectable company.' Roo smiled, mainly because she was able to make a joke about it which was a big step forward. She'd be okay, she knew she would be, give or take a little pain here and there. So now there was just the rest of her life to sort out.

'You are an insightful young lady,' said Jane. 'I laughed at so many points in that Christmas poem. I thought, how can she get into the head of someone so much older than her?'

'People don't realise how similar they are to each other, which gives you loads of material because it always surprises them when they realise it. For instance, what's the first thing that comes to mind when you think of a swan?'

'They mate for life,' said Elizabeth and Vincent together then laughing that they were in sync.

Grace went for a different fact. 'They can break your arm.'

Tim nodded. 'I would have said break your arm too.'

'Or that they all belong to the king.' Frank smiled smugly. 'Bet you didn't know that's not actually true.'

'Point made,' said Roo. 'It's either: they can break your arm, they mate for life or they're owned by the monarch – except when they're not. But people tend to think they're the only one who knows it and they're enlightening you.' Roo grinned. 'I used to watch my dad's girlfriends. They all had these common denominators. Like, for instance, they'd sit in front of the mirror plucking hairs out of their chins, swearing because they couldn't grasp the one that the tweezers couldn't find. Or they'd come in from work and as soon as they were through the door they'd fiddle about under their shirts and whip off their bras like a magician producing a bouquet, and make this groan of relief. Once you have your eyes opened to those sorts of patterns, they crop up time and again and I tap into them. A bit like Jane and her glimmers. I spot them everywhere, especially at work, how the bosses, who were probably normal once upon a time, speak management bollocks: *blue-sky thinking, having all our ducks in a row, circling back to* . . . When your job is as mind-numbing as mine, you need something to alleviate the boredom.'

'Well, you have a gift for observation and you need to utilise it.' Jane wagged her finger at Roo.

'I promise you, I'll give it my best shot, Jane.'

'Right. That's me done for the day,' said Tim, forcing himself to get up before he drifted off to sleep in the chair which was embracing him like an old friend who didn't want him to leave. 'Henry, you sure you don't want the second bed in my room? You don't know what you're missing.'

'Thank you, but I'm fine in "Maria Gloriosa", "the most beautiful bell in Europe".'

Tim's standing seemed to trigger everyone else into moving. They were all tired, but it took great effort to move as they were too comfortable. Yet the idea of an even more comfortable bed galvanised them. This could possibly be the last night they spent on board, if what Radio Brian was saying about the thaw was true. And all of them, without exception, had mixed emotions about that.

Chapter 40

'You and Roo are getting on well,' said Frank to Vincent, when they were both lying in their beds.

Vincent laughed at what Frank might be hinting at.

'I can talk to her easily because I think she's a good gel, fun, but no, there's nothing else in it.'

'He's a lucky bloke who's got Elizabeth,' Frank went on.

'Ain't he just,' said Vincent with a sigh.

Then Frank realised. 'Ah,' was all he said, but now he got it.

Jane was drifting off when Grace whispered, 'Jane, are you awake?'

'Yes,' she replied, opening her eyes, pulling herself back from the beckoning sleep.

'I just wanted to thank you.'

'For what?'

'For rattling the box in my head and making the pieces fall into a different formation,' Grace answered, because she couldn't think of how better to put it.

'Oh, Grace, I might put all my energies into the present

but I still contemplate the future and look back on my memories. Don't you think sometimes I have a good cry about what I've lost? The years don't make it hurt any less, but just less often.'

Grace fell silent but Jane could feel that she was building up to saying more. And she was right.

'Billy's girlfriend had a baby. They found out just before he died that she was pregnant. And she wrote to us after the baby was born. A little girl – she called her Billie, different spelling . . . she wanted to name her after her daddy, she said.'

'Oh, how wonderful,' said Jane. 'How—'

'I wouldn't entertain her. I didn't want to know.'

'Why?' Jane asked softly.

Grace opened her mouth to reply but wasn't sure she had an answer that could explain the fear properly.

'Were you frightened of getting attached to her and then somehow losing her too? Or was it that she'd remind you too much of your son?' *The son she could no longer hold.*

'At first I thought – and this shames me – how can she be alive and yet my son isn't, as if God had traded one for the other, which doesn't make sense, but that's how my brain was working. She's a part of him, Frank said, but not the part I want.' Out, it sounded worse than it felt inside. 'You must think I'm a terrible person.'

'I don't think that at all, Grace. I think you are trying to cope with immense grief and failing. You've managed to shut yourself in a room with it as your only companion. But there is no lock on the door and you can come out of it whenever you want to.'

'Frank's been seeing her behind my back. I was so angry when I found that out. I told him it was her or me.'

'That child could help you heal, Grace. And you could give her so many stories about her father to fill out her picture of him in years to come.'

'She looks just like he looked at four. Do . . . do you think I should see her?'

'That's up to you, Grace. But why would you want to stop Frank seeing her? I've never been a fan of ultimatums and the damage they bring.' Clifford's ex-wife was queen of the ultimatum. Jane knew only too well the misery that coercive control caused. She was only glad she'd managed to slip out of its fingers before they closed on her again.

'What have I done, Jane?'

'Undo it, Grace.' Jane decided she was too old for pussyfooting. 'If you want to know what I would do in your circumstances, then I'll tell you: I would hold fast to that lovely man and I would see Billy's daughter. Why would you choose to have nothing, when you could have it all?'

Was it really that simple? thought Grace. Did she really want to lose any more than she already had when maybe, just maybe, she had so much to gain?

'Do you like Vincent?' asked Elizabeth in the dark.

'Yes, he's great,' Roo said, the smile evident in her voice. 'And he gives top bantz.'

'I mean . . . *like*.'

'God no, don't be daft.' Roo hooted at the very idea of what Elizabeth was hinting at. 'He's big brother material, isn't he? Well, at least he is for me. What about you?'

Roo waited for Elizabeth to answer her. She had an idea what she might be about to fess up.

'Whenever we talk, I find we have so much in common, about what we want in life, and what makes us happy. They

aren't showy things like houses, money, prestige, promi-
nence, power . . .'

'He's not that type though, is he? He's a big old loyal
friendly mongrel as opposed to a Crufts champion. No airs,
no graces, what you see is what you get. I wish I could find
someone just like him, but obviously *not* him. But meeting
Vincent has made me realise that there are some top guys
out there, they're not all arseholes.'

'Yes . . .'

The air was sparking with words unsaid.

'What aren't you telling me, Elizabeth?'

'Nothing, Roo. Honestly.'

Roo didn't push it, but that claim to honesty was right up
there with Aaron Ewerin's claims that his car kept breaking
down and that's why he was so late home again from work.

Boxing Day

Christmas ain't over yet, folks!

Chapter 41

Roo was really was going to miss that little bathroom with its surfeit of wood, shiny brass, fancy glass and top quality smellies, she thought as she dried herself after what could be her last shower in it. She wished she could take the robe home, she might have been tempted to nick it if it wasn't so fluffy that it would take up a full suitcase. With her next wage, she'd decided to buy herself a nice quality one. It would give her an excuse to throw away that cheap shitty waffle one Aaron had bought her. Ooh, a thought of him that didn't bring a stab to her chest, she realised. Result. She was, as her new friends said, better off without someone who could do to her what he did. She was worth so much more.

She opened the cabin door slowly so as not to wake Elizabeth, but she was already up and dressed.

'Roo, I feel awful,' she said urgently, as if she had been waiting for her to make an appearance so she could tell her. 'I never asked you how you were feeling, about . . . your ex. You were so full of fun yesterday and yet I know you must still be hurting terribly . . .'

Roo was touched. 'Thank you. I'm okay, I think. Or

at least I will be in time. Not sure I would have been if I'd ended up on my tod in Whitby, but I'm on a train that would probably cost me a gazillion quid to stay on, with lots of lovely people, Santa Claus, a chef and an escaped convict. So I've had a bit of distraction from my thoughts.'

She and Elizabeth both snorted.

'I have plans now, things to look forward to,' said Roo. 'I'm going to move, find a better job, write material. Not sure what to do first though. It's not so easy when you've got no money, no real skills to sell so I'm just going to have to leap into the unknown and hope for the best. But it's deffo happening.'

'You're so brave,' said Elizabeth, who had money and skills to sell, but changing everything would be no less monumental for her. She couldn't guess how long she had lain in bed last night fantasising about a different life away from Reading and everyone she knew there, but to get to it she'd have to negotiate so many obstacles, the biggest being the wrath of her father and the meltdown of Gregory who was incapable of changes that weren't on his terms, so lord knows why he thought a career in politics, toeing a party line, would suit him. Where would she go? What would she do? It would be impossible to jump ship; almost too big a dream, even for her imagination.

'Did your dad leave you any money at all, Roo?'

'Not much. He had forty-three pounds and ten pence in his wallet. He hadn't paid the rent for a month, he'd can-celled his life insurance. I found an old pension fund from the short time he actually worked and the death benefit half-covered the cost of his funeral. I took out a loan for the rest. A couple of his old girlfriends contacted me wanting to help but I said no, though one of them insisted that I have the wake at her pub and she put all the food on which was kind of her. I honestly don't know what he had, my dad, but he could always get a woman. They all adored him and tried to sort him out, but it was only ever one-way traffic.'

It was one-way traffic with Gregory too, Elizabeth finally admitted the fact to herself. He didn't love her, even though he said it occasionally and she'd wanted so much to believe there was sentiment behind the words. But she didn't *feel* it. She'd tried to see it in his gifts of jewellery, or the showy gallantry when they were out in public, but she knew it wasn't really there. He'd never reached for her hand once, that would have said so much more.

She imagined that Vincent would be someone who would take his lady's hand, hold it firmly, raise it to his lips . . . She cut off that thought quickly.

Roo pulled up the blind and looked out at the whiteness. Her eyes were drawn to the solitary tree and she saw that the snow had melted off the branches.

They were last to the dining room where Frank was spooning out large potatoey clods from a frying pan onto the lovely blue and gold *Yorkshire Belle* plates. The whole carriage smelt absolutely delicious.

'Good morning,' everyone greeted them.

'Take a seat, ladies, you are just in time for the Boxing Day mash-up,' said Frank.

'I was hoping they'd stay in bed, then there'd be more for me.' Vincent rubbed his hands in expectant hope while giving the latecomers a cheeky lop-sided grin.

'I can't wait to try this,' said Elizabeth, sitting next to him on the only vacant chair, seeing as Roo had quickly claimed the one between Henry and Tim.

'Isn't Brian joining us?' asked Grace.

'Ooh yes, he must. Go and fetch the radio if you would please, Roo,' Jane asked her. 'He's still in the bar from last night.'

'How hungry are you?' Frank called after her, his big spoon poised over the pan.

'Think a cross between a starving elephant and a Tyrannosaurus Rex,' replied Roo.

'This is wonderful, thank you.' Henry plunged his fork again into his mash-up.

'Bit different to the food inside, Henry?' asked Tim.

'Oh, just a smidge.'

'You'll be out soon, I hope, and enjoying more of this.'

'My mum used to make me kippers every Sunday. I'd give anything to sit down at a table with her and have our breakfast again.' Henry smiled, but there was a sad wistfulness in his eyes. 'She hasn't been well recently, too poorly to visit us and my dread was that I'd never see her again.'

'Couldn't you get to her while you're out? Or maybe ring her? I wish the phones worked here,' asked Grace.

'Surely that's the first place they'd look for him,' said Tim.

Roo bounced in with the radio which she had already switched on. Bing Crosby was singing 'White Christmas'.

'You know who that is, Roo?' asked Tim.

Roo pulled a face as if that was the most stupid question ever.

'Course I do. Lovely song this, isn't it? I'd like to meet someone with a voice as deep as that who'd whisper nice things in my ear. And before anyone asks, no, Aaron Ewerin didn't. His was quite high-pitched for a bloke. As if someone had grabbed his gonads and was continually crushing them, which I would be doing if I had a chance.'

Grace coughed because Roo had made her chuckle as she was swallowing and sent it down the wrong way.

'Isn't that the most beautiful song?' said Brian. 'Although it has quite a sad background. The composer Irving Berlin lost his baby son on Christmas Day and because of his religion, he didn't celebrate Christmas himself but he and his wife would go and visit their son's grave on the anniversary of his passing. And many believe the melancholy in his heart was the fuel that helped him write it. It's a song that inspires all different feelings in people, isn't it?'

Under the table Frank took Grace's hand and held it, squeezed some of his strength into it. Giving always, never expecting to take.

'He's right, it always makes me a bit sad,' said Roo. 'But then, I've never really enjoyed Christmas that much, it was always too full of let-downs.'

Elizabeth didn't say 'me too', because she didn't have financially deprived Christmases but the presents she'd received weren't those that parents who truly knew their child would have chosen. She'd been given a pony one year, even though she'd had no interest in riding. But she'd loved him as a pet, got attached, and then the following year she'd walked into the stable to find him gone – sold with no advance notice. She could still get emotional about that if she thought about it too much.

'May all your Christmases be white ones is an interesting thought, isn't it?' said Brian when Bing had finished. 'I mean, we've had a lovely lot of snow in our corner of Yorkshire but I must confess I'm now glad it's going at the rate it is. I do hear that the further north you go, the fiercer the thaw. It's as if it never happened in Darlington, so I hear. I worry about flooding now . . .'

All of them looked up and through the windows of the dining car.

'Is he on a different planet to us?' asked Vincent. 'I mean, how is that a fast thaw?'

'The snow on the tree has melted, so it's definitely warming a bit,' Roo told them.

'After we've had this, I'm going out and I'm walking to that big building over there,' said Frank, nodding his head at the tall, square structure they could see. 'I'm intrigued and also I want to burn off some food. My trousers are getting tight.'

'You're too good in the kitchen, Frank. This is absolutely divine.' Elizabeth couldn't believe such simple fare could taste so good. She wished she could be somewhere next Christmas where she could have this again. *Well, you can be if you make it happen*, said a voice in her head. She'd ignored that voice too many times, even though it always spoke sense.

'I'll come with you. I'd like to stretch my legs,' replied Tim.

'If you don't mind, I would too,' said Jane. 'I'm no liability. I'm as sure-footed as a mountain goat in the right footwear.'

'I'll stay here in case the crew come back,' replied Roo, nibbling on a sprout; Frank had given her extra in her portion. 'If Brian's telling us the truth they might turn up and we don't want them driving off without us.'

But from the vista they were looking out at, that still seemed an extremely unlikely prospect.

As Roo was doing the washing-up, everyone else was getting ready to head out to the building in the fairly near

distance. There were some wellingtons in one of the cupboards in 'Pummerin' – all sizes, for Mr Ingleton's guests,
no doubt. All new, never been worn, though Jane preferred
to trust her safety to her familiar, faithful boots.

'If you're coming, Henry, I suggest you wear one of our
coats rather than the prison officer one,' Frank suggested.
'You don't want to draw undue attention if we happen to
bump into anyone.'

Jane had heard the low toll of the prison bell again the
previous day, though she hadn't said, so they were still actively sending out a signal. There was no point in making
mention of it to Henry and causing him stress though.
When the train began moving again, he would have a lot
on his plate to contend with. And not the nice things he'd
had on his plate since he had been with them.

Outside, the air was fresh but devoid of the biting bit-
terness that had been present the last time they'd been out
in it. Jane filled her lungs and felt another of her glimmer
moments because it tasted clean and pure as spring water.
She glanced over to find Vincent doing the same, savouring
it and on sensing her eyes on him, he said, 'I get it, Jane.'

'Parteeee ready,' said Frank, sergeant-major style.

'Yes, sir.' Tim saluted him and everyone laughed.

The snow was soft underfoot, the surface hadn't iced over.
It was like treading over the top of a Christmas cake.

'If you walk in our big footsteps, ladies, it might be easier
for you,' said Frank.

'I'm quite enjoying making my own,' said Jane. It reminded her of being a child in the fierce winters they
seemed to have. The seasons were much more defined than
they were now. She remembered building a snowman with
Susan and making him look like awful Mr Blenkinsop next

door. Dearest Susan who was so full of life and fun. She married someone who sucked it all from her, someone who made David Carteret look like Mr Darcy. They lost touch, as people do. She hoped she got out and had the sort of new start that she found with her dear Clifford.

'I see a church and houses and ... what's that? A pub?' said Frank, shielding his eyes from the blinding sunshine. He took his phone out of his pocket as he was walking and raised it in the air but there was still no signal. He thought there would have been with cottages there, a row of them, tiny workmens' dwellings by the look of them, old stone, prettily quaint with their snow-roof hats.

When they got to them, Vincent knocked on the first door, not really sure what he was going to say if anyone answered. But no one did. He risked censure staring through the window but it was too dark to see much and the windows had a long build-up of dirt and weather on them.

'Holiday cottages?' suggested Tim, working his way down them without finding anyone home. They went over to the church; it was a strange building, short and squat with the large square tower they'd seen from the train when the fog cleared. The tower was out of proportion to the rest of the structure, as were the double wooden doors which appeared to have been made for a church of twice its size. But the whole effect was curiously charming – as kooky as the rest of this little place, too small to even call itself a hamlet.

'Let's try over there,' said Vincent, pointing to what they could now clearly see was indeed a pub. There was a wooden sign over the three front windows but the name painted on it in what must once have been bold oxblood red was now too patchy to make out.

They had to cross a bridge to get to it, a bridge which

spanned a stream that was bloated with thaw water, probably from further up because not much was thawing around here.

The door was locked. 'There's no one in here either, surprise surprise,' said Tim, staring through each of the windows in turn. He even knocked on the glass: single pane. Blimey, he couldn't remember the last time he'd seen a commercial building without double glazing at least. The wallet in his pocket shuddered at the thought of all that heat loss.

'It says The Fog ... Figgy ... Hollow ... Inn,' said Jane, standing back to view the sign from the optimum reading distance. Squinting at it helped to fill in the missing lettering.

'Figgy Hollow,' repeated Henry: there was something about the name, about this place, but as much as he chased it around in his brain, it wouldn't be caught.

'How sweet,' said Elizabeth. 'It looks idyllic. Maybe it's just open in the summer months. It must be lovely here then.'

'Sitting by that stream having a pint outside, sharing a platter of scampi and chips,' Vince thought aloud. He imagined being there with a woman, the sun on their faces, a clean, pale ice-cold lager hitting the back of his throat, the aroma of salt and lemon and fried food in the air. He tried not to think of that woman as Elizabeth. As if she'd be the sort who ate scampi and chips with her fingers!

Elizabeth visualised herself sitting in this very spot in the summer; a table for two, a glacial white wine in a frosty glass to wash down salty crunchy chips and lemon-sodden scampi, licking her fingers because it would all taste so much better without using cutlery. She didn't imagine being here with Gregory though, but someone like Vincent, who'd eat all the small pieces and leave her the juiciest breadcrumbed nuggets. No, not someone *like* Vincent, but Vincent himself.

Grace appeared from around the back of the pub.

'There's a full log store but there's definitely no one here. And no phone signal either.'

'So we're still no wiser what's going on in the world then,' said Frank, hands coming to his hips, his stance telling of frustration.

'The walk was really nice though, I was ready for it,' said Elizabeth. 'Even if these big wellies make me look like a clown.' Even the smallest pair were too big for her.

Vincent couldn't think of anyone who looked less like a clown. She was beautiful, even more so with the sunlight on her face as if she were a flower that the sun had sought out to shine on before anything else. It was a good job there was a supposed thaw on and they'd soon be on their way because it wouldn't have taken him long to fall hook, line and sinker for a woman like her, especially spending so much time together in a relatively confined luxurious and romantic space. At least, at the *very* least, he should take from this that his ticker was still working perfectly and the right woman could easily increase its beat.

'Well, back home we go then.' Frank pointed across to the train. Its colours looked crisp and bright set against such a surfeit of white on the ground and ghost-grey sky above, as if an artist had painted it in his finest detail, leaving the background as a soft undetracting smudge.

'I'll follow you on,' said Henry.

'Me too,' added Jane. 'I'd like to take a look around here myself. I do like an old church.'

*

'You okay there, love?' asked Frank, turning to check on Grace. He crooked his arm, risking the rejection he'd had the last few times he'd done as much. *I'm fine, thank you.* But this time she took it, and he felt her close at his side, her familiar warm presence, like one of those glimmer moments Jane told them about, to be acknowledged for the bubble-burst of pleasure it brought. He slowed his pace, there was nothing to rush for, everything to savour.

Behind them, Elizabeth stumbled and Vincent's hands came out to catch her from falling if necessary.

'My feet are sliding around in these wellies,' she explained.

'Let's copy Frank and Grace.' Vincent offered his arm and Elizabeth stalled for just the slightest time before taking it because it felt like too much of an intimate gesture for what it was. It might not have been, had it been one of the others, but it wasn't – it was Vincent. She felt the hard bicep muscle underneath his coat. It shouldn't have had the effect on her that it did, it was tantamount to disloyalty, she should let go really. She loosened her grasp and her hand dropped and Vincent caught it and held it.

'What a beautiful church.' Jane stood and admired it, her head tilted so she could take in the outsized stone tower that must have stood there for hundreds of years. 'Not exactly Christopher Wren but I like it. Wonder where the name *Figgy Hollow* comes from. Can't be anything to do with fruit figs surely.'

Henry was deep in thought, still trying to find what was lost in his head, eluding all attempts to pin it down, like a savvy impish fly.

'I don't know how I know this, Jane, but I am thinking

it might just be that. I must have read it in a book in the Rose Garden library.'

'Rose Garden?'

Henry made a small noise of amusement. 'The prison. That's what someone clever renamed it. You'll never see anything less like a rose garden in your life.'

Jane wondered if some well-intentioned government official had decided to improve its reputation, make it sound less austere and daunting and more positive for the inmates' mental health. The way an accident-prone nuclear power station in Cumbria had been rebranded in an attempt to revamp its public image.

'I like history,' Henry went on, 'especially when it's about the local area, but I've read so many books over the years. Though ... something is telling me there was a monastery here centuries ago and the monks made brandy out of the figs they grew. Very successful they were at it too.' He knocked hard on his head, hoping it would help him remember. 'Come out, wherever you are.'

Jane turned a full circle while looking around.

'I suppose it's not outside the realms of possibility: shelter, plenty of water from the stream, maybe a fortunate microclimate all of its own. It happens; in Plockton in Scotland there are palm trees growing at the side of the sea. I'm guessing then that if the monks made themselves rich, they might have been battered by your namesake.'

Henry smiled and nodded. 'Good old King Hal, eh?'

'Is that a date on a lintel, Henry? I'm too short to see.'

Henry stood back, squinted. 'Sixteen forty-one.' *St Stephen*. It didn't say so but he knew it was the name of the church and it came with a flood of warmth, like a rogue summer breeze sweeping across him. 'I remember now.

The monastery was St Anthony the Blessed. Patron saint of the lost: lost things, lost people, lost faith.' He raised his eyebrows at Jane, who chuckled.

'Then I shall have to pray to him. Or maybe you can pray to him for me. He may not want to hear from a heathen.'

Henry placed his palm on the stone and closed his eyes. He didn't even know why, maybe to pull something from the fibres of the material, from the years. He saw no visions, sensed no psychic revelations, merely a sensation of peace, calm, happiness, one of those transient moments Jane was so fond of. When he opened his eyes again, Jane was beckoning him around the back.

'Look, Henry, how exquisite. Like something out of a fairytale.'

A churchyard with impressively ornate headstones and crosses, magnificent angels and baby cherubs, the chiselled letters worn away by time and the elements, but the most recent of the names and dates just about visible: *Walter Bellamy born sleeping.* At least her three babies had had as happy a life as she could have given them in the time allotted. To carry a child and never hear its cry, never taste the soft blow of its breath was a worse torture, thought Jane. Her sons had been beautiful, she wouldn't have missed having them for anything. But now, they lay under the ground, like baby Walter, a part of her heart in their graves with them.

'Time to go,' said Henry, putting his arm around her, sensing her sadness because moving as it was, tranquil as it was, it was too still and felt odd, as if they had strayed onto a different plane.

Chapter 42

Lunch was a simple buffet feast of baked potatoes, torn salad leaves, cheeses, hams, pickles, and slices of the picnic pie that hadn't been touched as yet. No doubt Mr Ingleton's staff would have factored in that his food on board would be no longer fresh enough and were busy scrabbling around trying to order more to pick up en route.

'I'm going to be the size of a house when I get home,' said Roo. Then she wrinkled up her nose. 'I say "home". Not sure that's the right word for it. It won't be a wrench to leave when I find somewhere else. At least wherever I end up can't be any worse than that damp dump.'

Frank cast a glance askance at Grace. They'd been talking as they walked from Figgy Hollow back to the train. Talking like they hadn't talked in a long time. She hadn't taken her locket off since she had put it on. And she'd asked if, when they got back, he would ask Ella if she could go with him to meet Billie. She confessed that she wasn't sure what she'd feel like when she saw her, but there was only one way to find out. Frank's heart had swelled to twice its size in his chest. Ella would of course say yes, it's what she had wanted from day one. Frank felt as if his wish made on Santa-Tim's knee was in the process of being granted. And they'd also been talking about Roo.

'You two aren't saying much,' said Roo, moving her finger between Vincent and Elizabeth. It wasn't that they weren't saying much, it was that something was unsaid, which was slightly different. She saw Elizabeth's pale skin begin to flush on her throat and there had to be a reason for that blushing. She switched off the too-bright spotlight she'd swung on them and aimed for damage limitation.

'I bet it robbed you of breath getting some fresh air after all this time. Your lungs won't have known what hit them. No wonder you're quiet.'

It was the best she could come up with, but it worked to take the heat away. She couldn't wait to hear the goss later though.

'Yes, quite the assault,' said Elizabeth, an artificial smile flickering on her lips.

'I was writing some poems while you were gallivanting, want to hear one?'

'I can think of nothing I'd like more,' said Vincent, his tone dry and deadpan. He winked at her and she stuck her tongue out at him.

Roo pulled her notepad out from under her bottom and opened it at her working page.

'This one is called "The Vow".

> *She said 'Let's not do presents at Christmas,*
> *Not when there's just only us.*
> *It's just something extra to think on,*
> *We don't need that bother and fuss*

'So let's make a pact here and now
And seal it in Jesus's name.
I will be buying you nothing,' she said
'And you promise that you'll do the same.

'We can buy what we want, when we want it,
There's nowt that I need anyway.'
So he stuck to the pact and bought her not a jot
And she filed for divorce New Year's Day . . .

'. . . Boom boom. Just carry on eating, folks, no need for a standing ovation.'

But she got a seated one anyway.

'I'm going to miss you, Miss Roo,' said Vincent, grinning fondly. 'I'm going to miss all of you. We should do this every year.'

'If only.' Jane smiled wistfully. 'It's been very special. Although I intend to be in the Bahamas next Christmas.'

'You better had be, Lady Jane, and not in some poky flat in Lancaster or we'll form a gang to rescue you,' said Tim.

'I promise, Tim. I won't be there. I'll be many many miles away in the sunshine.'

When Elizabeth shuffled position, something hard dug in her leg. She put her hand in her pocket and pulled out the little silver whistle that had been in the cracker. She blew on it lightly.

Vincent lifted his head. 'Is that a call for help?'

Elizabeth smiled weakly. Oh god, if he only knew how much she needed help.

'Can I see?' asked Jane, taking it from her and examining it. 'It's a pea whistle, I thought as much. I can tell from the pitch. And it's hallmarked. Those really weren't cheap crackers, were they?' She would find a chain for her enamelled orange pendant when she was home and wear it often. And she'd remember the significance of it when she did so: the fruit – the life – with all that juice in it still to savour.

Tim swallowed the last of his pie and his tastebuds sighed with pleasure. He doubted he'd ever have food that hit the spot as well as this again and he had eaten in some amazing restaurants around the world. It was enlightening how much good company made everything feel and look and taste as if it belonged to a higher state of existence and these people at the table really were the best of the best. Although he was very much looking forward to 'throwing another prawn on the barbie' in New Zealand. He was now desperate to see his girl. He needed to fold her in his strong, daddy arms and tell her that he would never let her down again and he'd be there for her whenever she might need him. But he would hold these days in his heart forever, because they had been the medicine he didn't know he needed.

He wiped his mouth with a soft cloth serviette and then addressed Henry. 'So, what's the plan of action then? Have you got one, or do you need us to brainstorm with you?'

'There's a station after the next one called St Hilda. I can get a train to London from there and lose myself for a while. I need a city law man. One of the big boys. And I need the newspapers drawn to my cause. So I shall walk down Fleet Street and knock on as many doors as I can.' Henry had taken their advice on board, it seemed.

'What about the fare?'

'I have enough money. I've been saving for a while from work and what my mam sent in for us. I always carry it on me for safekeeping. Just as well, eh?'

'If we can help you in any way, we will,' said Jane,

looking around the table. 'I'm sure I speak for us all. We'll give you our details and you call us if you need us.'

Everyone nodded or made small noises of agreement and it touched Henry because he had a brief moment of fidgeting in his chair to dispel the rise of emotion.

'I won't forget your kindness. And your trust in me not to murder you.'

'You've still got time, Henry,' quipped Roo, nudging him with her shoulder.

'I'm going to insist you sleep in the other bed in my cabin though,' said Tim. 'A bench in "Maria Gloriosa" is not a patch on what might be the last quality kip you have for a while. It's really not to be missed, Henry.'

'Aye, all right then, I'll give it a go tonight,' he replied.

Brian's voice came out of the radio and Roo leaned over to turn him up because he'd just been on a low babble in the background and this sounded important.

'I'm getting reports that most of the major roads in the area are now back to normal, although there is some very nasty flooding from the swollen rivers so let's hope your homes are safe and you all live on top of mountains. We live just next to a river but it's usually a piddly little thing and Cath's very concerned that it's going to burst its banks. Our friend, Malcolm, is doing nothing to allay her fears by offering to make up some sandbags for us.'

'I'm going to really miss Brian and his inane drivel,' said Roo with a loaded sigh. 'I'm going to miss Cath too and even Malcolm though I've only just heard about his existence.'

She walked over to the window. 'I can see green on those hills over there,' she said. 'The thaw is really happening now, isn't it? I reckon this is our last night, don't you? So later, I'm hitting that jar of cherries like there's no tomorrow.'

She smiled but she felt a hit of sadness, like the opposite of one of Jane's glimmers, because real life and her shit job and that bleak *bedshit* and shitty lonely existence was banging at the door and the hinges were ready to break.

Jane and Grace cleared the table. Jane volunteered them both to wash up because she wanted to talk to her in private. A change had come over the woman, she could feel it, a shadow lifted, her dark energy replaced with a much lighter one. Also, she looked a decade younger than she had when Jane had first laid eyes on her. Even the dull auburn of her hair seemed brighter, shinier.

'I'm going to see Ella – and Billie May,' Grace said, before Jane had even commenced with her interrogation.

'I'm so glad,' said Jane, giving her arm a comforting rub. 'Glad for you both. For you all.'

'Oh, Jane, I'm dreading it. I'm dreading scaring the little girl by exploding in front of her.'

'No, you won't. And you can always implode instead. You'll feel the glimmer of all glimmers, but yes, be prepared for a tidal wave of mixed feelings to knock the legs from under you. Grief and joy can react together like potassium and water. Brace.'

Jane dipped the first plate into the water and scrubbed at it with the brush.

'I have pushed Frank away for five long years and I can't believe I haven't lost him. He must be a fool.' Grace took the washed plate from Jane's hand and dried it with a fresh *Yorkshire Belle* tea towel.

'Oh, Grace, he loves you so much. Anyone can see that. You've come through a lot together. Both of you. It's time to fall back into step. Do something special for your thirtieth anniversary.'

'Yes, I've been thinking about that, I have an idea,' Grace said, then in a whisper added: 'I just hope he's not too sick of trains yet.'

Tim handed the piece of paper to Henry. He'd been round everyone for their contact details and written them down.

'We all genuinely mean this, Henry, if there's anything we can do. You ring us or turn up on the doorstep, though I'll be in New Zealand for a while, remember.'

Henry's hand reached out and took it as reverently as if it were a pertinent page of a prayer book.

'I promise I will.' He folded it up and put it in his jeans pocket and pulled it straight back out again.

'No, I better not shove it in there, Vincent will want these back.'

Vincent shook his head. 'Henry, keep the clothes.'

'I'll give you a few bits more in a bag from me,' added Frank. 'If you don't mind wearing someone else's boxers. They're clean, mind. I always bring way too much stuff with me.'

'And there's some money in an envelope for you,' said Tim. 'We've all chipped in.' Even young Roo had insisted on sticking a fiver in because she didn't want to be the only one not to contribute.

'If you can find a place that takes cash these days,' added Vincent.

Henry laughed, but he didn't understand the inference. Life outside prison changed quickly, he knew. He'd seen lags who'd left come straight back inside again because they couldn't cope with the changes the years brought, couldn't adjust and sought the familiarity of dysfunction. That wouldn't be him.

'I will keep you all in my prayers until the day I die and wish nothing but the best for you. You have shown me friendship and acceptance and wisdom. My life is richer for knowing every one of you,' said Henry, the envelope shivering in his hand.

Tim clapped him on the shoulder and said he was going down to 'Maria Gloriosa' to finish off the last of the *Great Bells of the World* book, because he wasn't good with raw emotion; but even he would admit, he was getting better at it.

Chapter 43

Jane collared Henry as he was standing by the window looking out at the tower of the church they had been to earlier. He was so deep in thought he jumped when her small hand touched his arm.

'Oh, I'm sorry,' she said.

'Don't worry, Jane. I was miles away, trying to remember something I'm not even sure I knew in the first place.'

She thought she understood what he meant, something akin to déjà vu, perhaps.

Henry had the list of their details in his hand; he tapped the bottom name before he read it out.

'Wutheridge, that's nice. Like *Wuthering Heights.*'

Jane huffed. 'Hated that book. Beautifully written, of course, but there was no one in it for whom I could find the least sympathy.'

'Me neither.' Henry smiled. 'Either nasty or spineless. But Wutheridge is ... classy.' *Like you, Jane*, he added to himself. Because she was, a wonderful lady, sprightly and sharp and he would pray that she remained so to the end of her days. But there was something about the name that was already familiar to him, tied up with the prison, the train, St Stephen, and it wouldn't come to him however much he tried hard to force it to the forefront of his mind. It was probably the blow he took to his head; its effect lasting, making him think he knew things when he didn't.

'We did try and trace where it came from as it's rare. Apparently, it's either derived from the old German for a tyrant or from the Devonian for a castrated ram.'

That made Henry hoot.

'Trust me, if you knew the Wutheridges, you'd plump for the former.'

'Formidable, were they?'

'Oh, you have no idea. Now, August Wutheridge, barrister at law. A man that could make the judge quake in court. He would have been a very good Wutheridge for you to have known. More weapon than human.'

Henry didn't sound convinced. 'He sounds terrifying.'

'As a tyrant, he was more Marcus Aurelius than Caligula. Although the last and worst of them – Michael Wutheridge – could give "Little Boot" a run for his money.' And thank goodness he hadn't procreated. She dreaded to think what his and Alison's mix of genes would have brewed.

'Marcus Aurelius – *Verissimus* – the most true of all.' Henry smiled.

Jane raised her eyebrows. 'You know your stuff, don't you?'

'Called so by his adoptive grandfather Hadrian, who recognised his strong sense of morality from a very early age,' Henry went on to prove he did indeed know his stuff. 'I've read a lot about the emperors. That's one good thing about the Rose Garden, we had a lot of books in the library. I think I'd have gone mad if we hadn't. I made a good case for us having more. Reading calms prisoners down, and it passes time and it educates them, gives them something to talk about, keeps them out of mischief. Men in prisons aren't good when they get bored. I don't know how anyone goes through life without being able to read. It must feel like half an existence.'

Jane was reminded once again of Elizabeth's proposed bookshop project. Books were more important than their small, humble form might suggest. Here, standing in front of her, was a prime example of their power. The more books that circulated in the world, the better good they did.

'Henry, I wonder if I could ask you a favour,' she said quietly, checking she wasn't being overheard.

'Of course, dear lady. Ask away.'

'May I take advantage of your . . . particular old skill set,' she said with a twinkle of a smile. 'One last time.'

Chapter 44

'Just the girl I wanted to see,' said Frank, collaring Roo as she came out of the loo. 'We've been trying to find you.' By 'we' he meant he and Grace, as she was hovering behind him. 'Come into the lounge with us for a minute, will you?'

He led the way and Roo said, 'Am I in trouble? You look all serious.'

'Massive trouble,' Frank threw the words over his shoulder.

'Ignore him,' said Grace. 'Although it is pretty serious, I have to admit.'

Roo hadn't a clue what they might want her for. Frank put another log on the fire to stop it dying out and stood square in front of her when she'd sat down. He clapped his hands and then came straight out with it.

'How do you fancy coming to live with us?'

'Oh, Frank, that sounds creepy as fuck,' said Grace, in the way the old Grace would have reprimanded him, the one who bantered with him, who chided him gently, playfully. 'Let me. Roo ... dear Roo, Frank told you that he wanted to start holding open mike nights in the inn. We need someone who'll be passionate about . . . humour and help organise it and bring people in, young talent . . . fresh voices. Frank has had the idea but he won't have a clue how to do it. Besides, he'll probably be too busy looking for a gym and getting involved in setting that up. Because I know how much he misses his boxing . . . his boys and his girls.'

When she turned she saw the look that Frank gave her which was like a gift of gold. She'd just surprised him with something far better than anything she could have wrapped up for Christmas. She hadn't planned to say it, but her impulse had been guided by something that knew it was right. She could see it in his face, the joy, the gratitude. She'd knocked him speechless and had to continue her pitch to Roo solo.

'We have a room which is bigger than the others, with its own sitting area, so you'd have some privacy – don't get too excited. But it will put you on until you can find something more permanent, if you want to stay in the area. And it's beautiful where we live. By the sea. We'd love to have you, Roo. We'd love to give you the chance to springboard to the Palladium.'

Fat chance, Roo was going to say, but she stopped herself. Because everyone who had appeared there must have thought *fat chance* once upon a time, but they'd done it. 'You serious? Really?'

'We are very serious. It's a chance for you to be involved in it right from the beginning. A learning curve for us all, an adventure. We could do with some help behind the bar so it would be half that sort of work, we'll play it by ear. We're quite good bosses. We don't take advantage and the locals are friendly – even to you northerners.' Grace smiled.

'We'd look after you. And if you hate it, Roo, we won't hold you to anything.'

'I love it already,' said Roo, almost breathlessly.

'Well, that's settled then, innit,' said Frank, still reeling from what Grace had said about the gym, about the life he loved. He had plenty of energy for it all and he couldn't wait to get started.

On her way back to the cabin, Roo took her coin out of her pocket and tossed it into the air. She caught it on the back of her hand.

'Should I go and live in Norfolk?' she asked it silently.

The answer was YES.

Elizabeth was lying on the bed having a catnap, she said, although it was really a battle with a stress headache caused by the journey to Topston becoming ever nearer.

'Roo, it will be a perfect opportunity for you, you must go,' Elizabeth said when Roo told her about the conversation she'd just had.

'They might even let me put on a Northern Soul night. I know all the dance moves. I could hold classes.' Ideas were falling over themselves in her head to be heard. 'I'll have to work some notice at my job but I'll be able to do that all right, knowing that there's light on my horizon.' Roo was giddy as a kipper and Elizabeth put on a good show of being thrilled for her, even though her head was pounding.

She hadn't wanted to let go of Vincent's hand when they were walking across the snow. They didn't look at each other, just held on as if their hands were a separate entity from the rest of them, and only when they reached the train door, did their contact end. She had read too much into it all: the contour of his arm muscle underneath her palm, the electric moment when his fingers curled around hers. She doubted very much he was reliving the walk from Figgy Hollow back to the *Yorkshire Belle*, imagining both of them in a sunny pub garden together sharing salty chips, remembering how her hand felt in his.

But he was.

'The A7501 is now fully opened. Train lines are thawed out as well, ice does something to the points apparently – I don't understand all that jargon though, but suffice to say that most of the trains will be running again properly tomorrow. But please take care in the Whitby harbour area because there is flooding. We just exchange one hazard for another, don't we, in this country – hee hee.'

'He loves doing his transmissions, doesn't he, old Brian,' said Vincent with a fond smile. He was going to miss him. He was going to miss everyone.

They were all sitting around the fire in the lounge having a mulled cider – made by Frank, but from Jane's recipe which included a hearty splosh of calvados. She and Clifford first tasted it made that way when they went skiing in France. Ridiculous pursuit at their ages, the holiday insurance had been astronomical. But what fun they'd had, and they emerged from the experience completely unscathed. Much to Michael's disappointment.

Roo had thrown the last five cherries in hers. Frank said he'd get a jar in for her when she came down, and plenty of sprouts as they'd still be in season.

First job when they got back was getting a room ready for Jane. There was a lovely airy one on the ground floor so there were no stairs for her to contend with, though she could probably do them better than he could. He hoped he was as sprightly at her age. He'd look after her as if she were his own mum. They both would. Until they loaded her cases onto the bus so she could sail off and start living her best life. The thought of the Jane they had come to know being cooped up in a small flat, having rings run round her by her seriously devious devil of a greedy bastard stepson made his blood boil.

Roo would bring her dynamism with her and he knew she'd make The Salty Cockle buzz. His own soul was already buzzing like a bee drunk on Jane's mulled cider recipe, because he knew where there was a unit that would be ideal for him to set up a boxing gym. He'd already had a crafty look, but turned it down because he knew it would be the end of him and Grace if he signed on the dotted line. It had still been on the market before they set off on their trip because he'd not been able to resist checking. If it was meant to be, it would be. And if it wasn't, he'd find somewhere else. He'd make it happen, one way or another.

He looked over at Grace, refereeing between Roo and Vincent as they had one of their playful verbal spats. It was so good to see that smile back on her face, the light back in her eyes. He couldn't wait for her to meet young Billie. Grace would fall in love with her, nothing surer, and that love would help her grow new tissue over her deep scars.

'Where you going when you get off then, Frank?' Vincent called over to him.

'Oh, I think we'll head back home.' He looked at Grace for confirmation.

'Home is good.' She dropped a nod of agreement.

'Back to the Rectory for me,' said Jane. 'I'll finish off what I have to and ring Michael to deliver the good news: that I'm spending the money his father left me – on me. I shall wait for him to try and have me committed.'

'Jesus, he won't, will he?' said Vincent. Mind you, this Michael geezer sounded a right sort and he really hoped Jane was joking.

'No, his modus operandi is more wheedling, more "poor me" than outwardly aggressive, he's too gutless for that.' The Wutheridge men must be rotating in their graves, she thought. The ones she met were all strong, fair, honest, fiercely loyal: Clifford's uncles Sutherland, Peregrine and Dennison, his cousin Cornelius, dearest August, her father-in-law and her beloved Clifford. Clearly Michael Wutheridge's genetic make-up was dominated by his mother's input.

'Don't worry, I shan't be drawn in. I'm too excited about going back to Venice.'

'Get yourself to that Taj Mahal,' said Vincent.

'I don't think I could go there, Vincent. Not alone. But there are plenty of other things to see in the world.'

'Good for you, Jane.'

'Myself and Mrs Cosgrove are booking our holiday this week,' said Brian from the radio, as if he was joining in with the conversation. 'We are splashing out this year and going to Scokland.'

'Oh, bless him, he can't get his gums around the country,' said Roo.

'Whereas you could get yours around the whole of the British Isles.'

'Hark at you, you cheek—'

'Shh, Vincent, Roo, I want to hear Brian,' said Grace.

'We are taking our trusty Morris Minor and setting off in early spring well before midge season. I'm going to book us into the little hotel on the island of Iona where Mrs Cosgrove and I honeymooned. Although she doesn't know that and she's not listening in because she's presently having a soak with her new bath cubes while reading the Mills and Boon love story book that Santa brought.'

'You old romantic, Brian,' said Vincent. 'Lovely Scotland. I'd like to do that myself, all the islands.'

Elizabeth opened her mouth to say, 'So would I,' and shut it before the words came out. Sometimes she felt as if Vincent could see into her head and everything in it married up with everything in his. She wished it didn't.

'He must be into his classic cars,' said Frank. 'I can imagine him tootling along in an old Morris Minor past a castle and a hill with a stag on it. I bet he's got it immaculately maintained.'

'Mrs Brian – Cath – in the passenger seat with a flask and some sandwiches for the journey.' Grace added to the portrait being painted of their expedition.

'Soft sandwiches though, milk roll probably, nothing he'd need teeth for,' said Vincent. 'She's a marg girl usually, but they'd have a scraping of best butter specially for the occasion, and he'd be in seventh heaven sitting by a loch with his best girl at his side.'

Frank knew how he'd feel. His best girl was at his side.

'Anybody want anything to eat?' he asked.

'I wasn't hungry,' said Tim, 'then you started talking about buttered milk roll sandwiches.' He rose from the sofa. 'No one dare get up, I'll knock us up some snap. Roo, you can be my sous chef.'

She jumped up, keen as ever, and both Frank and Grace thought that they wouldn't have any problems with her work ethic, that was for sure.

*

In the kitchen while Roo was buttering bread, which wasn't quite as thin as the milk roll Tim was coveting, he said, 'I asked you to help me because I wanted to say thank you, Roo, privately, for trusting me with the story about your dad. I don't think anyone else could have given me a perspective like that. And you opening up to me has . . . really helped me get my head into gear.'

'I wouldn't thank me yet, she might tell you to get stuffed when you talk to her,' said Roo.

Tim took that in and then barked with laughter, such a deep rumble he made the real Santa sound like a eunuch.

'She won't, I'm joking, of course,' said Roo. 'If my dad turned up now I'd throw my arms around him. I'd call him a tosser but I'd still love him, even though he was a rubbish dad. But you weren't rubbish, you were *good* to your girl. You have to stop beating yourself up and not judge yourself with the whip of hindsight because at the time, you were in a great position to get the very best for your family because you loved them and so that's what you went ahead and did. And so what if you enjoyed your work, there's no sin in that. You'd have been a better father being fulfilled and proud of what you could do for them. Maybe your work-life balance was a bit on the wonk, you're not the only one. But . . . I'd have killed for a dad like you, Tim.' She hoped she'd said that right. But from the look on his face, she thought she might have.

'I'm not very good with saying how I feel. I've never told my daughter that I love her. I find the words difficult. Never too late to learn a new skill, eh?'

'Well, I dunno about that. Not sure I'd try asymmetric bars at your age, Tim.'

'Don't ever change, Roo,' said Tim, taking the plate of

buttered bread slices from her so he could apply the filling. He wished at that moment he could have been her dad. But he didn't think a pony and a big bedroom with an ensuite and a swimming pool could have made Roo Cooper turn out any better than she already had.

Chapter 45

Things felt as if they were truly coming to a close now, there was a winding down in the air, a *change*. It came with different feelings to each of them. To Roo it brought the excitement of an unknown future she was ready to embrace. To Tim it made him want to just get home, talk to his daughter and then book his flight. To Henry, he felt galvanised by his time spent with these wonderful people to fight and carry on fighting until he was heard. Grace and Frank wanted to be back in the dear familiarity of their home, but enjoy it as they hadn't before with their old, loving connection restored. But Vincent would have been happy to stay, another day would have done, just to enjoy the company of them all for a little longer. To enjoy the company of Elizabeth. He shouldn't torture himself by prolonging their proximity, it was stupid. They'd have to part at some point. He could only delay getting out of the car, unloading her cases, saying goodbye, but he couldn't stop it. Then he'd return to a life where he was sort of content but it would feel paler by comparison now, so much more lonely.

As for Elizabeth, every time the lady came out of the

clock and the man struck the bell he delivered a fresh wave of dread for her. Her headache was lingering; she felt as if that brass man was in her skull, banging at the inside of her temple.

Tim was the first to break up the party. He yawned and stretched his great long arms.

'One last shower, one last time wrapped in that fluffy robe, one last night in that beautiful bed,' he said. The song on the radio ended. Non-Christmas songs were starting to infiltrate Brian's playlists now: 'Red Roses For a Blue Lady', though only Frank recognised it. Elizabeth looked blue, he thought, though he wouldn't embarrass her by saying as much and he hoped she was okay. She certainly didn't look like someone who was going to be reunited with her fiancé soon.

'Our last night as the *Yorkshire Belle* eight,' said Vincent.

'Nine, if you count Brian as an honorary member.'

On cue Brian spoke out of the radio.

'Well, I'll bid you goodnight,' he said. 'I'll not be around for a few days. I'm taking a break. I'm going to see my mum. She'll not know who I am, she hasn't for a while. She thinks she's still a bus conductress in Clitheroe and tries to charge everyone in the home fares, but she's happy. She keeps saying that she should retire at thirty-two, even though she's ninety-five on New Year's Eve. She's in a lovely home, they right look after her.'

Everyone exchanged glances. Oh, the pain behind the frontage of some people's lives. Frank was only grateful that he'd lost his old mum just when she'd started to slip. He wasn't sure he could have coped with her looking at him and not seeing the boy she made.

Elizabeth dabbed at her eyes. She was upset by Brian and

his mum but it also served as a cover for the build-up inside her that was threatening to burst its dam wall.

'So adieu, friends, because I never say goodbye. It's too final a word and there's no need for that. So thank you for listening to me. I hope anyone who is still stuck out there somewhere gets home safely now. And I hope you've had some enjoyment from my gentle tunes of yesteryear.'

'Brian, you've been a bleedin' legend, mate,' said Frank and stood up. Everyone followed suit and they gave Radio Brian a whole-hearted standing ovation.

'This has been the real BBC, Brian Bernard Cosgrove. Happy New Year when it comes to you all. May it bring you everything you've wished for.'

Then there was a click followed by a silence that resonated through them all like a seismic wave.

Frank walked into his cabin and had scarcely even put one foot inside when Vincent, who was in there, blocked his way.

'Change of plan, mate.'

'What do you—'

'No questions.'

Vincent pushed him out gently but firmly and beckoned his confused cabin-mate to follow down the train, one car forward to 'Sigismund'. Then he opened the door of the first, hitherto locked, room and thumbed inside.

'See you in the morning, Frank. Come on, in you go.'

Frank, dumbfounded, did as he was told.

When Grace went to her cabin, she noticed that her case wasn't where it should be and her robe was no longer on the bed.

'Oh, I'm sorry, Grace,' said Jane, who was already in there. 'You can't sleep in here tonight. Come with me.'

She bustled a bewildered Grace out and down the passageway, past Vincent and Tim's room and into 'Sigismund'. She knocked on the door of the first cabin and when she heard a 'Come in', she opened it.

'Have a nice evening, Grace,' said Jane, standing aside to let her enter the twice-bigger room with a sumptuous red and gold theme, pale burr maple walls, its own ensuite and a hand-painted ceiling that would have had Michaelangelo wolf-whistling.

Frank was sitting on the double bed, an ice bucket with a bottle of champagne and two glasses on the table beside him.

'I . . . I thought these cabins were all locked,' said Grace, still wearing a mask of confusion.

'Let's just say I know a man who knows a little about unlocking locks. Good night, you two,' and with that Jane closed the door.

Henry wriggled down the bed and made a gleeful noise that a small child might make rather than a grown man.

'Told you,' said Tim.

'I'm not sure any bed after this one is going to pass muster.'

'Yes, we are all going to have to get used to slumming it,' Tim chortled.

'I shall, however, make it my mission that – God willing – if I get out, my bedding will always be of the highest quality I can afford. That will be one of the many legacies from this . . . interlude.'

'You do that, lad,' returned Tim.

'I remember getting on board, feels like so long ago.

I remember the taste of that pie. I thought I'd landed in heaven after dying in the snow.'

'Aye, it's been a taste of heaven.' . . . *But it'll be nowt compared to being in a New Zealand airport and seeing my daughter at the barrier,* Tim added to himself.

'It's been a pleasure knowing you, Tim.'

'And you, Henry. It's a Christmas I'll never forget. Something to tell the grandchildren about. The day Santa got lost in the snow.'

He waited for a response but all that came from Henry was the softest snore of contentment.

While Elizabeth was in the bathroom, she had decided that she had to talk to someone, she had to get out the words that she didn't know what to do. She wouldn't expect Roo to direct her, just listen while she opened up her heart, and just maybe through the act of doing that, it might help get herself in order. She felt like a bowl of breadcrumbs, being tossed around by a baker's kneading hand, nothing binding, nothing coming together.

She couldn't get it out of her mind, Vincent's hand catching hers, such a small action but it had resulted in a big bang inside her, as massive as the creation of the whole solar system; she felt the heat from a newly born sun glowing in her chest. She knew he felt it too because he didn't look at her, they were both staring straight ahead as they walked, not knowing how to verbalise it. What did it mean? What could it mean? She was a jack-in-a-box that had sprung out, swelled in the air and the light, and had grown too much to return to its container. But what else could she do? She both had to go back and also . . . she couldn't. Jane's earlier comment to her was circling in her head like the vultures in the Bantam Cock poem: *Don't settle for a life without love, Elizabeth. You might think you can, but you shouldn't.*

Gregory didn't love her, she knew that. To him, she was just a key to the door that led to what he wanted. He would never hold her hand and send shivers through every nerve-ending she possessed. He'd crush her until there was nothing left of her but tears and regret.

The words formed in her head on the approach to the cabin. They were cued up ready in her voice box to splurt out.

'Roo, can I talk to you?'

She opened up the door to find Roo fast asleep.

27 December

*By the end of Christmas, we should
have realised that love weighs more than
any present, more even than gold*

Chapter 45

It was early the next morning when Roo awoke, but someone was already up because she could hear them walking
down the passageway. She lifted up the blinds to peer out
and saw many patches of green on the ground. The colour
looked too intense to be real, she could feel her pupils con-
tract to let it in slowly, cautiously.

Elizabeth stirred. She had no idea how she'd managed to
sleep with all that had been racing around in her head. It
was like a washing machine, her thoughts on a fast relentless spin.

'Morning, Elizabeth. I see mucho colour outside. We will
soon be on our way, I reckon.'

'Lovely,' said Elizabeth, affecting brightness. Last night's
bravery had retreated to the corner where it usually re-
sided, like a shivering beaten dog. Elizabeth the walkover.
Elizabeth the inconsequential pawn. Elizabeth the dutiful,
doing what was best for everyone bar herself.

'Goodbye, robe,' said Roo, giving it an affectionate stroke
as if it were a pet. 'You were the best.'

She was in such a good mood, so many things to look

forward to. The top one being telling her boss she was leaving. Mandrea Billington was one of those women who delighted in putting other women down, not a *sistah*; a sour-faced old cow, although she wasn't that old, but her many petty jealousies and resentments had aged her. If she'd bit into a lemon, it would have been the lemon that said '*ugh*'. Roo couldn't wait to tell her that she was moving to Norfolk to manage an exciting new creative venture after she'd been offered a job over Christmas, which she just happened to have spent on one of the world's most luxurious trains. Miserable Mandrea would spontaneously combust.

As she was brushing her teeth in the sink, Roo realised that Elizabeth had barely spoken a word. Something was up, she felt it. She swilled her mouth out and sat down on the bed where Elizabeth was putting things into her suitcase.

'What are you going to do when you get up to Durham?' she asked her.

'What do you mean?' Elizabeth replied.

'Well . . . I'm not being daft, but we've talked a lot and . . . are you really in love with Gregory? Is he what you want? I mean, you're not coming across as someone who is desperate to see the man you should have been formally engaged to this week. Also, I need a machete to cut the sexual tension in the air between you and Vincent.'

Oh my god, was it that obvious? Elizabeth felt her perfidious neck start to warm.

'I wouldn't worry, I don't think it's common knowledge, but you know me, I can read people. I harvest them for poetry. And you've got that face back again.'

Elizabeth halted her packing.

'What *face*?'

'*That* face.' Roo pointed at her and Elizabeth remembered the poem she had found in Roo's notebook.

You have sad grey eyes
Wearing the ring of your not-really prince

That reminded her. She reached into her handbag and pulled out her engagement ring, slipped it back onto her finger. It looked way too big and weighty for her small hand, as if it had grown in size since she'd last worn it.

'You and Vince . . . you have so much in common. You should have seen his face when you were singing that song about the bantam cock.'

Elizabeth wanted to ask about his face, she wanted to squeeze every detail from Roo like the juice from a Christingle orange. But what good would it do? Everything was heightened here with the romance of the train, the snow, the magic of Christmas. It wasn't real life and they couldn't exist in such a bubble forever. She'd got things all out of proportion, she was sure; silly commitment worries sending her into a reverse thrust. She would settle.

'I shall be going up to Topston as planned and hopefully we can arrange the party on a different date.'

It's a good job she wasn't a war commander. As a blueprint, it was weak as dishwater, but she also knew that she couldn't just run off from everything as if she were living in a fairy story. She'd talk to Gregory alone. Tell him that she was having doubts and needed time to iron out what was wrong between them. And she'd just have to hold firm and not be rushed into anything, whatever her father and in-laws said. Maybe in time, everything *would* be okay. And it would be easier, so much easier to mend their relationship, rebuild it even from the ground up, than upend her whole life because some man she'd known for a few days held her hand for a couple of hundred yards.

'Well, if you're sure.' Roo smiled. It wasn't up to her to try and disassemble someone else's life when she'd made such a crap job of her own so far. 'You'll stay in touch with me, won't you?' she said.

'Of course I will,' said Elizabeth, handing over her phone so that Roo could type in her number, though there was still no signal, no intrusion of the world outside bleeding into this one. Not yet.

'Morning, Mrs O'Carroll,' said Frank, as Grace opened her eyes and found him staring at her.

'You been watching me sleep?' she asked him.

'Only for an hour. Turns me on when you dribble and snore.'

He reached over, cupped her face in his warm palm and kissed her. They both had morning breath, but it didn't matter. It was a kiss that was loaded with sweetness and hope and love.

'I think you were right when you said let's sell up and buy our own train, Frank. I'm going to put another line on the lottery when we get back.'

Frank laughed. 'We're spoilt now, aren't we? How are we going to fit back into normal life?'

But normal life sounded good to Grace because normal was what she was craving. She was a work in progress and would be for a long time, but at least there was progress, there was light breaking through the cloud. She was looking forward to going home with her man. She didn't want to lose him and she didn't like to let the thought intrude that if Frank hadn't hurt his ankle, if they'd had to drive rather than catch trains and break down in a freezing carriage, she probably would have.

'Remember what you once said you were going to do to me on a train, Frank?'

'I do.'

'Well, you've still got time,' she said.

Everyone stripped their beds and left the sheets and towels and used robes in a big bundle in the upper vestibule of 'Uglich'. Tim and Vincent had given the galley a final spruce. Frank had checked the bar was as pristine as the first time he'd walked behind it. He was going to fill up the ice bucket, but someone had beaten him to it. He wished he could find one like it for The Salty Cockle. It must have been a really clever insulation design, for the ice never melted however long it was sitting there. He'd left a note half-tucked underneath it with his details on it should Mr Ingleton want to charge them for what they'd eaten and drunk. If he was contacted, however, Frank wouldn't be in touch with the others to divvy up the costs. What these days on board had given him would be cheap at any price. He felt like a man injected with a shot of new life this morning.

They assembled in the bar, where Grace distributed coffees. All their cases stood nearby. Outside, the thaw was making up for lost time. Roo had switched on the radio to see if Brian had changed his mind about not broadcasting, but all she could get on it was white noise.

When they were done, Elizabeth collected the cups and put them on a tray. She could feel Vincent's eyes on her, like the heat from a sun on a summer's day, holding her face in its hands as she sat outside a small pub, the air full of scent from salty chips and lemony scampi.

'I can see a car heading towards us,' said Tim, standing by the window. It was coming from the direction where they had last seen the guard and engine driver.

Real life had arrived.

Chapter 47

Elizabeth was in the back of Vincent's car again and it was as if time had looped back to the day before Christmas Eve. They had barely spoken since they had walked across from Figgy Hollow. Everything that formed in her mouth felt too big, too awkward to come out, other than the banal like 'good night', 'good morning' and 'thank you' when he helped her with her suitcase off the *Yorkshire Belle*.

She may have been surprised to find that Vincent's thoughts were running parallel. He had played it over and over in his head trying to work out how her hand had ended up in his when they'd been walking back from the abandoned Figgy Hollow, although he was glad it had. But what the hell it had done to the rest of him as a result was anyone's guess. There had been a burst of warmth in his chest when she took his arm, but when their hands clasped, there was a full-on nuclear explosion. He should have said something but all words fused together in his throat, he could barely get air past them to breathe. And now it was too late because she was once again his passenger and he was taking her to her fiancé and then going home to his cat.

The thaw was all that was needed for the train brakes to unlock. The guard had agreed to take Henry as far as St Hilda where he could pick up the line to London. They had all bid him 'adieu' because, as Radio Brian said, there was no need for a word as final as 'goodbye'. But it felt like one when the rest of them got off at Eskford, and Henry stood at the window and waved slowly as the *Yorkshire Belle* pulled away. The gesture said he sensed it too: the last vestige of connectedness, the flipside of a glimmer, a spell broken.

They didn't have long to wait for the shuttle to Derringbury where they found themselves back where it all started. Frank and Grace would be well on their way back to Norfolk now, Jane to her home in Derby. Vincent had been ready to get his tools out for Tim's car but it fired into life with one twist of the ignition key. He was giving Roo a lift as her village was just a short detour from his route back to Sheffield. They traded car pips at the end of the road where Tim turned south and Vincent turned to the north.

Elizabeth took a deep breath as she turned on her phone and waited for the messages to begin downloading. It sounded as if it had developed a fault: *bing bing bing bing bing . . . one hundred and twenty-seven missed calls.* Texts in shouty capitals. Voicemails too. She couldn't read them or listen to them; she deleted them and would pretend she never got them.

'Would you like to stop on the way for a coffee?' Vincent asked.

Bing bing bing bing. Even more coming through, demanding attention.

'No . . . I'd better just get there soon as I can,' she answered. She needed to face them, get it over with.

Vincent flicked his eyes up to the mirror and saw her

staring down at the phone in her hand. She looked differ-ent to how she had last night with the soft gold glow of the lamps lighting her features in the bar, making her lovely eyes shine; she looked drawn, stressed, sad.

She braced herself when the shrill *brrr-brrr* ringtone started up, the sound piercing the quiet of the car, an incoming call this time. Gregory's name filled her screen. She pressed 'answer' and didn't have the chance to speak before he did.

'Elizabeth?'

'Yes. I—'

'What the fuck is going on? Why haven't you answered my calls? Where have you been? Where are you now . . . ?'

A long string of questions with barely a break in between them for her to insert an answer.

'Gregory, I'm on my way. I've been stuck on a train with no—'

'What train?'

'A private train. We had a lift from—'

'What are you talking about, *a private train*? Are you still on it?'

'No, I'm in the taxi.'

'Where have you been for the past FOUR DAYS?'

'On the train, I told you. It was a sleeper. There were a few of us trapped on it. They couldn't move the train until today because of the snow.'

'There hasn't been any snow for two fucking days, what are you talking about? So I'll ask you again, Elizabeth—'

She couldn't stand it, the snapping relentless bark of his tone, a nail scraping down the blackboard of her nerves. 'I'm sorry, you're breaking up,' she fibbed and made a series of staccato noises that would intimate her voice was breaking up too. Vincent saw her disconnect the call and stuff the phone in her bag, where it continued to buzz like a livid wasp. She'd dropped her head as if it were weighted with more angst than it could carry.

'You all right in the back there?' he asked.

'Yes, fine.'

What else could she say?

Vincent switched on the radio, not the gentle sounds of yesteryear from Brian, but tunes, some of which Elizabeth knew, some she didn't. She couldn't really concentrate. All she could think of was what she had to face in less than fifteen miles because Gregory was fuming and the fact she was now actively ignoring his calls was tantamount to throwing petrol on a bonfire. Ten miles. Five miles. Two miles.

She could hear her heart thumping in her ears as if it had crawled there for a better place of safety. A horrible mix of emotions was tearing around inside her because they didn't know where to go, her whole body was in panic mode. She was glad that Vincent hadn't spoken to her for the last quarter of an hour because one kind word and she would have crumbled.

In the front, Vincent didn't know what to do. Every time he'd checked on her in the rear-view mirror, she'd looked paler, so lost in whatever was going on in her head that she hadn't heard him ask again if she was okay because she really didn't look it.

The satnav was showing a small chequered flag, they were almost there now. He slowed down, indicated right and they were on the long private drive down to the house. My, it was grand, even more so in the flesh than on a photo. He thought of his old mum again who would have asked how much the window-cleaning bill for such a pile would cost every month. Back to the beginning, a full circle.

Elizabeth reached into her coat pocket for a tissue to dab the discreet tears she'd been crying for a mile and a half. Vincent would have seen if she'd wiped them away before so she'd let them just roll down her face as she looked out of the window. She felt something else in there and pulled it out. The silver whistle she'd won in the cracker. She supposed she must have put it there when she was packing but she couldn't remember doing so.

The car pulled up next to a fountain in the centre of a gravel circle and a man marched out of the front door – Gregory presumably, thought Vincent. He wasn't smiling in relief that his darling was finally here, he looked furious; it told in his walk, in his expression and now in his voice.

'Finally, she turns up!'

He grabbed impatiently at the locked back door handle, trying to hoick it open which pissed Vincent right off.

It was just as he was about to press the door release switch that Vincent heard the high-pitched trill coming from behind him. In the frame of his rear-view mirror he saw Elizabeth with the silver pea-whistle in her mouth.

'Is that a call for help?' he asked, as he had asked her yesterday at the table. Yesterday he had meant it as a joke, but not today.

She nodded, unable to speak, she barely had even the breath to blow.

Gregory was rapping hard on the window with one hand, the other still jerking on the handle.

'Elizabeth, open this fucking door. NOW.'

Vincent slid the gear lever hard into drive, floored the

accelerator and slammed the steering wheel into a left lock, spraying Gregory with the family gravel as they sped away.

Vincent stopped at the first large service station he came to, somewhere where they could park themselves in a corner and she could talk to him. She was in a proper state. Even when he opened the door for her and she got out, for a moment he thought she might fold like a dynamited building.

They walked into the busy foyer, past the queue for Burger King and a noodle bar and into the large Costa. He bought two large Americanos and set one down in front of her. By the look of her she wouldn't live long enough to drink it. Her hands were gripped together in front of her as if they were the only things stopping her from falling off a cliff.

'What have I done?' she said. It was warm in the café but she was shivering.

'I think you should start from the beginning,' Vincent said. 'You've got about three hours before that coffee cools down enough to drink, that enough time?'

'Not even half,' she said.

She told him everything. Way too much detail that made her cringe as soon as it left her mouth, but once she started, it just rolled out under its own momentum. He listened to every word, fully invested, his eyes never leaving her. She was past caring how weak she sounded, how feeble and pathetic: how she had been fashioned and groomed, fooled and bullied to tread the path expected of her, marry someone suitable who ticked all the family boxes – and she confessed that she really did think he'd ticked hers too. Once upon a time. She left out the fact he made love like a machine that something had triggered into action by inserting a pound coin; it would have been one detail too far.

And at the end of her mighty diatribe, Vincent sat back in the seat and said, 'Sounds as if you've been played like a good'un, gel.'

'If I end it with Gregory, my father won't lose him from the business, he's too important, so I'll have to go. And my flat is in that office block so I'll have to leave that. And—'

Vincent held up his hand to stop the flow.

'Do you love him?'

Such a small question, such a big question.

If she said it, it would make it real. She didn't love him, but she would probably have still married him if a cab-driver from London hadn't held her hand in the snow and a million scales had fallen from her eyes.

'No.'

'Then you got a choice to make. Two doors, you imagine, one leads to Gregory and all his family, and your dad and your job and your house and a big fat salary and a life of privilege, kids in private schools, holidays in Bali ...' He paused.

'And the other one?'

'Takes you to a place called Cary's Pond. It's got a village green with ducks, couple of pubs, one of which does the best scampi and chips on the planet. It's got a few shops; one of them would make a great little second-hand bookshop. There's a farmhouse where you can hole up for as long as you want to get your head sorted out. And living in it, is a cat and a bloke who won't shout at you or use you, he'll just love you.'

Then Vincent reached across the table and scooped up her hands with his.

And there was absolutely no question which door she was going to walk through.

Chapter 48

Six months later

In history, Caffe Florian in the Piazza San Marco, Venice was the haunt of Lord Byron and Charles Dickens, Proust, Casanova. Seeing as the last time Jane saw her friends was in equally opulent and elegant surroundings, she thought it would be a suitable meeting place. Her cruise ship was in port for today and by lucky chance – or maybe more than luck – Frank and Grace were on their second day of holidaying in the city, after travelling here on the Orient Express. A present Grace had arranged for their thirtieth wedding anniversary.

When Jane saw them walking across the grand square, her smile expanded. It was weird seeing them out of British context, but wonderful too. They spotted her and waved and their pace increased.

'Jane, you look fantastic,' said Grace, releasing her from her tight embrace so that Frank could enfold her.

'I could say the same about you two.' Jane chuckled. It wasn't a lie. They looked glowing. They looked together.

'Sit and let's have coffee.'

'I'll get them,' said Frank, ever the gent.

'Absolutely not. Every penny I spend I'm denying Michael and that makes me happier than you could ever imagine.'

They ordered from a passing liveried waiter.

'In the end I told Michael there would be something for him in the will, but . . . on the understanding he got on with his life and let me get on with mine. Any request, however cloaked, for an advance on that money would result in me completely lifting up my drawbridge – one strike and out. He really has had no choice but to comply and not risk upsetting me. Nice to have the upper hand.' Jane grinned. 'I imagine he'll be absolutely furious when I pop my clogs and he finds out how little I've left him. I wish I could be around to see it.' She chuckled, full of mirth. She wouldn't feel guilty. Clifford had been overly generous with his son in his lifetime. Michael had had much more than he deserved from them already.

'You're having a good time then on your travels?' Grace asked, but it was a stupid question really because the answer was obvious.

'Yes, straight off one ship, straight onto another. Or a plane. Hotel rooms in between. It's very liberating not having possessions.'

'Well, you look great on it,' said Frank, meaning it.

'How's young Roo doing?'

'She's fine and dandy,' Frank replied, fond smile on his lips. 'Settled in like a dream, organising everyone, got herself a boyfriend. He's the builder we use. And he's doing a bit of boxing with me. Big handsome lad, treats her like a goddess.'

'Name?'

They both knew what she meant.

'Robinson. Roo Robinson would pass muster, wouldn't it?'

'It would indeed.' Jane nodded.

'Comedy Club's up and running, she's put her heart and soul into making it work and it's really taken off now the summer's come in. She's performing, making us all laugh, like a pig in muck she is.'

'Please give her my fondest regards,' said Jane. 'Tell her not to be too starry-eyed that she forgets to email me occasionally. There are computers on ships, I use them quite a lot, as I'll come to in a moment. And how is . . . everything else?' She looked pointedly at Grace, who dived into her handbag and pulled out her phone, pressed the photo icon.

'That's me and Billie. That's Frank and me and Billie . . . all five hundred pictures. I won't bore you but I think you get the gist.'

It had taken Grace a few weeks to build up the courage to see Billie. Jane had left for her cruise by then. Time was moving on and she didn't want another month to slip by so on 1 March, she and Frank made the journey to Cromer together.

Grace would always remember the moment she was sitting on the sofa in Ella's front room and in walked Billie May. Her eyes were brightest blue, just like her Billy's when he was that age, she was so like him. And when the little girl reached up to cuddle her hello, it was as if Grace were holding her son again. All the love she had stored inside her finally found its home.

'Had a message from Tim,' said Frank. 'He asked me to send his love when he heard we was meeting up. He's off next week back to New Zealand. I think he'll end up living there. His daughter's pregnant again – a little girl on the way this time.'

'He told me,' said Jane. 'He emails. He sent me a picture of him throwing a prawn on the barbie.'

'Yes, us too.'

He'd obviously staged the photo to make them laugh and they had.

He'd sent them all photos of him holding his grandson on the day he was born too. He got there just in time in the new year.

'Roo's always in touch with Elizabeth,' said Grace.

'Dear Elizabeth,' said Jane with a happy sigh. She'd wondered if what she'd said to her about not settling for a life without love had some bearing on what had happened when Vincent drove her back up to Durham. My, it was a good job she won that whistle in the cracker.

Jane's fingers came up to touch her own cracker gift, as they so often did: the orange enamel charm she wore on a chain. That big orange of life was certainly supplying a lot of juice and it wasn't done yet.

'I'm in contact with Elizabeth too because we are soon to be in business together. She's found the premises and we're just debating over the name of our bookshop. She wants to call it Wutheridges, I suggested Dudley and Wutheridge, but she doesn't want to use her family name – and I can't say I blame her after they cut her off like a gangrenous limb, although I'd argue the limb was healthy and it was the rest that was rotten.'

'Well, I shouldn't say but I'm going to.' Frank leaned in close as if the people he was about to talk of were in earshot. 'Vincent was asking me where I thought would be the most romantic place to propose.'

'Diamond and Wutheridge ... that sounds good. I like that very much,' said Jane.

The coffees arrived. Frank took one sip, coughed and said

that it would either put some more hairs on his chest or strip off the ones that he'd got already.

'I have to say, for romance, this place takes some beating,' said Grace.

Frank's eyes roved over the ceilings, the lights, the mirrors and artwork and sighed wistfully. 'The people that must have come into this café and sat here over the years. Thousands. Makes you wish you could rewind time and just be a fly on the wall.'

Jane nodded slowly. 'Funny you should say that, Frank, about time. And why I was so delighted that our itineraries overlapped.'

Coincidence.

Accept the mystery, Jane.

She had their attention.

'Have you heard from Henry?' she asked.

'Nothing,' said Frank. 'Not a dicky bird. I really thought we would have.'

'We keep looking on the internet but can't find anything,' added Grace. 'Then again, there are an awful lot of Henry Smiths but you would have thought there would be something somewhere, given his story.'

'I hoped he might have let us know if he'd been released. We took from his silence that something had gone wrong and he was back inside and maybe they have to block stuff like that on the net.' Frank sounded genuinely sad about it. 'I thought everything and everyone was on there. We couldn't even find mention of the bleedin' train. I suppose that if you're that rich and don't want anyone to know anything about your business you can pay to stop any unwanted coverage. Like them celebs having a bit of how's your father with people they shouldn't.'

Jane sipped from her cup. *Oh, where to begin.*

'I've also been trying to trace Henry. There are a lot of sea days on ships and I buy data packages, look things up on the internet. Easy to go down a rabbit hole when you have time on your hands, and I have been down a very, very deep one these past months.'

She reached down to her cavernous handbag and took out some papers.

'You might have found something about the train if you hadn't looked for it by name.'

Frank and Grace exchanged glances, wondering if they knew what Jane meant, but both were as confused as each other.

Jane unfolded one of the A4 sheets in her hand and put it on the table, the copy facing them. It was a printout of an old newspaper. The headline:

PLEDD BRIDGE DISASTER

It was dated 29 December, 1950.

It was hard to read, the typeface not conducive to eyes without glasses so Frank pulled his out of his shirt top pocket.

'You can take that with you to pore over the details later but I'll fill you in with the pertinent points for now. On the twenty-third of December 1950, a privately owned train – it doesn't give its name, possibly because it wasn't registered as having one at the time – was heading to Scotland to pick up its passengers when it was held up in a heavy bout of unforecast snow which interfered with the braking system, and so it had to sit there unmanned for four days between Derringbury and Eskford until there was enough of a thaw so it could be worked on.'

'Bloody hell, that's a coincidence,' said Frank, attempting to read.

'After Eskford – nowadays – the train line next stops at Helthorpe then off to Scotland via Middlesbrough. But once upon a time trains heading for Scotland would call in at St Hilda, Pleddington, Follyhead, all manner of tiny stations, along what was known as the Lochlann line, which doesn't exist any more. None of those stations exist any more. They haven't actually existed since the 1960s, because the route was one of many to fall under Dr Beeching's axe for being unprofitable, duplicated and underused.'

Jane paused to let that sink in, though she could see that it hadn't really.

'So ... the train. On the twenty-seventh of December 1950, it finally is able to resume its journey. But something goes horribly wrong when the train leaves St Hilda. The signalman on duty was not aware of a diversion in place to avoid a bridge which had been flagged for faults, and so he sends the train on the standard route over the River Pledd. The line should have been blocked, but for whatever reason it wasn't. The train goes over the weak bridge, which has been further weakened by the extreme weather conditions: the snow, the ice, the flooding. The bridge collapsed as the train went over it.'

'Good god,' said Grace. 'Was anyone killed?'

'Oh yes,' said Jane. 'Three died, three ... four were injured.'

Frank wasn't sure where this was going, vaguely interesting as it was, what with the coincidence of a train being held up as they were. But it would have been rude not to humour her.

She pulled out another printout. It was a copy of a copy

of a copy and so the photograph on it was unclear, hardly identifiable.

'PLEDD BRIDGE HERO' said the headline.

'That is a photo of a man called . . . Henry Smith. He saved three people, including the guard Albert Barclay and the driver Leonard Pitts, who was in a very bad way, but he did survive, thanks to Henry Smith. They were both trapped under metal and would have drowned had he not dragged them out. His own leg was badly cut open in the effort, he almost lost it which made what he did even more admirable. He couldn't save the newly-boarded engineer who was picked up at St Hilda along with a chef and a steward, but he went under the water and tried.'

'Listen to this,' said Frank, reading aloud. 'Henry Smith was pressing down on the chest of twenty-three-year-old butler-in-training John Tattersall when the ambulance arrived, an action which no doubt saved Mr Tattersall's life as his heart had hitherto stopped beating.'

Hark! Hark.

Grace remembered Roo teaching Henry how to do CPR, singing the carol in the lounge on Christmas Day. But Christmas Day 2025, not 1950. She couldn't quite connect the dots and that showed on her face.

Jane pulled out more sheets, unfolded them.

'Once I got my teeth into this, I couldn't let go. Henry Smith was arrested at the hospital. He had escaped from prison days previously. He'd served years for a vicious assault on a train guard in 1942. He was on the run, hoping to secure evidence to prove his innocence but instead of taking his chance to get on the London train, he ran to the scene of the accident to help.'

Frank, sipping his coffee, because at those prices he was going to savour every drop, suddenly spluttered.

'Eh?'

'Jane, what are you telling us?' Grace half-laughed, confused because she couldn't make head nor tail of this.

'I drew a blank with the prison ... at first,' replied Jane.

'Us too. We couldn't find *any* prisons in the area at all. Nearest is about thirty miles away from where we were stuck,' said Frank, flicking at the coffee drops on his shirt, glad he'd chosen black and not the white one.

'There was one, Harden Row, built in the eighteen hundreds, so bleak, grim and in such a state of dilapidation, inmates started to call it *Rose Garden* as their private joke.'

Henry had said to her, *you'll never see anything less like a rose garden in your life* and she hadn't twigged it wasn't its real name until she did some forensic-level digging. 'That was the one Henry was in. It closed in nineteen fifty-five and was demolished the following year.'

Frank looked over at Grace; it was plain she was still as befuddled as he was.

Jane presented them with another copy of a newspaper article: a clearer, more modern printout of a smiling old man in an armchair.

BELOVED VICAR AND HERO DIES AGED 105

'Recognise him?'

Frank laughed at the thought in his head. *It looks like a pensioner version of Henry.* He didn't need to say it though, Jane saw the answer in his expression.

She read aloud.

'"A much beloved retired vicar, Henry Smith, died peacefully in his sleep, 27 December 2025, in Belle Vie House, Whitby. As a youngster, Henry was a self-confessed reprobate who spent eight years in prison but for a crime he did not commit. He was named as part of a gang of robbers who targeted a goods train but was actually "fitted up" by a fellow gang member in revenge for him running away before the train was flagged down. When evidence was un-covered that could have proved Henry's innocence beyond all doubt, it was suppressed by the establishment, leading to Henry's desperate escape from prison to prove he was not responsible. He holed up over Christmas in a luxury train, heading for Scotland on its maiden journey, which had been temporarily abandoned when the brakes failed. When that train eventually set off, a signalman's error sent it over a closed bridge and both collapsed into the River Pledd. Henry, about to board a train to London where he hoped to find legal representation to clear his name, instead ran to help and saved three lives. He was returned to Harden Row prison after a stay in hospital where surgeons managed to save his mangled leg. But his story reached venerable legal persons of the day who volunteered to take on his case".

'Now this is where it gets very odd, if it can get any odder,' said Jane. She recapped a little for context: '"who volunteered to take on his case ... including celebrated barrister August Wutheridge KC, whom Henry chose to represent him".' Jane looked up to deliver her killer fact. 'August Wutheridge was my father-in-law.'

Frank opened his mouth to say something but nothing came out.

'He won the case, of course he did, because August was redoutable. George the Sixth pardoned Henry Smith in

January 1952, one of the king's last acts before he died just three weeks later.' Jane turned the page. 'Here's a photo of Henry and his mother outside the court on the day he was freed.'

Underneath it there was a quote from him:

I never doubted this day would come. My God was with me, and His angels. But He also sent me the best of secular help. The kindest of people.

'To cut a long story short, Henry Smith, upon his release, studied hard and for years to become a clergyman and for a while he was the incumbent vicar of St Stephen in the small North Yorkshire parish of . . . Figgy Hollow.'

Frank found something to say then: 'Fuck me!' for which he immediately apologised.

'I said exactly the same,' admitted Jane.

'This is screwing with my head,' said Grace.

Jane carried on. 'He married and stayed married for fifty-five years until his wife's death; they had a daughter – Jane.' She smiled fondly. 'Henry outlived her by five years. He was still holding services in his nineties. Did the owner of the *Yorkshire Belle* ever contact you about paying the bar bill, Frank?'

'No, he didn't,' said Frank, still in shock and trying to unscramble what he was hearing.

'A couple of carriages were salvageable but not much else was. There's a article from the sixties about a train that never accommodated a single passenger in its opulent rooms, apart from a lucky convict on the run who found it broken down in the snow in the Christmas of 1950. The owner – an American businessman – was paid out by his insurance firm but "considered the project cursed", so from that I'd guess he stayed away from buying another train, though I couldn't say for certain because that was as much as I could find out about Mr Dwight J. Ingleton.'

Jane stopped a passing waiter and ordered more coffees and a couple of large brandies. She thought Frank and Grace were in need of one.

'Henry Smith died on the day we last saw him,' said Jane, trying to pat it into a digestible shape for them. 'He was one hundred and five. We could never have met him at thirty. And we spent Christmas on a train with him that crashed and burned seventy-five years previously. It isn't possible. None of it.'

'But we did,' said Frank, doubting his own memories for a moment. 'Didn't we?'

'Yes, Frank. We most definitely did,' said Jane.

EPILOGUE

One year later

The sun was a bright yellow ball high in the blinding-blue Indian sky, but its heat was gentle as Jane Wutheridge sat down on the low marble seat in exactly the same place as Jacqueline Kennedy and Princess Diana and countless others had sat. Her eyes weren't large enough to take in the beauty of this place. Somewhere she had always wanted to be, something she had always wanted to see and now she was here and it was in front of her and it was every bit as superlative as she had imagined it to be.

She had no idea, still, what had happened to them all – the eight of them, the Christmas before last. But as her darling Clifford had waxed lyrical in his later years, some things could not be defined by science or reason and the mystery of them just had to be accepted. Science did not have all the answers and it never would. And so she had accepted it, as he had about his own 'experience', as a most special gift.

She had always said she would never visit the Taj Mahal alone but she wasn't alone, because she could feel him here, sitting beside her, the warmth of his presence unmistakable. He was never more than a mere breath away, barely anything separating them, a gossamer-thin barrier, his voice a soft whisper she heard often. There was no doubt in her head that he was there.

'Isn't it marvellous, Jane? I'm glad we came.'

And no one would ever persuade her otherwise.

Acknowledgements

As always, this book is not a solo but a team effort and I have the best of the best behind me. A superlative combo of agency and publisher, editors and PR lot. Thank you to the goddesses who are Lizzy Kremer, Maddalena Cavaciuti, Orli, Clare and all the Rights team who try and push me all over the planet. I'm so lucky to have you. And, at Simon and Schuster – my family: SJ Virtue, Matt, Maddie, Rich, Dom, Lou, Sarah, Odiri, Aneesha and the best editor on the planet – Clare Hey. Dearest God and my Fairy Godmother (Ian Chapman and Suzanne Baboneau) I will miss you so much. You were there at the beginning of this crazy dream of a journey and though I want you to enjoy a rest . . . selfishly, I want to wake up and find out I dreamt you'd said 'adieu' (as Radio Brian says . . . not goodbye) sort of like Bobby Ewing in the shower.

Thank you to Sally Partington – my copyeditor – here we've been again, Sal. And I loved it. And I love you for teaching me proper English and sorting out my cock-ups.

My lovely team at ED PR – Katie, Katey and Emma. Essentials in my author tool kit. Thank you for being patient and lovely and blinking marvellous at what you do.

Thank you to the blogging community and reviewers

who do so much for us authors, uncredited. Take it as read, I so appreciate your support. And to the people of Yorkshire, particularly Barnsley – who continue to carry me on their shoulders, shout about me, send coffees up the escalator in Barnsley market when I'm signing at Mike's Famous Book Stall – it never gets any less special to be owned by you.

Thank you to my pals who keep me on the right side of insane because you need good mates in this job, in and out of the game, and I have some GREAT mates. A special big THANK YOU to my writerly mate Debbie Johnson who is not only an uber talented author but makes Solomon look like a numpty.

And thank you to my family, here and above because I know Mum and Dad are looking down and still loving me and probably rolling their eyes sometimes as well. On earth, I continue to cling onto the apron strings because one never stops being a mum and I never want to. Tez, George, you are wrapped up in this booky adventure with me. A massive thank you to my OH Pete because I couldn't do what I do if he didn't do what he did. His parents named him well because he is a rock of the most solid granite.

Readers: I'd be an unpaid hobbyist if it weren't for you, so thank you for sticking with me.

It gets harder and harder doing this job. Brilliant romantic fiction authors are getting squeezed out of the market, so a little plea to book buyers and library lenders: don't desert the authors who have grafted so much year after year, who are still grafting, still writing their books for their readers – go seek them out. Sign up to their newsletters and turn up at their events. They're writing for you, and they want you to enjoy the books that they've crafted so lovingly, so do stay with us. And writing a nice review on Amazon is worth a LOT to us if we have moved you. Not for our egos, it does something to algorithms and helps with our sales, which we need to pay the bills and keep in the game. Okay, maybe a bit for the egos. We love it when you love us.

Couple of things I need to tell you about the book. You won't find the carol 'Hark! Hark' anywhere because I made it up. But there are plenty of other tunes to perform CPR to, though here's hoping you're never in the position of trying to bring someone back from the brink while trilling 'Eye of the Tiger' or 'Gettin' Jiggy Wit It'.

And the Toomey sisters don't exist either, not that I imagine anyone would want to listen to their 'Alone for Christmas'. Although I'd still take it over '(Simply Having a) Wonderful Christmastime'.

And for those people who really loved its 'sister book', *I Wish It Could Be Christmas Every Day*, you may spot some little easter eggs: cherries, diamonds, Norway, Sir Colin, Hollybury Farm . . . I put them there for you.

Thank you to the musical behemoth that is Roy Wood, yet again, for that song, because it's given me yet another story. It was bonkers to finally meet him, a wild coincidence, a mystery I have accepted, and I could finally say in person that I was the crank who sent him that Christmas book. He's going to get this one in the post as well. Not just any books, because these are beyond special. The first was written for Dad, this one for Mum, they are a beloved pair. My parents are present in every smile and tear these two novels pulled from me, they are watermarked in the pages, woven in the words.

My favourite Christmas film is *The Bishop's Wife*. You may find quite a few names crossed over from there into here as a homage if you're bored and want a puzzle to do.

Also – do pray to St Anthony if you ever lose anything, he's awfully accommodating and has helped me out loads.

And finally ... I really wanted to go back to Figgy Hollow, but we couldn't go back to the inn and I couldn't think how else to write another book. Then, blow me, as if by magic, I went into the lounge and there was a Christmas film on the TV featuring a train (no idea how as the other half had gone to the loo in an ad break during the snooker) and I knew instantly what I was going to do. It was beyond weird how the idea presented itself to me, like the best gift. The pieces gravitated together as if by enchantment and I am indebted to Katie at ED PR who suggested I contact the team at *Northern Belle* who might help me with some technical stuff. This beautiful train was on my doorstep – I never knew. And the chef is from Barnsley and he's blimming brilliant! From the off, everyone at the *Northern Belle* company could not have been more helpful, more friendly, or more informative. A special thank you to owner David Pitts who is rightly proud of his gorgeous train, and to Howard Barclay who has been a wonderful fount of knowledge, and never too busy to answer my queries. You've both been such a joy and a pleasure to work with. I have LOVED writing this book and I hope I've done you proud, too.

Dining on the *Northern Belle* is one of the loveliest experiences, oh my what a find, even better than I imagined it was going to be. It is like stepping back in time or even stepping out of time – into a world where nothing exists but a stunning train and the best fare that can be offered. It's the closest I've ever felt to being a queen. You should treat yourself, because you can. Because life is here and now and, as Roo would tell you, its juice is to be savoured – and it is worth every single penny. Go on ... you know you want to.

https://northernbelle.co.uk

**Enjoyed this book? Discover more
from your favourite author . . .**

For news, appearance dates and
information about Milly Johnson's
other books, visit her at
www.millyjohnson.co.uk

booksandthecity.co.uk
the home of female fiction

NEWS & EVENTS | BOOKS | FEATURES | COMPETITIONS

Follow us online to be the first to hear from your favourite authors

bc
booksandthecity.co.uk

X
@TeamBATC

Join our mailing list for the latest news, events and exclusive competitions

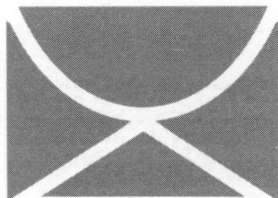

Sign up at
booksandthecity.co.uk